Viveck Rai Marwah was born in Delhi and has a degree in business management. Inspired by his proclivity for spiritual and philosophical discourses, his first book, *A Passage Through Life: A Saga of Life, Death and Beyond*, was published in 2004.

He has personally encountered many mystics in the last fifteen years on regular journeys to the lower Himalayas. His keen interest in philosophy, religion, and mysticism took him to Tibet and other regions in north-east India where Buddhist philosophy is still alive in ordinary life.

An avid theosophist, Viveck's journeys to such areas have helped him develop a better understanding of ancient Kangyur texts, rendering him deeply influenced by Buddhist culture and theology. His current work, a fable, is a culmination of all that he has seen, learnt, and encountered thus far.

THE MIND TRAVELLER

WARRIOR OF SHAKA

VIVECK RAI MARWAH

Om Books International

First published in 2024 by

Om Books International

Corporate & Editorial Office
A-12, Sector 64, Noida 201 301
Uttar Pradesh, India
Phone: +91 120 477 4100
Email: editorial@ombooks.com
Website: www.ombooksinternational.com

Sales Office
107, Ansari Road, Darya Ganj,
New Delhi 110 002, India
Phone: +91 11 4000 9000
Email: sales@ombooks.com
Website: www.ombooks.com

ISBN: 978-93-5376-957-4

Printed in India

10 9 8 7 6 5 4 3 2 1

In reverence to the Divine Mother,
the great sages, and Sai of Shirdi

Contents

1

A Tryst With Death

A long time ago, in the wilderness of the Himalayan mountains, a young lad slept curled up beside a fire that kept him from freezing in the Himalayan cold. He was Sankalp, a Tibetan boy driven from his home by invaders. The nomadic Yuan dynasty wanted to establish their dominion over the kingdom of Lhasa. This would not only give them control over trade routes to India and Persia but also a military base from which to claim the rich, fertile lands to its east.

The boy's family and many from his village were killed in a sudden and barbaric attack by a well-armed army that came across the Yarlung Pass, also known as Death Valley. The villagers were heavily outnumbered but preferred death to dishonour.

The boy survived, hiding in a small crevice in the mountain face. Much to his dislike, he chewed on wildflowers and ants to stay alive and live through the bitter Himalayan nights.

As the morning light slowly eclipsed the night sky, he flinched, and a groan escaped his lips. The sound alerted him to the stillness around. Startled into wakefulness, he slowly pulled his frail body up the steep rock face, keenly surveying the barren landscape for any signs of the ruthless killers. His tiny heart thumped with fear as he swept his gaze over the wilderness, listening for sounds other than those he was used to.

The clamour of hooves and hushed voices had passed him by at first light. He was safe for now, but the rain and hail from the night before had eaten into his bones. His tender hands and feet had almost given way, till the rising sun wove its magic, and the warm glow kissed every inch of the harsh mountain terrain, infusing life in the frosty desert morning. The Himalayan nights were unforgiving on mortals. Only a destined few survived.

The young boy had lived another night. His face grave from pain and shock, he hurried out of hiding but almost instantly retraced his steps, afraid that the enemy might still be close. However, he had to find a safe place to hide and protect himself from the cold, deathly winds that blew across the high mountain passes. Tired and hungry, he pushed himself and clambered across the steep terrain, which tested his abilities in every conceivable manner.

Covering a little distance, he faltered and fell to the ground, splitting the skin on his right knee. His face twinged as he watched a streak of blood trickle down his shin. Holding back his tears, he got up; this was no time to tend to bruises or cry out his pain.

Undeterred, he kept moving along an aimless path that led to nowhere, nibbling on the wild berries that grew in these parts. The dim afternoon light gilded the turgid clouds, turning them opaque. He could feel the air filling with a heavy, cold mist. It would soon be dark, and the night promised to be more unsparing than the one gone by.

Around sunset he crossed over a hump, an outcrop of earth and stone better known as the 'camel's back'. The beginnings of a forest appeared on the ridge and quickly expanded into a sea of green, connecting to the plains below. He sighed in despair, eyeing the tall dark pines and the forest they created. No one from his village had ever spent the night so far up in the mountains, and those who did often failed to return. The boy hurried his steps with a limp that had crept into his walk.

A faint light flickering through the darkness caught his attention. He stared hard in its direction. It came from inside a cave tucked between a narrow cleft in the rocks. The entrance was shielded by trees and shrubs. It was located to his left, just a few metres from where he stood.

He hesitated as these caves were the known dwelling grounds of the dreaded brown bear. Some also believed that they were home to evil spirits that roamed the barren mountains at night. But the young boy was too tired to fear either. Another night without shelter meant certain death. He watched for a while, considering how to make his approach through the few monstrous boulders that were precariously perched by the entrance. Treading cautiously, he made his way into the cave, the floor of which gently sloped inside. Its narrow entrance widened with every step and the ground flattened inside. Bright yellow flames of a fire danced in a far corner. Famished and exhausted, he curled up next to the fire. His senses quickly surrendered to exhaustion, his eyes almost immediately succumbing to the waiting darkness.

He lay still, unconscious.

Fate had played a cruel game on the young lad. The once happy family of Lin Thiampong, the village headman, was no more. Their beautiful home overlooking the mighty river Indus had been burnt down. The headman's wife and two of his three sons were done to death; only Sankalp survived. He had been grazing sheep near the high mountain passes that day. A fleeing family from the village had alerted him about the sudden and brutal attack.

His father, a brave man, was betrayed by an apocryphal truce and taken captive under the instructions of the renegade general Darqan Doodra, known for his savagery and lust for empirical expansion. Lin Thiampong was hanged along with the people of his community.

Now the invaders were searching for Lin's youngest son.

2

In the Presence of the Learned Monk

The boy spent the night slipping in and out of consciousness. The sun was almost overhead when he woke the next day, coughing in pain and filled with dread.

The boy had been asleep for over fourteen hours.

Although reluctant, he had shown courage by taking refuge in the cave, overcoming the many fears born of the stories that he had heard as a child.

He was still half asleep when the sound of footsteps alerted him.

'They have found me...This is the end...' He shivered at the thought and quickly ducked into the darkest corner of the cave, trying hard to conceal himself from the gaze of the intruder.

'Who is there?' a shadowed face called out in a forceful voice.

'Who is it? Speak up!'

The deep, commanding voice made the young lad tremble in anguish.

'It's me,' he murmured.

'Show yourself!' The voice resonated through the cave.

'Please don't hurt me.'

The boy winced as he reluctantly crawled out of the corner and stopped at the feet of the powerful man standing before him. Tall and broad-shouldered, his presence was accentuated by mesmerizing eyes. Draped in a maroon robe, the imposing figure radiated a meditative calm. He was Kalimpong, the mysterious wanderer of the mountains and protector of its forests. Much revered by the people, the great monk was known to have changed the course of the mighty river Indus when it had once ravaged the villages in its path. But for many years, nobody had seen or heard from him. Yet many in the villages around believed that he was there, somewhere, wandering the endless Himalayan ranges.

The little boy looked up, tears rolling down his sunburnt cheeks, until his gaze was lost in the serene vastness of the monk's eyes.

'Arise, my son,' said the monk, his voice softening. He affectionately laid his palm on the boy's head. His touch was consoling.

The boy's heart, despite his torment, felt lighter in the monk's presence.

'What brings you here?', the monk asked gently.

'Oh... Sir, my village was attacked. My father...' he sobbed.

'My father was killed and many in the village were murdered!' he continued to mourn, his voice choking in his throat. 'They killed them all! I ran away to save myself and took shelter here.'

The boy could barely speak for grief. He tried to stand, but his knees buckled under him, and he collapsed to the ground. His pain was overwhelming, hovering on the threshold of physical and mental endurance.

'It was not my intention to defile your pious abode.'

Kalimpong gave the boy a loving glance.

'The abode is in the heart. It cannot be defiled by anyone but the self.' He reached out and wiped the boy's tears. 'Now, bring me some water from that earthen pot,' he said, pointing towards the corner where a lamp burnt brightly.

The boy crawled to the pot and poured water into a copper dish lying close by.

He slowly limped back to the monk, his frail body trembling with the unbearable pain in his right leg. He had suffered deep bruises that went down to the bone. Kalimpong made him sit with his legs stretched out. He poured cold water from the copper dish over his feet and legs. For a brief moment, the boy shivered, and then to his relief, the pain began to fade.

The monk brought out a pot of *tu*, a nourishing cheesecake made from sweetened yak butter. The young lad hungrily ate it all.

'Can I have some more? I haven't eaten much in the last few days,' he said, licking the last bit off his fingers.

'Well,' said the monk, turning the earthen pot upside down, 'I wasn't expecting a guest.' A slight smile stretched his face.

'What about you, sir? You won't eat?'

'I just did,' replied the monk and refilled the copper dish with water.

'Drink. You look thirsty,' he said.

The water was refreshing—mildly warm. In a few seconds, the boy felt light and even strangely comforted.

Although the Himalayan winds froze everything that came their way, the inside of the cave remained remarkably warm.

'Can I sleep here tonight?' he asked after a while.

'Yes, my son, please do,' the monk said softly, placing his hand on the boy's head. 'And may you rise with fewer sorrows to a new tomorrow.' His face altered as he smiled slightly. The monk's eye then fell on the boy's tattered clothing.

'Let me get you something to wear.' The monk walked to a corner where the stone had been carved rather neatly into four shelves. He handed the boy a woollen robe, a bit large for him but warm and comfortable.

It wasn't long before the boy fell asleep, lulled by a sense of calm that he felt in the cave. He slept peacefully until his mind wandered into the past.

Hazy dreams of warm afternoons rekindled the joyous times he had spent with his father and brothers, hunting rabbits with their pet falcon, Zanzi. He could still sense his mother's loving touch, warm and comforting. He vividly remembered those lazy days spent wandering about the beautiful valley playing the flute. A fond gift from his grand uncle, the old man had taught him the art of making the hollow bamboo sing.

As he played, Zanzi would fly to his shoulder, mesmerized by the delightful sounds carried by the wind to the far horizons. The boy knew of no heaven greater than the one he had been born into, and there was nothing more he had ever wanted. It was bliss...

And then, like a mirage, it was gone. There was nothing left; his thoughts turned to tears. 'What have I done to deserve this?' He awoke with a jerk and a gasp, questioning himself in the middle of the night. But his sorrows soon drowned in the ocean of fatigue that covered every part of his body. He closed his eyes. His tears ran dry halfway across his bronzed cheeks; once again he fell asleep, sniffling.

Reflecting off the shiny rock face, the bright warm rays of the morning sun lit the cave. The boy opened his eyes and quickly sat up. He studied his surroundings, anxiously looking for the man who had provided him shelter the night before. He was nowhere to be seen. But the wound on his leg felt better. He could move around without much pain.

Famished, he looked for food and saw some fruits in one corner. He picked one up to eat but something held him back. He reluctantly returned it to its place. However, hunger soon forced him to leave the cave. He walked out, still fearful. From atop, he stared into the distance between him and the few houses that dotted the valley. It was a long way down and the only place he could get food. But he was afraid. The sight of fleeing families and teary-eyed children being carried on donkeys and makeshift sleds was still fresh in his mind. He paused before taking a deep breath, not sure what to do.

Just then, he saw someone approaching. The maroon shawl confirmed it was no enemy. It was the monk returning. He gestured to the boy to go back inside the cave. Sankalp immediately retraced his steps and waited for the monk.

'My son, where are you going? Don't you know they are still looking for you?'

He hesitated before answering. 'Sir, I was going out to find something to eat.'

The monk narrowed his eyes for a moment, and then his expression turned tender.

'What about the fruits I got for you?'

He hesitated again.

'Sir, I didn't know they were for me…' The boy lowered his head. 'I am already indebted to you for giving me shelter and saving my life...'

The monk was stunned by his reply. Who was this young, frail lad standing before him?

He put his hand on the boy's head with affection.

'What is your name?'

'Sankalp…sir.' He stood upright and straightened his robe before answering.

'Hmm…a powerful name indeed,' the monk said softly. 'You are a boy of extraordinary will and virtue,' Kalimpong remarked, his eyes closed in thoughtfulness.

'Perhaps there is a greater role destiny wants you to play. That is why…' he paused to gaze into the boy's eyes before continuing. 'That is why your path led you here.'

'Share my humble abode for some time. It will ease your pain and help you decide the future.'

Sankalp nodded. The expression on the monk's face was convincing enough, though he could not understand much of what the monk had said.

Kalimpong offered him a large bowl of apples before leaving the cave once again.

After eating his fill, Sankalp fell into a peaceful sleep.

Around sunset, he woke up refreshed. But the pain of losing his loved ones saddened him. As night dawned, he grew restless. Not from the fear of wild animals or ghosts who wandered the desolate mountains, but from the uncertainty of a future he could not see. He had no family or friends left. What remained were memories of a life filled with happiness and contentment, which now lay burnt and buried in a village he once knew as home.

Did he see a future here? Should he remain in the cave or run away towards the southern plains of India? Surely he could find refuge there. Sankalp stepped out of the cave, into the fading light of day. He sat quietly, looking at the sky and pondering over his grim and pitiful state. The sound of footsteps alerted him and broke his meandering thoughts. He flicked his eyes one way, then another, till they fell on a tall figure.

It was the monk coming back. The young boy felt reassured.

'How do you feel?' Kalimpong enquired.

'I feel sad,' he mourned, staring at the twinkling vastness with teary eyes. Calming himself with a deep breath, he continued. 'But there is something so peaceful about the night sky. The stars look so familiar and comforting.'

'Hmmm...Did you study the stars in school or did someone tell you about them?' asked Kalimpong.

'No, mostly I like to watch them sail across the night sky as seasons change.'

'There is a certain magic to them,' replied the monk. He smiled. 'Perhaps you can learn more from the stars one day.'

'Perhaps...' Sankalp nodded. 'Sir, I collected some seeds and planted an apple tree,' he said, pointing to the spot.

'Ah, the tree of life,' Kalimpong said with a broad smile.

'Sir, where did you go?' the boy enquired.

Kalimpong placed a filial arm around his shoulders before answering.

'I was in the village searching for survivors,' he replied and lengthened his stride, overtaking Sankalp.

Soon they were sitting by the fire sharing a meal. Wiping his mouth with the back of his hand, Sankalp queried, 'Did you meet anyone...anyone who asked about me? There must be somebody looking for me?' His innocent eyes beamed with hope in that instant.

Kalimpong lowered his gaze, unable to face his expression. An uncomfortable silence fell between them for a moment.

'I…' Kalimpong faltered, unsure of what to say. He drew a deep breath before speaking again. 'There are few people left, mostly old men and women.' For the first time, the monk's eyes grew mournful, deepening the fine lines of age that stretched across his sun-baked skin.

'The village seems empty. Most of the houses have been burnt down.'

Another painful silence followed.

'What about my home?' Sankalp finally spoke, his anxiety apparent.

Kalimpong silently stared at him and folded his hands in his lap.

'It's the largest one standing next to the village temple.' Sankalp's pulse rate increased, and his mind churned with a flurry of sensations.

'I believe even that has fallen to the ground,' Kalimpong whispered, pronouncing each word carefully. There was sadness in his voice. 'If you want, I can take you there tomorrow.'

Sankalp sadly nodded as regret and sorrow welled in him.

Kalimpong waited until it became apparent that the boy had nothing more to say.

'Rest for now, my dear Sankalp,' he said, looking at him with compassion. 'Empty your mind of expectations but don't lose hope.'

Sankalp looked downcast.

Night had descended quickly, as it does in the mountain lands. Kalimpong dimmed the oil lamp and placed it on a raised platform in the corner. He sat a little distance away from Sankalp and slowly pushed himself upright, settling comfortably into the lotus position.

Sankalp watched the monk quietly, struggling to hold back tears. The monk rested his hands on his knees and then let his eyelids drop; an unassuming smile etched his face. It seemed as if he had merged with some divine happiness—a feeling that appeared so distant to the young boy.

Silence reigned for several minutes. Sankalp wiped his eyes and drew a deep breath before quietly walking out of the cave.

A waning moon glowed delicately, its thin light barely touching the highlands. While he did not fear the dark, neither did he feel comfortable surrounded by the emptiness of a night that reminded him of his fate. Sankalp sat still on an elevated rock overlooking the tiny hamlet. Unblinking, he stared at the specks of light shining from oil lanterns, flickering submissively in the errant wind.

3

A Trek Back to the Ravaged Village

Early next morning, Sankalp and Kalimpong set out for the village to look for anything that could console the boy's grieving heart. They took the pass through Death Valley. It had steep slopes, which were the ideal nesting grounds for the saker falcon. Was Zanzi still alive? Had his pet falcon found a home somewhere? Or maybe it had come back and, finding no one in the burnt house, had flown away into the vast mountain ranges.

The young lad trudged on, his mind filled with anxiety. By mid-afternoon, they had reached the high mountain pass. From there, he got a fair view of the near-empty and ravaged village. The sky was still a dark hue, engulfed in the smoke billowing from the burnt-down homes. It was a heart-wrenching sight.

The moment they entered the village, Sankalp was overcome with sorrow and disgust. His eyes fell upon anonymous mounds where many from the village had been interred. While a few women wailed over their loss, many others had run away in fear. Birds of prey circled in the tortured sky, awaiting their turn to finish whatever had been left unfinished by the barbaric invaders. The boy's face contorted with both anger and fear. Had he made a mistake by coming back to his village?

A dark plume of smoke rising from nearby drew his attention. He stared at it with unwavering eyes. The destroyed structure seemed familiar. It was his home.

Most of it had been razed to the ground. A few pillars supported the broken roof, preventing it from falling to the ground. He went inside, only to find how mercilessly it had been plundered. Nothing remained as he remembered it. Sankalp stood frozen in place, tears rolling down his cheeks as he stared at the ruination that lay before him. Heartbroken at the loss, his body jolted with a shiver as he came to terms with the fear of being the only one of his family still alive.

He slowly raised his head and looked around. A few fierce-looking men on horseback were parading through the streets. But apart from them, the village seemed unnaturally empty, filled only with the sounds of hooves and anguished moans that slowly faded into silence. Doors were locked from the inside; windows were shut and curtains were drawn. The few people in evidence covered their faces and looked the other way to avoid talking or be seen offering sympathy. Sad and dejected, he turned away from it all and started to walk away. Just then, he noticed something familiar lying partly buried in the ground, close to the courtyard.

A glint of hope lit his face.

He hurried to the object, his small hands scrabbling at the rubble and speedily clearing the dust and debris. And there it was…His flute! The one little piece of happiness in the spread of dread, it was something the invaders had thought was not worth destroying.

He picked it up and blew out the sand. Could it still make music, he wondered.

Tears welled in his eyes as he filled the hollow bamboo with his breath, forgetting in the moment the pain of his present. Kalimpong looked on as he played. Just as the music pierced the cold mountain winds, something circling above caught the monk's attention. He pointed towards the sky. It was Zanzi! The wind had carried the sound to his ears.

Hearing the familiar tune, the falcon drifted towards Sankalp in great lazy spirals, drawing nearer to him. The young boy looked up and called out. The falcon immediately tilted its wings and circled one last time before landing atop his shoulders. It was his favourite perch.

Sankalp felt better. At least there was something from the past to console his grieving heart. With nothing more to wait around for, they made their way back to the cave. A painful silence hovered for most of the journey. A rising tide of rebellion consumed Sankalp, and though he tried hard to keep his face expressionless, he couldn't.

Later that night, Kalimpong consoled him.

'Sankalp, I understand your grief, but nothing can bring back what you have lost. I can only help lessen the pain,' the monk said kindly.

Sankalp nodded, his sorrow evident.

'Stay here with me for some time at least; it will help you heal from the grief,' the monk offered.

'Sir, there is nothing that can take away the pain in my heart.' Sankalp shifted uncomfortably and took a deep breath, his eyes filling with a rage that held back his tears. 'Not till… not till I have avenged the death of my family and driven away the invaders!' Sankalp clenched his fists as he made a vow.

Kalimpong cast his perceptive gaze upon him. He could sense passion, one that could never be claimed by adversity. 'One day you will, my dear Sankalp. Indeed, you will!' he asserted, raising his right hand in blessing. Sankalp bowed his head and slowly walked out of the cave.

He stopped in front of a large circular basin made of earth; from the light of a nearby lamp, he could see his face in its still water. For a moment, he had the feeling of seeing another. A resemblance so alike, yet so far from the pain that defined him. He stared, wondering if that was really him.

That night, the stars remained partially hidden by a blanket of low clouds. The wind flowed mildly, mixed with the hoot of the long-eared owl that drifted eerily through the silence. Unlike his thoughts, the world was calm as the night slumbered away. Sankalp sat unspeaking. He longed to cry out loud and share his pain with the quiet. But his heart, in silent throbbing protest, held back his emotions, and his eyes no longer offered an escape for his tears.

The following full moon night, after a day of fasting, Kalimpong initiated the young lad into the divine art of meditation. Days went by and Sankalp learnt from the master. Meditation offered solace to his grieving heart. It shifted his focus from the constant thought of loss that preyed on his mind.

The ways of the monk were hard, and he had little time to spare from his daily routine. Sankalp often accompanied him to nearby villages spread scantily across the valley. They collected food comprising the humble offerings of the villagers. At times, Sankalp went alone; the large bowl he carried never remained empty. The kindly girl who lived at the edge of the village would make sure to fill it with a generous helping. She never spoke, but her eyes offered affection.

After attending to the morning chores, Sankalp would trek down to the valley. The monk had entrusted him with the job of getting water from the nearby stream. Sankalp would playfully run down the rocky track; it was climbing back up with two pails of water that was exhausting. But it helped his limbs get stronger. Sometimes, he would sit by the stream. Much like its crystal waters, painful memories often flowed clearly through his mind. His dispirited eyes often questioned fate and what destiny had in store for him.

In time, Sankalp went deeper into the subconscious realms of his mind. He was able to control the pace of his thoughts and connect his mind to that of the learned master. Positive currents from the master energized his mental being; they helped fill the void in his heart. Yogic techniques and sacred chants helped unlock the power of his mind, while exercises strengthened his body. Gradually, his attitude towards events and objects began to change.

Winter was once again drawing to an end. The days had turned warm and the view more picturesque. The trees were dense and green, and the wildflowers were in full bloom. In the distance were snow-covered mountains through which flowed the mighty river. The lower part of the valley had lush grasslands and abundant wildlife. As Sankalp looked further, he could only imagine what he had heard—beyond the mountains was the amazing city of Lhasa. His father had often talked about it. He had promised to take him there some day. But that was one promise he couldn't keep.

The bright morning brought cheer to Sankalp for the learned monk began the day with praise for his disciple. 'My son, you have made steady progress in learning and understanding the sacred arts. Do remember, the most difficult battles are fought in the mind.' With these words, Kalimpong left the cave. The remark drew a broad smile from Sankalp.

For the first time in many months, he was alone.

Zanzi, his pet falcon, had ventured out in search of food. After cleaning the cave and readying it for the monk, Sankalp walked to a rocky ledge that overlooked a tiny village. To its south was a deeply forested valley that opened on to a flowing prairie. It was dotted with patches of brown, barren land and rocky formations. The boy often thought of visiting the beautiful valley. It lay beyond the village, across the river.

Despite the aura of expectation, the day went by as the ones before. The setting sun turned a crimson red and whispered the night in; Sankalp walked back along the grassy track that extended from the ledge to the cave.

He was up early the next day and was surprised to see that the simple bedding on the slightly raised stone platform lay undisturbed. Had the master not returned?

Kalimpong had once mentioned the secret rituals performed alone in the deep forests. 'Perhaps that is what kept him away for the night,' thought Sankalp. He scrubbed his face and hands then left the cave, walking a little distance from it. The jagged mountains that peeked beyond the clouds were clearly visible. They were still laden with snow, despite the spring greenery that had begun to spread across the valley floor. A single grey cloud cast a partial shadow on the village below. As he squatted on a rather flat boulder, a shaft of sunlight burst through the cloud. Within moments, the rift in the clouds widened. A distinct band of light slowly advanced across the landscape, creating an extraordinary ombré of colours.

In the distance, Zanzi rode the warm air currents, patrolling the land for signs of any furred or feathered prey. 'It is a bright morning, and the winds seem quieter than usual. It is about time I explore the valley,' thought Sankalp as a thin smile curled his lips. He whistled for Zanzi.

4

Wandering the Mysterious Himalayan Forest

For a long time, he had not dared to stray far from the cave. Sankalp's fears stemmed from stories of man-eating creatures that roamed the forested valley. The children were often told never to venture into the forest alone.

'Be afraid of the evil that roams the valley and the bear and the leopard that do its bidding,' an old man would say, blowing smoke rings from his opium-laden pipe. Most of these tales were implausible and seemed far-fetched, but they served to keep the villagers away from the valley. The children would listen in fear to these nightmarish stories and quickly snuggle back into their warm yak skin beds for the night.

That was then…

Sankalp was now beginning to overcome his fears, importantly his fear of being alone. His mind and body were becoming stronger. He was in an improved state.

He walked away from the cave, charmed by the beauty and vastness of the valley. Ahead ran deep forests, serenaded by the sounds of the mighty Kyi Chu that flowed along their edges. He recalled being told, 'If you follow the river for seven nights, you will reach the magnificent city situated on its banks. Lhasa!'

The mind is always intrigued by what it cannot see, only imagine. Curiosity and instinct drew him to the valley. Sankalp made his way down and across the tiny village. To the south, the forest went on, unbroken and unending. Towards its right flowed the river, wide and shallow. He passed through the woods, enjoying his walk through the dense mix of towering birch and oak trees. By mid-afternoon he reached a clearing; the air had grown warmer with the sunlight. A slight movement caused Sankalp to turn. Just ahead to his right, he saw a family of deer with a young buck grazing on the fresh green sod. A definitive white mark on its small forehead made it stand out. The sight brought a smile to his face. He stopped in his tracks, as if making a memory of it before moving on.

The valley widened ahead.

Clusters of apple and peach trees along with fruit-bearing shrubs began to appear in places where the sunlight came through the forest canopy. Then again, the forest became dense. He caught an occasional glimpse of the sun, but it was never clear enough to mark his direction. The landscape changed little through the walk other than the steep undulations of the terrain. The hissing sound of the river became more prominent as he came closer to it, albeit a bit tired.

A fruit tree caught his eye. 'Those peaches look ripe and juicy,' he thought and climbed up. After a hearty meal, he lay down near the tree, upon a patch of soft grassy earth. The boy stretched out and rolled to his side, enjoying the warm sunlight peeking through the branches. A pair of brush-footed butterflies floated noiselessly around him before spiralling upwards. The forest too was beginning to fall silent. He closed his eyes and was soon asleep.

Zanzi flew away to look for food in the forest. Blissful moments of sleep broke the shackles of dreadful memories. Sankalp slept dreamless for once, at peace with his past.

The sun was about to set. A whiff of cold mountain air woke him from his slumber. He gasped at the sight of the falling darkness that had begun to surround the forest. It would be night soon, and he had wandered a bit too far from the cave. Worried what the learned master might think, he turned back.

It was a long way through the dense forest and along the valley back to the cave. Pleasant thoughts gave way to anxiety over unseen dangers. He recalled tales of hungry leopards and ferocious bears that roamed the valley to hunt at night. The trees that looked beautiful by day had turned eerie, their boughs stretched out, waiting to grab him in the darkness of night. There were also stories of evil beings hounded from the celestial skies having an unseen presence here. Overcome with distress, Sankalp quickened his pace, walking briskly into the vast emptiness that lay before him. Sweat trickled down his forehead from angst and exhaustion; he tried to steady his breath but couldn't. The howling of wolves became louder, mixed with the cries of a hapless deer succumbing slowly to their deadly jaws. The frightful sounds of the jungle added to the dread of a dark, moonless night.

A shiver ran through his body. Partly from fear and partly from the cold mist that was slowly beginning to consume the forest.

'O God, why did I leave the warmth of the cave? I was so comfortable in its environs. This is a mistake! Please help me find my way back home,' he prayed and walked on, extremely wary of his surroundings.

All of a sudden, a thin shrill voice called out from behind.

'Are you lost, boy? I can lead you home...' It was followed by a hollow chilling laugh...

Aghast, he turned around, his heart pounding like a drum! There was nothing in sight. Was someone truly calling out to him in the middle of nowhere, or was his mind playing tricks? He stopped in his tracks and drew in a deep breath before calling out.

'Who is it?'

'Follow me, boy, I can show you the way,' the voice asserted.

Just then, he heard something brush against the low-hanging branches of a tree, followed by the sounds of footsteps. Sankalp stopped. His heart skipped a beat. 'Who could it be?' he wondered, afraid but hopeful.

'Please stop, I can't see you,' he stuttered as he followed the sound of footsteps.

'Hurry up boy… or you will be all alone, lost in the forest,' the voice sniggered.

He kept following the patter of feet, directionless, through a foggy maze. There wasn't much light to guide him. A faint sense of his surroundings made him realize he was running around in circles, climbing up and down the same damn path! A sense of dread replaced his hope.

'Please stop and show yourself. I can't keep up any longer,' he moaned, exhausted and out of breath.

'Ah…ha…You want to see me?' the voice cackled, not so distant this time and followed by a deafening silence.

An ugly figure, no taller than three feet, with queer eyes and a rather large head appeared! It let out a chilling laugh as it sailed down through the branches to the ground. Sankalp froze in fear. He wanted to shout out loud but couldn't, his voice benumbed, much like his feet. The young boy had heard of but never seen anything like this before.

Trembling, he looked up. The moon peered down brighter than ever.

'Please help me,' he closed his eyes and spoke in an almost supplicating tone.

Suddenly, a bright light flashed in front of him. Terrified, he opened his eyes; the glowing light took the form of a beautiful maiden!

'My son, don't be afraid,' she said softly and walked to his side.

Her presence calmed him.

'There is nothing to be afraid of. This djinn needs to be taught a lesson for scaring you.'

The woman then turned to the djinn, her eyes widening with an expression of annoyance.

Her powerful gaze lifted the djinn in the air. She bounced him up into the sky, turned him sideways, and then hung him upside down in mid-air.

The unseen force held him there, no matter how much he struggled.

'Mercy, mercy...Please have mercy on me!' he pleaded. A moment later, he melted away in front of them.

'My dear Sankalp, don't be afraid. The creatures of the forest derive strength from fear as much as from weakness. To overcome both, you must learn to control your mind.'

'Who are you?' asked Sankalp, completely unnerved and feeling more afraid due to what had transpired.

'I am Lasya, also known as the moon goddess.'

'I...I remember,' he stuttered, still trembling and trying to come to terms with what had just happened.

'My mother often prayed to you,' he mumbled. 'On full moon nights, she made offerings of rice pudding and kept them on the roof.'

'And you ate a large part of those offerings,' she smiled with disarming candour.

Sankalp hesitated a moment. 'I didn't believe you existed,' he said ruefully.

'Your mother believed in me. She always prayed for your safety.' She gazed at him, her angelic face radiating warmth.

'Do you believe in me now?' she quizzed.

Sankalp remained still, his eyes filled with indescribable emotions. A long moment passed between them, and then he spoke in a low voice. 'Yes, I do…I do,' he said and closed his eyes. A tear of faith trickled down his cheek. He opened his eyes, but she was gone. Trembling still, he sat down on a rock, thinking over what had just happened. He tried hard to compose his thoughts.

'If only I could find a light…It would make it so much easier…' he whispered into the emptiness.

Exhausted, he recalled the words of the master.

'Sankalp, meditation is a means of cultivating inner strength. It gives one the courage to fight shadows, the ones that lurk within. The mind, once relaxed, sees more clearly and realistically; fear and anxiety become insignificant. And you acquire the ability to think and go beyond your circumstances.'

Sankalp closed his eyes.

Drawing a deep breath, he uncluttered his senses and lowered the perceptions crowding his mind. Sankalp focused. For a moment he felt vulnerable, exposed to the shadowy whispers from the dark. He kept his calm and slowed his breathing. And then, he reached out from within…

In a few moments, the sounds of the forest fell silent. The dark images haunting his mind began to fade, and so did the fear of the unknown. Understanding prevailed.

Diving deeper into the subconscious reservoir of energy, Sankalp connected with the searching eye of the master. He was able to sense the sub-cosmic flow of a current guiding him in a particular direction. He came out of his trance-like state and opened his eyes to the view, which appeared to have changed. Or was that just the effect on his mind?

The twinkling starlight that had haunted the skies now illumed his path! He let his instincts lead him. He recalled the words of the learned monk. Sankalp understood better their deeper meaning and what Kalimpong had meant. He realized the power of a focused mind.

On his way out of the forest, he noticed a strange glow reflecting off the familiar rock face where the cave lay. Much like what he had encountered about a year ago. Was it from the fire burning inside, or was it a strange effulgence that surrounded the cave now and again?

Slightly bruised but otherwise unhurt, Sankalp emerged from amongst the trees and made his way up the valley. He quickly climbed up the familiar rock face that opened on to the cave and entered.

There sat Kalimpong, motionless but perhaps aware of his presence? A moment later, he broke his silence.

'Ah, my dear Sankalp, you are back!' the monk remarked, his eyes half-closed.

'Yes, master. I am sorry for making you worry. I left the cave thinking you wouldn't be back for a while.' He drew in a deep breath and continued. 'I got lost in the forest…and had quite an experience!

'Ah...you did,' Kalimpong replied with mild amusement. He leaned back a little, studying his expression. 'Lasya told me about your little adventure,' Kalimpong smiled.

Sankalp was perplexed. Kalimpong's reply was unexpected, and it stunned him. He sat unspeaking; it took him a few moments to gather his wits.

The learned monk rose to his feet and placed a plate of hot tsampa in front of Sankalp. In a blink, the boy gulped down most of it.

Placing his hand lightly on Sankalp's head, Kalimpong spoke affectionately.

'My dear...' His voice took on a sombre timbre. 'There are times when you stand alone, surrounded by nothing but emptiness. In moments like these, many look for strength on the outside, while some find it within.'

'But master, how...how could you—?'

Kalimpong anticipated his question and interjected. 'My dear, the universe is more responsive to the silent pleadings of the heart than to the loudness of words!' He paused for a moment before bestowing a compliment. 'You are gifted with an exceptional ability to see the unseen and unravel the extraordinary. I think you are ready for higher learning.'

A trace of a smile lifted a corner of the monk's mouth.

Sankalp looked bewildered as he sat thinking, quietly rolling a goji berry between his thumb and forefinger. He finally decided not to question Kalimpong anymore.

The monk moved to one corner of the cave and sat down in the lotus position. Closing his eyes, he once again sank into the still waters of sublime consciousness.

Though tired, Sankalp lay wide-eyed and sleepless. He found solace in trying to demystify the floating patterns drawn by the clouds of smoke rising from the burning incense.

Many seasons changed and so did the boy. He had wisely chosen to remain with the learned monk. The apple tree was taking root and growing. Kalimpong often referred to it as the tree of life. The short summer was beginning to fade once again. Everything seemed to have been affected by the wintry change, except the confines of the cave. It remained unchanged, and it seemed it would remain so till the end of existence. Time, though, had forged a deep bond between the two inhabitants. Kalimpong had reawakened faith and trust in the young boy. Sankalp was beginning to overcome his fears and live again.

On an early winter morning, while it was still dark and the cold mist hung low, the monk woke Sankalp.

'Come, son; let us leave before sunrise. We have a long way to go.'

Sankalp nodded. He hesitated for a moment, as if he were about to ask the monk something, but then decided to follow in the master's footsteps, unquestioning.

They descended from the west to where a tributary of the river Indus flowed. Its gushing white waters pooled in a lake. Sankalp watched as the learned monk waded into waist-deep water and faced east before performing his morning ablutions.

The sun was about to rise, turning the sky crimson. It was the magical hour of dawn. The most pious time in the physical world when gods from heaven descended to bathe in the holy lake.

Sankalp followed Kalimpong into the icy waters, his body trembling, shivering as he waded in deeper. Surprisingly, the water did not have the same effect on Kalimpong. His body remained immune to the vagaries of nature. Sankalp lowered himself into the lake, hesitating a bit before ducking his head under the freezing waters.

'Face the rising sun and welcome the giver of light to the world,' Kalimpong enunciated.

Sankalp nodded.

Kalimpong collected water in his cupped palms and offered obeisance to the sun god. He then turned his palms towards the sun as if absorbing the light into them. The young monk followed suit, his body shuddering, making it difficult for him to hold the water in his cupped palms. Kalimpong noticed his condition from the corner of his eye.

'Sankalp, don't let the mind be contaminated by external influences. What you feel is the reaction of the physical body. Ignore it! Concentrate instead on the warmth that flows from the magnificent light rising on the horizon.'

Sankalp shook his head with a strained effort to smile.

Kalimpong closed his eyes and started chanting sacred verses from some ancient texts, followed by serene gestures of offering water to the sun.

Sankalp braced his shoulders and joined his palms. His mind connected with the master; it too resonated with sacred chants. Within moments, the sounds reverberated through his every part. The power of the intonations activated energy centres in his body. Almost immediately, he felt a mild thermal surge! The quivering and shivering stopped. Sankalp stood calm, no more affected by the extremities of where he stood. A while later, the monk walked out of the lake. Sankalp followed close behind.

'Master, you have often mentioned the power of sacred chants. They work, I know by experience, but how?'

'Well, my dear, chants are powerful pronouncements that send vibrations out into the cosmos, which generate energy.'

'You mean random sounds, made by anyone or anything, can tap into this energy?'

'Sankalp, did I say random or just any sound? Let me make it a bit easier for you. Can you understand bird calls or the calls of various animals? They call in a pattern, at a certain volume and pitch that we don't understand. But they do, and they respond to this. My dear, sacred chants generate vibrations. Their semantics are understood by the cosmos and the space that surrounds us. The sounds unlock and gather power from the ether and help access energy stored within the body.'

'Hmmm…' Sankalp muttered, still confused.

'Sankalp, I can only explain so much with words, but in time you will come to understand the language of the cosmos and its sacred sounds and meaning.'

Sankalp nodded, still puzzled, but all the more inquisitive.

'Master, why do you pray to the sun instead of the much bigger and more powerful mountain god? His anger can destroy whole villages,' Sankalp said in a hushed voice. 'He can hurl down mountains of snow to hurt you! The sun seems to do nothing to harm us.'

'The God factor,' Kalimpong took a deep breath and chuckled. 'Is the universe a dream of the gods, or are the gods a dream of the universe? Sankalp, for everyone, even for powerful kingdoms, there exists a god. This is perhaps better summarized as belief. For the Indians, it is Siva, for some the Buddha, for the followers of Shinto, it is Kami. These gods are mostly portrayed in human form, while some might see them as powerful manifestations of nature, like fire, mountains, an animal or in some therianthropic form. It is what holds your faith.'

He smiled, his right eyebrow raised.

'And to some…' he stopped for a moment, drawing a deep breath and exhaling it slowly before continuing. 'My dear, god is something or someone beyond common comprehension. A being or force far superior to the normal. Perhaps a hidden hand that can control the outcome of situations, but to the wise…' Kalimpong held back his words as if he were reminiscing, and then a mysterious smile etched his face.

'To the wise, it is formless—a light that leads to awakening, divinity and immortality!' He paused and gazed at Sankalp, his eyes filled with delight. 'But are any one of these symbolic representations less godly than the others?' He pointed towards the wilderness. 'The majestic mountains are part of this great creation, and I offer obeisance to them too.'

Sankalp nodded, pretending to understand, though he was confused.

'My dear, everything around you in nature is a facet of godliness; the sun, the moon…' he paused and looked at Sankalp, as if reminding him of his experience with the deity.

Sankalp raised his hand in an impatient gesture to question but then held back his enquiry as an afterthought.

Kalimpong looked at him and smiled slightly before speaking again. 'The mountains, trees and all that you see, even the air that you feel, are part of a divinity that emphasizes the existence of a supreme. However, true understanding comes with awakening from within. I do pray to the sun, the harbinger of life to the world. I salute it so that its light may shine upon all. The magic of this light is imperative for the universe to function.'

He stood still and stared at the light. His eyes shut in silent prayer.

A moment later he spoke again.

'Sankalp, stand by me and look at the rising sun…' He paused. 'Feel the light enter within…' he whispered, his eyes still closed.

The boy did as he was told. The monk placed his hand on the boy's head and slowly tightened his grip.

'Tell me, Sankalp. How do you feel?'

Sankalp stood quiet, or was he just overwhelmed?

'I feel strange…the light is so magical,' he finally said softly, as if talking to himself.

'For once, I feel no longing for dreams nor desires. For once there is no yearning for what I lost. Just a feeling of nothingness that is so fulfilling.'

He fell silent again; the monk stepped back.

Sankalp turned around and looked at him, his eyes reflecting a sense of ecstasy.

Kalimpong smiled. 'You felt all that for a few moments?'

'Yes, I did.'

'Imagine if you felt this way every moment, through a timeless journey not bound by space or time.' Kalimpong's smile broadened as they began walking along a narrow track.

After a thoughtful interlude, Sankalp asked the monk, 'Master, I have noticed you eat little and mostly just once a day. How do you get the energy to follow such a rigorous exercise regimen and walk many miles in the mountains?'

Kalimpong smiled. 'My dear, you see those strong, tall oak trees? They don't eat. They absorb energy derived from a powerful concoction of water and sunlight. There are specific techniques I follow that work the same way, absorbing energy and energizing the cells in my body.'

As they walked, Kalimpong talked about the intricate web of light that unites all living beings in one single thread of existence. He spoke about the hidden meaning behind the rituals that were ancient yogic techniques to purify the body and soul. The monk described how the innermost parts of the brain were associated with subtle worlds of existence. And how through proper training in the ancient arts, these centres could be energized. Sankalp listened, baffled. He sought more explanation of what the monk was telling him.

'Sankalp, the real subtle activity takes place in the region situated between the two eyebrows. At the equinox rests the individual spirit entity; currents that flow from other senses converge at this point. This is what gives us life. Just as the human body is but a fragment of nature, containing in it all the vital elements that formed the universe, so too is the individual spirit entity a part of the cosmic being. To arouse this cosmic connection, all external activities of the body have to be brought to a standstill, at least momentarily. The essence of meditation, therefore, is to turn the current flowing through us inwards rather than outwards.'

Sankalp listened quietly, spellbound by Kalimpong's amazing assertions.

'My dear, just as water cleanses the dirt from the physical body, the practice of the ancient art of yoga cleanses the soul. This ritual, coupled with the chanting of sacred mantras, produces vibrations that energize the mind.'

Kalimpong looked at Sankalp and smiled as if he knew what he was thinking and that one day he would come to understand what he couldn't today.

After a brief rest, they continued their journey towards an unknown destination.

'How much further do we have to travel?'

'Are you tiring?' the monk asked with concern. 'Don't worry. We should be there soon.'

They continued their climb up steep mountain tracks. Sankalp thought back to the time spent with his father. He would often take Sankalp to the village fair. When the little boy tired, he would carry him on his shoulders. He recalled chasing the sure-footed mountain goats down steep slopes, his brothers trying their best to veer them off their path. The cold Himalayan evenings would be spent with family. His expression turned grim as he recalled how it had all ended. With many such memories playing on his mind, Sankalp became restless and missed a step, unaware that he was treading on dangerous ground. On the left was a gigantic mountain wall, etched with sharp stone edges that loomed large. The right opened to the valley and the river below. It was a steep fall that could take the life of any mortal!

He stumbled and fought to find his balance, coming dangerously close to the edge, but was quickly held by the monk. Sankalp winced as Kalimpong gripped his upper arm with bruising strength, preventing a steep fall into the rapids.

'Mind your step, Sankalp,' Kalimpong said, softly but firmly.

'I am sorry, master. It won't happen again.'

'You seem lost in thought. Tell me, son, what is bothering you?'

'Nothing, master. Just memories from the past,' he said, his tone resigned. As if he had recalled every gory thought down to the minutest detail. 'I can still hear the sound of approaching hooves and those hushed voices searching for me.' His brows furrowed at the thought. 'They continue to haunt me time and again!' A shiver passed through him. 'I have lost everyone and everything dear to me.' His eyes welled with tears. 'I feel so alone in a world that seems to have no place for me.'

'My son, adversity is the better part of penance. Don't let the fragility of emotions break your resolve. Nature sometimes chooses the best out of its creation to see, admire, test and behold all that it has. As in this, it sees the reflection of its own perfection.'

Sankalp looked at Kalimpong and drew in a deep breath. His words seemed beyond comprehension.

'My dear, we are part of an infinite energy. A universal force that transcends the laws of creation and destruction. This energy has the power to manifest in distinct forms, at different places and over various intervals in time. Death can claim the physical but never this immortal part of you.' He took a moment to compose his thoughts. 'The ones you weep for walk by your side, unseen. In another realm, a dimension that stands cloaked from the physical eye. In that realm, birth and death exist only as nuances of nature.'

Kalimpong motioned Sankalp to come closer as he slowed to a stop.

'If only you had the power to see beyond, you would realize that nothing has changed. The universal laws of karma have just played their part in unfolding this great drama of nature, and not without reason…' He paused for a moment. 'But to help elevate your inner being and cultivate the powers that lie within.' Kalimpong's expression turned sympathetic. 'That, my son, will eventually lead to the fulfilment of your destiny and that of the land and its people.'

'But why me?' Sankalp whispered to himself, sad and confused.

Dusk had fallen earlier than usual. The cold mountain winds pierced through the skin into the very bones. Through the trees, Sankalp glimpsed a clearing ahead. A tract of flat land which extended to the edge of the mountain from where it fell away in a gentle slope to the valley below.

They finally reached a cottage—a roomy hut that was tucked away from the mountain track, making it less accessible. The sun was about to set. A marvellous orange hue covered most of the plain blue sky. Sankalp stopped momentarily, and so did the howling of the winds in an ode to the spectacle.

5

A Magical Feast in the Abandoned Cottage

'Master, there is nobody here,' remarked Sankalp as he surveyed his surroundings, which had begun to acquire a sublime stillness.

'Don't worry. Make yourself comfortable,' said the monk, unlocking the small wooden door to the cottage. The hutment was sparse and without even a fire to shield the body from the severe cold. But it felt warm and exuded a certain comfort. A large incense stick burned in the corner; the usual cloud of fragrance floated amongst the wooden rafters above. The cottage had a few rooms, but the one adjoining the room where they stood looked different. Its carved door was larger than the others, and it seemed securely bolted from the inside.

While Sankalp familiarized himself with his surroundings, Kalimpong took a seat in the centre of the main room, his feet folded beneath him and his hands resting on his knees.

Much like the outside, a cold calm pervaded the inside. The learned monk closed his eyes momentarily.

After a few moments, Kalimpong broke his silence.

'Come, sit by me. We will soon be joined by our host. He is on his way back and slightly delayed by a storm in the upper reaches of the mountains.'

'Master, how do you know that?'

'My dear, it's a simple process that induces the transfer of thoughts from one to another. The limitations of distance and time are overstepped.'

'How does it work?'

'Thoughts are powerful feelings, capable of being channelled from the mind into the ether. They can be carried through this subatomic medium to the person you wish to connect with.'

While the monk was still explaining, the door suddenly opened. A young man bearing a striking resemblance to Kalimpong entered the room. His deep-set eyes gazed at them. The strange steadiness of his regard was almost puzzling, and then, almost immediately, he broke into an affectionate smile. Kalimpong bowed in respect with endearing humility, though his guest seemed much younger than him. Like his teacher, Sankalp too knelt in reverence to the stranger. The man smiled and raised both his hands in blessing.

'Arise, dear Sankalp!' said the stranger, studying the young man with a thoughtful smile.

He then placed his hand on Sankalp's head in blessing. The touch was disarming; almost instantly his innermost thoughts and desires seemed to flee his mind.

A charged silence filled the room. Kalimpong and the stranger exchanged glances, followed by a satisfied nod from the visitor.

'I am sure you must be hungry and tired,' he said, unlocking the door to the adjoining room with a gentle push.

It immediately swung open with a force that did not match his mild touch. He entered the room with slow, measured steps, followed closely by his guests. The room appeared different, strangely disconnected from the others in every conceivable way. Sankalp was stunned by the variety of fruits and dishes that he saw inside; they had been meticulously laid out on the carpet next to the fireplace. The seating around the carpet had cushions embroidered with gold. Hunger deserted Sankalp as he looked around shocked, in utter disbelief of what he was seeing… or imagining?

'Enjoy the meal. And do let me know if there is anything else you want,' declared their host in an almost teasing fashion.

'Thank you,' murmured Sankalp, entranced by the sight of it all.

The visitor smiled with a glint in his eyes, then waved his right hand in a circular motion. Lo and behold, from nowhere, some more dishes of an incredible variety appeared! A shocked Sankalp could no longer contain his curiosity.

'Sir, pardon my asking, but everything that just happened here…' Sankalp allowed himself a grim smile. 'It has taken away my appetite.' He drew in a deep breath before continuing. 'How did you create all this out of thin air? I want to know…' Bewildered, he spoke haltingly. 'How…how did this happen?'

'Is that all you want to know?' The visitor lifted an eyebrow, his large, captivating eyes searching him with a kindly expression. 'My son, shadows and light of thoughts and desires.' He paused with a smile. 'You will learn many more secrets from your teacher. For now, enjoy your dinner,' he said, pointing at the large assortment of food. 'A young man like you should not sleep on an empty stomach,' he smiled broadly, enjoying the expression of bewilderment on Sankalp's face.

Later that night, he departed, leaving no sign that he was ever there. The strange happenings of the evening had left Sankalp dumbfounded.

Seeing his perplexed state, Kalimpong remarked, 'My son, don't think too much about what you have seen. What seems like a trick is but a true occurrence. A combination of the power of the mind coupled with desire. It has the power to manifest as reality.'

'How?'

'All that you thought of while climbing up to the cottage manifested here. Your desires, Sankalp, were the source.' He smiled.

'In time you will know more. Now, go to sleep.'

Sankalp remained quiet and thoughtful for a long moment before speaking.

'Who was he?' Sankalp looked at Kalimpong, perplexed.

'Ah, the mind traveller.' His eyelids lowered slowly in reverence.

'My teacher. He taught me everything and has since moved on to a higher plane. I hold some of his powers for now.'

'A higher plane?'

'Yes. Another planetary existence, more sublime with no imperfections. Sometimes he visits here. I cannot explain with words, but some day you will understand.'

'He looks so young. How old is he?' Sankalp shook his head, amazed.

'He is ageless. The definitions of time, space and matter don't apply to them. They can appear, disappear and take any form at will. I wanted you to meet him. When the time comes, you will know him.'

'Are there more like him?'

'Yes, there are. Wandering the seen and the unseen worlds, some shining brightly in the night sky.' He paused for a moment before continuing. 'The league of godmen given the responsibility of keeping and restoring the balance.'

'He bears a striking resemblance to you.'

'Ah, my dear,' Kalimpong smiled slightly. 'When the minds become one, so does one's nature. A certain uniformity begins to appear.' Kalimpong's smile broadened mysteriously.

Sankalp was up early the next day. The morning was brighter and warmer than the days gone by. He walked down towards a small waterfall and waded to the middle, meditating and offering the customary obeisance to the sun god. After cleansing himself in the freezing waters, he made his way back to the hut. The learned master awaited him.

'From today, you start training in the art of chi, an ancient technique of hand-to-hand combat. It is a potent practice that combines the power of the mind and the strength of the body. I will also teach you the ancient art of swordsmanship, known as kenjutsu. It originated in the land of the rising sun, a region known as Yamato.'

Kalimpong retrieved some scriptures stored safely in an obscure part of the large cottage.

The art of hand-to-hand combat was something new for the young monk; he found it interesting.

It was also a good way for him to release the anger against the invaders that was so profoundly inscribed in his psyche.

'Sankalp, I want you to learn about the one hundred and eight pressure points located in the human body,' Kalimpong said, placing a very descriptive chart in front of him.

Sankalp looked distinctly nervous. 'It's so confusing.'

'Son, these points represent critical nerve centres and the axis that determines the flow of blood through the human body. Memorize them in the coming months.'

'Hmm.' Sankalp let out a breath.

'To be an adept, you must regularly practise everything you learn. It will keep you alert, both mentally and physically.'

'But, master, you always emphasize the virtues of self-control, sacrifice and non-violence. The ways of the monk. Why do I need to master fighting techniques?'

'Do you plan to preach the invaders out from your land?' Kalimpong's voice was stern.

'Fear rattles somewhere inside you!' Kalimpong stepped back and let out a sigh. He regarded his disciple with a penetrating look. 'Fear—the one true enemy. A mighty opponent that resides within.'

Kalimpong raised his finger and pointed at his heart. 'What you confront outside is only one of its many reflections!'

'Reflections? How will I know and see through them?' Sankalp queried after a moment's silence.

'You will feel it. By learning to overcome the appearance of fear, and importantly, the struggle it creates in your mind. Only then can you be fearless. A true warrior, indeed!'

Kalimpong smiled. 'My dear, most battles are between forces representing good and evil. You have to choose a side with the help of the values inculcated within by the higher self. Importantly, some battles are fought in the mind and others on the battlefield.' Kalimpong drew a deep breath. 'Sankalp, you slay the body, not the spirit. The body comes from the earth and goes back to it, while the everlasting spirit continues on its journey of realization, accumulating vivid experiences from the earthly plane.'

The days ahead were pleasant and Sankalp's progress anything but rapid. Though, he followed a strict regimen, learning and practising the more physical aspects of meditation. This was accompanied by important sermons.

'Sankalp, power is an illusion; true for those who subjugate to it. Real power is never expressed; it is evident,' Kalimpong emphasized. 'Anger is another decadent emotion; never use it as an instrument of aggression. It cripples the mind and disturbs focus. A true warrior must always stay calm; his action should be a quick, decisive reaction to his opponent's move.'

Kalimpong continued with his discourse, explaining every illustration in the ancient text that carried them through many, many years of history.

The sword fascinated Sankalp. The wooden katana became his favourite weapon.

'Sankalp, using the sword needs more acrobatic abilities than muscle. Your body needs to be supple and not rigid; now, clasp your hands together and raise them high.' Sankalp did as he was told. 'That is the easy part. Now, hold your arms up straight and bend forward from the waist and keep your knees steady,' the monk said, smiling.

This was hard for Sankalp; he could not bend very far forward, and his hands lost their grip on the sword. His shoulder muscles stretched and hurt.

'That is good enough for now. We can start with a few exercises for flexibility without over-exerting.'

Kalimpong added specific training methods to his teaching. Sankalp progressed well in the coming days.

'Sankalp, the key to fine swordsmanship is equilibrium with focus while maintaining momentum,' Kalimpong explained.

He taught him the correct stances and explained the eight directions, much like a compass, and the six ways of attack and defence in detail.

Sankalp practised hard, amidst phases of perplexity and impatience. The stances were difficult and the movements challenging, but he soon dispelled his wariness and flowed through the postures with perfect timing and confidence.

'There are many good warriors in the world, Sankalp. But being better is about expanding your mental reach and going beyond the limitations of the physical self,' the master remarked at the end of a rigorous session.

Sankalp nodded respectfully, but once again understood little of those words. They exchanged a glance.

'In time...' Kalimpong added with a smile, understanding his predicament.

By the end of their first summer at the cottage, Kalimpong had put Sankalp through a regimen as strenuous as his own. He taught the young boy the use of air currents and how they could exemplify the movement of the body.

'Sankalp, there is a saying that the sword that saves a man kills a man. The sword is a tool for killing, no matter whose hands it is in.' Kalimpong regarded him and drew in a deep breath. 'And if you truly want to master the sword, then be at peace with death first,' he asserted.

'Death?' Sankalp said in astonishment.

'Sankalp, the weapon might make you powerful, but it is emancipation from death that makes you invincible!'

Sankalp's training continued briskly.

They were nearing the end of their second summer there. And then, one day Kalimpong remarked, 'Winter will soon be here. We must leave for our final destination tomorrow morning.'

'Tomorrow?' Sankalp repeated, sounding surprised.

'It is a five-day journey from here if the weather remains bearable.' Kalimpong smiled.

'Master, where to now?'

'It is a small place in the mountains. Offering serenity to the soul and a sense of satisfaction to the mind, yet it challenges you to leap for a higher purpose!' A smile stretched Kalimpong's face as the two exchanged a glance. 'I was blessed with sacred teachings there, and it will be your place of learning. The intricate techniques, once understood, will guide you in your pursuit and unravel the secrets of destiny.' His smile broadened.

'Master, when will we return to the cave?'

'It will be a while before we do, my son,' replied Kalimpong.

'What about the apple tree? Who will take care of it in my absence?'

'Nature will. It always does!'

Early the next day, they started on the five-day uphill trek, led by the learned monk. Sankalp followed close behind. Kalimpong spoke little through the journey but occasionally glanced back with a reassuring smile. Sankalp knew well that the silence of this man carried more significance than his utterances.

They moved steadily up the mountain track, resting by sunset and starting at daybreak.

It was high noon of the fifth day; the monk finally broke his silence as they made their way past a few hutments to their right.

'We have reached the end of our journey. From here, we turn towards the valley, right ahead, amid all those beautiful trees,' Kalimpong remarked, pointing towards a cottage as he hastened through the narrow pass that led to the clearing below.

Sankalp rushed forward and hurried down the track excitedly.

6

The Teachings of the Sacred Art

The foreground was brimming with meadows awash with alpine flowers. In the distance, unending, snowbound peaks reflected the late afternoon light, giving the land a beautiful reddish tinge. A variety of melodious sounds from the exotic, colourful birds nestled amongst the fruit-laden trees filled the air. Sankalp had never seen such a beautiful place. He had only heard of the many heavens that existed in the Himalayan ranges. He stopped and wondered at it all. Was this one such heaven?

Zanzi had followed him and was circling close by, making him aware of his presence. Through the trees, he could see the cottage, set in the middle of a low-lying plateau with an enchanting view of the valley. It stood amongst a patch of green, mingling seamlessly with its surroundings. A soothing fragrance floated in the air, coming from the many flowers that grew all around.

Excited, he ran down the mountain track, carefully negotiating the steep and narrow trail. The sun was about to set when they entered the cottage. After resting for a while, Kalimpong called out to Sankalp.

'I will be gone for a few hours. You can take care of the cottage in the meantime; it has not been used for a while.'

'Will we be here long?' asked Sankalp

'As long as it takes,' the monk smiled, before walking out of the cottage and up the narrow track.

Sankalp made sure the cottage was sparkling clean and the master's room well-tended. He chose a room overlooking the south side of the valley for himself. The adjoining room was left vacant for guests. The kitchen was spacious. It had a large window overlooking the shrubs outside. There was also a small vegetable garden where coriander, sweet potatoes, green chillies and a few other vegetables grew.

After all his work was done, Sankalp sat near the large window in his room gazing up at the azure sky. A skein of geese flying in a 'V' formation caught his attention. They were migrating from the north of the Himalayan ranges towards their winter nesting grounds in the south. It was a delightful sight. For a long while, he sat still, entranced. Until he noticed the learned master making his way down the slope, towards the cottage.

He was accompanied by someone.

The minute Kalimpong reached the door, Sankalp was there to receive him and the guest.

'Sankalp, this is Titla. She will be staying with us and taking care of the cottage. I hope you have a room for her too?'

'Yes, master. She can have the room adjacent to mine,' he said, pointing to it.

'Thank you, Sankalp,' the girl smiled slightly. 'That has been my room every time I have come here,' she said as she placed a few loaves of bread along with four bags packed with cereals and grains on a shelf.

'So, you have been here before?'

'Yes, many times, with my father…until he passed away,' she replied with slight hesitation. 'But others do tend to the cottage in my absence.'

'I am sorry to hear about your father. I too have lost my family,' he said, trying to console her for her loss.

As night descended, Kalimpong asked Sankalp to accompany him. They walked to a clearing amid the pine trees. It was located to the south of the cottage, overlooking the valley.

'Sankalp, I have explained to you the aspects of the human mind and its control. We humans can think and also act on our thoughts. This makes us unique, since we can work on both planes of existence, the mental and the physical. Training thus must encompass both sides of our nature. It is therefore imperative that we raise our level of awareness and maintain a fine balance between both spheres,' Kalimpong said that smiled broadly, the deep horizontal lines of age merging.

'My dear, there is still a lot you have to learn, understand and, importantly, experience.'

The two sat beside a small fire in the thicket, a little distance from the cottage. Kalimpong explained the physical aspects of nature, comprising the human body, air, water, fire and earth. And about the supra physical aspect, which dealt with the unseen forces around us.

'Sankalp, the elementary body, comprising natural elements, is more reactive to nature since it is an integral part of it. While the soul, a luminous current we call consciousness, is more reactive to the cosmic consciousness. By cosmic consciousness, I mean the universal entity of which it is a part.

'While you must be active and aware of your surroundings, your reactions have to be more in sync with the cosmic laws that govern this physicality,' explained Kalimpong.

A shadow approached them from among the trees.

'Who is it?' Sankalp called out.

'It's me,' replied Titla. 'Have I interrupted something important? It's late, and I have been waiting with dinner.'

Kalimpong smiled at this pleasant intrusion. 'We will continue tomorrow,' he said and rose to his feet.

They followed Titla as she quickly made her way back to the cottage.

Sitting cross-legged on a woollen mat, Kalimpong could not help but compliment the young girl. She had laid out a sumptuous meal on the very first day of her arrival.

'Titla, I have known you since you were a little girl. Talented, you always were, and it shows in your cooking too. My dear, some day you will make a good wife to a lucky man,' he said, smiling broadly.

The shy girl blushed, bowed in humble appreciation and left the room.

After a refreshing meal, the learned master retired to his room.

Through that winter, Kalimpong simplified and explained the sacred texts to Sankalp. He delved into every aspect of his knowledge, from the history of the known world to statecraft and some of the more intense aspects of life.

'Sankalp, one must be ready to face whatever life has to offer. Be it happiness, sadness or grief. Struggle moulds and defines character,' Kalimpong emphasized.

Sankalp nodded in understanding.

'Today, let's talk about the tenets of war, though I do not recommend it. But it remains very much a part of the earthly world and casts a strong influence on human life.'

A smile overtook the seriousness on his face. 'My dear, I have said this before and I say it again. All wars are primarily fought in the mind.'

Sankalp nodded.

'If you lose on the mental plane, you can never win on the physical one. To win, you need to be dedicated, fearless and, above all, convinced that what you are doing is for the right cause. Only then can your actions be commensurate with nature. Consequently, in the face of death, you will stand fearless!'

Kalimpong looked at Sankalp; his eyes said more than he had in that quiet moment. He took a few sips of water from an earthen cup kept nearby before continuing.

'On the other hand, no matter how powerful your enemy, if his actions are not in accordance with the laws of nature and instead are motivated by material aspects such as lust, greed, ego and anger, then he will face defeat.'

Sankalp pursed his lips at the statement. He wanted to intervene but quietly continued to listen.

'Sometimes, in the immediate present, it may appear that an evil adversary has won. This could be because of positive karma carried from past deeds. But a victory of such nature is short-lived. In the long run, the cause and effect relationship reigns supreme and he will be defeated!'

Sankalp listened intently, his mind racing to the past. To the moment of disaster that had changed his life forever. He felt his chest constrict in anger and with the pain of losing his family and everything he loved. He silently questioned the reason for such an anomaly in his life.

Kalimpong understood his discomfort but continued his discourse without any change in expression or the slightest trace of emotion.

'One must understand that what we see and experience today is the cumulative effect resulting from a cause, which we cannot comprehend in the present time and moment.'

Kalimpong paused before continuing softly, 'My dear, the distress you feel today is the effect of a cause from a past life. Our memory is mostly limited to this birth. We cannot, under normal circumstances, remember our actions from a past life that may have led to our present. To do so, we need to awaken our inner subconscious eye and look beyond time and space as we see it.'

Sankalp understood little of what the monk said. Nor did he immediately grasp the purpose of his words. But he knew he was meant to remember them for another day and time.

It was the fourth lunar month. A bright star shone prominently in the night sky; the time of Saga Dawa was approaching. It was the most important of festivals for the people of the Tibetan lands, commemorating the birth of the Buddha and his attainment of enlightenment. With it, the Tibetan master initiated Sankalp into the more intricate principles and practices of the yoga of the mind and body control. Under this rigorous training, Sankalp began to develop powers that were beyond normal.

In time, Kalimpong taught him the penance of the sun god and introduced him to the secrets of light. He revealed more about the formless intelligence that surrounds us as space.

'Sankalp, the body derives strength from the food we eat. A part of the energy is spent converting this food from gross to abstract energy. This energy from food primarily helps us function and perform on a physical level.'

Sankalp nodded, listening attentively to every detail.

'The mind is much more powerful than the gross body and capable of achieving and performing incredible feats. The light derived from the sun is pure energy, ethereal but powerful. It is this extraordinary energy that powers your mind and helps propel the subtle body through the ether or the "sky paths". Your subtle body is a gridwork of light and sacred geometry. You cannot be a mind traveller without mastering the kinetics of light and thoughts,' Kalimpong emphatically stated.

'How does it work?'

'The outer layer of the body consists of millions of cells that form the skin—the first and the uppermost layer of the body. These cells contain within them many nano cells that connect to every iota of the human body.'

Sankalp nodded, giving the words his utmost attention.

'These nano cells are complicated dynamic structures, which can, with the right knowledge, convert photons of light into energy. It is an inexhaustible source of power!'

Sankalp listened, spellbound by the master's words.

Kalimpong cleared his throat and continued. 'You have to learn how to channel this energy, which can help power the subtle body through the sky paths.'

In time, Kalimpong taught Sankalp the mechanics of converting light into energy. The teaching of this complicated process continued for many months. By the end of spring, Sankalp had understood but not completely mastered the intricate science of it. His struggles, physical and mental, were often eased by Kalimpong's words of wisdom.

On one such evening, as they made their way back to the cottage, doubt and discomfort were writ large on Sankalp's face. Was he falling short of the master's expectations, he wondered?

Kalimpong could read his thoughts. He stopped short and spoke with affection. 'My dear Sankalp, you have always been precocious, and that is good. But higher understanding is more about unravelling,' he said and smiled in his characteristic way. 'Learning from your own experiences,' he explained as they walked together.

Placing his hand on Sankalp's shoulder, he continued, 'Interestingly, the deeper we go into understanding the complexities of life and science, the more do we begin to decipher its true hidden simplicities.'

With that, Kalimpong retired for the night, leaving Sankalp to ponder over his words.

The young monk sat quietly for a while, unable to sleep. A host of thoughts from the past filled his mind. He drew in a deep breath and let out a sigh before quietly walking out into the open, seeking reprieve.

The night was at its enchanting best. A gentle breeze wafted across the valley. Everything seemed brighter as a radiant moon slowly ascended the star-studded horizon.

7

The Soulmate

Sankalp walked across the length of the cottage's veranda, admiring what he saw, distracted briefly by the soft jingle of anklets.

'Who is it'? he called out.

'It's me, Titla. Am I intruding?'

'Not at all. I was out walking, thinking…' He spoke softly. 'Talking to myself, in fact,' Sankalp said and smiled lightly at his utterance, still engrossed in his thoughts.

'About?' Titla's question brought him back to the moment.

'What the master explained earlier.' He paused, perhaps not wanting to disclose the entirety of his thoughts.

Sankalp raised his right hand to his chest, feeling the soft evening breeze between his fingers.

'Ah…the winds are slower and soothing, a sure sign of the coming days.' He looked up at the night sky as he stepped past her. 'What a perfect night. I can't take my eyes off those peaks gleaming under the moonlight,' he said, pointing towards the expanse.

Titla smiled.

'Everything is so mesmerizing,' he concluded, turning his face to her. 'But why are you awake at this hour?'

Titla considered for a while before speaking. 'Well, I was lost in thought about my family, especially my mother, and couldn't sleep,' she finally said softly while deftly using her fingers to push back a lock of hair that swayed across her face.

Her slender frame turned to him as she slowly walked closer to him.

Sankalp looked at Titla, her lovely eyes shining exuberantly in the night sky.

'Don't you remember me?' she questioned, smiling.

Sankalp was taken aback. He looked at her intently. 'There is something familiar about you,' he said, staring into her big black eyes.

'You used to come by my village to collect food,' exclaimed Titla, holding his gaze.

'Oh,' he said, recollecting memories from the past. His expression quickly changed with recognition.

'Is it…? It really is you.' He gawked in amazement.

Shaking his head in astonishment, he continued, 'I remember now—the girl who never spoke!' Sankalp grinned and his eyes sparkled with amusement. He looked at her more keenly.

'I am so happy to see you here!' he said excitedly, in one breath.

'I am too.'

'Why didn't you tell me earlier?' Sankalp clucked his tongue in mild remonstration.

She smiled shyly, responding with a question. 'Why did you stop coming to the village?'

'Ah…' he rued, 'we used to travel from one village to another, but then, one summer we left the cave and travelled up the Sengg`e river.' He smiled. 'But I often wondered about you…'

Titla raised an eyebrow. 'Why are you here, in the middle of nowhere? Your heart is veiled, but I sense a burden in your eyes.' Titla's eyes remained on him.

'I have spent the last few years in the company of the learned monk, travelling, learning and understanding the finer aspects of the art of meditation. I need it…' He paused and looked up. 'I need it to help seek my destiny,' Sankalp replied, his voice deepening.

'I carry an unimaginable pain of the day I lost everything. My family, friends, all killed by the invaders! Memories often haunt me and shatter the tranquillity of my sleep,' he concluded, emerging from his thoughts.

'Sankalp, you cannot let your loss keep you from living life!' She continued to look at him, sensing his remorse. 'I am sure the learned monk will share secrets that we cannot comprehend today.'

Sankalp treated her words as he would a riddle. 'I hope that happens soon. I am trying hard to understand and learn what I can,' he sighed. 'So when the time comes, I can avenge the death of my family and my people!'

She moved closer to him and impulsively held his hand.

Sankalp stood frozen by the warmth of her touch. It was something he had never felt before.

He held on to her hand as they walked back to the cottage. It was a comforting moment for both.

Early the next morning, Kalimpong left for the upper reaches of the snow-covered mountains, towards Gang Rinpoche or Kailasa, as it was known. Sankalp watched him disappear behind a curtain of early morning mist.

'Why did the master leave so early without informing us?' he asked, puzzled. 'Do you know where he has gone?'

'No,' replied Titla.

She peeped out of the window, hoping to catch a glimpse of the monk, being as surprised as Sankalp by his sudden departure.

They spent most of the morning enjoying each other's company.

It was a sunny afternoon; the last few weeks had seen brief spells of rain due to the rising temperatures. Sankalp left the cottage to collect firewood while Titla prepared the day's meal.

'Ahh, thukpa at last,' Sankalp remarked over supper that evening. 'And it looks delicious. I could eat it all and still ask for more.'

Titla smiled, her eyes dancing with delight at his acknowledgment.

'It's been a while since I cooked thukpa.'

Sankalp heaped a spoonful into his mouth before raising his head and answering with a smile. He looked at her with a renewed sense of familiarity, of knowing her from another time and place. Besides being pretty and intelligent, she was a true companion, much like his mother was to his father. For a moment, he was lost in thought; his fazed look prompted a question from Titla.

'What are you thinking about? Did you like it?' she enquired as she sat down on the thick floor mat alongside him. Sankalp gestured his appreciation as he slurped down another mouthful.

'It is very well made,' he asserted.

Titla smiled as she began eating.

A while later, they strolled out for a brief walk.

'Are you going to leave soon?' Titla queried, tossing her hair.

'Not that soon,' he replied, raising an eyebrow. 'But once I have learnt all I need to.' A sudden burst of passion animated his face.

Inclining her head slightly, Titla waited a moment before asking, 'Sankalp, is that all you seek—revenge?'

He stared into her eyes briefly and then calmly replied, 'No, I seek freedom from it.'

Titla was confused and a bit saddened by his reply. He could sense her feelings and consoled her.

'Titla, my experiences have changed my perception of life and its very meaning. I have realized the futility of emotions and the unpredictability of time.' He paused thoughtfully. 'Moments that seem calm and blissful may have a storm brewing within.' He shook his head. 'One that can shatter everything you hold dear.'

Titla could see the anguish in his eyes as he spoke.

'In my tormented state, I am afraid to express happiness for fear of losing it.' He cringed at the memories from the past. 'There are times when I feel the futility of my own existence—of having no one to share the simple joys of life.'

Titla looked at him with affection. 'I understand. I have suffered a similar fate but not in the way you have. I too mourn the loss of my father, and I know how it feels.' The grief was plain on her face as she spoke. 'The learned master has taken me under his care, trying to make my life easier. After coming here, I feel at peace with myself. I know it might not last, but the love and care from the master have touched my heart, and I know his blessings will help me through life.'

'What about others in your family?'

My mother…she misses me. I go to the village sometimes to meet her.' A slight smile eclipsed the expression of unrest on her face.

Sankalp looked at her in understanding and nodded. Titla reached out. She took his hand in hers, entwining her fingers with his. The warmth of her hand touched his heart. In that moment he felt complete. They said not a word, preferring to stroll back to the cottage in companionable silence.

The study of ancient scriptures and the practise of various arts devoured most of Sankalp's days. They were now getting shorter, and the nights longer and darker. The brief summer of the high attitudes was receding once again. The winter chill was beginning to set in, and there was still no news from Kalimpong.

One fine morning, the two walked towards a small plot of green; the tiny kitchen garden adjacent to the cottage was dotted with patches of purple.

'We have a week's supply of the finest eggplant here,' Sankalp proudly stated and reached out to pluck a few.

'The master's favourite,' Titla responded instantly. 'I have been wondering about his return. He has been gone for a long time.' Titla sighed and looked up at the bright morning sky, now visible through the clearing mist.

'I have wondered too, but you cannot predict the master's course, can you? Something important must have held him back.'

'I hope he is fine.'

'I will try and find out tonight,' Sankalp muttered as they walked back towards the cottage.

'Sankalp, how can you possibly know the master's whereabouts?' jested Titla.

There was a brief pause, and then he spoke. 'The master has taught me a form of meditation wherein the subtle currents in the ether transmit your innermost feelings. Sending and receiving thoughts back and forth becomes easy once you practise enough.'

Titla's eyes sparkled with excitement. 'You must teach me before you leave; at least I will know whether you are safe and well.'

Sankalp responded with a chuckle in mild remonstration.

Titla, in a short time, had grown fond of him. His gentleness and care drew her closer. She felt at ease in his company. In his heart, Sankalp felt the same, but obedience to the master and to the laws that governed the sacred teachings made him less responsive. Titla cared for him even though she knew one day he would leave. Her feelings for him were unconditional and without demands. Humbling as it was, love had begun to prevail.

Sankalp requested to be left alone for some time. A sweet smile from Titla sent a humble message of acknowledgment; it also possessed his attention.

Sankalp sat down in the lotus position, trying to focus his mind on the centre of his forehead, the seat of great supramental powers in the human body. Reaching the state of conscious equilibrium was not always easy, at least not this time. As he moved deeper and higher into the subconscious state, his mind began to stray.

To an untrained practitioner, this was the most difficult phase in meditation. It was imperative at this juncture to hold the mind steady. Drawing upon his inner strength, he did so and let go of every other sensation and all his thoughts of her. Gradually, the oceanic movements within calmed. The initial restlessness gave way to a strange stillness.

The young disciple sat content and motionless for hours.

Steadily, his mind mastered the stillness within. With that, his perception became hypersensitive, deciphering and reading hidden messages in the ether. Slowly their minds bridged. His face lit up with a smile as Titla watched calmly through a window.

His thoughts connected with the master. The young monk heard his deep voice.

'My dear Sankalp,' the voice reverberated through the ether.

'Yes, master,' he whispered in his mind.

'I have been travelling deep within the upper Himalayan ranges, going through processes of transcendental meditation. I will be away for a while. Until my return, practise all that I have taught you and take care of Titla. I will return once the task here is complete.'

The voice disappeared.

Sankalp opened his eyes; dawn was breaking. A heavenly hour, when the darkness of night gives way to light and the world begins to slowly rouse itself from slumber.

He walked out of his room; Titla lay asleep close to the window. Through the night, she had been watching over him. His steps, though hushed, awoke her.

'Sankalp, is everything all right? Did you speak with the master?' she enquired, sounding anxious.

Sankalp nodded. 'Yes, I did.'

'Tell me, what did he say?' Titla insisted, still unbelieving.

'He has gone to the higher reaches of the mountains. He will be back after the winter is over. Till then, he has entrusted you to my care.'

'What is the master doing all alone in the mountains? I am worried about him.'

Sankalp smiled. 'There is nothing to worry about. The master is in deep meditation in the forbidden heights of the Himalayan mountains.'

Titla nodded, prompting him to continue.

'It is a divine place, meant only for elevated souls.' Sankalp raised his right eyebrow, conveying a sense of mystery. 'A well-kept secret; only the accomplished few can reach there.'

'Is that so?' Titla murmured, awed.

'He once described the magical aura of the place...' Sankalp fell silent and closed his eyes, as if reminiscing. 'It is a place of incredible power, where he mastered the language of the stars.'

Titla listened, wide-eyed.

His gaze fell on her undisturbed bedding. Distracted, he remarked, 'You seem to have been awake for most of the night.'

'I like to watch you sometimes,' she laughed innocently. 'When you sit in meditation, you radiate a certain calm that is so infectious—captivating, in fact.'

Sankalp smiled broadly, pleased with her words.

'Ahh, the lotus posture. It locks the feet together and holds the body steady, especially the spine, giving the human frame a solid base to sit upon, which prevents the practitioner from toppling over if they go into a deep trance,' he explained. 'And that sometimes can happen quite unexpectedly. A restless body will disturb the mind; the posture also brings equilibrium and eases the flow of the life force.'

Titla leaned forward—she was awed and wanted him to continue.

Sankalp paused to consume a few spoonfuls of tsampa. 'I need to collect firewood for the night and some fresh fruit.' He cut short his explanation with a grin before bouncing upright on his feet.

'Don't be long,' Titla smiled, her eyes beckoning his return.

Sankalp walked out of the cottage and made his way up the mountain, enjoying the early morning twitter of birds and the warm light streaming through the tall birch trees. Beams of light, trapped delicately in the early morning dew, covered most of the alpine shrubs and meadows. The dew drops hung low, like strings of pearls arranged artistically around the forest maiden. He could not help but think about Titla. Something had changed.

Was this what love did?

8

The Wrath of the Mountain Devil

Sankalp's life had gone through a major transformation; it had been difficult. He had learnt and realized much in the company of the learned master. He had met and fallen in love with a beautiful girl. But none of this had put an end to his anguish. He still felt bereft. His will tested his patience every now and then, while his soul yearned for answers to the happenings in his life. Was his life ready to be changed by love?

After collecting enough firewood, he climbed further up the path, which led to a dense cluster of trees. It offered a variety of fruits, including jackfruit. It was Titla's favourite. Sankalp plucked enough while feasting on some. With his bag full, he started to walk back to the cottage. On the way, he came across a shady pine.

'Let me rest awhile,' he murmured. Putting aside his bundle, he lay down under the open sky and closed his eyes. Almost immediately, thoughts broke out of his subconscious. He pondered what Kalimpong had told him about the hidden language of the stars. How easily then could he see through the uncertainties that surrounded life and learn about his destiny?

He lost track of time and fell asleep.

An uneasy feeling woke him. Dark clouds had eclipsed the bright afternoon light. The air felt heavy. Sankalp decided to head back to the cottage. Making his way down through the thicket, he heard a strange sound. Something had moved quickly through the shrubs behind him!

'Who is it?' he called out, turning around quickly. There was nothing. He hurried down the rough mountain path. A short while later, he heard the sound again. It was getting closer. The thick undergrowth made it difficult for him to see anything clearly. Then, at a point where darts of light pierced through the foliage, he caught a glimpse of furry dark spots moving stealthily. Sensing danger, Sankalp stopped and pulled out the longest piece of firewood from his bag. It wasn't much but offered some protection. He stayed alert as he carefully made his way down the trail.

On nearing home, he saw Titla standing outside. He called out to her, waving his hands in the air. Sankalp received a loving smile in return. Just then, a loud crack from somewhere behind him caught his attention. It was accompanied by a bone-chilling growl! Something had been watching and following him, probably waiting for the right time to attack! He headed quickly for the cottage, the menacing growl still ringing in his ears.

'Go back in and wait there for me!' he shouted from the fence.

'What happened?' Titla asked him as he entered the cottage, worried.

'I heard a loud growl and had an uncanny feeling of being followed here. I am sure it was nothing, but I was concerned about you,' Sankalp said as he placed the bundle of firewood and fruits on the floor.

Despite his words, she sensed anxiety, even fear, in his voice.

Sankalp walked to the other side of the cottage for a wash, thinking it would be unwise to end the day's conversation on a depressing note. Changing the subject, he engaged Titla in light conversation while she warmed the evening meal.

He stared out of the window. The sunset sky had turned darker and the stars brighter in the time they had been talking.

'I am ready for dinner,' he announced as the sound of cicadas rent the air.

'Eat the vegetable soup till I get the rice pudding ready,' she said, placing a large steaming bowl in front of him.

Titla quickly headed back to the kitchen. Barely a moment later, he heard a loud shriek from the kitchen!

'Sankalp, Sankalp!' shouted Titla, her face turning yellow with fear as if she had seen a ghost.

He quickly reached her.

'What is the matter, Titla? Are you all right?'

'I saw something moving outside the window. I only caught a glimpse of flaming eyes.' Breathing hard, she continued, 'And they scared me!' A cold shiver ran through her.

Sankalp grabbed her arm as she was speaking. 'Don't worry, Titla. I am here with you, but we must be watchful.'

Holding her close, he stared into the dusk that was quickly turning into a dark night. He scanned the cottage's surroundings with animal intensity. There was nothing in sight, but Sankalp noted a disturbance in the shrubs. A few broken twigs hung low, as if something big and heavy had recklessly passed through, and fallen leaves lay party buried in the path it had taken.

'Many fierce creatures roam the forest at night, looking for food,' Sankalp spoke with deliberate slowness.

He knew that strange and powerful forces inhabited the Himalayan valleys, having himself faced one some years ago. The learned master had told him to be alert whenever he left the cottage.

'Sankalp, in a world hidden from the one you see, there exists another. Unseen, unforgiving and immensely powerful! The forests and the mountains that provide the essentials of life also stand witness to your learning and growing strength. One day, they will put you to the test. Be ready to preserve what you value and protect the ones you love.' The master's words echoed from a near past.

Many moments in life test you, and this seemed like one such moment.

Sankalp stepped out of the cottage, armed with his staff. He reached the clearing outside, searching for the creature or any signs of it. Not finding anything, he walked towards the thicket on the other side. After a few excruciatingly long moments, fear stared him in the eye! A majestic creature, with an intriguing pattern of spots and stripes, appeared from behind the shrubs, its eyes glowing in the full light of a silver moon. It was hungry, and as their eyes met, the king of the snowy mountains let out a roar, letting the residents of the cottage know they were his chosen target.

A brief moment later, it disappeared, leaving Sankalp terrified.

Large cats had a habit of stalking their prey and coming back later to ambush it. The light of day had faded; it wasn't wise to go further and be drawn into the dense forest by the crafty predator. Sankalp quickly returned to the cottage. Titla too had caught a glimpse of the unusually large beast. She knew danger was lurking close, waiting for the right moment to strike.

'I am going to reinforce the fence with some wood and vine', yelled Sankalp. He walked into the room that was used to store firewood and objects of daily use.

'Will that keep it away?' Titla asked, shaken by her brief encounter.

'I hope so. Please make sure you lock all the doors and windows. The hungry animal might come back,' Sankalp cautioned.

Titla felt vulnerable; her body tensed with visible signs of discomfort as she walked away.

After taking precautions for their safety, Sankalp settled down in his room, close to the fire. It had been an unusually cold day, and the night could get worse. Titla was back in the kitchen, while Sankalp sat in meditation.

He was stressed. Fear and anguish threatened to break his concentration; both emotions were distracting and troublesome. They could make fine warriors fall before battle and kill the spirit long before the mortal body breathed its last.

'In the matrix of life, it is difficult to comprehend what the supreme consciousness has laid out for us. The death of the body is inevitable. It will happen the way it has been ordained for you. All you can do is perform your part with dignity and valour. And for that, you need to master your feelings and strike a balance between courage, compassion, defeat and triumph,' Kalimpong had explained many a time.

Remembering his master's words restored Sankalp's concentration.

In the coming weeks, there was no sign of the unusual animal. Until one day Titla remarked, 'Sankalp, I have had an uneasy feeling of late.'

'What is it?' Sankalp enquired as he helped Titla scour the dishes clean with earth.

'There are stories whispered in these parts, about devilish creatures that roam the highlands. They are powerful and can take any form.' Her worry was in marked contrast to the joyful verve that marked her every day.

Sankalp shook his head. 'Is that what the women you met from the village today told you?'

'Yes, the sisters deliver rations and milk occasionally. They mentioned the village had lost a few sheep and a calf a few nights back.' She paused, her expression becoming more disturbed. 'But now, a man from the village has gone missing.'

'Is it the leopard you are thinking about?' Sankalp smiled disarmingly.

'Yes, but now when I think back, it seemed large, much larger than a leopard,' she said and drew in a deep breath, 'and nearly as big as a tiger!'

Sankalp nodded. 'It could be a tigard,' he said slowly.

'What's a tigard?'

'A crossbreed. It has the stealth of a leopard and the strength of a tiger. Very rare, but they do exist.'

Titla's expression turned fearful at the description.

'Don't worry,' he reassured her. 'I will stay alert. We haven't seen it around for some time; I presume it has left the area,' he said, soothing her fears.

In the wee hours of the following morning, Titla woke up abruptly. For a moment, she had the strange feeling of being watched. She dismissed the thought as a reflection of the disquiet she had been feeling.

The next few days saw unabating rains, making the ensuing nights dark and devoid of moonlight.

On one such night, unable to sleep, Sankalp made his way towards the outer fence of the cottage. A misty darkness surrounded it. He laid out his mat in the front courtyard and lit a fire. As the night progressed, sleep got the better of him, but his slumber was short-lived. A blast of ravening wind tore him from his slumber. A large grey owl hooted loudly from up close. The forest suddenly came alive with sounds that were quickly drowned by a snarl. It had come from somewhere close! Sankalp jolted to his feet. He grabbed a large, half-burnt stick from the fire in one hand and a double-sided axe blade mounted with a spike in the other.

Just then, movement caught his eye. The fiery tigard emerged from the dark mist! It leapt out from behind the shrubs surrounding the cottage, covering an extraordinary distance. His blazing eyes stared at Sankalp from across the fire that stood between them. Using its powerful hind legs, he leapt soundlessly in the opposite direction, towards the cottage, to where Titla slept! The clever animal had chosen the weaker out of the two as its target. Sankalp ran towards the window that was only a few feet from the front door. He aggressively waved the burning piece of wood in the animal's face.

'That should scare him off,' he thought.

Roaring, the large cat backed away. Turning his head away from the burning stick, the tigard slowly paced towards him. From its flaming eyes stared the damned.

The commotion woke up Titla. She realized something was wrong.

'Sankalp, Sankalp! Are you all right? I just heard a loud noise!' she shouted with a flash of fear and ran to the door, not knowing the fiery animal was there, right outside!

As she flung open the door, her gaze landed on the beast. To her horror, it stood right between her and Sankalp!

'Titla, move back and shut the door!'

The fierce creature was closer to her and could strike at any time. Titla stood dazed, her body frozen.

Sankalp moved with lightning speed. He flung the axe at the tigard; the cat bucked its hind legs almost instinctively, and the axe narrowly missed its abdominal cavity. Not knowing what to do, Sankalp rushed at it, hurling himself at the animal, using the momentum of his weight to stop the beast from its intended strike. Sankalp quickly locked his strong arms around the large cat's neck. With an ear-splitting roar, the tigard struggled, its powerful muscles contracting and releasing.

The animal jerked itself free!

Sankalp lost his balance and fell. The tigard saw his chance and pounced on him. His large fangs skittered close, missing the jugular. Sankalp quickly rolled to where the axe lay, and in one quick move sprang back to his feet, his brow marked with a trickle of blood. Unrelenting, the tigard sprang forward, jaws wide open, aimed at his opponent's neck. Sankalp crouched low and thrust the spike of the axe in the beast's underbelly. The tigard roared in pain. Wounded and angry, it lunged with animal ferocity. Its powerful paws armed with long, sharp nails tore into Sankalp's chest and left thigh.

Sankalp stepped back; with his left hand outstretched, he held its neck. With his right, he thrust the spear into its chest. The tigard roared in pain and relented. Seizing the moment, Sankalp raised the axe with both hands and struck the tigard on its back and then again more furiously than before. The force of the blow cracked the animal's spine. The big cat struggled a bit before falling to the ground but not before it had drawn blood.

The tigard breathed his last. Sankalp staggered away from the animal, his robe dripping with blood, most of it coming from his wounds.

'Sankalp, you are badly hurt?' Seeing him in pain, Titla couldn't hold back her tears. She helped him as he slowly limped to his room.

'Stay calm and don't move. I will boil some herbs to clean your wounds.'

Sankalp nodded and closed his eyes as he struggled into a sitting position. The wounds were severe. He was losing blood. He could barely sit for a few minutes; he slumped helplessly to the floor.

'Are you all right?' Titla exclaimed with a hitch of fear in her voice.

'Oh, how I wish the master was here to help us,' she thought as she carefully examined the lacerations on Sankalp's chest and thigh.

'Your wounds are deep, and the blood isn't stopping. I will have to cauterize them; there is no other way to stop the bleeding,' her voice faltered as she spoke.

The pain would be agonizing, and she had to be careful. But it was the only way to save his life. She quickly tore a piece from her silk tunic.

'Go ahead...' Sankalp coughed, choking on his words.

The pain was becoming more and more unbearable. Titla placed the silken cloth on the open wound on his chest, and then very gently pressed it into the gash before burning it. His body twitched with the heat, and he let out a huff.

'Hold on, Sankalp,' she said, comforting him. 'It's nearly done; you will be fine now.' Her consoling did not elicit a response. Sankalp had crossed the threshold of pain and lost consciousness.

Titla was in shock.

She spent the night sitting beside Sankalp, keeping him warm, waiting for him to open his eyes again. She was afraid of losing him and prayed fervently for his recovery. The intensity of her prayers penetrated the ether. Kalimpong felt the distress; he realized something terrible had happened. Powerful healing currents made their way towards Sankalp while Kalimpong immediately started on his journey back to the cottage.

The following day was one of loneliness and anxiety. Titla sat for hours with her knees pulled up against her chest, watching over Sankalp. Every now and then, she fell asleep and woke up in anguish until dawn broke the next day. The wholesome rays of the rising sun brought relief. Titla felt Sankalp's forehead. The fever had come down a little, but he was still unconscious. Worried, she didn't leave his side. By late afternoon, he opened his eyes. He was in pain but had survived!

'Sankalp, how are you feeling?' She looked at him, smiling warmly through her tears and gently caressing his forehead with her hand.

'Ahh...' he moaned. 'I feel better, except for the terrible pain from my wounds.' His face contorted as he whispered his agony.

She ran out of the room and quickly prepared a vulnerary paste. It would not only help heal the wound but provide immediate relief from pain. Certain herbs plucked under a waxing moon held inexplicable healing properties. Titla had learnt the composition of the complex mix from her mother. She often tended to wounded soldiers returning from battle. Titla knew well that along with medicine, it was faith that healed. Pure thoughts and desires helped the process, and she wanted nothing more than for the young monk to be well and back on his feet.

'Let me clean your wounds and apply this herbal preparation,' she said, helping Sankalp sit and take a few gulps of water.

She spent the latter part of the day preparing porridge and tea. It was important for him to regain the blood he had lost. It took another three days for the fever to come down, and with that, he felt better. In about a week, the wounds on his legs began to close. He was able to walk around the cottage with ease, though he still felt bursts of pain from the deep lesions on his chest.

On a partly cloudy morning, Sankalp stepped out of the cottage and saw something hanging from the wooden fence.

'Titla, what is that?' he enquired as she came out of the cottage.

'That is a mat or, should I say, a tigard-skin mat.' She looked at Sankalp, smiling. 'You can sit on it while meditating or wrap it around your body. It will provide ample warmth and safety.'

'A very unusual mat,' Sankalp remarked, smiling. 'But how did you find the time?' His smile stretched to a grin. 'Looking after me for most of the day and taking care of the cottage and then this too?' he said, pointing at the mat.

'With a little help, of course, from the village sisters,' she replied, a small smile curling her lips.

Sankalp gently held her hands. 'These hands certainly hold magic.'

Titla glowed at the compliment. But almost instantly, a shiver ran down her spine as she remembered the ferocity of the encounter.

Sankalp stared into her eyes. 'I wouldn't be up and about so soon had you not cared and prayed for me as you did.' He smiled, caressing her hands, and then slowly moved them to where the wounds on his chest had healed. There was a momentary silence as he closed his eyes and recalled the past few days.

'What are you thinking about?' Titla asked with a smile.

'I was just thinking how happy my family would have been to meet you.'

'And why so?'

'Because…I am old enough to be married.' Sankalp gazed at her with gratitude. He reached out with both his hands and drew her close. The gesture held all the warmth and tenderness that he could not express in any other way.

He waited a moment before speaking. 'Who else could make me a better wife?'

Titla blushed. She wanted to say something but held on to her words.

A short while later, both sat silent over their meal. The moment, though, was charged with extraordinary affection. Love had taken strong root in their hearts.

Later that night, they strolled out of the cottage as was their routine. This night, they walked further to the edge of their home ground, where they stood looking at the stars.

And then reluctantly Titla spoke.

'My dear Sankalp, I am in a dilemma about the future. The present seems like a beautiful dream. A dream that will be gone a bit too soon,' she stated with a wistful shake of her head without taking her eyes off the brightly lit night sky. 'I ignore this reality and carry on dreaming. I know that one day I will awake, but I am afraid to.' She turned towards him and gave him an intense look. 'My feelings for you have made me weak.'

Sankalp looked at her with the same intensity. 'There is nothing to worry about, Titla.' He squeezed her fingers in reassurance. 'I feel the same way as you do, and my life has gone through a wonderful transformation. I have come to know and understand better what love is. I will never forget what you have done for me.'

Titla nodded but said nothing as Sankalp continued.

'I cannot be at peace. Not till I bring to justice those who killed my family and enslaved my people!' His voice was strained. 'I want to be here with you. But I can't.'

He hesitated for a moment and then looked up at the shining stars.

'You are an intrinsic part of my life, but I must avenge my circumstances and...'

'So you have made up your mind already?' Titla interjected. The words seemed harsh, but her tone was timid.

Sankalp looked at her, his eyes filled with love.

'I promise to return one day,' he said softly, sensing the theme of her thoughts.

Tears glistened in her eyes as she impulsively reached out to him, holding him in her arms. This was the first time he had embraced a woman. He had heard many a monk say how looking at a woman or even thinking of one while training in the sacred arts was strictly forbidden. However, he had crossed this threshold without doubt or regret.

'Love is an overwhelming force, an expression as profound as nature itself. Only in an exalted mental state can one feel true love.' Kalimpong's words held a new meaning. Sankalp had felt divinity in love. But was there caution too?

'Beware of love,' the learned ones would say. 'While true love liberates, attachment binds.'

Sankalp pondered over the time gone by. About the surprises life held. He wondered if the learned monk had had anything to do with Titla coming into his life. It was the first time Kalimpong had been away for so long. Whatever it was, it had made his life happy and more meaningful. With many questions on his mind, he bid Titla good night and retired to his room.

The next day, Sankalp's mind was calmer and more relaxed. He meditated and was able to connect with the learned master. A smile ran across his face; Kalimpong was on his way back. Sankalp was eager to meet him and share the host of thoughts that had been playing on his mind. But more than anything else, he missed his delightful yet sublime presence.

The morning sun ignited the bleary landscape with a fiery gold. A new day had dawned. Sankalp wandered outside, enchanted in a way he had never been before. The artistry of his surroundings touched his heart. What had kept him from feeling this joy in the past? Was it grief? He let go of such thoughts as so much seemed to have changed now. The air was filled with the fragrance of love, and the morning light carried delight. The sight of the beautiful mountain girl was enough to make his world go around. The young monk was overwhelmed.

This is what love does—it fascinates.

At the cottage, the summer day unfolded in its usual way.

After finishing his meditation, Sankalp called out to Titla; he wanted to share his thoughts.

'I think the master will be back tomorrow.'

Titla smiled, pleasantly surprised by the news.

'I had a vision and saw him cross the high mountain passes,' Sankalp explained.

'Oh, that is wonderful!' she said with a glint in her eyes. 'I have been waiting for his return.'

It was late afternoon. The sun was low in the west, intensifying the mellow orange light it cast over the alpine landscape. A familiar figure draped in maroon was seen coming down the mountain track. Sankalp rushed out of the cottage and ran up the mountain path to greet him. Titla too had seen him. She immediately got busy preparing his favourite meal, occasionally peeping out of the window to see how close he had reached.

Sankalp met Kalimpong halfway down the narrow track.

'How are you doing, son?" the monk asked, stopping briefly to hold Sankalp in an affectionate embrace.

'I am well and have been eagerly awaiting your arrival,' Sankalp's eyes beamed with joy as he spoke.

Kalimpong gave the young boy a warm smile, raising his right hand in blessing.

'How is dear Titla? I left her in your care.'

'She is fine and waiting impatiently for you.'

The smile on the monk's face unnerved him. The learned monk was a seer of the unseen. Surely he knew what had transpired in his absence. His feelings for Titla could no longer be hidden.

Within a few minutes, they were at the door of the cottage. Titla rushed out and hugged the monk. Tears rolled down her cheeks as she looked up at the fatherly figure.

'How are you, my dearest? It is good to see you cheerful.'

'I am well and happy to see you. I didn't know you would be gone so long,' she said in one breath.

'My dear, I left you in good hands. I knew Sankalp would take care of all your needs as well as I would. I hope you have no reason to complain.'

Titla nodded without speaking, a timid smile sketched on her face.

Later that evening, Kalimpong recounted some of his experiences. He told them about the secret abode. Cradled amidst the highest and most inaccessible mountains, somewhere close to the sacred mountain Rinpoche was the meeting ground of the learned ones. They had inhabited the earth, unseen and unheard, for hundreds of years. Bestowed with great powers, they could fly over mountaintops and make themselves invisible at will

His words sounded magical to both.

Kalimpong explained further.

'My dear, this journey was part of a learning process for the few. The elevated souls' thoughts have acquired the ability to understand the more intricate part of human existence.'

Sankalp listened carefully, trying to understand the master's words. The compelling experiences narrated by Kalimpong always enthralled Sankalp. The stories about mystics that he had heard throughout his childhood seemed so true. He was captivated by the magic that existed in the unending mountains, safely preserved by the custodians of its secrets. He was intrigued by the mention of sacred knowledge. The learned monk spoke of the hidden language of the stars. The spirits of elevated beings shone on the world in the form of starlight. And this starlight held the secrets…

Yes…Destiny! And to master its secrets, Sankalp purged his thoughts, reminding himself of the hardships he had endured to be here. He dreamt of being the learned one, 'the mind traveller', as they were known. He had mastered the physical aspects of meditation, but controlling the mind was the most difficult part. He was eager to learn the delicate process of mind control. It would not only give him dominion over the five senses but also help activate higher levels of energy in the sixth sphere. He needed these tools in his search for the invisible monk. The one who could unravel the secrets of light and destiny.

That night the learned monk continued to enthral the two with tales of his journey, till he finally remarked, 'Does no one sleep here anymore?' He smiled and lifted an eyebrow. 'It is late, and I need to rest. We will discuss what's on your mind in the morning.'

Kalimpong knew well what the young man was thinking.

Sankalp retired to his room, captivated by what he had heard. His mind was perturbed and he couldn't sleep.

Unblinking, he stared at the rafters of the ceiling, wondering about his life. Did it hold a purpose, or in time would it just fade into anonymity?

It was one of those nights when the light in his mind receded into a shadowy emptiness, and his existence seemed nothing but a mundane passage across this small transient fragment in the universe called earth. He was also worried how Kalimpong would react to his feelings for Titla.

Titla too was a bit worried. Had the master come to know about the happenings during his absence? She wanted to tell him about her feelings for Sankalp but couldn't. Beset by such thoughts she too fell asleep, thinking…

Kalimpong sat in meditation on the other side of the cottage. A slow fire burned in one corner. The thoughts that troubled the two minds were picked up by his powerful aura. A smile appeared on his face; he knew what there was to know.

The early morning saw the inhabitants of the cottage up and about. It was only later in the day that Kalimpong noticed the fine addition to Sankalp's room.

'That is a lovely prayer mat,' he remarked.

'Well, master, a very strange encounter happened some days ago. I fought to the death a large animal that attacked us. This tigard-skin mat is a gift from Titla.'

'It was brave of you to fight the large cat alone. I am proud of you.' Kalimpong rested his palm on Sankalp's shoulder in a gesture of appreciation.

'Thank you for saving my daughter. The mat should keep the memory of that moment alive for a long time,' Kalimpong remarked as he walked out of the cottage with a bag slung across his shoulders.

Sankalp followed close behind. 'Master, are you leaving again?'

'Yes, my son, but I will be back by nightfall.'

'We shall wait with supper for you.'

Sankalp meticulously followed the sacred teachings, but the lingering thought of being closer to Titla remained. He had to try harder than usual to control his thoughts. A strange conflict played in his mind—should he be here with the ones he loved most, or should he avenge his family and rid his land of slavery and injustice? The purpose of it all remained unclear. But he believed that one day the complexities would untangle themselves and he would come to understand the world and the events in his life.

His thoughts scattered as Titla walked into the room and gave him a most charming smile, displaying it long enough to make Sankalp smile too.

'Is something the matter?' she questioned.

'Just some thoughts,' he said, pretending to be carefree.

Sankalp felt it would be wrong to bring up what he was thinking.

Just then a honeybee flew in through the open window, distracting Sankalp. He shooed it away with a few gentle swings of a fan made of bamboo shoots. Titla laughed at his reaction and reached for his hand. She stared at him, momentarily deprived of words or perhaps filled with those she was too shy to express. She took a while to gather her thoughts before speaking.

'You and I face the same dilemma.'

Sankalp tilted his head in graceful admission.

'My dear Sankalp, it is more about the journey than the destination.' She smiled slightly before continuing. 'I understand what you have to do, and I would have done the same.'

He could tell she felt his struggles were in a way her own. Titla managed to hold her smile, though her eyes clearly revealed the tumult that played in her mind.

Sankalp kissed her hands gently. And neither spoke anymore.

The sun once again began to fade behind the snow-capped mountains; the stars had just begun to twinkle faintly. In the queer half-light of the two lanterns that decorated the entrance, Sankalp sat unmoving, his face marked with a trace of sadness, perhaps at the thought of his impending departure.

Just then, he saw Kalimpong walk down the track leading to the cottage. He was carrying something in his hands. As he came closer, the object became clearer. It appeared to be a sword. Sankalp's brows shot up. The sight of the monk carrying a weapon surprised him, although it was a well-known fact that Kalimpong was a fearsome fighter and that when the need arose, he would resort to the sword to save those in distress.

As the monk entered the cottage, Sankalp thought it best not to question him, at least for now.

Kalimpong went to his room, placing the sword in one corner.

Shortly after, Sankalp entered, holding a pan of hot water. He placed it on the ground, close to the raised platform where Kalimpong sat, a sure remedy for tired feet. His gaze flitted across the floor, towards the strange object that seemed to hover above the ground, its tip barely touching the earth. Sankalp was dumbstruck! He had never seen anything like it before. His eyes widened and his jaw dropped as he stood still in awe.

Gathering his wits, he spoke.

'Master, what kind of magic makes the sword balance itself on its tip, with no support?' he exclaimed as he walked closer to it, drawn by his fascination.

'Let me tell you about it,' Kalimpong replied.

The monk walked up to the sword and picked it up reverentially. He drew out the long blade with deliberate care in one steady, unhurried motion. The steel, a complex combination of different metals, moaned as it glided lightly against the sheath. The sound, a grim reminder to an adversary of their immediate destiny!

'The metal looks distinct; how old is the sword?'

'About one hundred and eighty years. A priceless gift from mother nature.' Kalimpong held out the weapon with both hands.

'Go on, hold it...'

For a moment Sankalp stood still not knowing what to do. And then, he carefully grasped the sword with both hands.

'It is so light, and its shape is distinct.'

'It's half the weight of any other sword.'

'What is it made of?' Sankalp questioned, his eyes glittering in amazement at what he was holding.

'It is made from a mix of nine earth metals. They were found in a volcanic eruption around the Kunlun plateau.'

'There is something extraordinary about it. And the metal displays a certain character, it makes you believe it has life,' Sankalp exclaimed.

'And it does,' remarked Kalimpong, raising his right eyebrow as Sankalp stared at him in disbelief.

9

The Incredible Sword of Balance

'Sankalp, this is the incredible sword of balance. It was given by my teacher to vanquish and bring to justice all wicked souls that terrorize the region. My dear son, like everything in this universe, the sword reverberates with the soul of its master. It stands in balance as long as its owner remains in tune with the three worlds: the physical or the conscious, the subconscious and the super conscious.'

Sankalp closed his eyes in concentration; he listened carefully to the words and attuned his mind to Kalimpong's thoughts.

'The physical world is the one that exists around us. The one we can see, hear and touch. The subconscious resides beyond the physical world and can be accessed only through higher intelligence or intellect, and lastly, the super conscious is a state of dynamic universal awareness, also known as the realm of light. The sword will stand in balance as long as harmony is maintained on all three planes of existence. However, if for any reason the wielder of the sword cannot maintain the balance, it will fall to the ground. And with that, it loses its miraculous powers.'

Sankalp stared in wonder, admiring the sword's impeccable craftsmanship. He had never known of such a weapon. The dazed look on his face prompted a remark from Kalimpong.

'Don't look surprised. You know about the sword. I believe you can handle it well.'

Sankalp gripped the sword more firmly. It had a rather long silver hilt inscribed with sacred chants. 'Maybe someday…' he said, staring at this mysterious weapon of destruction before carefully handing it back to the monk.

'The inscription—what does it mean?' quizzed Sankalp.

'It is a set of pronouncements that unlock the sword's energy and make you one with it,' replied Kalimpong. He drew in a deep breath before continuing. 'Let me tell you something more. I was in deep meditation when I felt danger lurking near the cottage. I could sense the encounter you had with the animal through the perturbed vibrations that I felt in the ether.'

'How is that possible? Thoughts you can read, you have taught me how to do so as well. But how could you sense happenings here, even though you were so far away?'

'My son, you must understand the phenomenon of universality. All happenings on the physical plane, like the extremities of joy and pain, resonate subtly through the ether. Sounds carry the influences of the person and place from where they emanate. And if you rightly focus your attention inwards, you can hear just about anything you want to, no matter how far the origin of that sound or disturbance. An attuned mind can pick up sounds and vibrations from many planes, especially from places and people one is connected to.

'My dear, this applies not only to the material; if you can tap into the spiritual band, you can hear sounds that are heavenly. The metaphysical forces that resonate on the earthly plane are truly a reflection of a subtler power. We can trace the force we hear on the material plane to a higher vibration, a force that escapes our physical ears simply because it exists on a different plane.

'With the mastery of specific yogic techniques, you can dive deep into the cosmic currents and hear even the more subtle vibrations. These constant vibrations are created by analogous waves emitted by the cosmic machinery. They resonate through the ether as Aum.' Kalimpong looked at Sankalp, a mysterious smile etched on his lips. 'Sankalp, you have to train yourself to harmonize this universal cosmic rhythm with that of the body,' he emphasized, resting his palm on the left side of his chest. 'This is essential.'

Kalimpong went on to explain many unusual phenomena in the universe.

Finally, he declared, 'That should be enough for tonight,' and smiled.

Sankalp managed a smile too despite the host of thoughts that played through his mind.

'Supper is ready,' Titla called out.

Soon, they were all seated next to the fire enjoying a sumptuous meal. Sankalp sat awed by Kalimpong's words. Though he had mastered most of the yogic techniques, the ones of the mind still eluded him. He couldn't help but ask the one question that had been bothering him.

'Master, with your blessings I have been preparing myself for the last eight years. When will I be ready for higher learning?'

Kalimpong smiled but remained silent.

'I want to learn the hidden language of the stars that you have often talked about.'

Kalimpong nodded, his smile widening as if he had anticipated the question and sensed Sankalp's desire.

He had also seen the sadness in Titla's eyes at the mention of Sankalp's going away.

After a thoughtful interlude, he spoke.

'My dear Sankalp, you stand at the crossroads of life. I have brought you closer to happiness and shared my knowledge. From here on, it is you. It is your resolve, coupled with a clear and reasoned thought process, that can take you further.'

The sudden change in subject and the onus of responsibility caught Sankalp off guard.

'I will retire to my room and leave you two alone. I hope the time you shared has given you a better understanding of each other?' He paused, his gaze gentle. 'This, my children, is also an essential part of life.' Kalimpong's words made it clear that he understood and had given them his blessing. It was now up to them.

Titla had long known Sankalp was in pursuit of his destiny. She could see it in his eyes and feel it in her heart. But she loved him. Love also meant sacrifice—to let go and not bind his destiny by her emotions.

As they walked out of the cottage, Sankalp was the first to break the silence.

'Titla, you know how I feel about you. Any man in my place would be happy to spend the rest of his life in this beautiful place with you as a wife and companion.' He stopped and looked away briefly before returning his gaze to her. He continued softly, 'But I know a time will come when I will regret the insufficiency of achievement clouding my life.' Sankalp shook his head. 'A life…less lived.'

Titla listened to Sankalp as if she knew his heart and had reconciled herself to his intent.

'Dearest Sankalp, it is not for me to advise you. The decision is for you to make.' She spoke from her heart. 'I realize that happiness and sadness are quite individual in nature, and we can see and share only a part of it.' Unlike her heart, her face showed no regret.

'You have endured so much loss, disaster…yet your fortitude is unwavering!' she said with a gentle shake of her head. 'A woman should be a source of strength for her man and not one of weakness.' Titla slowly lifted her solemn eyes to meet Sankalp's.

'I am happy that I have loved you and so have you.' She smiled uncertainly. She was young but demonstrated a maturity that was beyond her age.

A long silence followed between them.

And then Sankalp took her hands in his. He held them to his heart in a gesture that conveyed an unspoken promise.

'Titla, until now my heart and mind were pulling me in different directions. I was at a loss for words, trapped by my own beliefs and convictions. As you rightly said, let destiny lead us where it may choose to. But, there will be no other than you in my heart,' his voice fell to a whisper as he was overwhelmed by emotions.

It was an uneasy night, filled with deep inner conflict. The thought of leaving Titla played heavily on Sankalp's mind. He tried his best to focus, but his mind was restless. Oh, it would be so good to remain here and raise a family with the woman he loved! The thought brought a smile to his face. And the learned monk would guide the rest of their lives. This could be god's gift for all that he had faced earlier, his mind reasoned. Towards dawn, he finally succumbed to sleep, but that too was short. He awoke after a while, feeling restless. His eyelids felt heavy, but he could make out Titla's slender frame seated close by.

'What are you doing here so early?' he remarked, rubbing his eyes with his palms.

'I was not able to sleep.' She sighed. 'I saw you as I walked by your room to get some water and could no longer stay away,' she said with appealing candour.

Sankalp looked at her and smiled, his heart melting.

'Titla, my sleep has been disturbed too. The thought of leaving has made me extremely uncomfortable.'

Their conversation was interrupted by the presence of the learned monk. He woke before dawn as a matter of habit and had gone to bathe in the lake nearby. He returned to the cottage and partook of light refreshment, mostly fresh fruits. After a while, he asked Sankalp to join him.

The two sat in meditation on the freshly swept floor of the cottage. While Kalimpong sat calm, Sankalp struggled to concentrate. He tried to align his thoughts but failed. He needed the master's blessings to emerge from his perturbed state. Sankalp turned his focus towards Kalimpong and immediately felt his power flow through him. The turbulent emotions that were brewing within him began to calm. Soon enough, internal bliss opened its doors.

A smile of satisfaction appeared on his face. He was at peace. His meditation became calm and deep.

A while later, Sankalp opened his eyes.

'Master, thank you for being with me and helping me choose the right path.'

Kalimpong raised his right hand in blessing. He slowly stood up and pulled his maroon shawl over his shoulders. 'Sankalp, I cannot choose your path, only help you see it more clearly.' He smiled and walked out of the cottage.

Kalimpong enjoyed sitting out in the open courtyard. He was joined by the two for his morning sermon.

'My children, each and every thing in the world seeks to realize its destiny—it is part of karmic evolution. And as this inevitable process unfolds, no one, not even great rulers or their kingdoms, can escape their self-earned fate. But they may be protected through their troubles and even saved from dangers by an omnipotent force,' he explained.

'What is this omnipotent force?' asked Titla.

'It is the Great Spirit within us all, and it prevails throughout the universe. If you see something that soothes your eyes or mind, such as a beautiful landscape, rivers or mountains, do not worship it for its own sake, but do so for the divinity present within it, without giving it a religious face or identity. It is easy to be captivated by outer forms such that you forget the universal spirit that gives life to them.'

Titla nodded in understanding as Kalimpong continued to speak.

'Remember, the power of destiny is linked to the deeds of the living, in their present and earlier avatars; everything around us bears a reflection of it. All karma, good or bad, is returned to you. So, it is best never to tremble with sorrow but to look up to Him for divine guidance when in trouble. It is also imperative to concentrate on current action. Be aware that what one does is selfless and put the good of others before oneself.'

Sankalp listened attentively with a glow of peaceful beatitude on his face.

'Sankalp, the path you wish to take should be clear by now. Do what the mind and heart instruct. They are undoubtedly the torchbearers of your destiny!'

'Master, in your absence, many thoughts came upon me, but now I am sure. I await your guidance and help,' he said and drew a deep breath before continuing, 'to seek my path and master the secrets of destiny!'

'Ahhh, yes, my dear. A sublime journey into the immeasurable expanse of the mind.' A sombre expression crossed Kalimpong's face. 'Sankalp, it is not easy to master what you desire to learn and achieve. But your path will undoubtedly help you better understand the inexplicable.'

He paused and took a few sips of water from the earthen cup lying next to him.

'Son, the end of all human adventure is a certainty, which is better defined by the word "death". But it is irrelevant when compared to the experience, the adventure and the infatuation that life is, which so immensely expands the horizon of knowledge during the earthly passage of the soul.'

Sankalp considered the master's words for a moment, trying to understand the esoteric emotions that danced in his eyes, and then nodded in understanding.

'Is death the end?' Sankalp quizzed.

'It is just a pause.' A smile curved the corners of the monk's lips. 'My dear, the soul is an eternal light, a spiritual entity that resides within the physical body. All experiences the gross body undergoes during its natural progression enrich the soul. They take you closer towards understanding your true self.' Kalimpong stared intently into Sankalp's eyes as if studying his mind. 'Follow that inner voice; it will undoubtedly lead to what you seek.'

Sankalp bowed low to the master.

Kalimpong, who usually remained silent during supper, was chirpy. His eyes were filled with contentment.

'Sankalp, you will have to leave soon. It may be months or even years before you can reach your destination.'

'Is the journey that long? Do I have to travel to Gang Rinpoche?'

Kalimpong looked at him with mild amusement. 'There is something I need to share with you. The last but the most important: the principle of meditation. The control of the mind. And for that, we have to travel elsewhere; it cannot be done here.'

'When does he leave?' Titla's heart quickened. She was stunned by the fact that Sankalp could be leaving earlier than expected.

'We will leave tomorrow.'

For a moment, the girl seemed to lose her self-control.

'In the morning you will be joined by a new guest,' the monk stated.

He knew Titla did not like to be alone.

'She is your aunt and the wife of my disciple. They live in the lower reaches of the valley.'

Titla smiled at the news despite her feelings, trying hard to remain unmoved.

'She will stay with you till my return,' Kalimpong reassured her.

'Master, I will be ready to leave in the morning,' said Sankalp.

The monk nodded before stepping out of the cottage.

Sankalp took this opportunity to talk to Titla.

'My dear, please come with me,' Sankalp said as he walked to his room.

Titla followed him.

He pulled out an old bag from the corner and placed it on his sleeping mat. With a brief look at her serene face, he started to rummage through it and carefully pulled out something that was neatly bound in layers of white linen. He slowly unwrapped it for her to see.

It was his flute!

'Titla, this is something that belongs only to me and is a prized possession and my solitary companion. A reminder of the times...' The grief in his voice was clear. 'I want you to have it.' He handed it to her, slowly caressing her hands.

A strained silence followed. He quickly gathered his emotions and stood up with a calm expression. 'I will take the tigard-skin mat with me; it will always remind me of you'.

Titla continued to stare at him, unblinking. A long moment passed between them before she spoke.

'My dear Sankalp, this flute will be my most cherished possession.'

Titla leaned against Sankalp and put her arms around him. Together they stood for a short while. She took one last look at him. Her lashes glistened with tears.

'I hope you find what you are searching for,' she finally said and then quickly left to return to her room.

It was another unsettling moment.

Both spent a sleepless night, and it seemed longer than the others gone by. Once the heart was too exhausted to grieve, they slept. Only to be disturbed again by a knock on the cottage door.

'Who is it?' enquired Titla. She walked up to the window to see who was at the door.

'It is I, Sarvana, my dear Titla,' came the reply.

Titla recognized her immediately and unlocked the cottage door. Sarvana was her mother's cousin.

'Oh, please do come in! The master told me you would be coming.'

The elderly woman greeted her with a charming smile and a warm embrace. It was a cold but clear day. Dawn was about to break; Kalimpong had already left the cottage to bathe in the nearby lake. Sankalp had accompanied him.

'Would you like some tea?' Titla asked, putting her guest at ease.

'I would love some,' replied Sarvana and accompanied Titla to the kitchen.

'I hope we can enjoy each other's company for the time I am here,' she smiled affectionately as she helped Titla in the kitchen.

Through the window, Titla saw both men returning.

'Are you leaving already?' she questioned the moment they stepped in.

Sankalp remained quiet, while Kalimpong responded almost instantly. 'Yes, my dear, we must leave now to reach our destination in time. The days are getting shorter with the approaching winter. It will be difficult to find our way once it gets dark.'

Titla was momentarily taken aback by the answer; all she could do was nod and silently walk away.

Sankalp went back to his room and quickly packed his belongings, comprising mostly the tigard-skin mat and a set of robes.

After a light snack, it was time to depart.

Kalimpong picked up his belongings and bid the women farewell. He could see tears rolling down Titla's brick-red cheeks. They were for the young monk. Sankalp bowed to the girl who had so lovingly looked after him. The past three years wouldn't have been the same without her. Her words of wisdom would accompany him and so would her tender touch. Titla lowered her head, refusing to meet his eyes. Instead, she softly touched his hand.

Sankalp held back his emotions and whispered, 'Goodbye, dearest Titla. May God always bring you joy.' He walked out of the cottage with resigned steps.

'Sarvana, take good care of my daughter while I am away,' Kalimpong instructed the older woman before leaving.

Both men made their way up the narrow trail leading towards the high mountain pass. Kalimpong maintained a steady pace till they reached the point where the track turned sharply to the left, obscuring the view behind them.

Sankalp slowed his pace to a stop. He turned around to get a last glimpse of the wonderful cottage. He could see Titla standing at the door, waiting to catch a last glimpse of him.

A couple of steps more and the cottage disappeared; only memories remained.

The thought of turning back did cross his mind. He trudged along, weighed down by a heavy heart.

The afternoon sun was fading, and the wind had started to blow harder. Kalimpong stopped and looked over his shoulder. Sankalp was still a couple of steps behind him.

'Are you all right?' he asked, breaking into the young monk's reverie.

Sankalp took a deep breath before answering. 'Yes master, I am fine.' He sighed deeply. 'It is the pain in my leg…It…it hasn't healed completely,' Sankalp faltered, trying his best to do away with the thoughts that troubled him.

Kalimpong nodded. 'Don't worry,' he said, lifting an eyebrow. 'It is the heart that takes a while longer.' A slight smile edged his lips.

As the last rays of the sun streaked through the mountains, Kalimpong drew out his maroon shawl, his only protection against the bitter Himalayan cold. Throwing it across his shoulders, he remarked, 'Sankalp, we must move fast and reach the village. It is the only place on the high mountain pass where we can get shelter and something to eat.'

'Are we going to meet someone there?' asked Sankalp.

'No, I don't think so. But a lot of monks use the same passage. Kind people in the village arrange to keep the hut stocked with some food, water and firewood. I hope for your sake we find something there,' Kalimpong smiled.

'Ah, we don't have to worry about the food for a few days—Titla has packed enough,' Sankalp tried to sound enthusiastic.

'She thinks of everything, doesn't she?' Kalimpong smiled. 'We will spend the night at the village and leave early tomorrow. It will take us a few days to reach our destination.' He hastened his pace along the rocky track.

Sankalp nodded and hurried to catch up with Kalimpong.

10

Lessons From the Little Fish

It was the last day of their journey. The sun was no more than a thumb's breadth above the horizon. Sankalp glimpsed a small hutment. Close by flowed a narrow stream so clear it was almost invisible in the faint evening light. The only thing that betrayed its presence was the throaty burble of water pouring over the rocks. He had stayed here before while travelling up the high mountain pass. The very place he had learnt the penance of the sun god.

As they descended to the cottage, feelings of regret and anguish drowned his conviction. Now and again, he questioned his decision to leave.

'All this physical hardship and the pain of losing someone who loved me like family. Wouldn't everybody have been happy had I stayed back? I have been the cause of despair and grief to the one person who loved me so much.'

Then again, he speculated, surely the monk would not have allowed him to stay, and Titla would have done the same. He remembered how, on many occasions, his decisions had been sternly put aside by Kalimpong. His thoughts were momentarily swept away by gusts of freezing Himalayan wind that blew through the highlands at sunset. Much to their relief, the cottage was only a few paces away, just across the rivulet.

They crossed a narrow wooden bridge and within moments were inside the brightly lit cottage.

'Ahh, the people here are kind,' exclaimed Sankalp. 'We have enough firewood.'

He quickly lit a fire, using oil from the lantern that hung at the entrance. The fire would keep the air in the cottage mild.

'Sankalp, I am going to the stream for a bath and my evening meditation.'

'I'll be with you in a moment,' Sankalp replied, throwing a robe across his shoulders.

'Wait for me here.' An inscrutable smile touched Kalimpong's face. 'I am sure Titla has packed a good meal; nothing much grows in these parts,' he jested and walked away.

Sankalp followed Kalimpong's instructions and unpacked his holdall. He stared at the prayer mat. Holding it in his hands, he closed his eyes and thought of Titla.

He missed her.

He then went about the task of cleaning the hut before warming up the evening meal. Kalimpong returned past dusk. He seated himself on the neatly swept floor and asked Sankalp to join him for supper.

'Ahem…' Kalimpong cleared his throat before speaking. 'Sankalp, at the break of first light, go by the stream and meditate alone.'

'Why alone, master? What about you?'

'No, not this time Sankalp; you must meditate alone. This is the way it has to be. Your experience here will give you a better understanding of everything you have learnt and need to learn.'

'What about the hidden language of the stars?' Sankalp made a strained effort to smile. 'Won't you teach me about it?'

Kalimpong looked at Sankalp and continued lightly. 'My dear, it will come to you in time.' The monk raised the palm of his right in a calming gesture and smiled. 'For now, do as I say. When you are finished, you won't find me here.' He paused. 'I will wait for you at the cave. One is always comfortable in a place one looks upon as home.'

Sankalp nodded.

'You must stay here for the next three days and meditate alone. It will help cleanse your mind. It is only then that the journey from here on can be accomplished.'

After supper, they retired to their respective rooms. Sankalp sat quiet, perplexed by Kalimpong's words. His eyes alighted upon a lamp made of earth. It burned brightly atop the windowsill. The sight filled his mind with scenes from the past. Of bright mornings spent grazing sheep whilst Zanzi circled the clear blue skies. He missed his brothers and his father too; the feel of his strong arms as he playfully flung him in the air and caught him as he fell. The devoted care with which his mother looked after him. And of course, how amazed he was by the stories his uncles often narrated. And in a flash, it was all over. Alas, if only he could see them again!

The past weighed heavily on his mind that night, exhausting him of mental and physical energies. He felt anger, compounded by recurring thoughts of resentment. At times, his loss seemed constant and inescapable.

It was only after several hours that he was able to put his mind to rest and get some sleep. But that too was short-lived. He was reminded of the monk's words.

At the break of first light, braving the Himalayan chill, Sankalp strode down the stony path leading to the river. At first, he shivered; drawing strength from the sacred chants, he insulated his inner self from the outer. He carried the tigard-skin mat with him. He smiled slightly as he remembered the strange encounter that could have cost him his life.

He looked for a comfortable place to start his meditation.

A partly submerged rock alongside a stretch of riffles seemed to be the right place. It would give him a good view of the surroundings and keep him safe from the gushing icy waters. He climbed atop the large rock and spread his prayer mat. Then he slowly entered the stream and sprinkled water on his face and eyes. He felt refreshed.

The young monk settled down on his mat and gradually progressed to a stillness that enveloped his mind and body. Flowing steadily with the meditative currents he moved into a more consistent state of calmness. His mind was beginning to develop intent focus, a prerequisite to moving higher. His body became more relaxed, unaffected by the environment.

A penetrative sublimity began to settle upon him.

Then, all of a sudden, he felt the rock underneath him move! Unperturbed by the interruption, he continued in his meditative state, well aware that nothing could shake the huge rock. Distracted but calm, he quickly regained his composure. After a brief interlude, he felt the rock move again! It seemed as if something or someone was trying to break his focus and bring him down.

He came out of his meditative state, thinking, 'What on earth can shake such a big rock?' His thoughts began to run wild, falling prey to a host of imaginings. He tried to keep his face expressionless despite his unease as he tried to decipher the mystery behind the phenomenon. Or was it a sordid conspiracy? Something or someone was challenging his concentration! He was beginning to lose focus.

'The giant Himalayan brown bear is the only animal that can shake a rock of this size,' he thought, keeping perfectly still. Perhaps the bear would take him to be dead and leave him alone?

He sat motionless until the rock seemed stable and then opened his eyes to reassure himself.

But there was nothing in sight except for the barren landscape and the sun shining brightly overhead.

Convinced there was nothing near him, he once again started to meditate. Being adept at the practice, he was quickly able to recover his equilibrium. His mind began to relax.

The sound of footsteps passing by did not go unnoticed. He knew the learned master was on his way to the cave. Kalimpong reached out with his mind; he wished him well and continued on. Sankalp felt his thoughts and bowed in reverence, wishing him a safe journey. With his mind at peace, he turned his focus inwards.

Quiet reigned for several minutes; sublime stillness once again surrounded him. And then, all too suddenly, the rock shook again! This time, more vigorously than before.

Was somebody hiding in the barren landscape or was this the work of a mean spirit entity? How could the boulder come alive?

Angry, he decided to come out of his meditative state.

'Who are you? And why are you disturbing me?' he shouted. 'Don't be a coward. Show yourself and face me!'

The agitated monk stood up and studied his surroundings more closely. He had been on the rock for hours, and every time he had neared that state of perfect meditative stillness, something or someone shook the rock and broke his focus.

His questions did not elicit a reply apart from dislodging a wagtail bird from its nearby perch. He gazed keenly at everything around him in the falling sunset. Sankalp could see nothing that could move such a large rock. He looked down at the base of the rock. A small fish was caught underneath, struggling hard to find its way into the stream.

'Surely, it can't be that little fish,' he smirked at the thought. 'It couldn't move a pebble, much less this rock.'

He paused thoughtfully before stepping into the shallow stream. The icy waters whirled around his ankles as he placed both his hands on the rock. Firmly digging his feet into the soft stream bed, he gave the rock a push.

Then he heaved. Using all his strength he tried to move the rock but to no avail. His confusion was indescribable.

He looked around helplessly before drawing in a deep breath. Then he exerted the last bit of power in his muscles. 'Uhh…Uhh…' he panted, but the rock remained dead still. Tired, he leaned against it to catch his breath.

Just then, it shook again!

He quickly turned around, but there was nothing nearby.

He stared down. The little fish was struggling to escape from under the rock. He bent low to get a closer look. The little fish struggled again, its tiny fins brushing against the huge rock. That was when it moved again. Sankalp could feel the vibration in his hands. The large rock shook with every move of the little fish! Stunned, he stepped back.

'How can this be?' He looked around for a more palatable answer.

All his strength was nothing in the face of the steady rock. But the little fish, struggling to find its way out from under it, was shaking it with its tiny fins.

An astonished Sankalp was convinced that it was a cursed spirit in the form of a fish, making sure to disrupt his meditation. He decided to wait until the following morning and then kill the devilish creature.

He walked back to the cottage, feeling a bit angered by the entire experience.

Hunger deserted him, and tired and worried, he fell into a shallow sleep, his mind occupied with thoughts of loss. He missed what he had before and had left behind now.

As the night progressed, he felt his solitude more intensely than ever before. And from the stillness rippled a familiar voice.

'Sankalp, my child, don't let the mind horse carry you in different directions.'

The learned master was trying to tell him something.

'Master, I don't know how to explain this. But every time I sit in meditation on the rock near the river, it moves. And it happens just when I am about to enter the transcendental state.'

'That, my son, is the rock of will.'

'Master, it is amazing how a little fish is shaking the rock. The rock that…that even I couldn't move.'

Sankalp waited a while before speaking again.

'It's a damned spirit in the form of a fish that is trapped under the rock. Every time it tries to free itself, the rock moves. I will find another place to meditate tomorrow!'

'Do not leave the rock. Stay firm! Let go of the troublesome little "mind fish" instead,' the voice resonated before fading away.

'The mind fish?' Sankalp repeated, but there was no answer from Kalimpong.

Nonetheless, the master's words had given him a vital clue, which led him to introspect deeply about doing away with attachments in the realm of the mind. Only then could he be in a state of absolute lightness and break away from the perennial gravity that held one from being the exalted mind traveller.

'My dear, you are but the weight of your thoughts.' Kalimpong's words ran through his memory.

It was the hour of dawn; Sankalp left the cottage and reached the stream. He bowed to the little fish and climbed atop the rock. There, he sat down in the lotus position and released his mind from memories of the past and the yearnings that flooded his thoughts so often. He cast aside all the emotions that bound him.

'I set myself free,' the mind urged. 'And seek destiny without the weight of my past or the wants of a future.'

Sankalp sat in silence. Diving deep into the sub-cosmic currents, he reached a level of sublime awareness. In that state, the body and mind cease to react to the physical senses. He had attained a state of eternal bliss, and it flowed through his entirety.

In that state, he felt no hunger. The mind horse stood steady, and all desires merged into the sea of nonexistence. He migrated to a state of selflessness. The individual entity, the ego, stood subdued to a point of nothingness. His inner self became one with nature.

The day passed and night came. Sankalp continued in his meditative state. The Himalayan chill came down heavier than before. The night became particularly bitter, freezing everything in its wake. Dark clouds covered every iota of light as the sun refused to show the next morning. But the young monk continued to remain in a serene meditative state. The light remained thin for the entirety of the third day. And at night, the severe Himalayan winter froze every falling droplet of water into snow. Sankalp remained undeterred and silent.

This drama of nature continued through the night. By the dawn of the fourth day, the clouds had cleared. A subdued nature bowed to the resilience of the young monk and let its blessings flow through the warm light of the rising sun.

Sankalp slowly opened his eyes. At first, he observed objects that lay obvious, and then he entered a state of heightened awareness. He briefly noticed the subtle matrix of life that connected every living and non-living entity that existed in front of him.

Sankalp had gone through physical and cognitive changes. His senses were thrumming with a multitude of sights, sounds and feelings. Even with his eyes closed, he could see more and feel without touch. The feeblest sounds were audible to him.

His body, too, was flushed with unknown strength and vitality. He could accelerate the movement of the muscles in his arms and legs beyond human capacity and respond with animal-like speed and forcefulness.

Sankalp stared at a brightly coloured butterfly as it sat fluttering on a Tibetan blue poppy. A defining pattern of red spots caught his attention. The intense motion of its wings appeared slower as he stared and then slower still until it became steady, like his own breathing. Amazingly, he could see its flight path—it was visible as an array of colours that marked its trail from before it sat feeding on the flower's nectar. He could also see patterns that hazily marked multiple flight paths of a near future.

A white collared blackbird that sat waiting on a nearby branch swooped down on the butterfly. Sankalp watched keenly as it closed in for the kill. In one minute fraction of time, the butterfly suddenly spiralled up, narrowly missing the predator's beak! Sankalp had sensed its movement, with a feeling that it would survive. And it did as it fluttered away and faded from his awareness. Instinct, the silent whisper of nature, had become more cogent. Stunned, he stood overwhelmed by this para-sensory experience.

In his altered state Sankalp had momentarily accessed a realm that existed beyond common intelligence; a realm beyond the present. Nature had begun opening its doors to the fourth dimension. A world not encased in time—one that existed beyond the purview of natural laws. To understand the fourth dimension was to know the hidden language of the stars and unravel the secrets of destiny.

As Sankalp walked back to the cottage, a strange bright light danced around him. He watched it proudly till it diminished. He sat next to the fire and took a few drops of water to quench his thirst. That was all he needed. After a brief rest, he packed his belongings. It was time to meet the learned master.

The day had just begun, and the sun was shining brightly in the sky. Sankalp started on his journey back to the cave. As he walked across the wooden bridge, he looked for the rock, but mysteriously, it no longer existed. All he could see was a stretch of barren land running beside the river. Not finding the rock of 'will' upon which he had sat for three nights astonished Sankalp. But greater intelligence now answered every question.

He moved with surprising agility for a man who had gone without food and water for several days. But that was of no consequence; he could derive strength from the rays of the sun.

Relishing his experiences, he moved briskly and undistracted in a preordained direction.

It would take him about five days to reach the cave.

He walked through the day, trying to spot familiar landmarks on the way. The forest had changed from before.

Towards sunset on the fourth day, he had reached familiar ground. As Sankalp stood at the lip of a ravine and stared across to the other side, a wonderful thing happened. A large shadowy figure swooped down from above and started to circle him. It was so close Sankalp could feel the draft from the wings of the large bird. It swooped low, and then, with an acrobatic flip, rose up into the sky.

The distinct mark under its left wing was unmistakable. It was Zanzi, his pet falcon.

Sankalp had left the cave a long time ago. Zanzi had stayed, awaiting his return. The young monk was ecstatic. He looked up and whistled the familiar calling tone. The bird responded at once and swooped down to its favourite perch.

'You seem well, Zanzi. I am happy to see you. Now show me the quickest way to the cave.'

The cave was located on a steep mountain face. It was surrounded by thick pines, making it difficult to spot. The falcon soared high and then came down low, signalling the young monk to follow. It led him swiftly through the demanding terrain till it finally descended on a large apple tree. 'The tree of life' was how the learned monk often referred to it. The apple tree had passed through nine winters. It had courageously withstood the onslaught of the elements. Its roots held the ground firmly; it was branching out and beginning to flower.

The air was motionless when Sankalp entered the cave. A thick cloud of smoke, with a serene and familiar fragrance, floated within. It came from the burning incense. A few feet from it sat the learned master, in the lotus position, deep in meditation. Sankalp bowed in reverence and walked out. He sat on a rock from where he had an uninterrupted view of the valley below. Sankalp looked on; he drew a deep breath as memories from the time he had first found shelter here returned to mind.

'Sankalp, my dear,' the monk called after a while.

'Yes, master,' replied Sankalp and he went to where the monk was seated.

'It is wonderful to see you!' Kalimpong smiled as their eyes met. Sankalp smiled back, his hands folded in reverence. His eyes expressed maturity and gratitude.

'Well, my son, as you evolve and progress on the path you have chosen, be aware, you will be put to the test by nature itself.'

Sankalp nodded in acknowledgement. 'Your blessing of knowledge will guide me in my darkest hours,' he said as he sat down beside the learned monk.

'Sankalp, your higher self stands aware of the enormous power of nature. In time, you will find answers to questions and what you seek,' Kalimpong said softly, followed by a moment's silence.

'You have mastered the eighty-four postures in the yoga of body control and, to a large extent, have gained control over the mind. But my dear, knowledge is not enough. It is experience—I repeat, experience—that truly unfolds the subtle mysteries of life.'

Early the next morning, Sankalp accompanied Kalimpong; they walked down the serpentine path that descended into the valley. From there they turned north. Fording the Indus at its shallows, they continued northward for two days. By noon of the third day, the land, which had begun to slope gently upwards, got steeper. After a while, the mountain rose in a steep slope. At this point, Kalimpong stopped. He took a deep breath of the thin air as he scanned the horizon. His eyes came to rest on a ridge of peaks that lay further to the north.

'You see those snow-covered mountains,' he gestured.

Sankalp nodded as he looked at the immeasurable tract of mountains. A land incomparable with any other place he had seen or known.

'That is where your search begins for the unseen. The master of masters.'

Sankalp stood overwhelmed.

'And beyond them…' Kalimpong paused, staring in their direction.

Sankalp stood close, admiring the sight and waiting expectantly for him to say more.

'Do you see the peak rising more vertically than the others?' He resumed walking and raised his hand to point. 'That, my dear, is the much revered Kang Rinpoche or Kailasa…' Kalimpong inhaled deeply, his breath turning white as he exhaled.

'The axis mundi. The centre of the earth! A place so divine that its mere sight frees your soul from karmic cycles.' Kalimpong stopped. He bowed his head low and stood unmoving for a moment.

'Kang Rinpoche! Is that the abode of the invisible monk?' questioned Sankalp excitedly. 'That is an impossible climb, or so it seems from here.' Sankalp shaded his eyes with his hand as he stared at the majestic mountain.

'Sankalp, it is impossible for the mortal body to scale Kailasa. But the adjoining lower ridges are reachable.'

'Why?'

Kalimpong stood silent for a moment, his hands folded in reverence. 'How can you scale that which is endless? My dear, Kailasa rises beyond what your eyes can see.

'It is a connection—a bridge, an umbilical cord between the natural and the spiritual world.' He looked at Sankalp and then stared in the direction of the holy mountain. He continued softly, 'That, my son, is the physical representation of the supreme consciousness that resides within.'

Sankalp remained silent as Kalimpong resumed walking along the narrow path. Just ahead, it curved sharply to one side with a deadfall ahead. A three-foot passage with a rocky wall on the right led them closer to the sound of water, which fell from about two hundred feet above. A few nimble-footed mountain goats grazed at the very edges, which still held patches of moss and vegetation.

They followed the path along the ledge, carefully holding on to the jutting stones, which seemed to be arranged in a way that formed a natural balustrade. After a while, the ledge disappeared under a curtain of falling water. They entered a cave curtained by the waterfall. The small cave opened into a cavern.

'What kind of place is this?' remarked Sankalp, sensing a sudden shift in the atmosphere.

He looked around intently, his eyes slowly adjusting to the dim light as he tried to familiarize himself with his new surroundings.

'I can sense a strong magnetic field, an unknown power.' His heart quickened. 'And I feel lighter,' he concluded, drawing in a deep breath.

'This is a special place, Sankalp. It is impossible to discover or enter it without the guidance of a true spirit entity,' Kalimpong responded with a mysterious smile. 'Some of the most sacred scriptures relating to the yoga of Brahma-chinta, dating back to the thirteenth century, are stored here. What I am about to reveal cannot be let out.'

'Why?'

'My dear, its escape could spell disaster! The magnetic field holds the sound of my words within its confines. And the water curtain retains the energy here.

'Nature never ceases to amaze!' replied an astonished Sankalp.

'The energy created diffuses with time. Its remnants are carried by the water and neutralized back into the earth.'

They walked into the rather deep cave that sloped upwards. About fifty feet or so inside, it turned sharply to the right and rose steeply before gradually flattening out. An unseen vertical slit created a fast-moving draft of air from top to bottom. It formed a natural curtain of air that segregated the area ahead.

A few feet away, beams of light floated down in asymmetrical patterns from the ceiling. They lit the inside, just enough. Into one rock wall were carved four individual spaces to comfortably accommodate as many people.

'Sankalp, here we will focus our energies on aspects other than what you have learnt in the course of your training. I will teach you how to harness energy from your surroundings and magnify the strength of your mind. You will learn more about the power of sounds and vibrations. These powerful chants can create an impenetrable circle of protection around you.'

'Interesting. I remember you mentioned this before.'

'And now you are ready to learn about it,' Kalimpong smiled.

The revered Tengyur and Kangyur texts, written by the great saint Rinchen Drup, contained Buddhas teachings and details of sutras and powerful tantras. They had been passed down by word of mouth and partly written in the form of scriptures. The combination of spoken and written word ensured the scriptures never fell into the wrong hands. They were stored here, safely, in the remotest part of the Himalayan mountains.

11

A Treacherous Climb Into the Jaws of Death

In the coming days, Kalimpong delivered verses and explained and divulged meanings from the sacred Kangyur scriptures. They contained knowledge about transformative powers, including access codes to the unseen realms in the universe.

Sankalp devoted long hours to mastering the craft. The complex methodology combined not only yogic exercises but also a series of secretive chants along with intense energetic pronouncements. Delivered in a rhythmic pattern, they generated a high intensity energy pattern that acted as a shield and could also create and project optical illusions. He excelled, for he not only possessed the talent but also the zeal.

On a bright morning, with a smile that radiated satisfaction, Kalimpong remarked, 'Your learning here is complete.'

A profound pause followed. They had been in the cave for ninety-seven days.

'Sankalp, you are now ready to accept and hold the flow of energy that will guide you in your search.'

Sankalp bowed his head with his hands folded in utmost devoutness; he stood unmoving in that posture for a few moments.

'My son, the knowledge you have gained in the past nine years usually takes a lifetime to master,' remarked Kalimpong as he stepped closer to his disciple.

Sankalp immediately bent low and touched the master's feet with respect. 'With your grace, I have learnt much and in the process encountered moments that have enriched my mind.'

'You are now ready to seek and unravel the secrets of destiny.' Kalimpong looked intently into the young monk's eyes before speaking again. 'It is a challenging adventure. A difficult test for the human body and mind, it is a path that has taken many lives, but it also leads to wisdom and salvation.

'To reach your goal, you have to travel a long way to the north. It is a treacherous world in the heart of the Himalayan mountain ranges. A land inhabited by wild animals and the damned spirits and plagued by shadows and thoughts. The slightest slip in the mind can make the entire journey futile,' he cautioned.

'Even after reaching your destination, there is no surety of meeting the enlightened one,' Kalimpong sighed. 'Your journey could well be in vain,' he said, raising his voice slightly.

Sankalp was a bit surprised but acknowledged his words with a nod.

Kalimpong then turned his attention to the left of where they stood. He took a few steps and picked up the coveted sword of balance, holding it reverentially with both hands.

Sankalp bowed and extended his hands with a sense of elation.

'Master, I will uphold its honour and use it to maintain the balance it represents. I promise to guard the sword with my life.'

'And the sword will protect you,' replied Kalimpong as he handed over the sword. For a moment the sword hovered between their palms, amid two destinies, before it changed hands.

'Sankalp, head northwest towards the base of the three mountains. They stand alongside one another like links in a chain. The first two mountains are relatively easy to scale, but the climb up the third is rigorous. The lower half is covered with thick forests, while its higher reaches are masked with snow and ice. Once you near the summit, the bright North Star will be visible over its brow; its "falling lights" on a moonless night will show you the way to the valley.'

Sankalp listened attentively, every word reminding him of the adventure ahead.

'My dear, the other side of the valley stands separated by fast-flowing waters. Once there, look towards the incandescent glow. It comes from a sacred flame atop the hillock that appears to sit in a hunchback position.' Kalimpong paused, his eyes closed. 'It will take more than your eye to see it.' A slight smile curved the corners of his lips. 'Once there, seek the invisible master,' he concluded, as if narrating his own experience of it.

'Master, with your blessings, I will find him,' Sankalp replied with determination.

'Ahhh, I hope you do.' Kalimpong's eyes twinkled with an other-worldly charm, and a mysterious smile etched his face.

The learned monk embraced Sankalp and slowly stepped back. His extended hands lightly touched his disciple's forehead;

in that moment, Kalimpong let his powers flow. The intensity of the force was bedazzling.

In that overwhelmed state, Sankalp heard the master.

'Be aware! This journey will take you beyond the known laws of the universe. From this moment on, the dimensions of reality and illusion will fold and the limits of your mind will be put to the test!'

Sankalp could see the master standing close to him, but his voice seemed to resonate from afar. And then, a tranquil quiet prevailed.

It was a bright morning in the Himalayan wilderness. After refreshing himself in the freezing waters of the nearby river, Sankalp was ready to leave.

He bowed to the sun god in reverence, making a symbolic offering of water. Then he made his way down to the valley accompanied by his pet falcon. He made sure to carry the fruits of his labour. A few ripe apples from the tree of life would take care of his hunger for now.

To his left, the mountains were not very high and covered with forests of hardwood. But to the right, they peaked beyond the clouds. They were partly bare due to the extreme and harsh climate, save for a few densely wooded trails that ran up to their neck.

It took him about nine days to reach the foothills that marked the end of the simpler trail.

Before him, the chain of peaks rose unchallenged.

After a two-day rest, Sankalp began his climb. Cutting across the trail that led west, he headed towards the northern part of the mountain range. As he moved higher, he could see the entirety of the valley below.

Though apart, Sankalp and the master remained connected in thoughts. His link with the master grew stronger.

It took Sankalp another three days to top the ridge; from there the track curved steeply to the left. Facing west, it led down the mountain. He stopped and took one last look at the world that would soon disappear from his sight. Moments later, he began his descent. He continued to trail the setting sun until it disappeared below the horizon. The air once again began to chill with increasing intensity. Sankalp stopped for a few moments and wrapped himself in the tigard-skin mat; it did offer considerable protection from the icy winds. He then swiftly made his way towards the lower part of the ridge.

The air was warmer there, and he had a better chance of finding shelter for the night. Sankalp maintained a steady stride along the wooded trail that led to a small glade. From there, he could glimpse what lay ahead. His heart beat faster as he looked at the vast stretch of wild and ancient uninhabited lands and the seemingly formidable white mountains staring back at him. He wondered where it would all lead and how it would all end.

He collected pieces of wood and made a fire that would keep him warm through the long cold night that lay ahead.

The next day began early. Sankalp woke just before dawn, his breath turning white as he exhaled the crisp morning air. It was a cold day with the sun occasionally peeking through the thick cloud cover.

Within moments, he was on the trail, a light drizzle accompanying him. When it rained, the clouds and the forest canopy plunged the forest into a misty grey. The air turned chillier as the day passed, and it could get worse as he climbed higher. Till then, he had been lucky enough to find shelter in the high mountain passes. Sankalp had heard stories about the frightening brown bears that often made the deep crevices in these mountains their home, hibernating safely inside through the long Himalayan winter.

He continued his climb towards the crest that connected to the next mountain, the upper part of which was covered with snow and ice. Sankalp cautiously made his way through the dense forest. Eventually, the forest thinned and the sky was more visible. Rays of sunlight filtered through the canopy. The wind produced a low wailing sound as it blew unobstructed around him. Zanzi maintained constant vigil while gliding deftly upon the cold mountain currents.

It had been almost three weeks since he had left the cave. The journey had sapped him of his youthful energy. Sankalp was beginning to tire, but he continued to climb, ignoring his fatigue and the irrationality of the thoughts that questioned this deadly quest. As he walked on, the narrow path he had been following started to disappear. Most of it lay covered by snow and ice. His strength too was slowly but surely giving way. The most frustrating part of the journey was that no matter how clear and near the destination seemed, by the end of the day, it seemed no closer than it had been the day before.

Climbing higher towards the ridge, he noticed Zanzi had spotted something. It was circling in attack mode just a little ahead. The saker falcon, a natural hunter, had set his sights on a brown hare. His sharp eyes had spotted the hare feeding on the last morsels of grass before they were buried under the snow in the coming days. The rabbit was ignorant of the falcon hovering above.

A swift dive and pounce ensured a hearty meal for the two.

A break in the journey followed by a sumptuous meal was all he needed. Sankalp lay behind a rock in a narrow crevice that offered shelter. Tired, he fell asleep at once. By the time he awoke, it was late afternoon. The brief rest had refreshed him. Sankalp resumed his trek, moving quickly so he would cross a patch of dark, dense forest before nightfall. The freezing Himalayan winds made his journey more laborious.

By the time he reached the ridge, the sun had set. Sparse moonlight guided him on the rocky path, and he was still far from the rim that connected to the next mountain. To reach there, he had to climb down a few hundred metres and then climb back to the top. The lower part of the ridge was covered in tall pines and a jungle of ferocious density that extended to the valley below.

As the moon climbed higher, the land was lit with an eerie silver glow. Its light fell clearer through the rain.

The whistling winds were accompanied by occasional howls from hunting wolf packs. The ferocious sounds were answered by similar calls of acknowledgment from other pack members. The creatures of the night were out to make a kill.

Sankalp made his way down the mountain, with his face grim. An uncanny feeling of being followed accompanied him. Shadows seemed to come alive and vanish at sight. He could not see but only sense these creatures of darkness. Undisturbed but watchful, Sankalp extended his senses more intently to encompass his surroundings. That would keep him alert and safe from anything that could endanger his life. He continued to maintain a demanding yet sustainable pace through the forest, negotiating with care the thick undergrowth and low-hanging branches. Recent rains had made the ground under his feet slushy. It was covered with stones and a variety of flora.

Sankalp paused to rest when he was nearly halfway down. As he leaned against a tree, his eyes fell upon a beehive hanging from one of its branches. The nourishment was irresistible. Other than being a food source, the honey had curative powers due to its medicinal qualities. Wasting no time, he lit a fire under the low-hanging branch to smoke the bees out of the hive. The smoke stung his eyes, temporarily blinding Sankalp.

At that moment, a fiery shadow broke away from behind the trunk of a large oak tree. It came alive in the form of a ferocious bear! The brown mountain bear was a frightening creature that roamed the Himalayan jungles.

The smoke from the fire had dispersed the bees. They buzzed around for a while and then disappeared into the dark. Ignoring the effects of the smoke that continued to affect his vision, Sankalp shook the hive with his staff. Then again, he shook more vigorously until it fell right in front of him. He wasted no time in collecting his precious find. Sankalp sat close to the fire, enjoying the flavourful honey with some leavened bread, unaware that he was being keenly watched.

All of a sudden, a fearful cry filled the sky, conveying panic!

It was Zanzi. His piercing scream shattered the stillness of the night. Sankalp carefully scanned the dense forest but couldn't see anything. The fiery creature had retreated into the shadows. A while later, the ground under his feet began to shake. He heard the sound of branches breaking close by. A large brown bear suddenly appeared from the thicket, its prey in its sights.

Sankalp stood shocked. It took him a few moments to master his senses. The bear paused to stare at Sankalp, its ears tilted forward, listening to every breath exhaled, strategizing and trying to read signs of fear.

The forest went silent. The wind died and so did the sounds of the night. Then, with a sudden burst of speed, the bear charged at Sankalp, effortlessly negotiating the dense foliage and the undulating ground, picking up pace.

Sankalp couldn't outrun the animal. He quickly fell back, letting a large tree come between him and the charging bear.

Then he dashed to his left and grabbed a large piece of burning firewood. He waved it in front of the beast, trying his best to scare him away.

The bear snarled in anger, baring its exceptionally long fangs. It stood on its hind legs, asserting its massive weight and size. It roared, displaying its most deadly weapon—its five-inch claws!

Sankalp remained calm. He carefully watched the bear's every move even as sweat beaded his forehead. Moving swiftly, he thrust the burning piece of wood at the bear. It backed away, letting out an ear-shattering roar. There followed a sudden commotion in the jungle. Hyenas howled, deer bleated and an owl flew out of the comfort of its nest.

Sankalp moved closer to the fire and repeated the manoeuvre. His gaze unwavering, he picked up another piece of burning wood with his left hand and flung it straight at the animal's chest. The bear growled in pain and surprisingly melted into the night. Sankalp narrowed his eyes and scanned the forest. His view was partially obscured by the dense foliage and the rain that had started to fall and was quickly turning to hail. He swiftly added some more wood to the fire and sat close to it. His breathing was heavy as he sat there wondering, a pensive expression on his face. Reaching out for his urn, he took a long drink of water. Then he had a few more bites of food, wisely packing some away before he stood to continue his journey.

He carried a burning torch, feeling he would encounter his adversary again. Brown bears were known to stalk their prey. A cold tingle crawled down Sankalp's spine at the thought.

It was difficult to find safe shelter in the lower reaches at night. He knew this from experience. And the bear would surely track him with its keen sense of smell. His best hope of finding shelter lay in the upper part of the ridge. Sankalp picked up his pace, ignoring his fatigue. The brief encounter had taken its toll on his already worn-out muscles.

The rain fell to a drizzle and filtered through the cold mist that was beginning to cover the surroundings. Sankalp moved briskly, covering as much distance as he could, holding on to his torch. Zanzi kept a keen eye on the land, ready to raise an alarm at the slightest unfamiliar sound.

It was close to the witching hour. The night had turned dark, different from the darkness of other nights. Fireflies whirled, drawing strange patterns of light in the oppressive darkness. The air was colder, and Sankalp's torch was flickering to an end. Taking advantage of his debility, the forest once again seemed to be closing in, drawing him into a web of vivid imagination or a fearful dream from the past...

Just when he felt that he could go no farther, the dense forest ended.

Sankalp looked around him. He spotted a small cave that had probably been formed by years of erosion. He had to contend with the company of a few fruit bats hanging upside down from its roof. He quickly settled inside, whistling to his falcon as it perched upon the highest branch of a pine close by. He lit a fire and huddled close to it. Exhausted, Sankalp was soon asleep.

It wasn't long before his sleep was disturbed. A loud roar echoed in the vastness. Sankalp awoke with a start. He could hear Zanzi shrieking frantically outside the cave. The saker falcon was trying to warn him of the impending danger that stood at the mouth of the shelter! The brown bear had tracked him to where he was resting. A menacing figure, it stood on its hind legs at the entrance, its sharp claws outstretched, ready to tear him apart. It was a grim sight. The blood raced through Sankalp's body and flushed his face.

The fire inside was almost extinguished; it took a few moments for Sankalp's eyes to adjust to the darkness around. He wriggled to the farthest corner of the cave. Calmly, he wrapped the tigard skin tightly across his bare chest and drew his sword.

Seeing his prey cornered, the bear edged closer. Its eyes glowed like amber in the flickering flame of the dying fire. Sankalp remained composed and held the sword firmly in his hand.

'Go away and leave me in peace and I will spare your life!' he exclaimed.

Keeping his eyes firmly on his opponent, he stepped closer.

The beast was enraged! It charged, hurling his weight behind the attack. Sankalp parried the attack, moving swiftly to one side. Quick with his reflexes, he thrust his sword into the bear's left shoulder.

The beast roared and backed away in pain.

Sankalp moved cautiously, his back hugging the wall of the cave. His body, perfectly aligned with its contours and his form almost invisible in the fading glow of embers. He silently reached the opening of the cave. He stood a better chance in a fight outside.

Roaring with anger and in pain, the bear readied for another charge. Sankalp quickly edged past him and through the narrow entrance. Once outside, he moved back a couple of paces and positioned himself on firmer ground, anticipating the next move. The bear stalked after him, staring at its prey. Sankalp returned its stare and sent a telepathic message. 'Go away. I mean you no harm!' His thoughts reverberated through the ether.

This time, he immediately got a reply.

'I cannot let you go! This is my forest, and you will be punished for trespassing!'

The bear rushed towards him. Once again, Sankalp dodged the charge, moving aside with lightning speed. The bear raced past and stopped, aggravated.

What followed was a violent attack by the enraged bear; it wildly slashed the air with its deadly paws and ferociously snapped its large jaws. The force could break bones and instantly cripple any living being. At one point, the bear managed to hold Sankalp in a deathly embrace. Sankalp exhaled every bit of air from his lungs, and his body shrank just enough to help him slip out of the deadly hold.

Angered, the bear swung his right paw at his neck. Sankalp arched his body and threw back his neck in the nick of time; five razor-sharp claws missed his lower jaw by a whisker. Sankalp accelerated his movements; he ducked and slashed, parried and stabbed in a whirl of brutish activity. He knew this was the best way to exhaust the large creature. And then, seeing his opportunity, Sankalp leapt on the bear's back. Grabbing its long, thick hair in his fist, Sankalp took a firm grip around his neck.

He had to end this ordeal before the bear flung him off its back and got the better of him. Sankalp was about to thrust the mighty sword into the bear's neck when he heard a strange call reverberating in the ether.

'Spare me, warrior, and I will guide you through the mountains!'

The young monk took heed; he held the sword back, although he did not know what to make of what he had heard.

'You will live, for I am no killer.' He let go of his grip and dismounted.

Sankalp faced his fear, eye to eye. The bear sent another telepathic message.

'You are not only strong and intelligent but gifted with a gentle heart. From here on, you will have the gratitude and respect of all the inhabitants of this forest.' The bear was now calm, its disposition turned docile, and it rested its front paws on the ground. 'Spend a few days here and regain your energies. In time, I will lead you across the mountains.'

The bear merged with the shadows as quickly as it had appeared. The creatures of darkness retreated with the outcome of the night. A certain quiet prevailed. Sankalp sat down exhausted, his eyes closed in reminiscence. He recalled stories about this ferocious killer that very few lived to tell. 'A heavily muscled hairy beast, its blazing eyes tearing into your heart. What if I ever face one?' It was a thought that had haunted him since childhood but not anymore. The bear lived. The monk had slain his fear.

He understood the fine balance between courage and compassion.

Sankalp slept peacefully and woke to a bright morning. He inhaled deeply, the fresh mountain air filling and refreshing every part of his body. He clenched his teeth as a sharp prickle of pain emanated from a bruise on his shoulder.

Sankalp spent the next few days nursing his wounds and acclimatizing to the higher altitude.

True to its word, the fierce brown bear appeared on the fourth day. The unease Sankalp had felt earlier no longer existed. He was quickly on the move with the bear leading the way. They walked for two days, climbing over several high ridges, resting for short intervals for food and covering ground steadily. The high mountain stretched a league in either direction, except from a promontory, from where it dropped a few thousand feet. From there, the brown bear led him through a subterranean passage. It took them nearly a hundred hours to traverse the hidden trench that connected to the last of the high peaks. But it reduced the journey by a good two weeks.

By the time they came out of the long and narrow passageway, the sun was about to set. It had been four days.

Sankalp looked at the mountain face as they emerged; snow-capped, the mountain pierced through the thin low clouds. It was not higher than the ones he had crossed, but a thick mist covered the bare ridge that seemed almost vertical. The weather too was daunting, and the air had grown thinner. The brown bear had saved Sankalp a lot of time and energy. Had it not been for the strange encounter, he would still be far behind, facing the vagaries of nature.

At sunset, he thanked the bear.

'You have been a faithful guide, my friend. Without your help, I would not have reached here as quickly.' He stared ahead and remarked, 'And that is the last mountain,' Sankalp paused with a sigh. 'It could make all the difference between life and death.'

'Have faith!' With that final message, the brown bear vanished into the falling darkness.

The route that lay before him was tough. Sankalp decided to rest and gather his energy for the journey ahead. A storm broke that night; it continued for three days and finally abated during the wee hours of the fourth day.

Sankalp was well rested and up early. He was greeted by a pleasant sight—the sun was shining brightly through a thin cover of clouds. But it also gave him a clearer glimpse of the towering ridge and the steep climb that lay ahead. The last mountain on the trail looked truly imposing. Not letting his spirit be dampened, Sankalp plucked a few leaves from a low-hanging branch and scrubbed his face with their icy dew. It was delightfully refreshing and brought a smile to his face.

He took a long deep breath and began his climb while his trusted companion Zanzi hovered above. He made steady progress at first, but as he climbed higher the mud and snow made the steep and narrow path difficult to tread. He had to be cautious not to twist an ankle or injure his muscles. Carefully, he made his way up to the neck of the crest. From there, the rugged terrain dropped sharply towards the valley. He sighted the river from across the forbidding landscape, and the near-vertical hillock standing aloof, girdled by a chain of barren peaks.

The bright morning turned into a rather dull afternoon. He walked without resting, making his way slowly and steadily towards the narrow rim atop the mountain. The warmth of the afternoon sun soon surrendered to dark clouds. The air began to freeze, and the winds blew stronger than before. Sankalp hurried his steps; there was no way he would find shelter here.

Soon, a heavy rain came pouring down. He was drenched, and icy winds encircled him. His legs turned numb and his hands stiff. A sharp stinging pain in both often bothered him. The mountain track turned into deep slush. The mud and rock gave way wherever he stepped. He halted and leaned against a rough slab of granite and studied his surroundings. Sankalp sighted another route close by.

It stood shielded from the rain and icy winds due to its peculiar location. He could change course. However, the climb was tough. It was dangerously vertical and surrounded by steep slopes. If he fell, he would not survive. Grim and resolute, he took one last look at the ridge, and gripping the rock face firmly, he crawled up the challenging precipice.

After a while, the rain stopped. But the air grew colder and with that the pounding of his heart louder. For a while, he struggled, hoping the worst was over. Until fresh snow came down, completely covering the already slippery slopes. Sankalp was not only drenched but famished and a bit disoriented, given the altitude. He had to quickly crest the mountain and make his way down; no mortal could stay at this height for long and survive.

He carefully inched his way along and reached the most critical point in the climb. Just then, an eerie, high-pitched sound rent the air, followed by a loud crack of thunder. It was followed immediately by a brilliant display of lightning that blazed back and forth, a bit too close for comfort. Sankalp felt uneasy; he looked around, searching for any possible way to scale the ridge, but in vain. The weathered formation was too steep. It had no fissures, crevices or other faults near enough to give him a hold that he could use to climb up.

Then his eyes fell on a small ledge jutting from the mountain wall above him. If only he could raise himself up with the strength of his arms and reach it. And then, swing across a few feet over a deadfall that extended several hundred metres below. All this while clinging cautiously to a small part of the narrow ledge. If he could, he would be across…

Beyond that, the climb seemed easy, as the other side of the ridge sloped more gently. But the manoeuvre was difficult. Something even the mountain folk would never attempt. It was also unwise to stray from the given path, but his trail was as good as lost already. There was no way out, he had to either cross the ledge or freeze to death.

Sankalp paused for a moment, thinking. Reasserting his faith, he decided to go for it. He carefully stretched up and gripped the slippery ledge with his hands, the weight of his entire body resting on their strength. Using the last reserves of endurance, he swung his feet away from the ground, trying hard to pull himself up.

'Uhh…Uhhh,' he panted. 'Just a little more and I am done,' he mumbled. But he could not pull himself up. His legs moved in all directions to find a foothold, anything that could momentarily share the weight with his arms. The call of thunder grew louder, ear-shattering sounds that came from the bursts of forked lightning that streaked up close.

He dangled, vulnerable and exposed. Sankalp could feel his hands losing their grip on the slippery surface of the ledge. His physical strength was waning quickly and life seemed to slowly edge past him.

Had he reached the end of his journey?

Moments of emptiness stretched past eternity…

And from the void floated the blurred images of lost souls! They ghosted past him, howling menacingly, waiting for a chance to carry him into the jaws of death. 'Turn away while you can,' they called in his ears. 'You cannot withstand the winds! They are more powerful than the force that drives you!' The voices shrieked, making his skin prickle with the presentiment of evil.

'Not now…' a voice rose from within. 'Not till I have found my destiny!' A shallow whisper escaped his lips. Stronger than the words were the emotions that conveyed his conviction. Powerful thoughts pierced the ether. Sankalp coaxed every bit of strength out of his body and heaved one last time. The raging winds momentarily changed direction. Helped by a powerful gust that rose from under him and travelled upwards, Sankalp managed to pull himself over the ledge and roll to one side.

Exhausted, he lay there on the icy ground, composing himself. Recounting the moments gone by, he smiled with joy at his reprieve.

A while later, with a groan, he pulled himself to his feet. His head throbbed with the rush of blood, and he pressed his temples with his palms for relief. Then with a smile, he spread his arms in a stretch, soaking in the redolence that filled the crisp evening air. He spent about an hour recovering in a silence that was breached only by the sounds of his chewing on goji berries, found aplenty in this region.

A few white-bellied musk deer made their way past him, nibbling on the shrubs and the little blue flowers that sprouted at that height. Remaining oblivious to his attention, the deer came close, not fearing his presence. A large female, with a bright spot on her head, moved even closer to where he sat. Close enough for Sankalp to see the faint light of the evening reflected in her dark eyes. Almost immediately he recalled a memory from the past. The familiarity made him smile.

After a few minutes, Sankalp recommenced his journey. He quickly made his way to the lower half of the mountain, overlooking the sprawling valley below. Sidereal lights that occasionally streaked above were clearly visible in the darkened sky. At last, he lay down to rest. He gazed past the pines at the haze of stars that adorned the night sky. They seemed so close. The earth and the heavens seem to collide, merging ever so symmetrically the imperfections of the physical world with celestial faultlessness.

'Truly, it could only be here that the secrets of the past and the future, of death and destiny, could be known,' he murmured, before letting his eyelids close for the day.

12

The Land of Illusions

After a good night's sleep, Sankalp woke to a pleasant morning. It was a bright cloudless day. The air felt mild with the sun suffusing the valley in a crimson gold. His eyes keenly swept the horizon. The meandering white waters flowing through the valley caught his attention. It was a place of breathtaking beauty. Close to the riverbank stood what seemed like a small cottage. It was sheltered by three thick pines. Sankalp smiled, enchanted.

'Ah…I could live here forever,' he murmured with a sense of satisfaction.

He sat down and leaned forward, resting his elbows on his knees and enjoying his freedom from the misery of freezing winds and rain. He looked out at the valley, his brow furrowed with anxiety. He was nearing the end of his search. Across the river, he could see the sacred hillock. A molten glow covered its plateaued top. 'The abode of the invisible monk…' he murmured. And not very far, rising graciously towards the clear blue skies stood Kailasa.

He quickly made his way down. The trees were in bloom; the fragrance of wildflowers filled the air. He feasted on the fruit-laden trees that dotted the slopes, enjoying his trek through less feral surroundings. The weather was warmer than he had grown accustomed to. The sight of the afternoon light dancing delicately to the rustling sound of leaves added to the magic of the place. He thought back on the time he had spent with Titla.

As he neared the cottage, Sankalp was greeted by a familiar sound. It was Zanzi. He unlatched the front door. Though far from habitation, the cottage was clean, with an ample supply of fruits and honey stored in the kitchen. His steps slowed as he looked into the adjoining room. It had a large bed and a small fire burnt in the fireplace.

Sankalp was puzzled. Was someone living in the cottage? It was so far from the inhabited world. He walked out, looking for its resident.

He strolled along the stretch of water; its smooth-flowing currents beckoned him. A low-hanging vapour covered its entire span. Drawn forward by his fascination, he stopped at the riverside and plunged in. The waters were balmy as they flowed from the hot springs around the snow-decked mountains. His eyes glanced to the other side of the river; he could see the rocky path that led up the hillock. It was not very high, but the uppermost part remained covered in a nebulous mist.

Sankalp lazed a while in the warm and shallow waters that tingled through his body. Months of fatigue disappeared, and a sense of well-being pervaded. He felt light, energetic and happy, overcome as he was by the solemn beauty of his surroundings.

A low-hanging grey cloud appeared across the river as he walked back towards the cottage, still wondering about its occupant. His eyes fell on the undisturbed bed next to the fireplace. And a set of neatly folded maroon robes he hadn't noticed before. Sankalp felt grateful for the raiment. His own was badly travel-worn from months of exposure to the sun, rain and snow. The forest too had stripped it open in many places. He quickly donned a robe, enjoying the feel of its warm downy texture.

'I shall sleep here tonight and cross the river early in the morning,' Sankalp thought as he lay down on the bed. He closed his eyes, overwhelmed by a sweet but powerful fragrance that had begun to stir his mind.

A while later, and strangely awake, he found himself walking out of the cottage. The cloud had grown bigger and stood over the hut by then. In the thin light of the setting sun, he saw a figure approaching.

'I knew this cottage was occupied,' he murmured. The figure walking towards the cottage was of a young woman, but it was still a blur. As she came closer, the blur took on the features of the woman he loved, of how he remembered her. A shocked Sankalp stood frozen when he realized the young woman coming towards him resembled Titla!

'How on earth could she be here?' He couldn't believe his eyes and called out.

'Who is it?'

The approaching figure laughed mischievously, her hips swaying seductively as she came closer.

'Titla, is it you?' Sankalp exclaimed, louder.

'Yes, Sankalp. It is me,' she whispered, her voice a sound he had longed to hear. His happiness knew no bounds. He walked towards her and took her in his arms, his fingers threading through the dark waves of her hair. The faint aroma of wildflowers from her locks captivated his every breath.

'Oh, Titla, I have been thinking about you since I left the cottage! But how are you here, in the middle of the most treacherous of mountains?' he quizzed.

'My dear Sankalp, I have been miserable without you!' Her eyes fluttered with a hint of tears. Sankalp stared into her eyes, still unbelieving of the moment.

'Oh, Sankalp, I couldn't stay without you.'

'But how did you get here alone? It is extremely dangerous terrain,' enquired Sankalp, still in shock.

'My dear, I followed you to the cave. When I reached there, Kalimpong told me you had already left.' She sighed, still staring deeply into his eyes. 'Seeing my state and knowing I would not stop, he showed me a secret passage. That passage brought me here quicker than you,' she explained with a smile.

Sankalp was astonished at the sudden turn of events. 'But how did you…?'

Titla interjected, 'My dear, I knew you would reach me.' She held his gaze and slowly caressed the length of his arms, pressing them gently with her hands.

'You look tired and in need of rest. I have put together whatever I could find to make this our home,' she said, gesturing to the cottage.

Sankalp was overwhelmed with emotions. He slipped his fingers into hers and held her hand, the soothing sensation that he had been longing for. This is what he wanted; having the woman he loved by his side.

'My dear Sankalp, rest while I prepare your favourite pudding,' she said in a surprisingly casual tone before disappearing into the cottage.

'She must have been truly miserable,' Sankalp reflected. 'Miserable enough to follow me all the way here!' Thinking, he walked back inside the cottage and peeped into the kitchen, where she stood stirring a pot of stew hung over a bed of coals. 'How perfect she is in every which way and so caring by nature.' While engrossed in thoughts, he heard Titla call out to him.

'Dinner is served.'

He quickly seated himself on the mat in the main room, amazed at the sight of all the dishes she had put together.

'My dear Titla, I cannot thank you enough…' He struggled with words, being at a loss to describe his feelings. 'You…You risked your life for me,' he exclaimed as she filled his plate with generous portions of her preparations.

'It has been a long time since I had a meal like this,' he extolled, relishing the flavours that played in his mouth. 'Titla, my journey has been full of danger and challenges. The thought of turning back did cross my mind.'

Titla listened and smiled cryptically at his utterance.

'I wonder…Would I have been better off being with you? Rather than wandering alone in these desolate mountains.'

Titla looked at him and laughed softly. 'Sleep now, Sankalp. You must be exhausted after your long and tiring journey. We will talk about it tomorrow,' she whispered, tenderly caressing his forehead.

A distinctive change in his heart and mind took place with her every touch. While thoughts of her prevailed, his motive for being here seemed to desert him. Those moments of tenderness felt heavenly though, and he wanted them to last. But the hours flew by faster than ever.

It was another beautiful morning. He looked out of the window; there she was, bathing by the river. Titla looked at him, her expression playful, beckoning him to join her. There was so much in her that he hadn't seen before. His mind was quickly filled with words he wanted to say right then, in that instant.

Sankalp was about to step out when Titla met him at the door.

'My dear, are you going to the river to bathe?' she smiled, her expression mysterious.

'Yes, I was, but now that you are here, I want to ask you something.'

'Can I go first?' she interrupted with a bewitching smile.

'Whatever you wish,' he smiled back.

'I know you seek the invisible monk in these mountains. You want to learn the hidden language of the stars and unravel the secrets of destiny.' She paused and gazed at him, her long eyelashes fluttering to every beat of his heart.

'Don't you feel you have suffered enough? You have found a new meaning to life. Our meeting, too, is a play of destiny, isn't it?' She moved closer to him, her breath mingling with his.

'My dear Titla…'

She interjected before he could say anything further. 'Sankalp, let us start a new life, right now, right here.'

'But my dear…' he was interrupted again.

She held his hand and continued, 'Let us marry at daybreak tomorrow! And live in this beautiful place till we have our first child. Then we can go and meet Kalimpong and seek his blessings.'

Titla anxiously waited for his response.

Sankalp nodded, stunned that she had asked such a question. But then he quickly became aware of a curious sensation that had begun to play in his mind.

Perplexed, he slowly withdrew his hand from hers and walked out of the cottage. He tried to put all thought of her and what she had just said out of his mind, at least momentarily. He felt a certain lack of innocence in her words, and this happiness seemed like a fading glow compared to what he had experienced earlier in her company. Torn between conflicting desires, he closed his eyes and sought the teacher.

'Master, you know how I feel, caught in this dilemma. Show me the way that will make my heart feel lighter.'

He felt a subtle touch upon his subconscious that shook him gently. A familiar voice whispered across the distance. 'Awake! At some time or the other, we all fall prey to the sultry calls of inducement. Awake!'

Sankalp recalled words from the past. 'From this moment on, the dimensions of reality and illusion will blur, and the limits of your mind will be put to the test.'

The memory alerted Sankalp. He realized and understood the game of Maya! She had manifested as Titla to prey upon his mind. The conscious mind lifted the veil of ignorance; the illusion melted with the dream. It was time to cross the river that separated him from his final destination.

The river was formed by two streams joining into one. While one flowed down from the mountains, the other emerged from natural warm springs that welled from within the earth. A light mist hovered at the junction and blanketed the river for some distance. It gave the waters an obscure and formidable look. Being a mountain lad, Sankalp had never been taught to swim. At best, he had splashed and played in shallow streams during summer. Assuming the river was not too deep, he stepped into the water and began to wade across. After a point, the riverbed dropped steeply and the water rose rapidly, reaching up to his chin. He had no option but to retrace his steps to the shallows. He thought for a while and then set out for the nearby forest to look for a log that would be sturdy enough to hold his weight and keep him afloat.

An uprooted cedar tree caught his attention. It was partly hollow and seemed like an ideal raft.

'It is bulky but workable nevertheless,' Sankalp mumbled as he tried his best to carry it over his shoulders; it was heavy! A vein throbbed in his temple, and his knees buckled under the weight of the log. For a moment, he remained pinned in that position; then he dropped the log to the ground and drew himself upright. He paused, thinking. Then he tied one end of a vine to the log and the other end around his waist and finally managed to drag it to the river. An exhausting ordeal nonetheless!

'Let me catch my breath before I try crossing the river again,' he thought and sat near the bank.

A faint, almost equine splutter coming from nearby caught his attention. A mass of musk deer burst forth through the underbrush. They sauntered lazily towards the river and satisfied their thirst and then casually started to wade to the other side. A fawn, caught in the fast-flowing waters, struggled to keep pace with his mother. Sankalp focused on the deer. He recalled seeing her before, recognizing the bright white spot on her head.

'How can they wade across so effortlessly? Nobody taught them.' The thought aroused curiosity and envy in his mind, before settling into a conclusion. 'Is this what we call animal instinct? Sometimes you need it to survive!' Sankalp smiled and narrowed his eyes as something suddenly occurred to him.

There was no time to waste. The sun was about to go down. He quickly pushed the log into the water.

Sitting upright, he gripped it with his legs while using both his hands to paddle in the direction of the deer. The log, instead of moving forward, began to drift downstream. He paddled faster and harder, trying to cut through the strong current, but his efforts were in vain. The current started to drag him downstream, towards the waterfall that fell hundreds of feet below. He had to let go of the log that was keeping him afloat but taking him closer to his death!

Sankalp quickly jumped off the log and took to the river, frantically splashing his hands and legs. The river current showed its strength. It pulled him under, filling his lungs with water. Undeterred, he paddled harder with an almost obsessive energy, sinking then rising and gasping for air. He struggled, trying hard not to drown. His frenzied movements slowly acquired a more undulating motion. He managed to keep afloat.

Finally, to his relief, Sankalp felt sand below his feet. It was wise of him to have followed the deer through the shallows. He walked slowly to the other side, out of breath and drained of energy. On reaching the edge of the river, where the water reached only his ankles, he fell to his knees. Drawing in a deep breath, he coughed out the water from his lungs and then slowly crawled up the bank to dry land.

He lay motionless on the sand; though exhausted, his thoughts connected with the master. His face lit with eager anticipation, and he scanned the horizon. A pair of white swans floated across the dusky sky, the unerring motion of their wings emphasizing the sameness of their mind.

A thought caused a slight smile to be etched on his lips as he fell asleep.

13

The Invisible Monk: The Hidden Language of the Stars

The stars shone bright that night. He could see the crescent moon rising from behind the snow-covered mountains. A fulgent pattern of light from atop the hillock caught his attention. It resembled the one that had guided him to the cave many years ago. He stared at it determinedly till it faded.

The night was pleasant and the weather mild. Sankalp was too tired to look for shelter; he lit a fire and fell asleep close to the riverbank, his body cushioned by the soft dry sands. The next day was bright and beautiful. He stared at the misty hillock and exhaled deeply; his breath formed a white plume before mingling with the morning haze. After a quick dip in the refreshing river waters, he walked upstream, satisfying his hunger from a host of fruit-laden trees that grew close by.

The undulating land rose to a not-so-high peak. The ground then rolled down to meet the mountains and a clear blue lake on one side. He could see the barren hillock with its steep slopes. And the peak, hidden under a cloudy haze, lit with a mysterious luminosity, or so it seemed.

From afar, the comparatively small mountain seemed virtually devoid of vegetation. It was covered with loose, sharp-edged rocks, making it difficult to scale. Sankalp keenly surveyed the best possible route to the top. He stepped back a few metres and climbed down to a rather flat slab. It was perched close to where he stood, overlooking the mysterious blue lake. Some distance away, a trail had been worn up the steep ridge. He studied it closely, though the path was faint from disuse. And then, resting his hands comfortably on his knees, he assumed the lotus position. Closing his eyes, Sankalp reflected over past events. A smile covered his face briefly.

He sat in concentration, subduing his thoughts and synergizing his mental and physical energies. Undoubtedly, he would need both in search of the exalted monk. The cosmic energies floating in the ether assimilated around him. They surged through his mind, intensifying and filling every atom in his body with renewed strength. Sankalp passed into a silent prayer. Arising from this energized state he started the climb. Maintaining a steady pace, he scaled the lower part of the mountain in good time. From there, the path curved downward, skirting the edge of the small lake before rising again steeply. He stopped, considering the land ahead, his hands resting on his waist as he struggled to regain control over his laboured breathing. The rarefied atmosphere had begun to affect his body.

After a brief rest, he resumed his journey. By afternoon, he was treading the more difficult part of the terrain. The dark grey rock was slate; it was slippery and fragile. In places, the rocky surface gave way to soft ground strewn with thick patches of white flowers.

'What seemed like a day's journey will surely extend to another,' Sankalp murmured. The last remnants of sunlight began to disappear from the horizon. The sky was clearer than usual, but the weather was chilly and the fast-moving gusts unforgiving. He had inadvertently left his small pack of belongings in the cottage below. Undeterred, Sankalp inched closer to the summit, braving winds that seem to be born of the mist. He was still a few yards away from the small plateau, the highest point on the hillock, when a thick cover of mist began to engulf the area. A less resplendent moonlight made his movements slower still. And the thick veil of fog countered his every step. To find his way forward, he would have to depend on powers beyond sight and awaken the intuitive subconscious eye. He did so and, with utmost concentration, made his way through the haze.

Sankalp finally reached the small plateau, the sanctum. The atmosphere was charged with an inexplicable energy. The very air felt electrified! There was no one around and nothing on either side. The edges fell steeply from the shoulders to the bottom. Before him stood a monolith. The large rock stood unspoiled, unlike everything else that had been reshaped by the elements.

Shadowed moonlight trickled through the haze, creating an auroral effect. The gallop of time, unhindered through the day, came to a trot. Minutes passed by slowly.

His eyes wandered keenly over the plateau, seeking. Searching for signs that could lead him closer to his quest. But there was nothing here. Nothing that imitated life.

Tired, he began succumbing to the lassitude that had afflicted every muscle in his body. Exhaustion claimed the alertness of his mind too. With nowhere to go and not a soul in sight, he called aloud in desperation.

'O invisible monk, I am here from a faraway land. Bless me with your presence.' He waited eagerly for an answer but heard nothing. He called out again and again until his lungs ran out of the thin mountain air. Dazed, he fell to his hands and knees, gasping for air. His senses hovered at the threshold—that narrow dividing line between the conscious and beyond. Sankalp then experienced the strain that usually results from intense effort. But it wasn't fatigue.

Then suddenly, he felt a part of him being drawn out by an overbearing force. His body offered resistance, more as a reflex than a conscious defiance from the mind.

His mental senses continued to recede till he sensed a vibration moving through the air. It pulsated into a voice.

'Why do you seek me, Sankalp?' The voice was sharp and clear, compared to everything else that he was seeing and hearing around him.

'I am here to learn the hidden language of the stars, so that…' he faltered, 'so that I can seek my destiny…' Words turned to a mumble in his frazzled state, though the sentiment remained clear in his mind.

There was a pause. He could sense the howling of the wind. Then suddenly, his body jerked, and his heart felt a strange pull that was momentarily uncomfortable. Sankalp did not resist; he lay motionless. The unmanifested self rose and slowly floated away from the physical one. This detachment was real, but he still retained the sense of being himself. An indescribable peace surrounded him along with a realization that he would never be away from it.

Sankalp looked around, trying to determine the source of the voice. But all he could see was a vivid array of colours descending from above. Their magnificence was not of this world! The brightness pierced through the haze and was absorbed into the monolith. He moved closer, staring more intently at it. A reflection of him stared back. It was somewhat larger and mildly transparent.

'O invisible monk, I have come from a faraway land. My journey has taught me much about faith, love, compassion and courage,' his mind asserted. 'I have mastered all that has been taught and forsaken much in my search for you! Bless me with your presence.'

'I am here,' a voice resonated.

Sankalp looked more closely at everything around him, trying to discover the source of the sound, which seemed to emanate from the rock. He extended his hands, trying to touch and feel the reflection that looked so real. But his hand simply passed through the rough surface!

Sankalp was shocked. All of a sudden, the mist began to retreat, giving him a clearer view of the rock face. Still, all he could see was his reflection, but with a clarity that was hyperphysical.

'Sankalp, I am here, in front of you,' the faint susurration pervaded his hearing.

'But Master! I don't see anything except…' he stuttered, 'my reflection.'

'My dear Sankalp, the reflection that you see is of the pure and higher self. The invisible monk! The omnipotent force that rests within. Unseen by those who do not seek me with true resolve,' the unearthly voice echoed.

Almost immediately, a burst of bright light from the rock face struck him! It readied his mind for a new revelation.

And then he heard the voice again. 'I will now unlock the doors to the fourth dimension. Unleashing powers that will elevate you to a higher state of enlightenment, leading to the knowledge you seek.'

The voice receded, sending a strange current through the young monk. The force penetrated the central vortex in his forehead. It then moved down the spine, energizing all the seven life chakras, activating the potent third eye.

A pearl of omniscient wisdom invaded his consciousness. His higher self reached a more expansive state. Space and time merged in that moment of stillness, opening doors to a divine vision. His mind in that minuscule fragment of a moment stood attuned to the cosmic rhythm. It merged with the thread of divine light that bridged this universal vastness, yet consummated into nothingness. Bestowed with this divine vision, Sankalp could view the infinite vastness of the universe, its innumerable galaxies and solar systems.

In that moment of timelessness, he stood witness to many cosmic creations and their destruction. And to the rise and fall of worlds from times immemorial.

With this celestial vision imprinted in his mind, he could see and read the subtle movements of the nine planets and of the dancing starlight's in the sky that held the key to destiny. Then, suddenly, the vision disintegrated. His elevated conscious state dissolved, leaving within him a sense of penetrating sublimity. His body jerked slightly as he drew in a deep breath.

For a moment, his mind was blank, and then a picture trail of many images and emotions flashed through it. Some from childhood, some with his family and then others from a time he couldn't place. A few of the images were gory with an explicit show of life and death. He cringed as he saw the faces of people, many of whom he didn't recognize but felt the sensation of being close to.

He had never experienced this before; a rising tide of tension consumed him. Then again, the mind became unfilled, and the expression on his face calmed. His breathing returned to normal.

Sankalp slowly returned to awareness.

A familiar figure materialized and floated towards him.

'Of shadows and light, my son. Of thoughts and desires.' The sentient figure spoke in a shallow whisper.

Sankalp looked at him; as their eyes collided, he instantly felt the warmth of his touch and love in a way he had never felt before.

'I have seen you before…in a time gone by.' He paused, reminiscing. 'Ah, I remember now…after we left the cave. It was at the cottage…' He drew in another deep breath before speaking. 'The magical feast.' Sankalp closed his eyes. A tingle of awe and inexplicable joy ran along his spine. 'I saw you then,' he said, his voice fading. An understanding smile sailed across his face. He whispered slowly, 'The little fish, the bear… and the high winds too. I recognize you now, Gedun Drupa, the mind traveller. The master of masters!'

Sankalp folded his hands in reverence before falling into a deep sleep.

He awoke hours later, amidst the spread of noon light. Atop the heights where he had witnessed the miracles his destiny had stored for him. Sankalp bid farewell to the land of the invisible monk, smiling and thanking the master of masters.

He had observed briefly the power of the cosmic light and understood the subtle interplay between time, space and matter. A dominating thought in that moment had freed his mind from the others. Reaffirming that the identity of the supreme was truly singular in nature. Yet, through its infinite power, it had given rise to many millions of cosmic bodies, all transient. They would live out their given path and, in time, disintegrate to become one with the supreme. All beings existing in this temporary cosmic reality functioned within the confines of their individual worlds, enacting a part in the universal cosmic theatre.

Through the power he now possessed, he could read the cosmic lights. The prophetic language of the stars. But for the first time, everything he held dear seemed minuscule, including his destiny. Though he understood well that other than the living, even powerful kingdoms were tied to the threads of destiny, that every village had its destiny, deeply intertwined with its inhabitants and rulers. And all that ever transpired or would transpire in these lands was part of a universal objective.

Destiny, then, was no preordained superimposed reality for the living but a metamorphosis of various deeds determined by a set of choices at various intervals across time.

Along with these thoughts, his experiences of life from the past and his present ratiocinated with unbridled clarity. A sublime realization dawned. This life, too, was part of an inexplicable journey. Every hardship he had ever encountered had only proved to be a learning experience. An experience that had helped him overcome the obstacles in his path towards enlightenment.

Sankalp had gone beyond *nang-mchod* and tamed the ego. He had acquired control over *sa ayatana* and *vijnana*, the senses and the mind consciousness, and conquered the five *kleshas*. The doctrines of the yoga of Brahma Chinta lay clear. His mind stood in harmony and complete obedience to the higher voice of conscience.

Armed with many treasures of knowledge, he started his journey down the steep hillock.

Climbing down was as difficult and tiring as climbing up the demanding terrain. He finally reached the riverbank by afternoon. Wading through the strong currents exhausted him more. Dusk had fallen by the time Sankalp entered the cottage.

The monk was greeted by the warmth of a fire that burnt brightly. There was no one, but the air was laden with a mesmerizing fragrance, emphasizing an invisible presence. He quickly walked to the adjoining room, looking for his meagre but precious belongings. To his surprise, except for a fruit-laden basket, there was nothing there.

Unperturbed, Sankalp smiled, his face lit with palpable serenity. He sat quietly in the centre of the cottage; closing his eyes, he concentrated on the fragrance filtering through his breath.

A moment later, he called out in a confident voice, 'Show yourself, the one who hides behind the fragrance. My eyes do not see you, but I feel your presence, O Maya!'

The pronouncement forced her presence. Almost instantly, a beautiful maiden appeared, holding his belongings. With eyes lowered becomingly, she spoke softly.

'Your awakened self sees through me,' she smiled. 'I hope you don't hold me responsible for the tricks played on you, mind traveller.'

Calmly, with a smile, Sankalp nodded in acceptance. The maiden dissolved to a sparkle and vanished, leaving with him his belongings.

14

Back to the Village: The First Encounter With the Invaders

A burst of early morning light reflecting off the shiny rock face woke him. Sankalp opened his eyes and blinked to adjust to the light. He then drew in a deep breath and coughed it out. A radiant aura encircled him. He smiled and once again closed his eyes briefly.

Sankalp had glimpsed the master! Having divested himself of his yogic powers and thus moved beyond his physical body, Kalimpong had transcended to a higher subconscious plane.

It took Sankalp several minutes to bring his body to a stir. He stretched his arms and slowly shook away the mud that had accumulated on his body over the past few months while he had been immersed in a meditative state. After a while, the mind traveller walked out of the cave.

The first thing he noticed was that the trees were budding. The apple tree was in bloom and had borne fruit. He bent low and examined the small shrubs and found that every plant, large or small, had acquired new growth. He strolled further down to the stream and enjoyed a long refreshing bath.

On starlit nights, he pondered, looking back at the challenges he had faced and at every contest that had contributed to taking him higher, making him one of them. A greater purpose awaited; higher intellect guided him in a preordained direction. On the far side of the mountains was the village where his family had once lived.

It was a nine-day walk to the little hamlet of Shaka.

The sky was clear. Bright afternoon light suffused the entire valley. To his right, the high mountain tops were still capped with snow. To his left was the valley, dotted with terraces. These mountains had been neatly carved by the earliest settlers in the area, making good use of the most fertile ground at this high altitude. While some terraces had been ploughed and soaked with water, others waited to be planted.

As he neared the village, he saw that nothing much had changed in the years gone by. But although the streets were filled with people going about their daily chores, a forced stillness prevailed.

Sankalp walked towards a small grain shop owned by an elderly man and inquired, 'My good sir, I am looking for work. Is there anything I can do in exchange for food?'

The diminutive old man stopped in his work. He stared at Sankalp with gloomy eyes. He looked around cautiously and murmured, 'Have you been spared by the rascals, or did you run away in fear? You look able-bodied and yet are still in the village!' He kept his eyes on the young monk for a long moment.

Sankalp kept his voice level, his hands behind his back in respect. 'I have come back after a very long time.' He fought to keep his face expressionless. 'I don't quite understand what you just said. The streets are the same, but the people seem different. The once sparkling eyes of the village women look subdued and full of fear. Can you tell me what is going on?'

The old man's expression saddened as he stared at Sankalp with stony eyes. 'Can't you see? They took away everything... everything! Except for the gloom we carry on our faces.' The old man lowered his eyes and whispered, 'Now, come in before anyone sees you.'

He led Sankalp by the hand to a small courtyard, where an old lady sat weaving in a corner.

'My dear, we have a visitor. Please get him something to eat.'

They sat on a mat that was neatly spread on the floor. The old man proceeded to tell Sankalp how the invaders had taken most of the able-bodied men to serve in their army, while some, along with the women, had been sold as slaves.

'The village is nearly devoid of youth. And those not taken by the invaders have left the village for the city of Lhasa.' He paused. 'To find safety and work.'

Sankalp could feel the agony in each word as the old man spoke.

'My son too...' His face grew shadowed with more sadness. 'His name is Rabten. He was taken captive and forced to serve in their army. We don't even know if he is dead or alive.' It took him a moment to regain his composure before he spoke again. 'He was our only child. The one who would care for us in our old age.' His eyes moistened with grief. 'My wife has been heartbroken ever since.'

The old woman came with some food and water. She gave Sankalp a motherly smile and then quietly left the two alone. Sankalp could sense the pain beyond her expression; it was evident in her eyes. The old man looked inquisitively at Sankalp's robe and then stared at the small pack he carried.

'Are you a warrior, young man?'

'No, I am a monk looking for shelter.'

'But you carry a sword and dress differently. Do you know that anyone found with a weapon in the village is called a traitor and killed by the invaders? '

'Hmmm…' Sankalp's expression turned thoughtful.

'If they come to know I fed a traitor…they…they will kill me!' the old man stuttered. 'I suggest you eat quickly and leave the village!'

Sankalp placed a gentle hand on his shoulder, saying, 'You are a kind man, but I must decline your offer. I have decided to spend a few days in the village and visit my house.'

'Are you from our village? Where is your house?' the old man asked, taken aback by Sankalp's answer.

'It is the large, broken-down house close to the village temple.' His tone was detached and devoid of emotion. 'Somewhere over there…' Sankalp raised his hand and pointed.

'That house!' The old man's eyes flickered with a glint of surprise. 'That belonged to a friend…Lin Thiampong was his name. He was the village headman. His family was murdered by the invaders about ten years ago,' he said, barely able to hold his grief.

'But how did you know him?'

'I am the youngest son of Lin.'

The old man stood there shocked. It took him a few moments to recover from what he had just heard.

'You are a brave man to say that here!' He put his hand on Sankalp's shoulder, offering sympathy.

'My name is Rangdol. Your late father was my friend. You are the only survivor in the family.' He looked at Sankalp, his eyes barely able to contain his pain. 'It would be better if you left. Save yourself while you can! As it is, there is nothing much left in the village now,' he said, his voice pained as he walked Sankalp to the door.

'I am here to stay a few days.' Sankalp stared at him, unblinking. 'And if I am to be done to death for that, then so be it.'

Sankalp thanked the old grain merchant for his hospitality and left the house. He walked along the dusty village track reminiscing, while his eyes anxiously searched for familiar landmarks. Close by, a few men worked a forge—a small one good enough to produce farming tools and horseshoes.

A youthful girl worked the bellows with single-minded intensity. She smiled a little and tossed her hair over her shoulders, staring briefly at Sankalp's attire as she watched him go by. After a brief walk, he came across the temple. A prominent site, it had been badly plundered; nothing of interest or value remained. A few metres from the temple stood another ravaged structure. His house!

Sankalp stopped and stared at the fallen structure, remembering what it had looked like before the invaders had destroyed it. He walked in after a long moment, his hands brushing against its broken walls.

All of a sudden, he heard Zanzi's cries alerting him to danger. They were followed by screams for help from a girl!

Sankalp immediately stepped out of the house. He was horrified to see a girl being chased by two men on horseback. He immediately recognized her as the one who had been working the bellows at the forge. Her cries for help rang through every nook and corner of the narrow streets.

'Help! Please help me!' she pleaded.

But no one opened their door to her. To avoid being trampled by the horses, she ran inside the ruins of what was once the courtyard of Sankalp's house. Responding to her cries, Sankalp quickly ran to her and planted himself firmly between the horsemen and the girl. The men stopped and urged their horses into a trot, advancing towards the girl.

'Do not enter!' warned Sankalp, his hand resting on the hilt of his sheathed sword. His presence was comforting to the visibly shaken girl.

'Move away while you can, monk!' shouted one of the horsemen, pointing his sword menacingly at Sankalp. His eyes were charged with a shameless passion.

Sankalp took a step forward, making his challenge clear. He drew his sword and stared at the two advancing men.

'Go away and leave the girl alone,' he said, his tone calm.

Though surprised, the men paid little heed to his call of caution and quickly dismounted. They moved together, goading him to fight and swinging their swords at his shoulders. They wanted to maim him and ridicule and kill anyone who raised a voice against them. A gory lesson taught to anyone offering resistance. But the two men were no match for the kendo master. He let them close in, dodged their blades and then jumped; it was more like levitating in a swirling motion. His sword circled as he moved, severing their heads effortlessly.

The skirmish was bloody but soon over. The girl's family had arrived at the scene by then.

They stood shocked at the sight! The girl, shivering in fright, quickly ran into her mother's arms. She was bruised at the knees but otherwise unhurt.

'Are you all right?' questioned the elderly woman, firmly clasping her arms around her.

The girl, still in shock, could not reply but nodded in affirmation.

Meanwhile, hearing the commotion, a large crowd had gathered around the house. The girl's father had also arrived at the scene. 'Are you all right? Did anyone hurt you?' he questioned in a low voice and hugged her instinctively, his hands trembling as he ran them across her face and wiped away her tears.

'I am fine, Father,' she whispered. She then looked at Sankalp with unfeigned surprise. 'Thanks to that man over there. He saved my life!' she declared, pointing at him.

Sankalp stood calm in the midst of the tumult. No one from the village had challenged the invaders in a long time.

'Thank you for saving my daughter from the evil designs of these barbarians,' the mother sobbed.

The villagers stood dazed. They didn't know what to say or do, especially as some among them were suspected informers of the invaders. While many stood shocked, a few stared at Sankalp with incriminating eyes. He met their stares and unuttered accusations without flinching.

A voice called out from the crowd, 'What have you done? You have killed two of their men, and now many more will come to seek revenge!' The man groaned in resignation. 'No one will be spared! We can't fight an entire battalion.'

The villagers murmured amongst themselves and then fell silent.

'No, we can't,' replied Sankalp gravely, 'but neither can we be silent and let them kill our people and destroy our lives!' He drew a deep breath and exhaled, shaking his head. 'Just because you fear for your life. Aren't you dead already?'

The man offered no response to Sankalp's call. A silent moment passed before Sankalp addressed them again.

'I once knew of brave men in this village. I don't see any now,' he remarked with disdain.

Another voice called out from the babble around. 'You are a stranger and will leave soon. We will end up paying the price for your damn actions!'

Sankalp did not reply but noticed the flash of anger on the man's face.

An old woman cried out, 'Too many have died from our families. We live in acceptance of what is left of our forsaken lives.'

Then, an elderly voice called out in a pacifying tone, 'He is no stranger, people, but the youngest son of Lin Thiampong!'

It was Rangdol, the old grain merchant. He had arrived with the others on hearing the commotion, which had reached a feverish pitch. His statement drew an immediate response. Surprise showed on the faces of those gathered there. Lin Thiampong had been much loved and respected by everyone in the village. And for long, he and his family had been presumed dead by the villagers.

The crowd took another look at Sankalp, wide-eyed and one of utter disbelief. An unspoken consensus of quiet settled in. The old grain merchant was the first to break the silence.

'Long live the son of Lin Thiampong! Long live the son of Lin Thiampong! Death to the invaders!'

A few cried out along with him, and then suddenly the crowd began to chant more loudly.

'Death to the invaders! Long live the son of Lin Thiampong!'

Sankalp stood awed by the sudden change in response now that they knew who he was. He bowed low with humility. For the first time, he saw how loved and respected his father had been.

The old grain merchant walked up to him. 'Your father was a brave man. He sacrificed his life to save the village. Lin Thiampong died with dignity while fighting for his honour. We remember him proudly!' Rangdol declared, his voice shaking with emotion. 'Come now, rest with us till we find a suitable place for you to stay.'

'I have decided to stay in my home.'

'You mean the ruins?' the old man stated without lenity.

'Yes, let me seek solace in the shadows of its broken walls.'

The grain merchant was a wise man and understood his intent. He signalled to the crowd to follow him, leaving Sankalp alone.

Everybody in the village was intrigued. They wanted to know more about this strong and handsome man, introduced to them as the son of Lin Thiampong. While many were happy with his return, some had mixed feelings. They were confused, wondering about his strange attire. He was dressed like a monk, but he fought like a warrior!

While Sankalp rested amongst the ruins, his pet falcon found a perch atop a nearby tree.

Rangdol took it upon himself to bring food and water for Sankalp. Perhaps he wanted to know more about the monk. A few men from the village accompanied him. Meanwhile, the village settled into a restless repose; there were murmurs going around.

Many expected the invaders to be back in greater numbers to teach the villagers a lesson. As evening fell, a bright moon lit the night sky. Sankalp strolled out to get a feel of the village. He recalled walking the muddy paths in the happier days of yore. Though wistful, he was excited to be there. The village had not changed much. But there were fewer men to be seen, and an unnatural calm prevailed, especially after sunset. Perhaps this was due to fear of the invaders, who usually raided the villages at night. He stopped and looked around before walking back to his house.

On the way, he was greeted by the old grain merchant. He was accompanied by the girl Sankalp had saved from the invaders.

'I have brought you some food. The girl has specially cooked rice pudding for you.' The shy girl nodded with a smile. 'Moreover, the villagers say they will help rebuild your old home.'

'Thank you for that gesture of kindness, but the effort could be in vain. I may be here only a few weeks,' replied Sankalp, relishing the rice pudding.

Rangdol waited awhile, choosing his words carefully.

'My son, sometimes it is good to see things as others do, even if it is for a short duration.'

Sankalp nodded understandingly.

'Tell me about yourself. How did you escape the clutches of the invaders? As I recall, they searched all across the Yarlung Pass for you.'

Sankalp recounted the events of the past ten years to the grain merchant. He told him how he had managed to escape and find refuge in the cave and about the time he had spent with Kalimpong.

'I am here at the call of destiny, perhaps for an unfulfilled purpose,' he emphasized.

The grain merchant listened with awe. He concluded that Sankalp's return was more than mere chance.

'My son, despite their fear of retribution, most people will stand by you. We have lost many of our men.' Rangdol shook his head in despair. 'They put up a great resistance and fought to the death. But the battle-hardened invaders had an edge.

They ruthlessly killed those who raised their voices against them. We have lived in fear ever since.'

Sankalp nodded in understanding but said nothing.

Rangdol furrowed his brow, deepening the creases that stretched horizontally across his forehead. 'Sankalp, these people are seeing something they haven't seen in a while—hope!' he emphasized, drawing in a deep breath. 'Most of them see you as someone who can win back their freedom, their happiness.'

Sankalp sighed before speaking softly. 'My dear man, everyone has to fight their own battles and face what destiny has in store. Let them not think much of what happened today. I only did what the moment demanded of me.' After a thoughtful interlude, he spoke more intently. 'Can you arrange a meeting at the village square tomorrow?'

The old grain merchant nodded and left.

As the night progressed, the broken walls of his home came alive with memories. He recalled the unconstrained, atemporal afternoons of childhood, but his fatigued body soon got the better of his mind. Sankalp slept peacefully and more comfortably than in the past despite being amidst the scattered ruins of his home.

The next day, at the appointed time, people began assembling in the village square. Sankalp walked the path his father once had. He sat under the shade of a large oak tree, surrounded by the village elders.

The old grain merchant introduced Sankalp, recounting to the villagers the boy's escape from the invaders. The villagers were captivated by the story. Many were curious, some were awed, while others were sympathetic. But they were starting to believe that the son of Lin was indeed their saviour.

Prompted by the elders, Sankalp took his father's seat amidst loud cheers from the crowd.

He then addressed the villagers.

'Please don't get carried away by the small incident that happened yesterday. Like you, I have lost everything to these barbaric invaders! They have disrespected our people and our culture and have taken most of our young men and women as slaves,' he spoke in a raised voice, his contempt apparent. 'I cannot fight them alone! So you must decide whether you will fight and live or die as honourable men, or suffer every day like cowards!'

A few responded with mixed feelings, but most applauded his words. 'Son of Lin, we will fight along with you!' they shouted, encouraged by his words.

Rangdol had been chosen as the village headman after the death of Lin Thiampong. He addressed the gathering next.

'I will no longer be the headman of Shaka,' he declared.

The announcement drowned the light chatter. A quiet followed.

Sankalp too was surprised, but he waited to hear Rangdol out.

He raised his hand to the crowd, seeking their attention.'I propose to appoint the son of Lin Thiampong, our beloved friend, as the village headman.'

An ecstatic crowd applauded in acceptance.

'Now, as per our tradition, you may choose a name to address him.'

'He is a monk with a unique attire,' a voice called out.

'But an incredible fighter,' declared another with a booming voice.

The voices deliberated amongst themselves for a few moments.

'We shall call him "the warrior of Shaka"!' proclaimed an elderly lady holding a gaily attired child.

The crowd cheered in acceptance.

'From now on, the son of Lin Thiampong will be known as "the warrior of Shaka"!' Rangdol announced to the ecstatic crowd.

Sankalp finally broke his silence. 'I cannot accept the position of the village headman.' Sankalp looked at Rangdol. 'I cannot…I am a slave to the call of destiny and may leave soon. Perhaps to return another day,' he smiled slightly. 'Till then, Rangdol will continue to be the headman.'

Rangdol was a good man. The people accepted the proposal with little reluctance.

Sankalp then requested Rangdol to gather all the able-bodied men from the village and bring them to his house.

When they had gathered at the ruins, he told them, 'I will train you in the art of combat and fight the invaders with you.'

The men roused to his words.

'In return,' he smiled thoughtfully, 'you can help rebuild my home.'

'We won't disappoint you, warrior of Shaka!' a young man with a limp said with fervent zeal. His words were immediately acknowledged by the others as some in the gathering were trained masons.

Rangdol looked at the young lad and smiled. 'Perhaps we can offer you something other than being a warrior.'

'Why?'

'My boy, I don't wish to offend you, but you are lame.'

'Perhaps you see me as lame, but I don't!' the young man replied with conviction.

Impressed, Sankalp walked up to him and placed his hand on his shoulder. 'What is your name?'

'They call me Bhumiputra the lame, but—'

Sankalp interjected, 'Bhumiputra the fighter, I would say!'

The crowd cheered again in acknowledgement of his words.

The evening passed without a retaliatory attack from the invaders. And the following day, the warrior of Shaka began training a handful of very determined individuals to fight.

The invaders were battle-hardened. But the village men compensated for what they lacked with dedication and a fierce determination to break free from tyranny. They wanted to put an end to slavery and were willing to die for it.

Most of them felt quite comfortable with whatever weapon they were given to handle. They spent several hours a day learning and perfecting their fighting skills. The men Sankalp trained were honourable; they were not afraid to fight or die in battle. It was in fact a desirable end, being one that led to immortality in the stories that would be told of them in the times to come. What they lacked was a leader. Someone who could draw them from behind the veil of fear and uncertainty and fill them with confidence and the assurance that they could win. That they could once again be free!

The men spent their leisure hours in helping to rebuild the fallen house. Thanks to their skilled craftsmanship, it was beginning to take shape. The masons from this region were known for their fine work, and many were summoned by the king to work in his palace at Lhasa. Every night when Sankalp returned, his heart filled with joy on seeing the fallen house beginning to take shape again.

One morning, as Sankalp was about to leave, Rangdol hastily entered the courtyard accompanied by a shepherd boy.

'Sankalp, this boy has some information to share. He was out grazing sheep on the high mountain passes and spotted some activity in the invaders' camp.' He looked grim. 'I think they are regrouping, preparing…'

'Do you know the whereabouts of this outpost?'

'Sir, it is on the other side of the valley, connected by a narrow rope bridge,' the boy replied.

'Can you take me there now?'

'Yes, sir. I can,' he nodded.

Sankalp set out with the boy and a couple of men for the outpost on the far side of the valley. A few men stayed back to protect the village in case of an incident. The outpost was about half a day's walk from the village. As they neared the valley, they saw the rope bridge. It had been built by the invaders to enable them to make routine checks on their territories and ward off any potential threat.

The outpost had a small number of horsemen, not more than fifteen. And it seemed that the shepherd boy had been right! They were readying a scouting party to search for the two missing soldiers. Sankalp assessed the situation with his men. They decided to return at once and ready themselves to confront the invaders.

They reached the village by sunset. Sankalp asked the men to meet him with the others later that evening. Meanwhile, he headed for Rangdol's house. Sankalp explained his plan to the headman and suggested he convene a meeting of the village elders.

Rangdol listened intently; there was a pause before he responded, his eyebrow raised. 'Are you sure of your plan and its implications?'

Sankalp understood his reluctance. It was a result of the suffering he had seen and experienced over the years.

'It is time to put an end to this misery,' he urged and patted Rangdol's shoulder.

Before leaving, he told Rangdol to inform the villagers to stay vigilant and not venture far from their homes.

That evening, the people assembled in the village square under the half-light of a crescent moon.

'My brothers,' Sankalp exhorted, 'this is our chance to seek revenge for everything the invaders have done to us! I know many of you have lost loved ones to these merciless marauders. They have been raiding and looting our villages for too long. Let us not give them another chance!'

The crowd roared out, 'Death to the invaders! Death to the invaders!'

'Let me warn you—battle is a volatile situation. There is no certainty, and anything can happen. You may live or die, but promise yourself that whatever the result, you will accept it with honour and dignity!'

He drew a deep breath and continued more softly, 'I know some of you may change your mind after meeting your family. If you do, don't come back here.'

There were young and old people and some with little children in the gathering. He saw faces turn morose as he called for the young and able to gather again after supper.

Sankalp had shared the truth, and to some, it had sounded fearful. But all he wanted was to make them understand his vision and share his sense of purpose, which could eventually set them free. While he understood what was required, the simple village folk did not. They did not yet grasp that only courage and selfless action could redeem their present.

Later that night, Sankalp and the old grain merchant waited patiently for the men to return.

The moon slowly climbed higher in the sky, but there was no one in sight. The two exchanged a reluctant glance, reaching what seemed an obvious conclusion.

Suddenly, the quiet night was interrupted by a queer noise, the tapping of wood against the stone-paved road. The sound drew closer, followed by scores of torches marching towards them. They were led by Bhumiputra the lame. Holding a sword in one hand and a crutch in the other, he made his way towards the two men. He was followed by a large group of hardy men. While most were from the village, a few had joined them from the surrounding areas.

Sankalp had shared his thoughts with the old grain merchant—he had expected many to stay away, fearing death. But to his surprise, not one had stayed back!

'We are all with you, warrior of Shaka! Now tell us what to do,' Bhumiputra said with calm determination.

'I respect your courage and feel proud to be one of you!' Sankalp replied in admiration. 'Come, sit with me and listen carefully. I have a plan.'

The meeting lasted well into the night. Everyone was told what to do before they retired for the night or what was left of it.

The next few days went by uneventfully. Until one night, Sankalp woke with a start in his makeshift bed, nudged awake by an innate intuition. He immediately ordered his men to gather. It was still dark. Before dawn, they had taken up positions in and around the village. With the first rays of the sun came the thumping of hooves. The sounds originated from the narrow path that led to the village. The horsemen were on their way!

The morning light was yet to grow when the invaders entered the village. Ground frost prevented them from seeing the ropes that were stretched across the narrow streets. With one pull, Bhumiputra had the first two horsemen on the ground! He looked at them, his heart pounding for revenge and clamouring to attack the men who had brought death and destruction to their quiet land. The horsemen riding behind realized a trap had been set and jumped over the ropes.

Undeterred, Bhumiputra and his two companions charged at the fallen men. Their sharp axes emerged through the thick mist and quickly struck the enemy, killing one and badly injuring the other before retreating into the haze.

The invaders were shocked at the nasty surprise! Seeing just three men, one of whom was lame, their leader shouted out in anger, 'Go, get them! Don't let them get away!'

Two riders immediately broke away while the leader and a few others galloped into the village, hurling their torches at everything in sight.

As planned, the old grain merchant had emptied the hutments along the streets. The villagers were safe, but the hay barns burnt ferociously, as they were meant to. The smoke and the mist favoured Sankalp; it was the ideal camouflage.

With a shrill whistle, Sankalp alerted his men. Two of them moved forward, challenging four of the enemy's battle-hardened soldiers. Confident of their superior numbers, three of the attackers dismounted and surrounded Sankalp.

'Spare no one. Kill them all!' shouted one and charged, his sword aimed at Sankalp's neck.

Sankalp swerved back in a flash to avoid the charge. And in the same smooth motion, he pirouetted with speed, his blade slicing through the enemy's neck in quick retaliation. Finishing the move, he planted his feet and moved his sword skilfully from the front to the back, tearing into the second attacker's chest. The man screamed in pain. He struggled to find his balance and dropped his sword. Two more moved in unison towards Sankalp, who arced his sword upward, deflecting their strikes. Lowering his sword to a horizontal position, he slashed their rib cages in one quick, punishing move. The powerful sword of balance appeared demonic to the eyes of the invaders! The enemy was not ready for such retaliation.

Just then, a single arrow whizzed towards Sankalp. He caught it on his wooden shield and looked in the direction from where it came. It was the fifth horseman; he had shot the arrow in a desperate bid to maim, if not kill him. Sankalp swung the shield to his back with the help of a leather cord. Then, sheathing his sword, he drew out his bow and retaliated with a quick and precise discharge. The horseman stumbled and slumped on his horse.

Defeated, the captain signalled his men to follow him. 'Retreat!' he shouted, staring at Sankalp as he rode past him.

Meanwhile, the two armed invaders sent to confront Bhumiputra had not lasted long—they were done to death! The lame Bhumiputra emerged as the youngest and fiercest of all the fighters.

The leader of the invaders fled with his remaining men, followed closely by Sankalp and his band. They had daringly grabbed the horses of the fallen men.

The enemy was shaken by this sudden and furious resistance. They had never faced anything like this. Though more in number, they were on the run, chased by a handful of villagers! The invaders headed back to the bridge, followed closely by Sankalp and his men. The attackers wanted to cross the narrow rope bridge as quickly as possible. It was the only escape for them. But the men from the village were in no mood to give up.

There ensued a wild chase. Seeing the enemy flee had boosted the villagers' morale. Spurred on by anger and disgust, they would settle for nothing less than the heads of the ruthless invaders!

The invaders were good riders. It was difficult for the inexperienced village men, and even Sankalp, to catch them on horseback.

Soon, they were nearing the bridge. The narrow bridge could support only three horsemen, maintaining a respectful distance, at a time. Once the invaders made it over, they would be seen by their comrades camped on the other side.

'They're crossing!' shouted Sankalp over his shoulder. The last fleeing horseman had climbed the already overburdened bridge by the time Sankalp reined his horse to a stop. He quickly dismounted and struck at the ropes that held the bridge with his sword. The first strike frayed a few knots. The bridge jerked hard, emitting a loud creaking sound, followed immediately by shouts of panic. The horsemen were finding it difficult to maintain their pace and balance. They rode on with great difficulty. The last horseman glanced back and realized what was about to happen.

'Ride faster! They are trying to cut the ropes!' he shouted.

Bhumiputra and his men joined Sankalp. They slashed at the ropes together. The tremors racked the bridge vigorously. Only two of the riders had managed to reach the other side. The others were caught in the middle! A few more strikes, and with a mighty crack, the partially frayed ropes snapped, sending the bridge along with the horsemen down to their deaths! The men rejoiced as the invaders fell, asserting their defiance of what they had endured and would no longer do so.

With the rope bridge gone, it was difficult for the invaders to return. The triumphant band rode back to the village. Flushed with the thrill of victory, the village celebrated that night. Rangdol and his wife temporarily forgot the pain of losing their son. As did many others who had lost members of their family. Everyone joined in the celebration.

'It has been a long time since the village rejoiced,' Rangdol said and smiled through the creases that covered almost his entire face. 'It takes me back to the time when your father was the headman and festivals were celebrated!' He nodded in contentment. 'I see those times coming back.' His age-creased forehead wrinkled further with joy. The village priest, who was seated nearby, agreed and acknowledged his statement with a slight smile.

'Yes, I do remember the happier times,' Sankalp reiterated. 'But today's victory is not the end. They will be back, and you must be prepared for them.' His expression turned grim.

'You will lead us now, son of Lin. With your battle skills, we will defeat the invaders once and for all!'

Sankalp stared at him. 'Ah, my dear sir, I shall soon be on my way, but the village has many brave men. I am sure you will be safe in their hands.'

The old grain merchant sighed. 'Do you have to leave, son of Lin?' Rangdol pleaded.

Sankalp smiled but said nothing.

'You are the rightful heir to your father's legacy. The people need you more than ever before. This village could be prosperous once again.' He looked at Sankalp expectantly.

'I will stay for a while.' A tentative smile crossed Sankalp's face. But his eyes betrayed the tumult of the thoughts that played in his mind. 'Then, I must leave for the kingdom of Lhasa.'

The old grain merchant knew better than to be astonished by his statement and considered his words wistfully.

'But I do hope to return one day and get rid of the invaders,' Sankalp reassured him.

Rangdol smiled in relief.

Sankalp rose to his feet and paced a few steps, his hands clasped behind his back. 'Their general was once a great man, but now stands corrupted,' Sankalp said thoughtfully. 'He does have a large army though, and I presume they will be back with reinforcements. We must prepare for that.'

The enemy forces stationed nearby suggested a motive, and it did not escape Sankalp's suspicious mind. But for now, the villagers dismissed any further threats from them. After a long time, there was fervour and gaiety in the village.

Towards the end of the evening, Sankalp approached Bhumiputra and called for the attention of the villagers.

'This young man, whom you see as lame, is the bravest of the brave!' Sankalp held him close in a warm embrace. 'Today's victory would not have been possible without him. He has the blood of a warrior. A true warrior is not one who is physically invincible but one who stands undefeated in his mind.'

Bhumiputra smiled at the recognition. He possessed a soldierly spirit despite his disability and was pleased at being recognized as more than an equal. He immediately proposed establishing two outposts at vantage points to help them keep track of the enemy's movements.

For now, peace seemed to have returned to the small hamlet. The villagers celebrated and slept without fear in the coming nights.

Sankalp slept too, but memories played on his mind. Images from childhood, of eating and merrymaking, came back with brilliant clarity. Then he thought of more recent times. He thought of Titla and appreciated the sacrifice she had made. But did he have a choice? Could the murder of his family and the freedom of his people go unavenged?

The thought lingered in the silence of his mind.

The months of work done by the village artisans was now showing. The ruined house had begun to take shape. The basic structure stood secure and erect. It took another three months for the more skilled craftsmen to make it look as it had many years ago. By the full moon of the new year, it stood completely restored. The house was simple; the doors and windows were rather large, and the walls were rustic. Yet the simplicity gave it a distinct character—a classical severity that no opulence could bridge. Sankalp looked at it with awe; his mind was filled with scattered memories from the past. A fervent expression covered his face.

Many from the village had gathered in its courtyard to celebrate the festival of Saga Dawa.

'Sankalp, now that the house is complete, why don't you stay here and raise a family, like your father?' a woman suggested and was supported by a loud cheer from the people.

'With you as the headman, our village will flourish. Many who fled in fear have started returning. They see hope in you,' the priest reasoned.

'My dear sir, if only you could see what I do,' Sankalp said slowly, his tone resigned. 'You would then understand that my leaving will give this village a future.' Hesitantly, he continued, 'Otherwise, it will perish! I cannot submit reasons today, but in time you will understand. The lights forbid me to stay here any longer.'

Rangdol looked at him wistfully. 'Then why did you spend the last ten months reconstructing the fallen house?' he finally asked, breaking the awkward silence.

'I wanted the people to feel I am here to stay. That I won't be gone long…' He looked up, staring intently at his home. 'Let the people see it as a mark of resurgence, of change, and believe in it.' He slowly looked away from the elegant structure before continuing, 'More importantly, I am here to resurrect everything that was destroyed by the invaders!'

'The house of Lin will be empty once again,' Rangdol said thoughtfully.

'It will be…' Sankalp paused and then declared boldly, 'But it will always stand as a symbol of the valour and sacrifice of the people of this village!'

Rangdol was a wise old man and understood the deeper meaning of the words that came from the warrior of Shaka. He nodded in agreement as he thought about past events. 'My dear, you have given us more than a symbol! You have given us the hope and trust we needed to combat past events and stride towards a better future.'

He led Sankalp into his house. Bright moonlight compensated for the dim light of the lamp hanging across the courtyard. The two men then settled down for dinner and talked of how the village could improve its farming and livestock and produce more than what they needed.

'You know what we must do?' Sankalp paused as he tore a loaf of bread in half.

Rangdol looked at him in anticipation.

Before putting a piece of bread in his mouth, Sankalp suggested, 'The council of elders must help establish trade with nearby villages. This will make them interdependent and help bring people together.' He raised his right eyebrow. 'And hopefully unite them for a common cause.'

Rangdol considered Sankalp's suggestion thoughtfully. He was a wise man. What Sanklap was suggesting could indeed have positive implications.

'You are right. Prosperity will give them the confidence that the days ahead will be better. It will also help establish trust.'

He looked outside the window to where a few men sat around a fire.

'And yes, there is always strength in numbers. Let us hope we can give them wisdom too.' For the first time since they had met, Rangdol laughed.

The days ahead were important, and both understood that well. There was peace for now and no news of the invaders coming back. They had probably moved the cavalry from the high mountain post to the plains for the coming winter months. This was a good time to reassess, learn and improve from past happenings.

New fortifications were set up around the villages in the area. They were not only stronger but also more extensive than before, though Sankalp noted that some places still required a few more days of work.

While he still enjoyed grazing sheep as he used to, he spent much of his time training the men from the villages. They were divided into three groups based on the skills that they excelled in; body dynamics influenced the selection of the ideal weapon for each man. Each group practised archery, swordsmanship and handling the long spear. While they were taught the use of all three, each group practised hard to gain mastery over one.

The lame Bhumiputra was undoubtedly the best warrior. He was not only dedicated but also single-mindedly committed. It was as if he foresaw his role in the coming events. He was in charge of a band of highly motivated fighters. They trained hard and often conducted mock fights among themselves, keeping well prepared for any eventuality.

15

The Wondrous City

Never before had the villagers rallied together as they did now, under the able guidance of the warrior of Shaka. His fame and stories of his feats of valour had travelled far. Many came from far-off villages to train under him. This was a good sign. Petty differences had kept many villages apart for years, but that was beginning to change. There was hope of unity amongst them.

The lean months were closing in, and with that, the morning light was getting thinner. On one such morning, Sankalp asked Rangdol to assemble everyone, including the elders from neighbouring settlements. His expression suggested it was something important.

Early the next morning, under a partially clouded sky, they gathered at the village square.

'I will be leaving at dawn tomorrow,' Sankalp announced with a touch of regret.

The crowd looked at him, dumbstruck. They knew he would be leaving, but none had imagined it would be so soon. The look on their faces was indescribable.

Finally, a voice called out from the crowd, 'Please don't leave now! We have seen peace after a long time.'

'Stay with us, let this happiness last. I can't see any more being killed by the invaders again!' cried an old woman.

'I wish I could stay. But I must leave,' Sankalp sighed. 'I want you to hear me out before you give voice to your thoughts.'

The crowd murmured but was urged into silence by Rangdol.

'Whatever be the circumstance, accept it or change it. But don't live in fear of it! Not now, not ever. Fear, my friends, is an illusion that imprisons your potential. Do away with it!'

His pronouncement was followed by a loud cheer, especially from the young men in the crowd.

Sankalp remained silent for a moment, as if considering his next words. 'You can survive and live better by giving up petty differences and staying together. The enemy could be back in more numbers. If you are together, you have a better chance of defeating them!' His tone was honest and warm and aimed at the village elders gathered there.

'I will be back one day!' he reiterated.

The crowd rejoiced at his words and felt much more at ease.

'In the meantime, I suggest the name of Bhumiputra, the brave young lad who has proven himself to be a formidable warrior!' Sankalp paused. 'Do you take him to be your captain?' He spoke not from impulse but from an enhanced perspective.

'We do! We do!' the crowd cheered.

'He will be our leader! We all stand together in this war against the invaders,' roused the men.

With the day's proceedings over, the mind traveller sat in meditation for the last time in his house.

Early the next morning, he left the village. Rangdol and Bhumiputra were there, watching as he faded from their sight.

As Sankalp walked along the mountain track, he remembered what Kalimpong had once said—'Lhasa awaits you! You will visit the beautiful city soon. That, my son, is a certainty.'

It was a pleasant day. Sankalp made his way briskly through the high mountain pass. He was followed closely by Zanzi.

By mid-afternoon of the next day, he had reached the Death Valley, so known for its notoriously hostile terrain. He remembered the village elders had often told him about the volatile westerlies. They would blow violently, striking at steep slopes and dislodging great amounts of snow and rubble. It would all come crashing down, covering and destroying everything in its path. There were stories about trade caravans being destroyed year after year. Many people accompanying them lay buried under the snowy debris. But the mountain folk could read weather conditions and avoid dangerous situations. With the knowledge gathered over years, they could with reasonable accuracy predict when the destruction could begin. The village elders relied on their experience to identify signs, such as the prevailing wind pattern, speed and sound. They could also predict the area that would come under its influence.

It was a near seven-day walk to the city of Lhasa from the village. As he descended the steep mountains, the terrain began to flatten, and the air felt warmer. On the fifth day, he crossed the mighty river that flowed into the plains, close to the city. He came across fertile lands and scythed fields. There were canals and water wheels, which helped irrigate the land round the year. While rice grew in some fields, a variety of vegetables and cereals grew in others. There were also large orchards full of delicious fruits bordering the well-paved roads leading to Lhasa. He had heard that people in the city were rich and generous too.

Sankalp decided to rest for the night. He sought refuge in a large orchard not very far from the city. In the middle of the greenery was a palatial house. 'It must belong to a wealthy man,' he thought and decided to ask permission to stay there.

Two burly soldiers manned the main entrance. They led him to the house.

Sankalp knocked on the door, which was opened by a young man. He was thin, angular in appearance, and attired in expensive clothes of silk. He wore several rings, and the jewelled hilt of his sword further emphasized that he was a noble and the owner of the property.

'Sir, I am a monk on my way to Lhasa. May I get a place to rest for the night?'

The young man looked at him, his face exhibiting clear signs of confusion. He had never seen a monk dressed in animal skin. And the faint outline of the hilt of a sword that was visible from under his robe had not escaped his piercing eyes.

'Hmm, a monk you said,' he rubbed his chin for a moment, 'Or an assassin?' His tone turned accusatory as he continued, 'A monk carries a begging bowl, not a sword!'

Then quickly drawing his sword, he pounced on Sankalp! His movement was swift. Tired and taken by surprise, Sankalp did not have time to react. The young man had his sword at his neck. He held his pose, making his threat clear.

'You are an impatient young man, and that may land you in trouble. Now remove that sword and talk to me,' Sankalp said calmly.

'Disclose your real identity, stranger, or else you will not live to talk!' The young man's tone was agitated, and he was reluctant to stand down.

Sankalp reacted quickly. In a flash, his hands changed the direction of the sword staring at him. And before the young man could recover, Sankalp held his neck in a firm grip. A platoon of about ten men in battle gear emerged from the shadows and surrounded him. The young man raised his hand, a signal that he would tackle the intruder himself. Then in a surprise move, he dropped his sword as if to surrender.

The move distracted Sankalp. Taking advantage of the moment, the man tugged at Sankalp's legs, throwing him off balance. Then he quickly turned around and held his worthy opponent in an arm lock. His movement was well coordinated and technique flawless.

'You are a persistent young man!' Sankalp regained his balance and unlocked himself from his opponent's grip. A powerful angled thrust into the man's rib cage threw him a couple of yards across the grass, where he landed flat on his back, the wind driven from his lungs.

'Are you willing to listen now?' Sankalp levelled eyes with his aggressor.

'Ah…Ahh…' the young man groaned, his face flushed with a mix of pain and anger.

He tried to stagger back on to his feet but could not. The impact had caused his muscles to spasm, rendering him motionless and writhing in pain. Sankalp sat beside him and closed his eyes. He put his palm on the point of impact, followed by a series of quick, dexterous rubs at specific vital points on the body, relieving him from the temporary spasm.

'I am a monk—a warrior if you see me as one,' Sankalp spoke softly with a slight smile, his hand resting on the fallen man's shoulder in a manner that exhibited camaraderie.

'I only seek refuge for the night. By tomorrow, I will be on my way to Lhasa.'

The young man got up slowly, staring at Sankalp's strange attire and assessing the monk. Finally, he gestured to Sankalp, saying, 'Please come in.'

He let Sankalp lead the way on the marked pathway while he walked a step behind, still cautious and studying him keenly.

Sankalp entered the large house. It was decorated with fine linen that looked Persian and filled with expensive artifacts. It was evident the owner was a man of considerable power and wealth. Sankalp noticed the walls were covered with armour befitting highly decorated men in the army.

'Who wears this celebrated armour?'

'It belonged to my father,' the young man replied. His gaze was firm, though his voice was warm and courteous. 'You can rest here for the night, but do tell me who you really are. And why are you here?'

The young man seemed suspicious of everything. It was imperative to change his opinion of him.

So Sankalp decided to satisfy his curiosity. 'I am Sankalp; some know me as the warrior of Shaka.' The calm on Sankalp's face altered for a moment. 'My father, Lin Thiampong, the headman of our village, was slain by ruthless invaders many years ago.' He drew in a deep breath and spoke with composure. 'Destiny draws me to the city of Lhasa. I have stopped here just for a night's rest.'

The young man's expression was neutral. It was impossible not to admire his calm confidence. He waited a while before answering.

'My name is Divya Drishti.'

He considered his guest in a moment's silence. 'I sense honesty in your words,' he finally said as he fixed his visitor with a piercing look. Even in defeat, he exuded a certain confidence.

'I will be gone tomorrow,' Sankalp reiterated. 'But if you still find my presence upsetting, I will be on my way,' he finished, his tone subdued as he picked up his belongings.

Divya Drishti put his hand on Sankalp's shoulder and smiled, his condescending demeanour lessened by Sankalp's yielding words.

'Please, be my guest,' he said as he led Sankalp to an adjoining room.

'You can stay here for the night,' he stated and quickly left.

Sankalp was tired after his long trek through the rugged mountain terrain, and the tussle with the young man had quite exhausted him. After refreshing himself, he sat calmly on the wooden floor, reining his mind into silence.

A knock on the door alerted him.

'My master awaits you in the dining room,' an attendant informed him.

Sankalp followed him through a large carved door to a finely decorated hall where Divya Drishti was seated.

'I am sorry about what happened. It is not advisable to trust unfamiliar people in these parts,' Divya Drishti explained.

The attendants meanwhile started to serve them with the variety of dishes that adorned the table.

Sankalp nodded. 'And why is that?'

A fierce laugh erupted from Divya Drishti. 'It is a sign of the times. My father was a general in the king's army. He had successfully led his men to war many times. And then we heard about the invaders coming from the north, destroying many villages as they moved south. My father was given the task of driving them away.' He drew in a deep breath before continuing. 'Twice they attacked but the invasion was repelled. Our strength prevailed! Tempa Dargaye, the commander of the invaders' army, an evil man, sent his ambassador with a pledge for peace.

'The ambassador approached the king with a peace treaty,' he sneered. 'Much against the wishes of the council, the treaty was accepted, and the ambassador, Asudai, found favour with the king. However, the invaders continued to raid and loot villages.' Divya sighed.

Sankalp nodded in grim understanding.

'The attacks continue in the mountain villages. Many have fallen victim to the treachery of the invaders,' Sankalp confessed.

'My father tried to convince the king to teach these invaders a lesson, but his voice fell on deaf ears,' Divya replied, his expression bitter.

'Where is your father now?' asked Sankalp after a thoughtful silence.

'He is dead.' Divya Drishti could not help but yield to his emotions. 'He died fighting…but rumour has it that he was poisoned on his way back home.' Divya paused and narrowed his eyes. 'Since then, we have faced only discrimination and oppression. And that makes us cautious of overbearing strangers.' He smiled, sipping gently on a glass of wine. 'I live here with my mother; she is visiting a nearby village.'

'Overbearing? Is that what the attire of a monk seems to you?' replied Sankalp with a friendly smile.

'It is not the attire, but the rather large sword concealed under it,' came the artful reply from the witty Divya Drishti.

'Ahh, that is a special gift from my master,' Sankalp smiled. Then his expression turned serious as he said, 'I am sorry to hear about your father.'

He shook his head, encouraging his host to speak. He had a feeling that Divya had finally reached the subject that he had been driving towards all along.

'Do tell me more about the king and his people.'

'Lhasa...' Divya let out a sigh. 'It lures all kinds into its abundance—the adventurous and the pious from all over the world. 'But,' he huffed, 'it also draws the deceitful and the vicious, to say nothing of the political traitors who have found a safe haven here!'

'What about the king?'

Divya paused before answering. 'The king seems to have weakened with time.' His expression changed to one of discontent. 'I await mine, to set right the wrongs! You might find my intentions somewhat revolutionary, depending on your perspective.' His expression was spirited. 'But truly, all I wish for is the betterment of the kingdom and its people.'

Sankalp was impressed and he let it show in his words. 'Your intentions seem resolute. But, my dear, are they to bring about a change or create one by force?'

Divya raised an eyebrow as he smiled. 'To be honest, either way, without conceding my beliefs or the future of Lhasa.'

They talked long into the night. Divya Drishti explained past events to Sankalp. The monk understood why the people of Lhasa lived with the same fear as they did in the mountains. The invaders were not there just to loot the villages. It was a well thought out strategy to enslave them.

After a hearty meal, Sankalp thanked Divya Drishti and retired to his chamber. He slept well till a ray of sunlight filtering through the stained-glass window awoke him. He walked up to the large windows and pushed them open. They opened on to the green that rolled in an unending verdure resembling a wild meadow, save for the delicately placed stone statues and fountains. The furthest parts were dotted with bright yellow mustard flowers spreading their pungent odour.

Sankalp had heard about the large, beautiful fields that people owned in the valley. In the higher reaches, such large fields weren't possible. He was amazed by the variety of fruits that grew on the farm.

After a while, he was ready to leave and sought out the owner of the fine estate.

'I will be on my way now. Thank you for the hospitality shown to an overbearing stranger,' he said with a twinkle in his eye. 'And, as you can see, I have nothing to offer in return…'

'But you do,' interrupted Divya Drishti. 'Stay here for a few more days. Teach me how to fight and knock people out as you did, and we could be even,' he laughed and continued. 'I promise to ride with you to the city gates in a few days, if you accept my request, that is.' Divya stood gazing at the monk with appealing eyes that would not take no for an answer.

Sankalp stood in quiet thoughtfulness for a moment. 'Your words come from the heart, and of course, I am indebted to you for your hospitality.' He smiled. 'We will have a few days before I leave.'

The decision was not taken lightly. Perhaps the warrior of Shaka had found a reason to stay.

Divya Drishti thanked Sankalp for accepting his offer.

As promised, his training proceeded apace, with Sankalp teaching Divya Drishti the arts he was accomplished in.

'My dear, you must first learn to control the mind, be it preparing for war or during meditation. Concentration is the silence of the mind and the key to controlling it.'

Divya chuckled. 'You are a learned man for sure. Are you going to make a monk out of me too?' he jested.

'Given your disposition,' he smiled, 'just a better warrior for now.'

Sankalp couldn't help but grin at Divya's light-hearted banter. He knew well that behind it was a lot of seriousness.

'Divya, you must learn to keep your senses in check; your thoughts and decisions are affected by them. My training is about conquering the self and then the enemy.'

Divya Drishti was an eager learner and would practise alone for hours. So engrossed would he become that he would often miss his meals and not allow his attendants or any audience-seeker to interrupt his routine.

Sankalp was delighted by his dedication. Night and day, Divya strove to master the lessons. In the few weeks they spent together, both duelled together almost every day. On other days, Sankalp shared his knowledge of the sacred texts, and, importantly, how to use the learnings in everyday life.

'My dear, it is imperative to remain at ease. Neither subdued at the sight of a stronger opponent nor aggressive with a weaker one.'

Divya nodded and Sankalp continued in a lighter vein, 'Divya, you must stand unyielding to emotions. This makes more sense for you than anyone I have known,' he smiled.

'Sometimes I do tend to get emotional. Especially when someone knocks at my door in the dark, wearing strange attire and concealing a weapon,' Divya quipped. 'And later introduces himself as a monk, or was it a warrior?' he clucked his tongue and smiled. 'And as it turns out, he is a bit of both—a thaumaturgist!' Divya burst into a good-natured laugh, gesturing with his hand at the dilemma of it all, in a way that showed no disrespect.

Sankalp couldn't help but smile at the lively young man. 'Divya, I have spent years practising what I have taught you. Follow my instructions ritualistically. You might not be very successful in the beginning, but don't give up and keep trying harder.'

'I am not planning to give up in your absence, oh holy one,' Divya remarked with mild amusement.

Sankalp chuckled at the statement. 'The more dedicated you are, the sooner the finer secrets will be revealed. And one day, you will master what I have taught you.'

'Perhaps,' Divya nodded.

'And promise me that you will share this knowledge with your people,' Sankalp urged.

'I will do as you say, warrior of Shaka,' said Divya, sounding serious for once.

Sankalp took a step closer to Divya Drishti. 'My friend, the days have stretched to weeks and the weeks into almost a month…such is your hospitality.'

He rested his hands on Divya's shoulders in a brotherly gesture. 'It is time to take your leave.'

Divya nodded at once. 'When would you like to go?'

'Tomorrow would be a good day.'

So Divya ordered his attendant to ready two of his finest horses, and early the next morning, they set out for Lhasa.

It was a clear day. A light breeze had replaced the high winds from the previous day. The roads leading to the city were wide and fairly busy, with farmers bringing in wagonloads of rice and vegetables every day to sell in Lhasa's markets. Many carried fine silk and paper, which they got from far-off lands. They were auctioned to the highest bidder in the market square.

Divya Drishti was young but well respected, as was evident by how he was greeted by everyone they came across on their way to the city. He too warmly acknowledged their greetings with a polite nod and a gentle wave of his hand. This did not go unnoticed by Sankalp. He felt proud to be riding with him and smiled.

The two horsemen reached the well-guarded gate to the city by noon.

'This is as far as I go, Sankalp. I am not allowed to enter the city gates,' remarked Divya Drishti.

'Why?'

'As I told you earlier, Asudai, the ambassador, found favour with the king and now has a strange hold over him. He managed to convince the king that my father was a traitor.' Divya hissed out a laugh at the insensitivity and mindlessness of the ruler. 'We are forbidden to enter the gates of the city.'

He pulled on the reins, and his horse immediately stopped at the command.

Sankalp closed his eyes and smiled. 'Don't be disheartened and never give up hope for a better tomorrow.'

Divya looked at Sankalp, hesitating before he finally spoke. 'It seems as though I have been waiting for fate to bring me to this juncture—to this moment of knowing and having you as a brother.'

Both riders dismounted and Sankalp held Divya in a brotherly embrace. He bid the young man a quick farewell and walked towards the city walls while Divya remounted and spurred the horses in the opposite direction.

Destiny had finally bought Sankalp to the gates of the enchanted city of Lhasa.

16

A Plot to Kidnap the Princess of Lhasa

The imposing outer wall stretched around the city, towering at almost seven metres. The main gate was impressive, artistically engineered to give it strength and beauty. It was made from a combination of aged teak wood fortified with iron. Beyond this intimidating outer wall was a second defensive wall.

Both walls had several openings of different sizes. Those towards the base were rounded so spears could be thrust through them, while those near the top were narrow slits, ideal for firing arrows through.

Beyond the main gate were two control points. The alert guards watched every visitor with a practiced eye. They keenly checked all carts carrying goods.

Near the main gate were the guards' quarters. Some were located on top of towers and manned around the clock to alert the army to any danger. Once the main gates were closed, it was extremely difficult to enter the city. It could only be taken if the formidable city gates were unlocked. This was one reason why Lhasa had withstood invasions by the many armies that had come to conquer and rule.

Sankalp passed through the gates with ease. He was dressed in a monk's robes and hid his sword to avoid a confrontation with the guards. No one stopped him. The guards took him to be a travelling monk. He walked on and stopped at a street corner to quench his thirst. An old woman sat offering water to all those who came by.

On both sides of the road were shops selling everything from fresh fruits and vegetables to wheat, rice and pulses. Some of the larger shops also stocked silk that came from the far lands of the east and spices from the southern plains of India.

A short walk along the weathered road opened to the view ahead. Sankalp stood enchanted by the city, with its magnificent gardens and many golden gompas dotting the landscape. The pagodas were richly carved and decorated with quaint statues. The gardens had fountains running through the middle, with flower beds laid out alongside. A little ahead, on slightly elevated ground, was the entrance to the city square. A gate, which was in the form of a temple, overlooked the enormous rectangle. One could glimpse the beautiful tree-lined road leading to the palace from there.

The rest of the neighbourhoods spread out towards the north and the south, occupied mostly by the residents of the lovely city.

After spending an entire day exploring Lhasa, Sankalp returned to the main entrance looking for a place to spend the night.

He slowed to a stroll as he approached the old woman who sat offering water.

'May I have some water, please?' he asked politely.

The old woman looked at him and then casually poured water into an earthen bowl and handed it over.

'You are a traveller, aren't you?' she enquired.

'Yes, and I am looking for a place to spend the night. Can you guide me to a suitable place?'

'There are many here, but I don't see how a monk like you could afford one.'

'Maybe you are right, but surely someone can offer me a place to sleep and give me food in return for work?'

The old woman looked him over, from his Gyiachin shoes up to his face, stopping as their eyes met.

'What is your name?'

'Sankalp,' he answered softly.

'I am Dolma,' she replied and, after a brief pause, made him an offer. 'You will have to bring water from the city well to my house,' Dolma said and raised an eyebrow, continuing, 'Twice a day, in return for a day's shelter and food.'

'Sure!' Sankalp readily agreed.

The old woman lived close by in a comfortable house. She seemed well provided for and served water only to pass the time. She gave Sankalp a room with a fireplace that kept the room warm through the cold winter nights.

The next morning, Sankalp woke up much before the old lady. He left for the well to fill water in the two large wooden buckets kept outside the house.

The old lady was pleased with his effort. As she served him a plate of hot tsampa for breakfast, she enquired, 'May I ask the purpose of your visit?'

'Well, I come from a village far up in the mountains. I have long wanted to see this beautiful city,' Sankalp replied.

'Hmm,' she murmured, her expression sceptical and her age-wrinkled eyes not missing a thing. 'I have an uncanny feeling that there is more to you than meets the eye. For one, you wear an animal skin and carry a weapon of some kind. And that's no dress for a monk! But more than that, it is the look in your eyes,' she said and paused to draw a deep breath. 'Do you pose any danger?' she concluded.

Sankalp smiled lovingly as if he had anticipated this conversation. 'You knew the answer to that question before you let me in. These are gifts from people I love,' he said simply.

Then he thanked her for her help.

As he was about to leave, Dolma made him an offer. 'My dear, if you want you can spend a few more days here. In return, you can ferry water from the well, like you did this morning.' She smiled. 'I am getting old, and my back hurts.'

'I would be happy to do that for you,' Sankalp replied with a smile.

He spent the rest of the day wandering the city. The streets were packed with residents and visitors alike. He came upon a roundabout with a large fountain and a garden filled with a variety of seasonal flora. It was a pleasant sight indeed. From there, a series of narrow cobbled streets branched off into four directions leading to various parts of the city. His eyes fell upon the ornately carved buildings of stone and wood flanking a wider road; these were residential houses.

Sankalp walked down a street that was the most crowded with hawkers selling all kinds of mouth-watering eatables. He interacted freely with the people, and his attire drew respect from everyone. He spent the day trying to find out as much as he could from the people he met before returning to the old woman's home in the evening.

'Do you have any family here?' he asked the generous old lady over dinner.

'My husband was a soldier. He died some time back. I worked in the queen's palace till she passed away from an ailment. I was entrusted with the task of bringing up the princess, who was a little girl at that time. And that is all the family I have known.'

'How did the queen die?' Sankalp was curious.

'It was an incurable disease that took her. The king was shattered; he never married again. The princess has now grown into a fine young woman and often comes to see me. I am too old to go to the palace now,' she sighed.

Soon after, she retired for the night.

It was getting bitterly cold with the approaching winter. Sankalp sat quietly in the open courtyard. He closed his eyes and opened his vision to the sky; within moments, he received answers to the doubts that plagued his mind. The starlight wanted him to be there, at that very place and at that time.

Returning his attention to his surroundings, he noticed Dolma sitting at the window of her room, observing him keenly.

At first light, Sankalp was off to the well to get water. It was still early when he returned with the pails full. He was surprised to see a couple of guards outside the old lady's house. Near the front gate stood a decorated carriage drawn by four white horses.

Sankalp entered the house and put the buckets down in a corner. As he turned, he blinked at the sight of a beautiful young girl who stood motionless next to the staircase leading to the upper level of the house. Her thick lashes fluttered, and her large, captivating eyes fixed on him for a moment. She then proceeded to climb up the stairs. Her attire and gait showed grace and dignity, a sure sign of her royal upbringing.

'She is undoubtedly the princess the old lady spoke about,' Sankalp thought as he went about his chores. After a while, she came down the stairs, crossed the small courtyard and entered the carriage. Their eyes met briefly before the carriage drove away, followed by her guards.

'That is Princess Mayuri,' explained Dolma coming down the steps.

'I am sure she gets her name from the fabled bird found in the lower Himalayan lands of India, which is known well for its beautiful eyes.'

Dolma nodded with a smile. 'Did I mention she occasionally comes to see me?'

'Yes, you did, and I must say she is not only beautiful but very dignified,' Sankalp said as he followed Dolma into the house and sat on a thick woollen mat for his morning meal.

'Intelligent and gracious too, much like her late mother,' Dolma added.

Sankalp nodded in acceptance.

'She will make a fine queen one day. But she is quite unhappy these days.'

'Why?' Sankalp quizzed.

'It has to do with her father's decision to marry her off to someone whom she has never met,' the old lady explained.

'She does have a choice, I presume?'

'Not in this case,' Dolma emphasized.

Dolma told Sankalp that their king, Trinyen Tsenpo, was a good man but was being ill-advised by someone who had come from the kingdom in the north. He had been sent to Lhasa as an ambassador of General Darqan Doodra.

Darqan Doodra was known to be a ruthless ruler and warrior. He had engineered a revolt against the Mongol king and had carved out a small domain for himself by treason. If he gained control over the kingdom of Lhasa, he could well challenge the monarch of Mongolia.

'This ambassador, Asudai, is sly as a fox, a rogue, and is definitely brewing something. I am old, but I know the ways of the world. He is hatching another conspiracy to rule our lands. Darqan Doodra will not go unpunished by the gods.'

At the general's name, a slew of images flashed across Sankalp's mind, and he grimaced. 'I have heard the name before.'

'Trinyen Tsenpo is a noble man and was once a good warrior. But since the death of the queen, he has become a recluse. Rumour goes that Asudai has been boldly taking advantage of the situation,' the old lady explained.

Later that day, Sankalp met many people in the town square. He gathered that most of them respected the king, but they also understood that something was not right.

As night fell the streets lit up, and the shops continued to do business. There was singing and dancing in the square to mark the coming of the annual Ongkor festival.

Sankalp's interactions with the people had led him to his own conclusions. The king did have a strong army to defend the kingdom, but in his current state, he was hardly in a position to lead his men.

The invaders came from lands devoid of vegetation and beauty. They had never seen such prosperity as they found in Lhasa. Though they were not physically bigger or stronger, the wealth of the land was motivation enough. They had nothing to lose but only to gain. Greed had turned them barbaric and uncompromising.

On the other hand, the people of Lhasa were a satisfied lot. They had a bustling trade, profitable agriculture and lived in comfort. With their needs met, they had become nurturers from fighters. Material wealth had lulled them into a false sense of security. They were not inclined to give it up and take on the hardships a war brought. But sooner rather than later, the invaders would arrive and take away everything they had!

The word on the street was of concern, given the times. And although the preparations and celebrations for the festival continued, the people did not know if the princess had consented to join the celebrations on the final day of the festival, given the uncertainty and fear of an attack.

The next morning, Sankalp told Dolma what he had heard.

'The people are wondering if the princess will take part in the festivities being held in the town square.'

'She mentioned that she would when she came visiting the other day. It is quite unusual,' Dolma sounded hesitant.

'Why?'

She walked to the window and drew the curtains wider before speaking. 'Well, the final day of celebrations used to take place in the palace. Many people from the city attended; it was always a very large gathering.' She looked at Sankalp and pensively added, 'But the king has refused to hold celebrations this year. So, the princess has decided to join the festivities that are held in the celebration grounds instead,' she explained as she poured him a bowl of sweetened rice pudding for breakfast.

'Can you take me there?' requested Sankalp.

'I have agreed to accompany the princess to the celebration. I can request her, and if she agrees, you can accompany the royal carriage to the grounds.'

Sankalp nodded. 'How far is it from here?'

'About three miles; it's the large open ground close to the city gates.'

Sankalp spent the rest of the day wandering the streets. The sky was mostly clear, except for a few white clouds that provided occasional relief from the glaring sun.

As he neared the city square, the chatter of excited voices caught his attention. He saw a group of people sitting under a tree, keenly watching two men absorbed in a game of *chandraki*. He had heard of it but did not know how to play. A crier explained the moves and gestured expansively to the few men present there, trying his best to get the attention of other passers-by. Curious, Sankalp sat under the shade of the tree, watching the men play while a few peddled their wares in raised monotones.

The two men were engrossed in the game, while others sat around casually, watching and applauding their moves. They gossiped and cheered in low voices so as not to disturb the players.

Sankalp heard one of them say, 'I hear the princess has agreed to join the celebrations tomorrow in the city.'

'Yes, she has,' said another, with a disapproving shake of his head. 'It is a risk.'

'It certainly is. I have reason to believe that her life may be in danger,' his companion added.

Sankalp listened to the ensuing conversation keenly. Then he quickly made his way back to the house and shared what he had heard with Dolma.

'I was roaming the streets and saw a few people deeply engrossed in a game of chandraki. I sat there, trying to learn a bit about this very interesting game.'

'Well, did you?'

'Very little, but I overheard two men talking in hushed tones. One of them mentioned a threat to the princess when she comes to town on the day of the festival.'

The old lady smiled, her expression one of both amusement and mild irritation. 'Their conversation is frivolous, more the result of the poppy that has smoked their brains out. My dear, the townsfolk, especially the kind you met, have nothing better to do. If not such conspiracy theories, then they talk of flying saucers, eight-legged beasts and so on,' Dolma laughed. 'Not to mention dancing debauched witches out to corrupt the town's men.'

'Perhaps,' Sankalp gave her a grin. 'But what about now? These are different times.'

'Ah…' Dolma pursed her lips. 'It is a rumour—an unbearable one at that,' she muttered. 'Nonetheless, the princess is guarded by eight warriors. The best in the land! And on the day of the festival. The city gates are closed to outsiders. You must have seen that it is almost impossible to enter the city when its gates are locked.'

So saying, Dolma went about her work.

Sankalp realized that the old lady would not understand why he feared for the princess.

Later, in the middle of the night, an uncomfortable thought entered his mind, forewarning him of impending danger.

The coming of the full moon foretold trouble for the princess. And that was the day of the grand festival. The ensuing night, Sankalp sat in solitude and readied himself for the coming day. It would decide not only the fate of the princess but the future of the kingdom too.

Though he had slept little, Sanklap felt refreshed and was up early. He went about his morning chores before setting out to fetch water. He walked to a well that was near the celebration grounds. The preparations for the festival were in full swing. A podium had been set up on one side, and it was being decorated with fresh flowers.

'What is the podium for?' Sankalp enquired from a man holding a bunch of wild blue irises.

'The princess is coming,' he said, his excitement clear. 'She will be seated there for the annual celebrations.'

Sankalp nodded before heading to the nearby well. On his way back to Dolma's house, he saw three men examining the grounds rather intently. They were standing under the shade of a large fig tree; one was on horseback. Something about them seemed suspicious.

Sankalp slowed to a stroll and moved towards the men. As he neared them, he struck up a seemingly frivolous conversation.

'Can I offer you some water?' he asked the man on the horse. The rider looked askance at the young monk. He was bearded, with rather osseous features.

'Give some water to my horse, monk,' he said with a mirthless smile.

Sankalp placed the wooden pail in front of the horse.

'You must have had a long journey; your horse seems tired and thirsty.' Sankalp noted the men's sweat-drenched clothes. The stocky horseman remained quiet. He looked away, ignoring Sankalp, but kept a close watch on the grounds and the people there.

'We have been travelling for two days,' replied another in a lighter tone. He was about to say more but was abruptly interrupted by the stocky horsemen.

'Enough! Be on your way!' he said rather firmly and then turned to the other two. 'I am going to the palace to deliver a message from the captain. Meanwhile, keep a close watch here. Everything must go as per plan or we will lose our heads!' He then quickly rode away.

The conversation convinced Sankalp that what he had heard the previous day was no rumour. There was indeed a threat to the princess!

The day went by. Sankalp readied himself to accompany Dolma and Princess Mayuri to the celebration grounds. He wore the tigard skin around his chest for protection. His sword was concealed under a long woollen shawl that was draped over his shoulders.

A violet darkness began to spread across the sky. With that, the city lit up with the glow of many thousands of lamps. Sankalp heard the princess' carriage pull up outside the old lady's cottage. It was drawn by four white horses and surrounded by eight guards. Four of them rode ahead of the carriage and the others rode behind.

Dolma and Sankalp entered the carriage. The old lady sat beside the princess and introduced the young monk to her.

'This is Sankalp, a monk. He is here to see the fair.'

The princess looked at Sankalp, recognizing him from her earlier visit to Dolma's house.

'He comes from a small village far up in the mountains. With your permission, can he accompany us?'

'Of course, he can. He is a guest in our city.'

'Princess Mayuri, I cannot allow a stranger to accompany you. These are my strictest orders,' pleaded one of the guards.

'He is a stranger to the city and a monk. He poses no danger; let him sit alongside the carriage driver and ride with us,' the princess asserted.

The carriage made its way towards the celebration grounds. The stone-paved road was lined with a large number of people cheering for the princess.

'Long live Princess Mayuri!' they shouted.

She waved to the crowds from the carriage window.

The royal carriage proceeded without any hindrance. Sankalp sat vigilantly in the front. Finally, they reached the grounds. The princess was taken in a procession to the podium, followed closely by Dolma.

Mayuri then lit a large lamp that stood at the centre of the podium, signalling for the festivities to begin. This was followed by the bursting of crackers, which added sparkle to the clear night sky.

The princess sat close to Dolma, enjoying the dances that took place on the stage that had been specially built for the occasion. There were folk dancers from many villages of the kingdom. They all came to her with an offering; Mayuri enjoyed every bit of the attention.

Sankalp was seated on one side of the podium. He had a good view of the princess and everyone around her, including the guards who had accompanied her.

Mayuri occasionally glanced at him as people lined up to offer her customary gifts. She confined her observations to those near her, moving only her eyes while keeping her posture gracefully steady. This was expected of a princess. She was served with a variety of delicacies prepared by the townsfolk. Mayuri took a small amount from each and requested the rest to be distributed among the people.

Everything seemed to be going well, and sounds of celebration filled the crisp night air.

The merrymaking continued well past midnight. Then, one of the guards went up to the princess and whispered something to her. He stood there briefly, staring at everything around, and then, with a final look, he left. Sankalp recognized him as the horseman he had met earlier near the grounds! He was also the 'guard' who had objected to Sankalp accompanying the princess. Sankalp remembered that he had two accomplices, but they were nowhere around.

The princess was enjoying the celebration as much as the people. She freely mingled and danced with them till the old lady came up to her.

'My dear, it is getting late. We must leave now. Your father must be worried. This is the first time the celebrations have been held outside the palace grounds.'

Mayuri was quick to heed Dolma's advice and descended from the podium, ready to leave. She waved to the crowd and walked towards her carriage, accompanied by the guards. Sankalp followed the princess and the old lady to the carriage. He took his seat next to the carriage driver.

'What a lovely evening,' Sankalp remarked.

The carriage driver gave him a blank look. He finally gave a strained smile, and without saying a word, he urged the horses into motion. He seemed to be a different fellow, not the one who had driven them to the venue earlier. The new driver drove the carriage fast. The ride remained uneventful till they neared a junction. While one road led towards the palace, the other led to the city walls, and that was the road the driver took. It followed a narrow winding course through an area where the buildings were few and the paths more deserted.

'This is not the way we took on our way here,' cautioned Sankalp.

'This way is faster and better,' the driver said, his expression hardening.

An innominate fear made Sankalp uncomfortable. There was imminent danger to the princess and Dolma. He had to act fast and stop the princess from being carried away!

He was still thinking when a loud cry rent the air.

Sankalp looked to the right. To his horror, he saw that one of the guards had managed to strike another down. Then all of a sudden, the guard riding to his left drew his sword and struck the one riding alongside him.

'Faster! Faster! Move towards the city gates!' he yelled out to the carriage driver.

Grinning, the carriage driver instantly obeyed. He whipped the horses, making them gallop at top speed.

Using all his strength, Sankalp pushed the driver off his perch. Grabbing the reins firmly in his hands, he barely managed to steer the horses off the road leading to the city gates. The wheels screeched and the carriage shuddered as it swerved to the right.

'What is happening?' Dolma shouted from the small window that looked from the coach box on to the front of the carriage.

'Someone is trying to abduct the princess,' yelled Sankalp.

The words struck fear into Mayuri.

'Stop the carriage!' shouted the horseman riding alongside the carriage.

The old woman's heart stopped as the voice rang out—the princess' security cover had been breached. The guards riding alongside were all traitors. The princess was indeed being kidnapped! The abductors were desperately trying to overtake the carriage. They had killed the only two guards loyal to the king.

Meanwhile, one of them raced close to the carriage. Swinging his sword menacingly at Sankalp, he tried to board the carriage from the front. Sankalp immediately tugged on the reins. The horses responded and shifted a little to the left, increasing the distance between the carriage and the rider. Holding the reins firmly with one hand, Sankalp drew his sword from under his robe with the other. He brandished the sword, making his adversary swerve further away. Two riders closed in from behind, their horses galloping much faster than those drawing the carriage.

Sankalp had barely managed to steady the horses when he heard the princess scream. One of the riders had managed to jump on to the back of the carriage, while the other was about to. Mayuri realized what was happening. She could no longer be a mute witness to this deathly spectacle. She quickly came out of the side door and climbed on to the driver's seat alongside Sankalp.

'Give me the reins and you try and keep them away!' Mayuri called out.

The scared horses were running wild!

The carriage swayed to the left and then to the right until it finally balanced itself.

'*Hyah*!' shouted the princess, swinging her whip. She was not one to be intimidated by fear or panic and used all her skill to try and control the horses. Sankalp quickly made his way to the back of the carriage and engaged the two men. He slashed at one, his deadly sword piercing his opponent's shoulder, and kicked the other on the chest, throwing them both off the footboard.

The second group of four horsemen challenged Sankalp. Their eyes were filled with rage as they watched their plan go awry! As luck would have it, the carriage struck a stone on the pavement that broke its left wheel. Sparks flew from under the carriage as the metal rim ground against the cobblestone road. It overturned with a terrifying crash and all its occupants were thrown to the ground. The old lady fell unconscious as her head hit the pavement. Mayuri tucked in her head and rolled to the side, bruised but otherwise unhurt. She lay still, the world still spinning before her eyes. Sankalp landed on his side. His back and shoulder took most of the impact, while the hard ground scraped the skin off his arms. He took a few rolls and used the momentum to flip back up on his feet, surprising the enemy!

The horsemen quickly surrounded them.

'Be on your way monk! We need only her!' the one in front growled, clenching his fists. 'Run now, boy, before I change my mind!' he ranted as Sankalp continued to stand there.

'Surrender, while you still breathe!' he countered.

The horseman considered his words with an amused expression.

'Very well then. Die if you must!' The lead horseman jumped off his black steed, quickly followed by the others. They closed in on him from all sides.

Meanwhile, the sounds of distress had alerted the neighbourhood. People came out of their houses and the shadowed alleys and began to gather around the scene.

Sankalp planted himself firmly between the princess and her kidnappers, his sword pointed at the traitors. The first two men charged him with drawn swords. The warrior monk leapt to one side, pulling the princess along with him. He ducked the second attack; Mayuri matched his movements. Sankalp curved low as the enemy's sword sliced through the air above him. His spine stretched and flexed as he bent low with his sword hand extended, and he thrust his weapon into the attacker's thigh. The enemy screamed in pain!

The other three pounced on the monk. He dodged the assault, pulling back his neck just enough to let a blade scythe by. He instantly moved his sword at an inverted angle, blocking a body blow by the second attacker. But the third attacker managed to pierce him through the tigard skin. The blade skimmed Sankalp's shoulder, drawing a trickle of blood. In a flash, Sankalp's sword changed hands, confusing his attackers. Flowing with the move, Sankalp jumped high and struck down; the sword was aimed at his attacker's neck. His opponent was fast and blocked the blow, but the mighty sword of balance broke the man's weapon on impact.

Sparing the unarmed man, Sankalp leapt towards the other two. He executed a series of defensive moves, blocking blows from the aggressors. Then, there was a sudden burst of speed and intensity, quite unmatched by the enemy! Within moments, it was over and the two men lay dead, their heads severed from their bodies.

By now, the princess had recovered her wits; she wasn't the kind of woman who would stand and watch. Mayuri drew out a thin sharp dagger from the scabbard attached to her thigh. She flung it at the guard who had overpowered Dolma.

The dagger found its mark, and he dropped dead. For a moment, everybody stood still, surprised at what they had just seen.

Sankalp moved fast in that moment, and a powerful swing from his mighty sword sent the leader of the kidnappers to his death.

'Are you all right, princess?' asked Sankalp, his sword resting on the neck of the lone survivor.

'I am fine,' she replied, moving closer to the man, who was on his knees, begging for mercy.

'Who are you? And why did you attack us? Tell me or you will meet a terrible fate…much worse than that of your accomplices!' Mayuri said angrily, pointing at the lifeless bodies lying nearby in a pool of blood. 'Talk!' she demanded, 'Or you will be bound in chains, destined for slavery for the rest of your life!'

'In a place that is beyond your worst imagination!' Sankalp added. 'Answer her, and she may spare your life!' Mayuri stared down at the prisoner and nodded.

'I know you planned to kidnap the princess.' Sankalp looked him in the eye and slowly thrust the tip of the blade deeper into the fellow's chest, making him squirm.

'We...we were ordered to abduct the princess and return to our camp,' he stuttered and shut his eyes for a moment before speaking again. 'It's located beyond the Yarlung Pass!'

'Who sent you, and how did you enter the city?' asked Mayuri, still seething with anger.

'I...I don't know much,' he squealed. 'We were told to follow the orders of our leader. You just killed him!' he said, pointing to one of the fallen men wearing a captain's attire. 'Someone from the palace helped us enter the city and was to ensure our escape through one of the secret tunnels constructed for our getaway,' he continued reluctantly. Mayuri bristled, looking for the slightest inconsistency in his admission. 'Do you want to be a free man and see your family again? Or rot in prison for the rest of your life!'

'Will you set me free now?' he asked hopefully.

'Tell me everything you know, and I will set you free,' the princess retorted.

'Lhasa will soon be invaded! Your king is to be taken captive. A large brigade has already entrenched itself in the mountains and taken control of nearby villages,' he answered, shivering at the thought of impending consequences.

'What else?' questioned Sankalp.

The man shifted on his knees in fear and blurted, 'They will be joined by a large army coming from beyond the Yarlung Pass and being led by General Darqan Doodra. That's all I know,' he hung his head and whispered. 'Please let me go before the guards come. And don't worry about anyone finding out about this conversation. I cannot go back. They will hang me for my failure. Please let me escape to safety!' he begged.

'Run away and don't be seen in our lands again,' said the princess before asking Sankalp to set him free.

Meanwhile, the people who had seen the royal carriage running amok on the road had alerted the guards stationed nearby. The soldiers were on their way. A messenger had also rushed to the palace to inform the king about the incident.

In a short while, Sankalp, the princess and Dolma were surrounded by the royal platoon.

'Princess Mayuri! We are here to escort you safely back to the palace. Please come with us immediately.'

The princess cast one last look at the fallen men. Her would-be abductors.

'The men who planned to kidnap me are your guards!' she protested. 'It was the monk who saved me!' she shouted angrily while one of the guards checked the identity of the fallen men.

'I haven't seen these men before. But they wear our armour ...' the guard looked puzzled.

The princess appeared unconvinced.

The captain, meanwhile, stripped the armour from the body of one of the kidnappers, revealing a black military outfit underneath. It was the uniform of the invaders! They had cleverly disguised themselves to look like the royal guards. This would have made their escape after kidnapping the princess easy. Anybody who saw them would think the royal guards had kidnapped the princess. It could have sparked discontent in the army, which was what the invaders had wanted. A rebellion in Lhasa!

The king and his bodyguards also arrived at the scene, much to the relief of the princess.

'Are you all right, my child?' The king enquired and immediately hugged her. He appeared rattled but only briefly.

'I am all right, Father,' Mayuri replied, visibly shaken by the events. 'Thanks to the monk. He fought bravely to save my life!' She then turned her eyes to Sankalp with a gentle nod of appreciation.

Sankalp nodded back, acknowledging her courage. He then retreated to one side, watching over the proceedings while the old lady spoke to the king about him.

'Thank you, monk, for saving the princess from these rascals!' Trinyen Tsenpo reiterated. His look of surprise turned to disdain for the royal guards who were supposed to protect the princess.

'Please honour us by coming to the palace once your wounds have healed. I would like to reward you suitably.'

Sankalp said nothing but nodded gracefully.

At a gesture from the king, the charioteer brought up the carriage and lowered the mounting block. The king and the princess returned to the palace escorted by the guards. The crowd came out of its stunned daze and began to disperse.

Trinyen Tsenpo and his men had no idea what Sankalp and Mayuri had learnt from the man whose life they had spared, and Mayuri thought it best not to disclose anything at the moment.

The king instructed his personal physician to take care of Sankalp. The royal physician duly attended to him through the night. He applied a paste made from mountain herbs, which soon relieved much of Sankalp's pain. By morning, his wounds had stopped bleeding and had healed considerably.

Sankalp had realized that the princess was no ordinary woman but one endowed with intelligence, beauty and strength. She was courageous too and would fight to the death for her honour. He complimented Dolma for bringing up the princess to have such depth of character.

As they were speaking, the clatter of hooves drew his attention. He looked out from one of the square windows that looked on to the street below. The royal coach was at their door. The charming Princess Mayuri stepped out. She was accompanied by only two attendants and was without the retinue of escorts placed at her disposal.

She entered the house and headed straight to the guest room. 'How are you feeling today?' she asked Sankalp, smiling as she checked his forehead for signs of fever.

'I am fine, Princess. Thanks to your father's physician, my wounds are better already.'

Mayuri walked across to a wooden settee and sat on it shyly, with an air of vulnerability. Her demeanour was different from that of the woman who had fought her kidnappers so bravely the day before.

'I wanted to thank you for saving my life. I couldn't do so yesterday…'

'My dear princess, I did what the moment demanded of me. I am happy you are safe.' Sankalp's expression turned earnest. 'But you and I both know what awaits your kingdom in the near future.'

The princess gazed into his eyes. 'Who are you, and why are you here?'

Dolma intervened, 'I think the time has come to tell you more about my guest.'

She then proceeded to tell the princess about Sankalp. Dolma's story astonished Mayuri. She could not help but ask Sanklap more about his life.

'There is nothing more to my life, Princess. I am here at the call of destiny.'

'I knew there was something about you.'

The princess then proceeded to disclose the state of affairs in the kingdom. What had transpired and the reason why it was under threat from the invaders.

'My father wants the best for me, I know. But he is completely under the influence of his advisor. Asudai is a wily man, and he represents the kingdom of the north. He wants me to marry their general…' Her lids fluttered and her eyelashes shimmered with a hint of tears. 'His name is Darqan Doodra,' she whispered, drawing a deep breath. 'My father feels this is the only way peace can reign in our lands. Without a successor, our kingdom has become vulnerable to attacks.' Tears filled her eyes as she spoke.

Sankalp was startled into silence as he considered what the princess had just disclosed.

He was beginning to understand the enormity and depth of the conspiracy hatched by the invaders. They were raiding and looting the land to terrorize and instil fear in the people. At the same time, Asudai was misguiding the king at every step. Now, for the final assault, he had made an offer to the king to marry his only daughter, Princess Mayuri, to their general, Darqan Doodra. He could then easily gain control over the kingdom. If Trinyen Tsenpo refused, he would bring war to his very doorstep.

'Princess Mayuri, don't worry,' Sankalp took a deep breath and pushed himself upright on one arm. 'Just like us, even kingdoms have a fate. Let the stars decide their destiny while we do what we can to prevent a war.'

Mayuri looked at him with respect. 'After learning about your life and knowing what you have done for me…' Mayuri stirred slightly in her seat before continuing. 'I see no reason not to trust you. Moreover, I strongly feel you are the one person who can help Lhasa survive!'

Sankalp smiled. 'That's asking too much of a monk, Princess.'

Mayuri merely smiled and invited Sankalp to the palace the next day.

'I will be at the palace not for a reward but to meet the king,' he replied and bid her goodbye.

That evening over supper, Dolma remarked, 'Why do you want to get involved with matters of state? You are a monk; your pursuits are higher. Be on your way.'

She looked downcast as she gently stroked his shoulder. 'My dear,' she sighed, 'I sincerely fear for your life here.'

Sankalp smiled politely, intending to ignore the remarks but respecting her emotions.

'My destiny has bought me here. The village headman I told you about, the one who was killed by the invaders, was my father! I foresee death, destruction and the kingdom being subjected to many cruelties once the invaders conquer your land.' Sankalp sounded grim but his eyes radiated calm.

'I cannot overlook my past nor be afraid of the future. I have decided to stay and do whatever is in my power to save the princess and her kingdom. This will also help my people,' Sankalp gently explained.

'Well, then, be very careful, for traitors abound. And some in the palace are enemies of the state. Watch out for them, and may God be with you!'

Sankalp slept later than usual, but he was up early and so was Dolma. She was more excited than him about being invited to the palace.

17

A Visit to the Grand Palace

The following morning, the royal carriage came to fetch Sankalp at the appointed time. Upon his insistence, Dolma accompanied him for his audience with the king. As they sped along the tree-lined avenue leading to the palace gates, Sankalp was kept busy by the carriage driver narrating stories about Lhasa, its residents and places to see.

Soon they entered the palace gates. Sankalp looked with amazement upon the beauty and splendour of the structure. It was built not only by artisans from the city but by many who had come from other lands to lend their skill to this magnificent complex.

Four royal guards on horseback were waiting at the gates to escort the carriage. The air was redolent with the fragrance of peach blossoms.

They dismounted in front of the main palace door. The court crier banged his staff once against a hollow dome, signalling their arrival. Breaking tradition, the princess was waiting at the entrance. She was pleasantly surprised to see Dolma. Mayuri led them through the foyer to the main hall. The king sat on a beautiful gold-encrusted throne in the large hall, surrounded by his ministers and a host of attendants. This was the royal court, where he met people and discussed matters of state.

The hollow dome sounded twice as the princess entered, accompanied by her guests. The king immediately noted their arrival. Dressed simply in a monk's robe, Sankalp radiated a certain charm and sense of calm. In the midst of the august gathering, he showed no signs of nervousness. He approached the throne and bowed in reverence.

'Welcome, my brave young man,' announced the king and leaned back in his throne, his hands resting on its cushioned armrests. He narrowed his eyes as a thought crossed his mind. 'Did this monk—a monk—save my daughter?' A slight smile etched his lips as he proceeded with the formalities of the hour.

'I am indeed happy to know that my kingdom has people with your courage, strength and honour,' he gestured to Sankalp to take a seat.

An attendant seated Sankalp on a chair not too far away, while the princess occupied a seat opposite him. Dolma sat right behind her. Sankalp swept his keen eyes across the hall. His gaze fell on a rather obnoxious-looking person with an imperious and cold disposition. He was middle-aged, dumpy and had small beady eyes. He was definitely not from these lands. His features were much like those of people from the far north. And he did not seem as happy as the others on seeing Sankalp.

Trinyen, on the other hand, looked at the young man expectantly.

'Introduce yourself to the audience, my brave man, so we may honour you and your family for saving our princess,' announced the minister standing to the right of the throne.

A few whispers and discreet conversations filled the hall. Sankalp stood up and walked past the seats occupied by the high council. He stopped in the middle of the hall.

'I am Sankalp, the last of the family of Lin Thiampong, who was the headman of Shaka.' He smiled sadly.

Regaining his composure, he spoke again. 'And a disciple of the learned monk Kalimpong.' His pronouncement resonated clearly through the palace hall. There was complete silence for a while. The name of the learned monk had that effect on people.

Meanwhile, King Trinyen signalled to an attendant, who placed a large basket of gifts in his hands.

'Accept this humble offering as a mark of gratitude from my people and I. My daughter has told me much about you and your bravery. So knowing, there is but little that I can offer in return,' Trinyen said warmly.

Sankalp bowed low with humility. 'I am delighted to be in your presence and humbled by the honour you bestow on me. This is more than I need,' Sankalp nodded in respect, 'As you can see, I am just a wanderer, a monk. The weight of your gifts will only make my journey difficult. Without offending your kindness and with your permission,' he said and turned his attention to where Dolma stood, 'I would like to give this basket to the old lady.' Pointing in her direction, he said, 'She has been kind enough to give me shelter and food, and above all, she has given your daughter impeccable values that few in her place possess!'

Trinyen Tsenpo was intrigued. He rested his chin on the palm of his left hand and looked at Sankalp with renewed interest. 'So be it,' he spoke softly after a long moment and gestured to the courtier. He immediately handed the basket to Dolma. Besides many expensive items, it contained a purse of fifty gold coins, assuring her a better life.

Dolma, unlike others, knew without a doubt that the guest in her house was more than just a wandering monk. She blessed him from her heart for all that he had done.

Sankalp walked up to her and whispered, 'You remind me of my mother's warmth, and that makes it my duty to look after you in your old age.'

Sankalp returned to his seat, and shortly afterward, he requested the king's permission to leave.

Trinyen Tsenpo, in the meantime, had been passed a written message. He read it carefully.

'Sankalp, before you leave, I have but one request.' Trinyen paused and raised his head. 'You are aware that these are uncertain times for my kingdom and its people. You were a witness to the drama that unfolded some days ago.' The king's expression turned sombre.

Sankalp nodded.

'It could have put my kingdom at great risk. I request you to stay here with us and take charge of the princess's safety. It will relieve me of one of my many worries.' He glanced at Mayuri before looking expectantly at Sankalp. 'This is also the wish of the princess,' he added.

'My king, I am indeed honoured by what you ask of me. I am but a slave to the will of destiny. Please give me a few days to consider and decide.'

'Very well. Till then, please accept my hospitality and honour us by staying in the palace.'

Sankalp considered his words thoughtfully; he then looked up to reply but was interrupted.

The beady-eyed man seemed to have lost his composure. He walked up to the throne and demanded, 'My king, how can you have a stranger come into the palace and take charge of the princess' security? We need to find out more about him before you make a decision.' He spoke with unquestioned authority, his tone malevolent and without humility.

A short silence followed.

Then the princess confronted Asudai. 'I have seen your security and the guards that accompanied me to the city. So from now on, I will be in charge of my own security!'

Asudai frowned. He did not miss the quick glance exchanged between the king and the princess. He hissed something under his breath. But it was clear the princess would have only Sankalp and none else as her bodyguard.

Trinyen Tsenpo nodded; Sankalp's valour and demeanour had won the king's trust.

Before there could be any further deliberations, Sankalp replied, 'I accept your offer and will remain in the palace for a few days.'

The princess took a satisfied breath and nodded.

Sankalp then thanked Dolma for all she had done and bid her farewell. He was escorted to his living quarters, which were located close by.

The warrior of Shaka became a favoured guest in the palace, but its splendour and magnificence had little effect on him. He meditated for hours and spent a large part of each day practising his arts in its sprawling gardens. On some days, he would accompany Mayuri to the royal court. He keenly observed the proceedings and the behaviour of the people who constantly surrounded the king. The complex game plan hatched by the enemies from the north was becoming clearer. They wanted to create a state of chaos and anarchy across the kingdom. The small cavalries stationed at strategic points were doing a good job of this by regularly raiding nearby villages and spreading terror.

He did not want to share his views with anyone, not till he was sure.

It was a dark night. Sankalp sat with a blanket pulled over his legs. He stared unblinking at the starlight, drowsy but unwilling to sleep. His mind was invaded by a host of thoughts. The inner eye screened the starlight for a long while, before he finally succumbed to sleep.

Early the next morning, he met the princess.

'Princess Mayuri, I have decided to accept your father's offer.'

For the first time, a smile, if only a small one, brightened Mayuri's face. 'It is our privilege to have you here,' she replied softly.

'But my decision may not be pleasing to everyone in the palace,' replied Sankalp, clearing hinting at Asudai.

'Ah, as if that matters.' Her smile broadened. 'Your decision has made me immensely happy.' Continuing to smile, she raised her face higher. I see a reason for you being here,' she paused briefly. 'Given our limited knowledge of the future, we sometimes cannot decipher the true reasons for present happenings.'

Sankalp had noticed the intensity of the aura surrounding Mayuri. She was gifted with the divine light of knowledge and was definitely special. Not only was she courageous, but she was also humble in her bearing, and her learning surpassed that of many intelligent men.

'You amaze me, Princess, and some day you will be a well-loved and respected queen'.

Mayuri smiled humbly, accepting the compliment.

Sankalp requested the princess for a horse and permission to leave the palace for a while. Mayuri nodded unquestioningly.

Sankalp had decided to pay a visit to Divya Drishti, the young man he had met on his way to the city.

It was a pleasant trip to Divya's home. He rode from the city and through open fields.

He entered the grounds of Divya's mansion, and in the far corner of the beautiful gardens, he saw Divya Drishti. He was engrossed in the practise of fighting techniques. Seeing a rider approach, he dropped his hands in a signal and alerted his bodyguards.

'Greetings to you!' shouted Sankalp.

The expression on Divya Drishti's face turned cheerful. He had immediately recognized the warrior monk, with the customary maroon shawl flung across his shoulders. He rushed across the garden to receive him.

'This is a pleasant surprise,' exclaimed Divya, holding Sankalp in a tight hug. He could barely contain his excitement on seeing the warrior of Shaka.

'You look happy. That is a good sign,' Sankalp smiled.

Divya laughed. 'Come with me,' he said as he walked towards the mansion.

Sankalp followed the young man to a courtyard, where he introduced him to his mother.

'Mother, I want you to meet Sankalp. I mentioned him earlier; he was my guest while you were away'.

Sankalp bowed in reverence.

Divya's mother immediately placed her hand on his head and blessed him.

'How did you find the city? Was it worth the visit?' Divya questioned cynically.

'I am very impressed with the city and had a chance to meet the king and his daughter, Princess Mayuri.'

'How is Mayuri? Is she well? How does she look now?' His expression suddenly became gentle.

'She is a remarkable woman, beautiful and intelligent.' Sankalp smiled slightly. 'That is a rare combination.'

'It is,' Divya smiled back.

'Do you know her?'

'We stayed in the palace once, when my father served as the captain of the royal army.' Divya let his thoughts wander into the past. 'She was ever so playful…Those were wonderful times.'

Sankalp nodded and smiled.

'But do tell me more about the city and your stay there.'

Sankalp narrated the events of the past few days, especially the plot to kidnap the princess. He explained how he had managed to save her and what they had learnt from one of the imposters dressed as a royal guard.

Divya looked unsettled as he said, 'The enemy seems to have the upper hand.'

'It seems they do,' Sankalp concurred.

'The conspirators continue to rule while a weak ruler watches mutely. And now, his daughter will pay the price for it!' Divya shook his head in disgust. 'I am baffled by the discrimination against those who are loyal and the oppression that rule the royal court.'

'It is a little more complicated than that.'

'What is complicated about using common sense, Sankalp? How can one allow such injustice?' Divya protested.

Sankalp merely smiled at his irritation.

After spending a few days with Divya Drishti, Sankalp bid farewell to the family. He thanked them for their hospitality and sought permission to return to the palace.

'I was hoping you would be able to spend some more time with us,' Divya's mother said. She had grown fond of Sankalp and looked upon him as one of her own.

'Mother, under the circumstances, I must return today. I promised the princess I would be back soon.' Sankalp bent low with folded hands and took her leave.

Divya walked with him to the gates.

'Be prepared, my friend, for one day you will help decide the fate of Lhasa,' Sankalp said softly.

Divya Drishti smiled slightly, a look of consternation on his face.

Sankalp said no more; instead he held Divya in a brotherly embrace and bid him farewell.

Sankalp understood that the king was a fine ruler. A generous and just man, he was well-loved and held in great regard by his people. But it seemed he felt that he was always being watched and judged for his actions. Was he afraid of something? The thought hovered in Sankalp's mind as he rode back.

He reached the palace by sunset, where his arrival was eagerly awaited by the princess.

18

A Dangerous Game: The Invasion of Lhasa

Mayuri reminded Sankalp of the apprehensions she had expressed about her marriage and the danger posed to the kingdom and its people.

In a low voice that held a touch of regret, she explained further. 'Sankalp, as I mentioned earlier, my father has been under considerable pressure from Asudai—the man who resisted your stay here. Ever since he came here as an ambassador of the rulers of the north, our kingdom and its provinces have been under constant attack. Many villages and families, including yours, have faced their wrath! When my father asked for peace, he was advised that I marry their general, Darqan Doodra,' she spat his name hatefully.

'This would ensure peace for our kingdom and my family. My father has been resistant to this offer,' she said, clearly uneasy at the thought of this alliance. 'I guess that is what led to the attempt to kidnap me.' Mayuri sighed and was unable to speak any more, overcome as she was with emotion.

'I have heard of the general. A ruthless man!' Sankalp grimaced and walked to the window overlooking the palace lawns. 'We both know he is no advisor but a spy planted by the invaders.' Sankalp looked into the distance before abruptly turning to Mayuri. 'Why can't the king see and understand his real motives? He is an intelligent man.'

Mayuri closed her eyes for a moment. 'Perhaps it is the thought of an invincible enemy that has cast a net of fear around him. My father has been a wise ruler. He comes from a famed and powerful clan of savant warriors. He was one of the best fighters in the region, but after my mother's death…' Mayuri stopped and sighed. 'He has lived in grief and has been ailing since.' She shifted uncomfortably, her voice filled with grief.

'His fears have gotten the better of him now.'

Bristling slightly at her words Sankalp stood up from his seat. 'My dear princess, often grief numbs our finer senses. When that happens, it impairs your vision to see and understand rightly. We fail to see things in the correct perspective.' Sankalp's brow furrowed as he looked at Mayuri. 'That is the only thing that ails the king.'

'What should we do now?' Mayuri queried, sounding morose. 'I am happy you have decided to stay. I hope you can help my father see the true motives of his advisor,' she paused briefly and shrugged in a gesture of grim acceptance. 'Before it's too late!'

'Have you told your father what we learnt from the man who was part of the plot to kidnap you?'

'No, I haven't so far.'

'Let us wait for an opportune time to tell him. At the moment, his mind is filled with a mix of emotions, and his heart is feeble. I will need your help to persuade the king to join me in my morning ritual.'

Mayuri's excitement was palpable at the offer.

Sankalp smiled and added, 'There are methods that can help get rid of the grief and negativity that seem to dominate his mind.'

'I will convince him,' she stated with the authority that only a daughter can have over her father.

In the coming days, Sankalp encouraged the king to practice a particular form of meditation. Specific breathing techniques helped uplift his subconscious and do away with the feeling of helplessness. The princess too joined them.

All this did not go unnoticed by Asudai. He was angered by Sankalp's presence and his growing proximity to the king and the princess.

Gradually, there was a perceptible change in Trinyen Tsenpo. He was more energetic not only physically but mentally as well. A strong bond developed between Sankalp and the king. He started trusting Sankalp more and more in matters of state.

The cloudy winter mornings had given way to pleasant blue skies. On one such day, Trinyen Tsenpo asked Sankalp to accompany him to the palace gardens. His eyes reflected the conflict of thoughts that had kept him awake for most of the previous night.

'Sankalp, I asked you to come here alone,' he said hesitantly.

Sankalp gave him a slight nod, encouraging him to continue.

'I have something important to discuss and need your advice.' He stopped for a moment and looked at Sankalp. 'You are aware, my daughter, the princess, is too young to understand the implications of state politics.'

'The princess is a fine girl, mature and extremely intelligent,' Sankalp responded.

'She gets that from her mother, the queen.' The king looked pained for a moment and then smiled slightly before continuing. 'She was just a child when her mother passed away. The queen was not only beautiful but extremely intelligent. She participated actively in matters of state. Her death shattered me,' Trinyen Tsenpo said sorrowfully. 'I have not been myself ever since and have carried the burden of grief while bringing up my only child. Can you, the disciple of the learned monk Kalimpong, help me overcome my sorrow?'

'My king, life is in a continuous state of flux—enslaved by time and led by karmic currents towards an unknown finality. You must understand the transient nature of life, of which death is a part. However, the power of death culminates at the physical level, that being a necessity of nature. The divine light or soul within us is indestructible. It either becomes one with the supreme or, depending on its karma, seeks rebirth.'

He had the king's undivided attention. 'Joys and sorrows are very individual in nature. We can share only a small part. Grief is imminent to those who get caught in the present.' Sankalp paused. A mysterious smile edged his lips. 'Every moment is a new painting on the canvas of life. Enjoy it. Grieve too but not so much that it claims the better part of your being,' he added.

'My king, you must go beyond the confines of personal grief and the open doors to the higher intellect. In that refined state, you might hear the voice of the one who you think is dead,' concluded the young man.

Trinyen Tsenpo fell into deep thought on hearing Sankalp's words. A pleasant quiet followed before he snapped out of that state and finally responded.

'Thank you, Sankalp!' He put both hands on Sankalp's shoulders in a gesture that conveyed far more than simple affection. 'Your words give me solace. My mind feels relief from the grief that has constantly inundated my thoughts.' He shook his head. 'I cannot go on like this anymore. I have been hiding behind my plight to avoid confronting my fears and have been ignoring the circumstances of today.'

Trinyen Tesnpo looked at Sankalp with gratitude; the monk seemed to understand his confusion and his thoughts on the marriage of his daughter to a powerful adversary, an enemy!

That night, Trinyen Tsenpo stepped beyond the cloak of rationality as he experienced a rather unusual dream.

As he slept, his subconscious awoke to a fragrance he knew well. It was of the jasmine flower, frequently used by his wife, the queen. He felt her come up to him. She ran her fingers across his forehead and then slowly rested her head on his chest.

'My dear, do not grieve or worry about me. I am there, by your side, watching over you till we are together again,' she said softly, with a loving smile.

He could sense her presence and feel her touch upon his heart. The vision was as clear and vibrant as any waking experience. He opened his eyes, startled. 'Was she here or was it just a dream?' he wondered, drawing in a deep breath that still carried traces of jasmine. He excitedly drew another; the fragrance floated throughout the room with a telling presence.

The king carried his happiness to the royal court the next day. The transformation was unmissable.

In the days that followed, the court churned with effusive energy. The council was happy and so were the others. All except the beady-eyed Asudai. He seemed perturbed, and one day, in the presence of the ministers, he addressed the king.

'There is some grave news, my king. I have been forewarned of a rebellion brewing in the southern provinces. Before it spreads, we must suppress it!'

'How is that possible?' The king went pale, an unusual reaction from an able king. 'We have not faced dissidence in our lands for many years. I believe the people living there are honourable and content.'

Although the king was surprised to hear about the unrest, this time, instead of listening to his advisor and acting on the matter, he secluded himself from all those present in his court. He proceeded to the inner chambers lost in thought and summoned Sankalp to join him.

'Sankalp, have you heard? There is news of a rebellion in one of my lands. I know the people of that province. Many of my fine warriors come from there, all of whom are trustable beyond doubt. However, many years ago, one of my captains did betray me,' he rued.

'My king, sometimes what appears true may not be so. I imagine you are referring to your trusted captain and brother-in-arms. The one who fought alongside you in many wars and whose family was banished from the city,' said Sankalp.

'How do you know all this?'

'Before coming to the palace, I spent a few days with his son, Divya Drishti. He told me what had happened between his father and you. He is my disciple, and a friend too,' replied Sankalp.

At that moment, Princess Mayuri joined them.

Sankalp felt it was time to share the compelling piece of evidence that they had kept between themselves.

'Princess, please tell your father what the captured soldier, or should I say the kidnapper, revealed to us,' he urged Mayuri.

The princess related the incident in detail. 'Father, the plot to kidnap me was indeed hatched by someone from the palace. It's a conspiracy of mammoth proportions!'

The king gasped, visibly annoyed. 'Why was I not informed earlier?'

'We were waiting for the right time,' replied Sankalp.

The king shook his head slowly as Sankalp continued. 'We waited till your mind was more open to understanding the depth of this conspiracy, this nefarious plan being hatched by the invaders to take over your lands one way or another!'

'Do we go to war then? Or is there an alternative?'

'We cannot afford an all-out war,' Mayuri contended.

'We can't but we do have an alternative,' Sankalp paused thoughtfully for a moment before continuing. 'A counterplot…'

Sankalp explained what he foresaw, and the king too realized the gravity of the situation. The three sat well into the night to put a plan in place. The audacity of the proposal shocked the king, but on Sankalp's advice, Trinyen Tsenpo made an announcement the very next day in the main palace hall.

'I was informed of an uprising in our southern provinces. We will send a small contingent of royal guards to subdue the revolt and restore peace in the area,' the king declared.

'Your majesty,' Asudai raised his head. 'Who will lead this group of soldiers? I suggest you send someone who can be trusted and is experienced in this kind of warfare.'

'If you permit, I will lead a small army of my best men,' replied the captain of his army.

Trinyen Tsenpo looked at his captain and waited a moment.

Asudai interjected quickly. 'I suggest we send someone else. We need the captain with his military skills here. The city cannot be left unguarded in these times.' He stared at Sankalp contemptuously. 'Why not request the disciple of the great Kalimpong to handle this matter? He has already been entrusted with the important task of guarding our princess. This expedition will give him a chance to prove his skills and dedication to the kingdom.'

'I would be honoured to do so if the king gives his permission,' stated Sankalp.

Trinyen Tsenpo smiled. 'Sankalp will lead the men to settle matters in our southern outpost.'

The declaration was accompanied by nods of approval from his council.

'But there is one condition,' Sankalp raised his voice just enough to be heard by the gathering.

'Ah and what is that?' demanded the beady-eyed man with an unpleasant smile.

'I will select the men for this expedition myself.'

'You may do so, by all means,' replied Trinyen Tsenpo. 'The campaign is approved and Sankalp is authorized to proceed as he deems fit,' the king declared, his right hand raised as a sign of authority. 'We eagerly await the news of your success.'

'My king, these are not dissident tribes rebelling against us; they are the backbone of our army. We trusted them! They must be dealt with harshly; no special treatment or appeals! I propose mass execution to teach them a lesson,' fumed Asudai.

Trinyen Tsenpo looked at Asudai and frowned slightly, ensuring that the others present saw his disapproval.

Sankalp smiled and left the audience hall with alacrity.

That same afternoon, Princess Mayuri met Sankalp. She seemed worried but was comforted by what he had to say.

'Don't worry, Princess. Everything will be all right. Right now, I need your help to send a letter to my friend. And permission for him to enter the palace.'

'It will be done.'

Sankalp nodded as he pieced things together in his mind. 'With someone you trust,' he added.

The following day, Sankalp handed over a letter to the princess; it was meant for Divya Drishti. At the same time, his pet falcon carried another message for Bhumiputra.

The following day, Divya Drishti arrived at the royal palace. He was greeted by Sankalp at the palace gates.

'I am happy to see you here,' Sankalp beamed, holding Divya in a friendly embrace. He led him to his chamber and explained the recent developments.

'Sankalp, I am fortunate to be of help to you and the people of Lhasa.' He looked at the monk before continuing. 'In spite of being treated with contempt by the king and his council.'

Sankalp merely smiled thoughtfully at his choice of words.

'But the king might not be too happy to see me as a part of the campaign,' Divya mused.

'Leave that to me. Take this challenge as a call of destiny to seek your rightful place in the kingdom and avenge the death of your father.'

Later that day, Princess Mayuri joined them. She had come to know about Divya's presence in the palace.

The princess seemed a bit nervous as Sankalp introduced them to each other. 'This is my friend Divya Drishti.'

Mayuri stared at him for a moment. 'Yes, I know,' she said softly, sounding a bit perturbed.

After the greetings, Sankalp requested Mayuri to show Divya to his room while he attended to matters at hand.

The princess, accompanied by two attendants, walked the young warrior to his room, making sure he was well taken care of.

'Please rest a while till we meet again,' Mayuri said as a mix of emotions struck her.

She walked away quickly and then turned around as an afterthought. 'I want to thank you for your help. I know what happened to your family and share your pain.' There was genuine concern in her words. 'Before long, we will know who the real culprits are,' she concluded with a sad smile. Mayuri found it hard to pretend. She knew what she felt and let it show.

'I don't know what draws me here—my destiny or an inexplicable bond with the warrior of Shaka,' Divya answered. It was evident that he carried the pain of the dishonour faced by his family after his father's death.

The princess was at a loss to explain that she wasn't responsible.

Mayuri and Sankalp met again the same evening. Sankalp explained part of his plan. With Mayuri's help, he identified a group of men from the royal army. They were loyal and dedicated to Lhasa.

The following morning, Sankalp took Divya with him to the royal court. The gong sounded twice to mark the beginning of the day's proceedings. Sankalp walked up to the throne and bowed in respect. Trinyen Tsenpo nodded, acknowledging his presence, while he looked enquiringly at his accompanying guest. Divya said nothing; he glanced around the hall, waiting to be introduced.

'My king, I would like to present a trusted friend and the captain of my contingent. His name is Divya Drishti.'

Divya bowed low in respect.

'He will lead the contingent against the uprising in the south. Of course, with your consent,' Sankalp stated.

Trinyen Tsenpo took one look at the young, handsome, able-bodied warrior and nodded his acceptance. 'Your personality reflects nobility, and your name sounds familiar. Go forth and claim victory'!

'I have also handpicked the men who will come with us,' Sankalp declared.

Asudai was keenly watching the proceedings, especially Divya Drishti. He did not say a word, looking dismissive of the proposition. The king appeared to be taken aback, but only briefly, by his behaviour.

Meanwhile, Sankalp informed the court that his contingent would be departing the next day. He deliberately made this common knowledge to all present. Notably to the one man he did not trust.

Sankalp and his men left the same night when the city was clothed in a blanket of darkness. The men carefully weaved their way towards the city gates, their faces covered to avoid being recognized. Divya Drishti took the lead, with the rest following him. He knew the best and fastest way to the southern provinces. They rode like the wind through the night, crossing a series of barren mountain ranges till the break of dawn.

The warrior monk had deliberately planned to lead his men at night. They had a better chance of reaching the southern province without being noticed. The element of surprise was crucial for the success of this mission. There was another reason too, but one that he wished to keep to himself until the time was right for others to know.

The men rested and prepared food during the day, and by dusk, they were ready to ride again. They would cross the Death Valley, and Sankalp wanted to reach there before dawn.

The light was fading. Grey clouds had started covering the sky as they reached the narrow mountain pass leading into Death Valley. Sankalp swung off his horse and focused his attention on the stretch of undulating land that lay ahead. The mountain pass they stood on was part of the vast range that stretched from the north to the south. A river ran alongside at places and, from a point, curved sharply from the south towards the west. At the foothills, close to the river, the landscape changed from light brown to dark green with dense forests stretching to the plains.

'We will be at the border of the southern province later tonight,' Divya Drishti assured him. 'We can lay siege to the rebels tomorrow morning.'

Sankalp nodded and mounted his horse, spurring it to a trot. He rode past Divya and stopped a few metres ahead of where the ground rose a few feet, scanning the high mountain pass. Divya followed the movement of his eyes keenly. His instincts prickled.

'Sankalp, I don't have a good feeling about this place. Let us move on quickly.'

'What you say is quite right,' Sankalp responded as he pointed to the east side of the mountain pass.

For a moment, Divya saw nothing in the distance. Then suddenly he blinked as the evening light reflected off metal—the metal of shields! Many men were marching towards them, and as they drew closer, Divya could make out their armour. It was the enemy! Someone had tipped the invaders off on their movements. A shocked Divya assessed the approaching force and realized they were heavily outnumbered.

His eyes filled with rage, and his chest heaved. 'This is a trap! We have been led into a bloody trap!'

He turned to Sankalp, who was still surveying the high mountain pass intently.

Sankalp remained calm. 'Do not fear, my friend. I knew this journey would not be without surprises. I sent a letter to my village through Zanzi. I have no doubt that reinforcements will be ready and waiting for my signal.'

'But we have been betrayed…betrayed by Lhasa.' He shook his head sorrowfully.

Sankalp looked at him silently, his expression telling him he understood.

Divya's brief outburst was quickly replaced by more pressing problems at hand. 'Sankalp, under the current circumstances, we cannot descend into the valley by day. Any movement of our men and material will expose our position and make us vulnerable to enemy arrows.'

Sankalp nodded in agreement. All they could do was sit tight and wait for reinforcements. But no one was in sight. The sun was about to set behind the barren landscape giving rise to strong wind currents.

Sipping on a hot cup of tea, Divya reluctantly posed another question. 'What if Bhumiputra did not receive the message? What do we do then? Our rations won't last long, and I am sure the men waiting in ambush are well supplied.' He sighed in frustration.

Sankalp understood Divya's worries but remained calm. 'We will try and do the best we can with the means available. I see no reason to fear these mortals and their dirty game plans.' He pursed his lips. Let us stay vigilant and leave the rest to the gods of destiny!'

Divya nodded with another sigh.

They rested for the evening but did not light any fires. Divya suggested they descend from the mountain pass later at night, failing the arrival of reinforcements. It would give them a better chance to escape the siege laid by the enemy.

Close to the midnight hour, Sankalp heard a familiar call from somewhere close. It was Zanzi. Just then, he noticed a ruddy glow. A few torches were moving towards them from a low-lying trail on the northern side.

'Bring me a light,' Sankalp asked one of his men.

He drew a pouch from the belt around his waist and sprinkled some powder on the flame of the torch he was handed. The flame immediately sputtered and changed to a deep blue. He waved it in a pattern. The signal was recognized and reciprocated. A platoon of well-armed, fierce-looking men on horseback came out of hiding. They followed the blue flame to where Sankalp waited.

A smiling Sankalp looked at Divya Drishti. Both men mounted their horses and tugged at the reins, urging their horses into a gallop to meet the others.

'Greetings to the warrior of Shaka! I hope we haven't kept you waiting long,' exclaimed Bhumiputra.

'You are just in time!' replied Sankalp and introduced Divya to Bhumiputra. While the two men talked, Sankalp gave instructions to gather the soldiers.

The men rallied around in two semicircles as he explained the plan. 'We will rest for the night and descend the mountain pass in the morning.' Sankalp marked a point to the south, overlooking the mountain pass where Bhumiputra would lay siege.

The next morning, Sankalp and his men headed for the valley, galloping over the high pass, making sure they were visible to the enemy. Bhumiputra had already ridden with his men towards the narrow, steep, rocky track of the pass at first light. This would keep them a little ahead of the enemy and give them time to position themselves at vantage points.

The invaders, oblivious to these preparations, mounted an attack on what they saw was a heavily outnumbered contingent. Confident of victory, they opted for close combat and charged the enemy.

'On my signal, we race down the mountain track,' explained Sankalp. 'We must descend halfway to the valley before engaging the enemy.'

They galloped cautiously down the treacherous mountainside, aware that even a small slip could spell disaster and lead to a horrible death below! They were followed closely by the invaders, misled into believe they were fleeing. At one point, the track curved sharply as it skirted a jagged outcrop of rocks bulging from the hillside. The riders had to slow down and negotiate the curve carefully. The moment Sankalp and his men negotiated the obstacle, he gave the signal!

The men pulled on their reins, forcing their horses to a stop. They turned around with military precision and drew their weapons, ready to attack. Seeing the men in attack mode, Bhumiputra gave out the battle cry! His men came out of hiding from the steep slopes overlooking the narrow track. They emptied their quivers on the enemy with precision. The narrow passage prevented the easy movement of men and horses. The enemy stood cornered. With nowhere else to go, they ran into Sankalp's men and clashed in bloody combat!

With his quiver empty, Bhumiputra dropped his bow. So did one hundred archers at his command, and drawing their swords, they charged across the slopes!

Sankalp's powerful sword of balance danced through the air in a finely tuned rhythmic motion, drawing blood with every swing! The enemy was surrounded. They stood little chance in front of these fearsome warriors, though they were good riders and fought bravely.

The fear created by the warrior of Shaka and his menacing sword dampened enemy morale; many began to flee, fearing for their life. While Bhumiputra and Divya Drishti engaged the others, the leader of the invaders fought Sankalp in a fierce battle. By noon, the very air smelt bloody. The narrow mountain path leading down to the valley was laden with corpses. The cries of the men and the clatter of hooves began to fade with the day. The leader of the invaders was severely wounded in his sword hand.

By sunset, they had no option but to surrender.

'Spare the life of my men! We surrender!' shouted their captain, waving a white flag.

Sankalp raised his right hand and signalled to his men to cease fighting. It was a decisive battle and they had fought hard for victory. A whisper of appreciation ran through the warriors of Lhasa, and many impulsively saluted Sankalp. The newly appointed captain had proved his leadership in battle.

The commander of the invaders led his horse up to Sankalp. 'Spare the life of my men and take mine instead,' he spoke softly with composure and offered his sword in surrender.

'I will spare your life and whatever is left of your army!' replied Sankalp.

He told Divya Drishti to strip the aggressors of all weapons.

He then consulted his men. They decided the enemy would be of more use to them alive than dead. So Sankalp proceeded to make their captain an offer of surrender.

'I am well aware that you are following orders without knowing the reason for or consequences of your actions.' Sankalp stared down at the enemy. 'Answer my questions truthfully. Give me a reason to believe in you, and you shall have my mercy. Otherwise…' he stopped short of saying what would happen but was well understood by the enemy.

A heavy stillness descended. The captain of the invaders was quiet but evenly met Sankalp's gaze.

After a brief, thoughtful pause, he replied. 'I respect your words and accept your terms. We, as soldiers, only obey orders and are trained to do so without questioning the reasons behind them.' So saying, he handed Sankalp his sword.

That night, the soldiers of both camps nursed their wounds together.

'We have some powerful medicinal herbs that are very helpful in the healing process,' said one of the invaders, looking at Bhumiputra and seeking his permission.

Bhumiputra nodded. The man applied a combination of herbs on his wounds. To his amazement, Bhumiputra felt immediate relief from pain.

And so the men who had fought a bitter battle in the morning shared medicine and food that night. There was no difference between friend and foe; they treated each other to the best of their abilities.

However, sleep evaded the captain of the invaders. He got up in the middle of the night and, finding everyone asleep, quietly walked to the furthest corner of the camp, avoiding the sentries that patrolled the perimeter. A fire nearby cast its light upon his face. It seemed stricken with fear. He sat deep in thought. Unseen, Sankalp had followed him in silence. The captain drew out a thin sharp knife from a scabbard attached to his boot. He aimed for his heart.

Sankalp quickly pounced on him. Firmly gripping the hand that held the dagger, he shook it out of the captain's grip.

'Leave me alone! Let me die a soldier's death. I know you will kill us in the morning.'

'No, I will not,' Sankalp assured him as he gazed into the fear-filled eyes of his enemy.

The enemy saw compassion, not anger, in Sankalp's eyes.

'How can I go back and tell them about this defeat? I will be tortured to death! My master is ruthless and shows no mercy.'

'Tell me your name and who sent you here?' Sankalp asked as he sat beside the captain.

'I am Tshangpa, the captain of the contingent. Our orders were to ambush your patrol near Death Valley.' His eyes met Sankalp's. 'And take no prisoners.'

'How did you know about our route? And when we would get there?'

'There was information about your departure from Lhasa. But you arrived earlier than expected.'

'Hmm.' Sankalp rose to his feet. He kept silent for a long moment before finally speaking. 'Trust me and sleep without fear, Captain. I will tell you what to do in the morning.'

The man gave a slight nod of acceptance and walked a few steps before abruptly turning around.

'Sir, you seem different from the many warriors I have known. Who are you?'

'A monk,' Sankalp replied.

'And what do you want?'

'Want?' Sankalp smiled. 'Now, when do we ever know that?' he quipped.

He walked the fallen warrior back to his tent before stretching out under the open sky, staring silently at the twinkling expanse.

The next day, Sankalp told everyone in the camp to gather. He and his men sat facing the captured soldiers. No one except the two leaders knew what had transpired the previous night.

'I am giving you freedom from being my prisoners or anybody else's.' He drew in a deep breath before speaking again. 'A choice of being truly free, physically and mentally, to be the masters of your own destiny!' Sankalp announced to the gathered men.

Murmurs ran through the enemy ranks as surprise replaced fear.

'But this freedom comes with a condition—a solemn promise by you and your captain to follow my instructions. If you do not, you will face dire consequences!'

The enemy's contingent was comprised mostly of captured men from nearby villages. They had allied with the enemy under duress and fear of reprisal. So it was an easy decision for them to forsake the invaders. The captain and his men swore allegiance to the warrior of Shaka.

Two young men edged forward and introduced themselves.

'I am Lieutenant Rigzin,' said the taller of the two.

'And I am Lieutenant Rabtin,' announced the other.

The name immediately caught Sankalp's attention. He stepped forward and rested his hand on the young man's shoulder in a friendly gesture. 'I know your father, Rangdol.'

Rabtin stood surprised by the words. He took a minute to gather his thoughts before speaking. 'How is my father?' he quizzed softly, his voice full of emotion. 'And my mother?'

'He is well and so is your mother. I will let them know about you,' Sankalp replied affectionately.

Sankalp then instructed Lieutenant Rigzin to send word to their camp and report the mission as successful. Captain Tshangpa would be reported killed in battle.

'Do we still ride to the southern provinces? We know this was a plan to lead us into a trap,' said Divya.

'We will. Just to convey our regards from the king. In the meantime, I will alert the princess and let her know what happened,' Sankalp replied.

Zanzi carried Sankalp's message back to the palace. He wanted the princess to be careful till they returned and not get swayed by any false news that would no doubt soon reach the palace through the traitors.

Sankalp and his men then proceeded to the southern borders of the kingdom. As expected, they found everything to be peaceful there.

'My doubts are confirmed. I am convinced the king's advisor is a spy, an enemy! He and some others had planned to kill us,' Sankalp confided to Divya Drishti.

'Yes, and the enemy soldiers had enough provisions to last for weeks. Someone carried a message to the enemy camp with instructions to ambush us on the way.' Divya shook his head and sighed in disbelief. 'Making the king believe there was indeed a rebellion!'

Divya looked at Sankalp. 'Who could be the enemy's accomplice? Another traitor in the palace?'

'Hmmm…' Sankalp drew in a deep breath, his eyes fixed on the ground. 'That is what I am thinking about.' He looked at Divya and, shifting his weight to one side, he sat at ease.

'There is another thing. I am sure the men who ambushed us will follow your instructions. I hope they understand it is the right thing to do. But what if they don't?' Divya queried anxiously.

Sankalp paused for a moment as the flutter of red-spotted butterflies caught his attention. 'My friend, the cavalry is formed of captured men—slaves. They have great respect for Captain Tshangpa and little for their captors. The lieutenant, Rigzin, happens to be the captain's brother-in-law. And Rabtin is the missing son of Rangdol, the headman of Shaka.' He smiled. 'So we do have some security on their commitment.'

'Hmm…' Divya replied sceptically.

'There is a plan—an exceedingly difficult gamble. Will it work? I don't know yet.' Sankalp's eyes in that moment defied description. 'It is still too incomplete to draw any meaningful conclusions.' He locked his hands behind his back and took a few steps. 'But why deliberate now?' Some of his former levity returned as he smiled slightly. 'My dear Divya, sometimes we must rely more on faith than reason.'

Divya smiled with a nod. He could not help but acknowledge the validity of the monk's statement.

'So let us wait and see what new picture is painted on the canvas of life at the hands of destiny. But I can see the certainty of battle looming large, though I am not one for it.' Sankalp spread his hands in a placating gesture before continuing. 'Moreover, when the outcome is bound to cause suffering to many. But sometimes, it becomes imperative to fight against injustice!'

Divya drew in a deep breath and nodded, not sure what to say. He watched the fire for a while and then stood up. 'I need to get some rest. And you should too.'

The following morning, the men were greeted warmly on their arrival at the small but important town that marked the beginning of the southern provinces. The village elders and the local magistrate received them.

'My dear sir, welcome to our town,' said one of the elders as he led Sankalp and his men to the town square.

'What brings you here? I hope all is well?' the local magistrate enquired as they sat, surrounded by the elders.

'Indeed it is, and I hope your town is blessed with peace and prosperity,' replied Sankalp.

'This is the way it has been, and I hope it remains so,' an elder responded.

That was the answer Sankalp had hoped to hear from the people. The three men leading the king's army exchanged glances of satisfaction. Sankalp requested the elders to provide food and accommodation for his men. They were battle-fatigued and in urgent need of rest.

They were immediately led to the nearby barracks.

'You may rest for the day, but please accept our hospitality for tonight as a token of our love and respect for the king and his soldiers,' the magistrate smiled warmly.

That evening the townsfolk laid out a grand feast for the visitors. They enjoyed the evening, eating and making merry, which they so deserved.

The magistrate, a wise man, approached Sankalp later in the night.

'Sir, your men and horses are fatigued and some are wounded.' He paused. 'Please tell me the real purpose of your visit,' he said with a look of scepticism.

Sankalp studied the man before him, allowing him to continue.

'I know from experience that there is more to it than meets the eye.'

Sankalp could sense the unease in his words as he waited for an explanation.

Sankalp smiled. 'You are right,' he said softly and rested his hand on the magistrate's shoulder in a comforting gesture. 'I want you to assemble the elders early in the morning before we leave.'

Early the next morning, the magistrate and the elders assembled at the barracks.

Sankalp explained the reason for his visit and the danger facing the kingdom. A heavy silence fell over the gathering.

'Now that you know the truth, are you ready to fight and make sacrifices for your motherland and the king?'

His words were met with a loud cheer.

'Tell the king we stand by him! No sacrifice is greater than defending the honour of our motherland! Long live the king!'

The elders presented Sankalp with a silk robe encrusted with precious jewels as a token of their love and respect for their ruler.

As the men and their horses had gotten some much-needed rest, the contingent bid farewell to the people and thanked the magistrate before walking back to their horses.

As they were preparing to leave, Bhumiputra remarked, 'Sankalp, it is astonishing to see the love and respect the king commands.'

'My dear Bhumiputra, no one can command love and respect. It is a thought that comes naturally when you are happy and feel liberated. Anything that is demanded or forcibly extracted is short-lived. Sooner or later, rejection of this authoritarian force is bound to happen. It is only a matter of time before suppression finds a way to transgress the threshold of self-control and become vindictive.' He paused with a shake of his head. 'No ruler has been able to govern people with force for long. In time, people tend to make their own choices on how they want to be governed, depending on their circumstances and those of the state.'

Sankalp straightened up and crossed his arms across his chest.

'The sad part is that some rulers forget that it is through a privileged destiny that they are put in this position. Instead of thinking about the welfare of the people whose trust and devotion have put them in a position of power, they act as absolute masters and rule with might to further their desires. In the process, they subject their people to misery and suffering,' Sankalp pointed out and mounted his steed.

Divya looked at Sankalp. 'You are right, my friend. It is the common people who suffer, whereas the mighty enjoy the privileges of destiny.'

'Not for long,' Sankalp smiled. 'Sooner or later, the universal law of karma catches up with them, making them go through the same plight and suffering they inflicted on others. The karmic law does have its own checks and balances. The universal balance has to be restored, no matter what!'

'Ah, another set of mercurial laws?' quipped Divya.

Sankalp smiled. 'Many people do not believe in any such law; for them, death is the end. They don't realize that the end is just a doorway to a new beginning.'

So saying, Sankalp spurred his horse into a gallop.

The men rode through the day without stopping. The sky remained overcast as they crossed the plains across the Yarlung Pass by night. By late afternoon of the next day, they entered Death Valley. Here, a small tributary of the Indus flowed. Sankalp stopped his horse by the riverside, and so did the others. He dismounted and, laying aside his battle attire, waded into the refreshing water.

Later that night, Sankalp sat with his two trusted aides and shared his thoughts about the future of the kingdom.

The shrill cry of the falcon marked the beginning of a better day. Zanzi had delivered Sankalp's message to the palace. The princess had been duly informed of what had transpired during their journey to the southern provinces. The falcon had also carried back an important message from the palace. The cavalry immediately set a quick pace back to Lhasa.

The expedition had led to strong bonds being formed among the men. The royal guards accompanying Sankalp had begun to trust and have faith in his abilities. It was because of his foresight that they had survived the ambush at Death Valley.

By mid-afternoon, they had reached a high mountain pass. Sankalp signalled his men to a stop at a vital intersection. He wanted to make an announcement.

'My dear Bhumiputra and Divya Drishti, your bravery and courage are unsurpassed. I am indeed fortunate to have you on this expedition that may well decide the fate of Lhasa.'

Both soldiers accepted his words with humble nods and a quietness of the mind that underlined their character.

Sankalp's voice was distinctly hoarse with emotion as he continued. 'The depth and strength of a warrior's character will once again be challenged in battle. You will see many fall and some survive as the gods of destiny decide our fate.' He paused for a moment and then raised his voice to be heard by each of his men. 'Death will once again stare at you, and all you can do is smile back without remorse! I ask again, will you fight for this land and seek your destiny, or will you chose to retire to the comforts that await you?'

'Like you, we too seek our destiny! Let it lead us where it may. If it means death, then so be it!' The men roused to his words.

Sankalp acknowledged their enthusiasm with a raise of his sword. He then turned his attention towards the high mountain passes. 'Bhumiputra, you must return to Shaka and keep a watch on the invaders. Send some soldiers to the other side of the Yarlung Pass and watch out for any suspicious movement of men and material. Being forewarned is being forearmed!'

With matters settling somewhat in the south, Bhumiputra and his men rode back towards Shaka. Sankalp, accompanied by Divya Drishti, made his way towards the kingdom of Lhasa.

The princess had sent an important message through Zanzi, instructing them to avoid entering the city from the palace gates. Instead, they were to use a secret passageway, which was known only to the royal family. A drawing showed the location of the passage. It connected to the palace gardens from a water body that ran along the north side of the outer wall.

It was wise to keep their return a secret from the conspirators working within the palace walls, who could well have presumed them dead. It was a well thought out plan, one that would encourage the plotters to lower their guard and thus be caught unawares. It was a smart move by Princess Mayuri.

Sankalp and his men found the secret tunnel near a small water body about three hundred yards from the palace wall. The opening was narrow, just wide enough for a single horseman to enter at a time. Sankalp bent low over his horse and entered the passage, followed by the others in a single file. The tunnel gradually rose from under the ground and led to a secluded spot at the edge of the palace gardens. Here, the thick foliage had been arranged to form discreet areas enclosed by shrubs and bushes. It was quite impossible to see the opening of the tunnel.

Princess Mayuri had learnt of their arrival and was waiting expectantly a few metres from the entrance.

Relief broke out on her face as Sankalp emerged, followed by the others.

'I am surprised to see you here, Princess. How did you know the time of our arrival?' remarked Divya Drishti.

'Well,' a mischievous smile touched her lips. 'This is one secret I must keep, for now, at least.'

'You are far cleverer than I thought,' Sankalp smiled and arched an eyebrow.

The tired men dispersed into the night. They were told to keep their return a secret, at least for now. A few along with Sankalp and Divya disarmed in a makeshift tent that had been set up in one of the discreetly enclosed areas.

Divya returned to where the princess was waiting. Mayuri wanted him to stay but knew he wouldn't. She led him through the palace gardens. A quiet followed, disturbed only by the sound of noisy crickets.

Mayuri tried to keep pace with Divya's quick strides. Finally, keen to draw him into a parting conversation, she spoke. 'I am grateful for your help in this hour of crisis. I will never forget what you have done for me and the kingdom despite what happened to your family.' Her voice was mellow and her eyes moist with emotion.

'I have only done my duty to the people and a friend. A friend I deeply respect. I also need to find the culprits who bought dishonour to my family.' So saying, Divya bid a quick farewell to the princess and rode back to his home under the cover of darkness, followed by his men.

Meanwhile, Sankalp had entered the palace from a secluded location. He was led to a secret chamber by a close aide of the princess. None in the palace knew of his return. The secret chamber had a small opening into the main hall where the king conducted his business, allowing Sankalp to be privy to all happenings there. He was eager to see Asudai and hear what he had to say.

Sankalp woke to the sound of people assembling in the large hall.

The proceedings were resuming after a week-long break. The king first attended to the people who had come to seek justice. After a while, the crowd in the large hall thinned and many left feeling satisfied. By noon, it was time to attend to matters of state. Only a close group of advisors along with allies from neighbouring regions remained in the hall.

Trinyen Tsenpo addressed the beady-eyed advisor, Asudai. 'Tell me, in the presence of all seated here, what you have come to learn about the fate of our men?' The king flinched slightly at his own words. 'About the contingent sent to quell the uprising in the southern provinces?'

The courtiers eagerly waited for Asudai's response.

Sankalp, meanwhile, was keenly watching the proceedings from the secret chamber.

'Your majesty, the man known as Sankalp or the warrior of Shaka or by any other name,' Asudai began to say, raising his hand dismissively with each pronouncement as his words oozed contempt. 'This so-called disciple of Kalimpong, entrusted with the job of quelling the uprising in the southern provinces, is dead! And so are his men! He was not the super warrior he was made out to be by the princess.' An almost offensive grin spread across his face.

Princess Mayuri merely smiled and looked away from Asudai's gaze. It was best not to be drawn into a conversation at this time.

'How did you arrive at this conclusion?'

'Your majesty, I know some people in that area,' Asudai said without the slightest trace of any emotion. 'They brought the news to me.'

'How could they have been ambushed? Only a few I trust knew about the plan. Surely, there is a traitor among us, and he will not escape my wrath!' Trinyen Tsenpo glared at Asudai.

The men in the hall were shocked at the king's utterance, but Asudai remained unmoved. His arrogance conveyed that he was untouchable and enjoyed the protection of a powerful adversary.

'Your highness, surely you are right,' Asudai said, looking suspiciously at the man sitting to the right of the king. He was one of Trinyen Tsenpo's most trusted lieutenants and had been resisting Asudai from the very beginning.

'Tell me, who do you think ambushed Sankalp and his men? And what should we do now? I have lost some of my best warriors,' the king asked.

'Your highness, I think they were renegades, mostly from the southern provinces,' Asudai declared and raised his bony chin. 'We have to crush this uprising before it spreads further. Let us not wait.'

'Hmmm...' Trinyen Tsenpo huffed and stared down at Asudai from his throne, wondering whether the man was truly ignorant or if this was a charade.

'So what do you suggest?' he finally quizzed, holding his stare.

'I suggest we send out the elite group—the top fighters reserved to defend the palace.'

His advice seemed contrived, suggesting something more sinister.

'How many fighters do we have?' questioned the king as he rested his chin on the palm of his right hand.

'About four thousand,' Asudai replied, raising his bony chin higher. 'We can send about a thousand men, and the rest can remain here. The reserved fighters are formidable warriors and have proven themselves on many occasions. They are specially trained in tactical battle skills and can easily rout the dissidents,' he declared, feigning a false sense of pride. 'And this time we will be more careful.'

Trinyen Tsenpo nodded in grim resignation. The act held good. Asudai was convinced his plan was working.

He coughed slightly and cleared his throat to attract attention before continuing. 'I would also like to remind the king that the powerful general of the north still desires peace. He can be of help in this hour of need.' He turned to look at the princess. 'I feel it is in the best interest of the kingdom that Princess Mayuri give up her stubborn stance and agree to marry the general, the respected Darqan Doodra!'

Mayuri had heard enough of his chauvinistic jabber. She stood up in a huff and threw Asudai a penetrating look before leaving the royal court.

The king was now well aware of Asudai's true intentions. The beady-eyed man appointed as advisor to make peace with the northern rulers was without doubt a seditionist. Asudai had only one motive—to perpetuate the surrender of Lhasa!

General Darqan Doodra knew the king was a brave man. He commanded the respect of his people and the army; a battle would be disastrous even if they succeeded. So the general had opted to send a spy, disguised as a peace representative. His main task was to convince the king to marry his daughter to the general. And the attacks on the villages were a tactic to exert pressure on the king.

However, the tables seemed to have turned for now. The ambush party sent by the northern invaders had been annihilated and their captain had changed sides. On Sankalp's advice, the king played ignorant and continued to act on the advice of Asudai. They would once again play truant and send a small garrison under the command of one of the oldest and most trusted commanders in the king's army.

Trinyen waved the court into silence before dismissing it earlier than usual. He later summoned his commander.

They met with Sankalp in the chamber where he was in hiding. He explained to the commander how he and his men had managed to escape the trap laid for them and win the allegiance of the enemy soldiers.

'My dear Sankalp, will it work a second time?' the commander voiced his worry.

'We have to take that chance and do unto them what they wanted to do to us. We must induce fear and reduce their numbers in the forward areas,' Sankalp reasoned.

With a plan in place, the king made the announcement in the royal court. 'We will send a contingent to the southern provinces on the advice of Asudai.'

None, except for Trinyen Tsenpo, his trusted commander, and Sankalp, knew that Bhumiputra and Divya Drishti with their battalions would once again join the contingent across the Yarlung Pass.

Sankalp had decided to remain in the city and keep watch. He wanted to catch Asudai along with the others who were part of the plot. There had to be someone inside the palace who was conspiring with them and passing relevant information to the invaders.

Sankalp had been informed by one of the captured men about the enemy's numbers. The northern invaders had three battalions of about two thousand men each. They were posted in the nearby mountains and any one of them could act immediately on receiving an order to attack. It was important to apprehend the traitorous messenger without alerting the others. He was the crucial link in this dark game of betrayal.

Sankalp shared his thoughts with the princess.

'Princess Mayuri, as you are aware, there is another scoundrel in the palace. The one carrying messages for Asudai! We must keep a close watch on things; it is imperative we catch him red-handed.'

'I will have my trusted maid keep a watch on Asudai's movements within and outside the palace.'

'And on everyone who comes to meet him. Tell her, the moment she senses something wrong, I should be informed,' Sankalp added.

'Don't worry, I will be extra vigilant from today,' she smiled and left with her waiting attendant.

Sankalp was still in hiding, meeting only the king and the princess for short intervals during the night. On some nights, he would be transported by the power of the blue light to the small cottage in the high mountains. His astral body could glimpse Titla as she slept. He would penetrate her dreams and feel her emotions. Her heart longed for him…

One night, a strange sound snapped him out of his sublime state. Sankalp peered into the audience chamber through a small peephole. His eyes narrowed as he heard the sound of soft footfalls.

Moonlight cast partial light into the pillared chamber, illuminating portions of the large hall. A robed figure briefly stepped through the shadows and then disappeared into the dark. Sankalp was surprised. Who could have managed to enter the palace hall in the dead of a cold winter night?

It seemed the intruder had climbed in through a large window that had deliberately been left open and had slipped. The noise had alerted the guards, who now entered the hall. They looked around, trying to find the source of the disturbance. But the robed figure had quickly disappeared behind one of the many pillars. Finding nothing wrong, the guards returned to their posts. The robed figure stood unmoving for a few moments till another emerged from the surrounding darkness. It was difficult to recognize either of the two. They both wore dark burlap robes with hoods.

Sankalp saw one of them handing over a small piece of paper to the other, which the latter quickly put in a tiny box. The first then whispered some instructions, which were inaudible to Sankalp. The two figures then silently made their way across the hall.

Sankalp unlocked the hidden door that opened into the hall. He followed the figures, making sure to remain completely hidden from sight. While one crossed the long corridor and turned towards the main entrance, the other climbed out through the opened window and moved towards the palace walls, followed closely by Sankalp. The robed figure quickly walked through the tree-lined gardens, building up speed with each step. The gardens lay adjunct to the royal living quarters. Taking cover among the tall dense trees, the figure moved towards the palace gate. Sankalp had to act quickly and confront the person before they crossed the tree-lined garden.

Advancing with lightning speed, Sankalp pounced on the figure, grasping the neck in his powerful arms! As they scuffled, the hood slipped off his adversary's head. It was a woman! Sankalp was shocked. The hardy woman struggled to free herself from his grip.

'Don't shout or I will break your neck,' Sankalp ordered. His arm firmly clasped around her neck, he retrieved the little wooden box from her hand. The robed woman realized the futility of struggle.

'Let me go. I have done no wrong,' she mumbled.

'What have you been doing inside the palace, and who is your accomplice?' questioned Sankalp. He dragged her to the nearest tree and tied her to it.

Meanwhile, the maid who had been keeping watch alerted the princess. Mayuri rushed out of her room and ran down the spiral stairs armed with a dagger for protection. She crept into the garden thicket, drawn by the sound of low voices. She could make out Sankalp's voice.

'Who is it?' asked Sankalp, drawing his sword and fearing it was the other.

'It is I,' replied Mayuri, moving closer and trying to get a glimpse of the prisoner through the foggy night air.

'What is she doing here?' she said with a look of surprise. 'I have seen her; she works in the palace gardens.'

'I was about to ask her that. I saw two robed figures, their faces covered, meeting in the palace hall. One of them handed this box to the other then both left. I nabbed the one who headed to the garden, while the other must have disappeared within the palace halls.'

Sankalp walked up to a decorative lantern that hung low from one of the branches of a nearby tree. He opened the tiny wooden box. It had a small piece of paper rolled up inside. The lettering was tiny but readable, and its contents shocked him.

'What is it?' The princess asked, seeing the seriousness of his expression.

Sankalp handed her the tiny piece of paper. Mayuri's eyes narrowed and brow furrowed as she read the note. An expression of fear spread across her face.

'Tell me the name of your accomplice, the one who handed over this box or else…' Sankalp's eyes widened in anger as he said, 'I will make sure you rot in prison for the rest of your life!'

'Tell us the truth, and I will try and save you from this misery,' Mayuri added.

The prisoner stood rooted to the ground. Indecision weighed heavy on her mind for a few seconds, and then words rattled out of her.

'I will be murdered if I do that! No one can save me from him,' she sobbed and hung her head in shame.

'I promise to protect you. I promise. You will remain in our custody, and no harm will come to you or your family,' Sankalp reassured her.

The next day, Sankalp waited in the secret chamber along with the king and the woman, while the princess and the others sat in the main hall. Mayuri, knowing that her father still hoped that they were mistaken about Asudai, wanted to prove that he was indeed the culprit responsible for all the miseries in the kingdom. Soon, the beady-eyed Asudai entered the hall. The woman trembled in fear at the sight of him.

'He is the man! He has been using me to take messages back and forth,' she whispered.

'Are you sure it's him?' Trinyen Tsenpo asked.

'Yes, your highness, it is him!' the woman replied and dropped her head in shame.

The king now knew beyond a doubt that Asudai was indeed a traitor. He needed some time to digest the implications. He did not attend the gathering of elders that day. The princess informed everyone that her father had taken ill. The same evening, Trinyen Tsenpo met Sankalp and Mayuri in the secret chamber.

'We must stay quiet! I repeat—must! We cannot alert Asudai. Let's take the woman into confidence. She can help identify the last pawn in this circle of deceit. There must be someone carrying the messages to the invaders,' Mayuri exclaimed.

It was agreed that the woman and her family would be given protection in return for her help in nabbing the others. She was instructed to continue with her usual routine and keep receiving and delivering messages while also keeping the princess informed of her every move.

Unknown to Asudai, a counter-strategy was being laid out.

Things were therefore quite different from what they seemed to the invaders. The man carrying the message did not know the original note had been replaced with a new one. For once, the tables seemed to be turning in favour of Lhasa. They would be able to use the same network of foes to better their chances in the war that now seemed inevitable.

Within a fortnight, the king dispatched a small contingent led by his trusted commander to the southern provinces of his kingdom. Asudai was happy, convinced his plans were working.

The false message sent to the invaders had instructed them to mount an attack on this group with a small contingent of about a thousand men. Once again, the enemy was surprised by a second band of warriors lead by Bhumiputra and Divya Drishti. They landed a crushing defeat on the invaders and took many captive. But this time, all the captured soldiers were taken as prisoners. Lieutenant Rabtin took them to the southern provinces to be held there. It was now just a matter of time before the enemy realized something was amiss.

It was also time for Sankalp to come out of hiding and face the traitor, Asudai.

A day before the victorious contingent was set to enter Lhasa, Trinyen Tsenpo made an announcement to the royal court.

'All those loyal to the kingdom of Lhasa, we have in our midst a man who betrayed my trust and the faith of my people! I am ashamed of acts that I may have committed because of my trust in him.'

Trinyen Tsenpo rose from his throne before continuing.

'Today he will stand exposed, and you will decide his fate!'

Asudai caught the seriousness of the king's tone. He froze and paled with fear at the announcement.

At that very moment, Sankalp walked in! Astonishment was evident on everyone's faces. The warrior of Shaka, presumed dead, appeared holding his sword in hand! The sight of Sankalp sent shivers down the spine of the beady-eyed man. He realized something had gone drastically wrong.

'My king, he is the culprit who has been deceiving you and the people of this kingdom!' exclaimed Sankalp, pointing to Asudai. 'He is the one who has been plotting to betray the people and hand over the kingdom to his masters in the north. That was the real purpose for which he was sent here!'

Sankalp related the ordeal of the ambush and how his men had not only vanquished the attackers but made them change sides.

Advancing upon him, Asudai shouted, 'Your ignorance of statecraft betrays you, monk!' He turned to the throne and addressed the king with false contrition. 'He is a liar, Your Majesty! He is the one betraying you and the people. He was behind the plot to kidnap the princess!'

Meanwhile, Sankalp signalled the guard to bring the woman out of hiding. Two guards marched in with the messenger in tow. She related the tale of deceit spun by the beady-eyed traitor.

Enraged, Asudai knew his game of deceit and treachery was up. He drew his sword and pounced on Sankalp but was no match for the warrior of Shaka! The monk blocked the blow and retaliated with a cross swing that severed Asudai's sword hand. He fell to the floor.

Sankalp stared into his enemy's eyes as scattered memories from the past raced through his mind. Once again, the wails of despair from the women of his village echoed through the walls of his mind.

His expression turned fierce as he raised his sword and said, 'My sword yearns for your head! It is men like you who are responsible for all our troubles.'

Seething with malice, Asudai turned towards the gathering.

'You will pay for this with your lives! Surrender to me while you can. Our army will be here soon, and in no time, they will turn this…this pitiful kingdom to dust!' Asudai barked out a harsh laugh as he reeled in pain.

'Well, let me enlighten you on your little game plan,' Sankalp smiled.

He signalled to a courtier standing close by and whispered an order. The courtier immediately left the hall, followed by the eyes of those in attendance. A stunned silence filled the hall yet again, perhaps in anticipation that yet another bizarre event was about to unfold.

The courtier appeared moments later with Divya and the king's trusted general in tow. Asudai was shocked to see Captain Tshangpa with them! The men standing before him narrated the details of the ambush to everyone present.

Captain Tshangpa had arrived with six hundred soldiers the previous night. He had presented himself before the king and sworn allegiance to Lhasa.

Sankalp turned his attention to where Asudai lay. Staring down at him, he declared, 'The men sent to ambush our brigade are either dead or have joined forces with us. You had hatched a plot to get rid of our elite warriors, but we surprised your men instead. Your game of treachery is over!'

The guards surrounded the traitor, Asudai.

'Take him to the prison and hold him there,' ordered Trinyen Tsenpo.

Asudai turned to the warrior of Shaka. 'Surely, no one man can defend the kingdom against an entire army!'

Sankalp let his gaze drift slowly up and down the fallen man before he spoke. 'The passion, the fury that you see in one resides in many today!'

Still mumbling, Asudai was chained and dragged out of the hall.

'Don't hurt him. We may need him,' Sankalp instructed the guards.

Trinyen Tsenpo then addressed the royal court.

'No one—I say no one—will speak of this incident to anyone, at least not for now.'

A moment of silence ensued as everyone present absorbed his words and the seriousness of his tone. It was quickly followed by nods of approval.

Princess Mayuri was happy. A surge of emotion rushed through her, bolstering her with a sense of confidence and happiness.

The king, on the other hand, was infuriated for having trusted this man for so long but was thankful to Sankalp for bringing him to justice.

However, they all knew war clouds loomed large over the kingdom. The enemy had already begun massing across the Yarlung Pass for a possible invasion of Lhasa.

19

A Kingdom at War

Trinyen Tsenpo was ill at ease. He sat quietly in the gloom of the palace hall, knowing the invaders would soon launch their attack. His army was comparatively small, and the chances of an outright victory were slim.

'Father, you look worried. Tell me what ails you,' consoled Mayuri.

'My child, a host of events have conspired against us. I see the inevitability of war being brought forth on the kingdom and my people. The invaders have nothing to lose. But we, on the other hand, will pay dearly for peace!'

Princess Mayuri's euphoria from the previous day was marred by her father's words.

'But, Father, I remember you telling me that in life, there are times when one's resolve, patience and courage are tested, and it is in times like these that the destinies of nations are made or destroyed. Let us not think much and do what is right.'

Trinyen Tsenpo did not reply. A long quiet moment passed as both remained grim considering what lay before them.

The next morning, Mayuri met Sankalp. She looked uncomfortable.

'Princess Mayuri, is something the matter?'

Mayuri told him about her father's worries.

'Do not worry, Princess. I too have been thinking about the possible repercussions of our actions.'

'It bothers me that they could be preparing an invasion even as we speak.'

'We will have to face the invaders in battle one way or another. But there is something on my mind. I will discuss it with the king,' he assured Mayuri, much to her relief.

Sankalp spent the afternoon by himself. His thoughts focused on the future of Lhasa.

More than ever, he saw the uncertainty of life. Every moment was filled with infinite possibilities and choices that would determine the destiny of a kingdom and the lives of its people. The way ahead seemed harder than ever.

He sat with his eyes closed. For three nights, he remained in a world beyond sight, seeking answers.

Sankalp broke out of his trance to the soothing sight of a full moon. Exhausted!

Summoning the forces did consume a lot of his energy. He slowly walked out to the large veranda overlooking the palace gardens. He was surprised to see the princess there.

'Princess Mayuri, is everything alright? It's close to midnight.'

'I am fine, Sankalp,' Mayuri spoke softly. 'I haven't been able to sleep for the last two nights.'

Sankalp smiled with warmth. 'Don't worry, Princess. I will meet your father tomorrow morning.'

Mayuri smiled. Her delicate frame belied her unbreakable strength.

'You are indeed a daughter to be proud of and a counselor to cherish,' Sankalp remarked understandingly. 'In the meantime, get some sleep. I need an alert and attentive princess tomorrow, for you are indeed a daughter to be proud of and a counsellor to cherish,' Sankalp reassured her as he walked her to the door.

The next day, he met the king along with the princess. The king shared his worries and asked Sankalp for his advice.

'Your Majesty, I know what you have been feeling and understand the troubles weighing on your mind. There is no way out but to fight the evil designs of the invaders. Like you, my concern for the people is paramount, and I understand our chances of winning this war are slim.'

'What do you suggest? Is my marriage to Darqan Doodra the only way out?' Mayuri said and then grew silent and pensive.

'That will never happen…Never!' Trinyen Tsenpo declared, his eyes brimming with the affection that only a father can feel for his daughter.

Mayuri was surprised and, at the same time, extremely happy at her father's firm rejection of her words.

Sankalp nodded with a smile. 'Princess Mayuri, that is not what I meant, and neither is it the way out. I reckon his proposal of marriage is just another ploy to achieve the final objective of taking over the kingdom, but I have a plan that might work.'

'Will it save the people of our kingdom from the perils of war?'

Sankalp took a deep breath and paused for a long moment.

'Will it save Lhasa?' the king questioned again.

'I cannot be certain,' Sankalp said with a shake of his head. 'But we must take a chance. A chance that can save us from an all-out war.'

Sankalp put forward what he had in mind. Undoubtedly, the plan was ambitious yet pragmatic, given the circumstances. Trinyen Tsenpo nodded thoughtfully. Being an accomplished military strategist, he understood the finer details, the risks and gains alike.

The very next day, he summoned his captains and trusted generals and explained the battle plan. They worked through every eventuality. The generals, who had fought many battles alongside Trinyen Tsenpo, were convinced. They would be putting some of their best men at risk, but if the plan worked, they would be able to save the people from the horror of an all-out war.

A day later, Trinyen Tsenpo proceeded to make a formal announcement of war.

'My loyal men, you have stood by me in many battles, and many times I have trusted you with my life. You are well aware that we once again face a threat from the northern invaders. They have been like wolves in sheep's clothing. They ask for my daughter's hand in marriage on the one hand, while on the other, they continue to loot and plunder our land, their sole objective to enslave our people and rule Lhasa!'

He paused as the assembly roused with passion.

'Let me say that I was a fool not to see the reason they sent an emissary to my court. Under his influence, I may have committed some grave mistakes,' he paused again, his eyes solemn. 'But that is in the past. It is now time to face the enemy!'

The crowd murmured but fell quiet as the king stood up.

'We have amongst us a brave young man.' He raised his right hand and pointed towards Sankalp. 'He has proved his valour, courage and intelligence by leading us from one victory to another in the most daunting of circumstances. It is because of him that the treachery of the invaders stands exposed!' He turned to face his ministers. 'I propose we appoint him as the general in command of the royal army to lead the people of Lhasa to victory.'

There was unanimous approval and everyone cheered the appointment of the new general.

'To the brave and valiant!' their words resonated louder than ever.

Sankalp rose and nodded gracefully.

Princess Mayuri was more than happy, and unable to control her emotions, she hugged Sankalp.

That night they all celebrated his appointment to the highest post in the kingdom. The son of Lin had come a long way. The shepherd boy who enjoyed grazing sheep had become the general of one of the most powerful armies in the land.

Though he had more than earned his place in the palace and was looked after well by a retinue of servants, he did not entirely feel that he belonged there. His perspective had been moulded by a life that was like no other. Sankalp would often cast aside the comfort of his warm bed draped in silk to sleep on a mat on the floor. The warrior of Shaka had encountered life, mastered much and understood more than many men of his time. But he still missed his family. And as they looked upon him from unknown horizons, he knew they felt proud. He had given up much to tread the path and reach this far. But it could all be in vain. Pushing such thoughts out of his mind, he focused on the task ahead. There was so much to be done in very little time if at all his plan was to work.

Over the next two days, he sent messengers to Bhumiputra and Divya Drishti, requesting them to assemble their men and reach the city of Lhasa. Lhasa's trusted commanders were also told to assemble their best men. They would all embark on a rigorous training schedule together. This was important to establish better coordination among the soldiers.

Meanwhile, Princess Mayuri had been able to find out more about the man who had been meeting the woman from the palace and carrying messages to the enemy outpost. A trap had been successfully laid and executed by the princess. This man, a hired hand, had befriended the woman working in the palace. She had identified him, the last link in the chain of deceit. He was kept under watch but not arrested.

With the help of the woman, Sankalp cleverly replaced the messages being carried to the invaders' outpost. So far, the enemy remained unaware of the developments in Lhasa.

The rigorous training had begun apace. Sankalp instructed his soldiers in the art of guerrilla warfare, among other techniques. The men trained hard under his guidance, mastering not only the physical but also the mental elements of war.

'My men, the most important war is fought in your mind. If you win there, you can win anywhere,' he would emphasize. His words of encouragement helped his men strike a key balance between the mind and the body. It was all part of reinventing the self for what lay ahead. He spoke about the symbolic nature of war and how it tested one's capacity for sacrifice, courage and mental strength.

'Brave soldiers, trust my words when I say that the finest way to die is on the battlefield, where the brave meet death face-to-face, staring it in the eye without fear, to be born again as powerful men who shall forever live with grace and dignity till the cycle of life turns a full circle.'

These sermons were important as they kept the force motivated.

At dusk, the captains would deliberate on strategy on how best to use their resources. Captain Tshangpa was well aware of the enemy's tactics and offered valuable advice.

War undoubtedly brought suffering—more so upon the people who were largely at the mercy of their rulers. Was committing to this action part of a sacred duty, a solemn obligation to the motherland and their king? While some did question the motive behind the war, others were emboldened by the thoughts shared by Sankalp.

The monk explained to his men the finer dimensions of selfless action—how the action they were committing themselves to would not only save the kingdom but also ensure the freedom and survival of the coming generations. The complexities of physical action and its inevitability, including why it was one of the most important means of survival in the living world, had often been explained to Sankalp.

'Action can more fully be defined by the words sincerity, intention and, importantly, motive, and these combined result in honourable action. The spirit of freedom and reverence to our land and the spirit of sacrifice for the sake of others are all part of noble action—a superior motive. Inspired by such ideals, humans have performed great and ennobling acts, the fruits of which have been enjoyed by successive generations. Hence, the higher the ideal that motivates an individual, the more selfless is the action.' The words of Kalimpong were more inspiring now than ever before.

However, the simple folk feared what they were about to be a part of. Taking the life of another human did not come easy to them. Many had never been in battle. Sankalp spoke to them without betraying his fears regarding the daunting task ahead.

'Some of you have not witnessed the gruesome realities of battle and may wonder about the action you are committing to. What we are about to do—is it right?' He drew in a deep breath and then spoke with determination. 'Be sure, we do not fight because we covet another man's land or his possessions, but to save what is rightly ours! We are at war to resist the greed and hunger for power of an enemy. Fight and you will be remembered as martyrs in death! If you surrender, you will forever remain slaves. So fight and be liberated!'

The men listened to him intently, and in the days ahead, many of their doubts were cleared. They were ready to dedicate their lives to a greater purpose. They stood inspired by the cause.

The warrior of Shaka had gained time by replacing the messages being carried to the invaders. This allowed him to develop a complete battle plan. Bhumiputra was a master of the terrain that surrounded Death Valley. On Sankalp's advice, he had begun to entrench his fighters in the surrounding areas. This would give them a strategic advantage over the invaders.

The weather had remained extreme during the year. The mountain passes had witnessed quite a few landslides during the rains.

While the debris had covered a few of the known passes, newer passageways had opened up as a result of the ground shift caused by the landslides. Bhumiputra had gathered men from the nearby villages to clear the openings and establish newer and more accessible routes. These routes were not known to many. Knowing the enemy had vast resources at his command, and to ensure their own survival in the harsh terrain, Bhumiputra had established a supply chain along the new routes, which extended from the borders of Lhasa up to their forward positions. There had to be an uninterrupted supply of food and water, for men and animals both, in a battle that might last through the long fierce winter.

Divya Drishti, who commanded one of the battalions, instructed the captain of the royal guards to station his men between the enemy camp and the mountain pass close to Death Valley. Their objective was to cut off enemy supplies. Sankalp took it upon himself to lead another battalion comprising about two thousand men towards the Yarlung Pass for the first encounter.

On a night that had the royal family and the other generals in attendance, Sankalp proposed his thoughts.

'My king, we must send an emissary to the Mongol king. As you are aware, Darqan Doodra is a renegade general in his eyes—a deserter. We must inform him of our intention to bring this deserter to justice. The Mongol ruler can prove to be a powerful friend and ally,' explained Sankalp.

'Hmm, a brilliant thought. ' Trinyen arched an eyebrow. 'And we can use this opportunity to gain favour with the Yuans. I will request one of my ministers to leave immediately for the Mongol court.'

Trinyen walked up to Sankalp and rested his hands on the monk's powerful shoulders. 'My dear Sankalp, how can I thank you for what you have done? But I am sure we will have our chance once you are back, victorious!' Trinyen's eyes filed with gratitude.

'My king, as of now, this battle is reward enough. I have spent many nights waiting for my time…' he paused, as if reminiscing. 'For this very moment, when I stand face-to-face with the enemy. Destiny has given me that chance.' He paused and looked at Trinyen Tsenpo.

'I do have one request though.'

'Speak. It will be granted,' Trinyen smiled.

'Please take my advice and remain here.'

Trinyen Tsenpo was taken aback, albeit momentarily.

'That is not possible, Sankalp! I may be old, but I understand my duties well. A king has to lead his men and not remain in the comforts of the palace while his men fight to the death.'

There was a brief silence before Sankalp spoke.

'Your words bear the character of a man who is worthy enough to be called a king, even by a monk like me!' Sankalp folded his hands in a gesture of respect. 'I ask you to stay back not out of weakness but to protect the city. With your presence here, the men who leave their families behind will stand assured of their security. You will have a small contingent under your command.'

King Trinyen said no more; he only smiled.

Sankalp returned to his room and lay down to rest. A light knock at the door awoke him. He removed the silver shade from the lamp, and in its dim light, he walked to the door and opened it with caution. Mayuri stood there quietly in the thin light of the crescent moon.

'What is the matter, Princess? Why are you still awake?' He was surprised to see her.

'You will be leaving soon,' she regarded him quietly for a moment. 'And I wanted to see you before you left.' She slowly walked across the room to the veranda that it opened on to. Sankalp followed close behind, rubbing his eyes with his palms, a bit perplexed.

'My dear Sankalp, I don't know how to thank you for all that you have done for us. There is no way to repay your kindness, nor do I know the reason for your generosity.' A tear glistened in the corner of her eye as she spoke. 'Moreover, your presence has become a source of strength for us all.'

'Princess Mayuri…' Sankalp searched for the right words as the pause in their conversation stretched longer. 'I am just a monk, a wanderer. It is the magic of the stars that has bought me here. Do not fear; trust in yourself. For one day you will be queen.'

'But will you be here, with us?'

Sankalp smiled as he once again searched for the right words. 'Let the stars decide…when the time comes.'

Mayuri merely nodded before stepping through the shadow of the doorway. She returned to her chamber with many an unspoken word in her heart. This was no time to ponder over such matters. A war loomed large over the kingdom!

Fate had turned an indolent young lad into a wandering monk. A revolutionary to his people and a warrior that many now knew him to be. Unafraid, he had made this perilous journey. Yet, often enough he was caught in that beautiful and mysterious web of feelings. Even for men of his intelligence and understanding, the power of human emotion was overpowering. But eventually, it subsided into a calm acceptance.

That night, Sankalp shuttered his mind from the outside world and sat in solitude. His meditation was broken abruptly by a vision of battle, flooded with the terrible sounds of bloodshed mixed with defeat and victory alike. The terrain looked difficult but familiar. A large red-spotted butterfly danced close by. And then the vision faded as abruptly as it had begun.

He would confront the invaders amid the mountains, across the Yarlung Pass, he concluded.

Within three days, he prepared his battalion and set out for battle. It would take them at least a week to reach the ridge that connected to Death Valley. Captain Tshangpa was chosen to lead the brigade trained specifically in guerrilla warfare and mountain tactics. They were entrusted with the job of luring the enemy towards the high passes.

As Sankalp's battalion crossed one of the many mountain valleys on the third day, heavy rain poured down on them unabating, and the weather turned daunting with icy winds blowing relentlessly. While the horses marched ahead, the foot soldiers followed behind with a large retinue of animals, notably yaks. They were sturdy mountain animals; not only could they carry heavy loads but also provide the men with their nourishing milk—its nutritional value was unmatched in these cold lands.

The icy winds subsided as the clouds cleared after two days. Zanzi was by the side of his master, flying high in the skies and keeping a close watch on the ground. Sankalp wanted to meet Bhumiputra at the earliest. His men were well entrenched in the mesa around Death Valley. They had strategically stored their supplies in the previous days; this itself could prove decisive in battle. By the ninth day, Sankalp and his battalion were nearing Death Valley, and with that, the weather once again started to turn.

Divya keenly observed the skies as he said, 'Should we set up camp and wait for the storm to pass?'

'It would be better to keep moving. This area is prone to landslides,' Sankalp responded.

He was eager to meet Bhumiputra at a prearranged place and share his final battle plan. A decisive meeting between the two commanders before he moved his battalion towards the Yarlung Pass.

They travelled swiftly through the day, covering as much distance as they could on horseback. Until the light of day began to fade, and the icy winds made it difficult for both man and animal to climb the steeper part of the mountain.

'We cannot go any further,' Divya declared, raising his voice high enough to be heard over the whooping sounds made by the winds.

'Looks like we have some bad weather coming upon us,' Sankalp huffed slightly and raised his hand, signalling the convoy to a stop.

They set up camp for the night, taking shelter along the narrow mountain track. It gave them some relief from the bone-chilling winds. The men huddled close around their fires to survive the night.

Tired, the cavalry fell asleep earlier than usual. In the middle of the cold winter night, the winds changed direction, bouncing off the mountain face with increased intensity. They came down strongly on the sleeping men, extinguishing the flames that kept them warm and alive. Much as they tried, they could not light the fires again. Without their warmth, surviving the night would be impossible.

'We cannot remain here, the winds are dousing our fires. We must find another place to rest,' the camp leader shouted out.

'How will we find our way without torches?' a soldier asked.

The sound of his men's voices drew Sankalp out of the tent he shared with Divya. It did not take them long to understand the gravity of the situation.

Meanwhile, a soldier walked up to them. 'Sir, just ahead there is a path that leads down to a narrow gorge. It will be safer than here.'

'Hmm...how do you know about it?' Sankalp stared intently at him.

'Sir, I have taken my sheep to shelter there in the past. But the trek into the gorge is difficult.'

Brushing aside a host of uncertain thoughts, Sankalp patted him gently on his shoulder. 'Lead us,' he requested.

Divya quickly made the announcement to the soldiers. It did not take long for the men to prepare for departure, for they were accustomed to quickly breaking camp and moving.

The nimble-footed soldier took the lead of the convoy. Sankalp waited, letting a few soldiers pass by, and then along with Divya joined in the ranks. The area was covered with jagged rocks, some of them rising to thirty feet, and criss-crossed by deep and narrow gullies. It was not advisable to ride, so they walked alongside the animals.

It was a test of courage and endurance; the freezing winds wreaked havoc on both man and animal alike. They had to keep walking to keep their bodies warm; death was certain if they stopped. Slowly, the convoy kept moving forward. The best that Sankalp could do was get his cavalry to safety. Around him, many tried to help their fellow soldiers, but for the most part, they could only watch as tragedy struck.

After a few gruelling hours, they finally made it to the narrow gorge and felt immediate relief from the gelid conditions. But the trek had not been without loss—a few men and some animals had succumbed on the way.

At last, the cold dark night lost its grip to the warm rays of the rising sun.

Sankalp ordered the men to rest and have food. Despite the challenges of the night, their strategy seemed to be working. There were no reports of any enemy movement coming in from their scouts. By noon they were well rested and ready to leave. Sankalp wanted to descend the high passes before sunset. The weather at this height was always temperamental. He could not risk going into battle with a group of fatigued men.

They rode down the steep tracks as fast as their horses could carry them, finally reaching another narrow pass at the end of the ridge. The sun was low in the sky and the freezing winds swelled again. The cavalry came to a stop at a critical juncture. As planned, Sankalp rode ahead with about a thousand men. Divya took the lead and masterfully negotiated the tricky slopes. He led the rest of the battalion towards the plains below; there, they would set up camp for the night.

By the afternoon of the next day, Sankalp had covered considerable ground. Up ahead, the Yarlung Pass was within his sights. Interestingly, the advance party of scouts had sighted movement of an enemy platoon on the north-western side. The moon was high in the sky when his cavalry entered Death Valley.

As the faint glow of torches became visible on the other side, a look of relief crossed Sankalp's face. He was on familiar ground. They stopped and set up camp for the night. Sankalp consulted with captain Tshangpa before riding alone towards the lower part of the ridge. It was a place he knew well. Bhumiputra waited outside the cave close to the large apple tree. Little did he know that this cloistered domain had been Sankalp's home for many years.

The cave had offered him refuge then, and now he was out seeking the enemy from the very same place. Sankalp fought back the tears that welled in his eyes at such thoughts. He dismounted a few metres away from the cave. It was uninhabited but not deserted, though everything around it had either withered or evolved. The cavern, though, remained quiescent, magically preserved from the decay of time.

Sankalp slowly walked to where Bhumiputra waited and held him in a friendly embrace.

'I hope you did not have a problem finding the place?'

'No, it seemed as if I was almost led here,' said Bhumiputra, sounding curious.

A mysterious smile edged Sankalp's lips. 'Come with me,' he said as he led Bhumiputra inside the cave. Both men then sat comfortably within its confines. They spoke long into the night as Sankalp explained the finer parts of his strategy to Bhumiputra.

'I will take your leave now. Please get some rest while I arrange something for you to eat,' Bhumiputra said with concern.

'Pluck me a few apples from the tree outside,' Sankalp smiled. His eyes were lost in reminiscence as he remembered the time he had spent in the cave. 'My teacher called it the tree of life.'

'Will that be enough?' asked Bhumiputra.

'That is all the hunger I have left.' The smile stretched to a grin with a twinkle in his eyes.

Later, Sankalp sat in deep meditation. The ethereal powers prevailed upon his mind. The past and present retreated into oblivion. Slowly his subtle form transcended the here and now. He was joined by Kalimpong on a higher plane, in the parallel dimensions of time. He bowed to the learned master in reverence.

'Arise, my son. I see you enjoying the fruits of your toil,' Kalimpong said, exhibiting an esoteric smile. 'The apples from the tree of life do taste good.'

Sankalp saw beyond his smile and he understood.

'Master, O Master!' exclaimed Sankalp and held him in an embrace. The presence of his teacher on this unearthly plane calmed him.

'Master, I go into battle with my mind haunted. Not from the fear of death, but due to knowing that many of those accompanying me will not return. My conscience is plagued with just one thought…' He paused and then continued with a trace of hesitation.

'What I am about to do—is it right? Is it personal vengeance that has led to this war?' He hung his head and whispered, 'That would make me a murderer…' Sankalp hesitated briefly. 'Or is it truly the collective will of the people to rise against these tyrants?'

'Sankalp, you have become what you were meant to. And you are doing what is expected of you. What the world reads as right or wrong, good or evil, is a perception based on circumstance. Let higher consciousness lead your actions,' Kalimpong paused and gazed into the eye of his mind.

'My dear, you must use higher intellect to understand and define your true motive. Rise above this duality through the trueness of selfless action. Your conscious will then become one with the Shiva, the Brahma and the Vishnu. Centred at the equinox of these formidable forces, the world will then become a slave to your thoughts and your actions and words will be the very definition of dharma.'

He placed his hand a few inches above Sankalp's head. The force jolted his mind across past lives. It refreshed his memories, giving him an enhanced perspective. An uninterrupted view of the lives lived.

And then he heard the master say, 'You have indeed been placed in this position by the divine and collective will of those who knew you then and are with you now so that your physical conquest may eventually lead to annihilation of evil from this land!'

As this realization dawned on him, Sankalp's mind became clear in purpose. He became aware of what would lead him to a higher plane of existence. The chain of events that started many lives ago lay untangled.

Kalimpong floated closer to him.

'Sankalp, shadows of your past life will always motivate current action. Go forth and do what your destiny demands…' The vision dissolved into a tiny fragment of light before disappearing.

Sankalp emerged from his trance. The morning light was spreading across the night sky. It promised to be a cloudless day. Sankalp walked out of the cave to the small stream nearby. He refreshed himself in its freezing waters and emerged with a new resolve. It was time for battle.

In the meantime, Divya Drishti and his battalion had made their way towards the base camp of the invaders. They had positioned themselves strategically to target enemy supply lines and hold their movement. By afternoon, Sankalp started his descent from the bare ridges. The northwest terrain was rugged and dotted with clustered formations, which made the men less visible, giving them a better chance to catch the enemy unawares. The element of surprise would be crucial in this battle.

However, a lone horseman posted at a strategic vantage point keenly watched their movements. But as soon as Sankalp spotted him, the horseman bolted. If he was one of the invaders, he could be on his way to alert the troops stationed nearby. The slightest whiff of an attack could undermine Sankalp's plan and jeopardize the campaign.

Sankalp scowled as he considered his options. Moments later, he gave a command.

'Continue forward. We will join up with you soon!'

Sankalp knew the mountains well. He and a handful of men broke away from the others. They cut across the track and took a narrow culvert towards the ridge, riding briskly through the narrow rocky tracks, which were just wide enough to accommodate the sure-footed horses. It was a risk; the presence of the horseman confirmed the enemy soldiers were close. They could well be sighted by them. But this was the only way to stop the horseman before he descended into the valley and alerted the others.

The men rode like the wind till they reached an intersection. At this point, two paths merged into one and led down into the valley. They could see smoke rising from the camps not too far below. Just then the lone horseman passed them by under the ridge. He had outpaced them and was a turn ahead!

'Let us turn back, Sankalp. We cannot pursue him anymore,' shouted captain Tshangpa, wiping sweat off his brow.

Sankalp reigned in his horse; the stallion snorted and flared his nostrils before coming to a dead stop. Sankalp pulled out his bow, which was strapped to the horse's flank. He nocked an arrow, holding it delicately as his eyes followed the fleeing horseman and calculating the speed of the rider and the winds. Waiting for the right opportunity.

The pounding of hoofs and the rattle of armour slowed to a silence behind him. All eyes converged on the bowstring in bated anticipation. Calmly, without any nervousness or anxiety, Sankalp measured the distance. His hand pulled the bowstring a little further back than usual and then he let the arrow fly. It streaked through the air with a whizzing sound towards its intended target. Moments later, the horseman stumbled and fell into the deep gorge on the side of the mountain. A shrill cry from Zanzi rose to a crescendo as it circled above.

The arrow had found its mark! The men stood in silent deference to the demonstration of exemplary skill they had just seen.

The riderless horse was taken into custody. The men rode back to where the rest of the battalion waited. It was getting dark, and the enemy was close. Sankalp thought it was best to give his men an early break.

'Rest while you can,' he announced. 'We mount an attack on the enemy camp at first light!' On a more solemn note, he added, 'This battle could be long and exhausting.' Captain Tshangpa unsaddled his horse and sat beside the fire. A hand dropped on his shoulder; he looked up to see Sankalp.

'Take this shield,' he said, handing him one with a distinct red mark.

'I have mine,' Captain Tshangpa replied, a bit perplexed.

Sankalp smiled. 'You will need this more than the other.'

Captain Tshangpa said no more as Sankalp explained the reason.

The men were ready at the break of dawn. Sankalp spent his final moments before battle in deep meditation. Placing the incredible sword of balance in front of him, he drew its magical powers unto himself; steel and flesh merged in essence. The sword became him!

At first light, the men charged towards the camp of the invaders. The guards saw them coming and alerted the others. But it was too late! Sankalp and his men wreaked havoc on the troops. Minutes into the battle, Captain Tshangpa raised his shield. Lieutenant Rigzin and his men immediately responded. They broke away from their cavalry and joined forces with the warrior of Shaka. The plan worked with meticulous precision! Their shields bore a red mark in the centre, differentiating them from the others. None other than Sankalp and captain Tshangpa had known about this till before battle.

The sudden turn of events had a cascading effect. Most of the warriors ran amok, not knowing what was going on. Sankalp used the element of surprise to his advantage. The invaders were good fighters but could do little. The fearsome sword of balance drew blood with every strike! The enemy suffered heavy casualties, but it wouldn't be long before enemy soldiers stationed nearby would be alerted.

By afternoon, the invaders had rallied their second column. Their archers had taken up fortified positions. In fact, for the first time, the enemy seemed to be gaining ground; it became increasingly difficult for Sankalp and his battalion to break through their ranks. The sun set early for their sake. Curtains of smoke mixed with the failing light, deepening the darkness. The scent of blood clogged the air as men and beast both wailed their pain.

The warrior monk lifted his hand; Captain Tshangpa responded by raising the battle flag high and waving it twice. Both sides sounded retreat and led their men back to their respective camps, leaving a few to take care of the wounded and the dead.

Sankalp rode up the ridge with his cavalry to where they had camped the night before. From the heights, he noticed the third flank of enemy soldiers; they were on their way to join the others. It comprised nearly a thousand men! The message of the attack and the heavy casualties inflicted on the invaders had obviously been conveyed to the nearby enemy camp. So also the fact that the local unit of their ground forces had deserted. The invaders, though, had quickly rallied. Reinforcements were on their way and a new battalion would soon be forged, impatient for battle.

A small contingent of enemy soldiers followed Sankalp. They set up camp halfway atop the valley, keeping them in close view. The rest of their battalion continued to march and set up camp a few hours from where Captain Tshangpa's men were stationed. They were up to something. The invaders wanted revenge and the warrior of Shaka could feel it in the cold mountain air.

'Keep a keen watch through the night. Let me know of any movement that seems suspicious,' Sankalp told the guards.

He then sat with his close aides planning their next move.

'We have lost some good men and the wounded are being treated,' said one of his captains.

'Take good care of the wounded and bury the dead along with their armour.' The captain nodded. 'We must be extra vigilant. This stormy night might change the course of the battle,' Sankalp added.

'We will,' they affirmed and retired to their tents for the night.

Captain Tshangpa was the last to leave. He stopped and turned around with a question. 'Bhumiputra…where is he? I could do with his courage,' he said and a smile broke through his troubled expression.

'So could many of us,' Sankalp smiled in response and patted his captain's shoulder, putting him at ease.

In the dead of the cold winter night, a soldier posted at the checkpoint came to Sankalp's tent. 'You must come and see what is happening! There are thousands of torches illuminating the night sky and they are marching towards us.'

Sankalp came out of his tent. He was followed by his commanders and they quickly understood what was happening. The invaders were making up for lost ground by moving slowly through the night. This battle would not wait for the morning!

Sankalp stood in silent thought. The westerly winds had begun to pick up speed.

'We cannot rest,' he finally declared. 'You must get the soldiers ready before it's too late.'

Captain Tshangpa went still at the utterance and in an undertone asked, 'What are we going to do in the dead of the night?'

He was interrupted by a sentry who rushed in with more news.

'Sir, there is someone from the nearby village to see you. It's urgent, he says.'

'Send him in,' said Sankalp.

Two guards marched in with the messenger in tow.

'The winds have spoken,' he stated in a low voice. 'I bring word from the wise elders...' The man conveyed the message.

Sankalp listened attentively; the news was of significance! He gave thought to the circumstances before speaking.

'We must stop them at the narrow culvert. Only a few men can pass through at a time. We have a better chance to hold them there and thus gain time.'

'How will that help? They might send part of their large force from atop the ridge to surround us,' Captain Tshangpa expressed his doubts.

'Morning light will break early—the sky is clear to the east,' Sankalp declared. 'Trust me,' he reaffirmed. 'Now get the men ready and let's meet the invaders at the culvert!' Captain Tshangpa nodded, convinced.

Sankalp washed his face with water and then donned his armour. He quickly scribbled a message and let his pet falcon fly with it.

The soldiers had endured a long journey and fought a bitter battle, but no one slept that night.. Even a slight delay could cost them dearly. Sankalp guided his horse carefully down the stony slope that formed a large part of the narrow mountain pass, while the men silently followed. The darkness of the night aided their mission, keeping them invisible to enemy eyes.

The men drew their swords and laid an ambush, positioning themselves on either side of the passageway. The enemy narrowed their flanks, with only six horsemen leading the cavalry through the tapered path. The rest followed in one long and slow procession. No sooner did the first group emerge on the other side than they were charged at, the clamour of steel and metal echoing through the narrow passage. Sankalp and his men dominated the rhythm of the battle, striking deadly blows on enemy soldiers. The warrior of Shaka and his men slashed at everything that dared to cross the narrow entranceway. They managed to hold off the large army at this strategic point.

As expected, the invaders had dispatched a part of their large cavalry along the ridge. They were to mount an attack and surround Sankalp's force from behind. It was a clever move, given their superior numbers while they struggled to make headway at the narrow pass.

As the night progressed, Sankalp heard the cavalry moving along the snow-covered ridge. The drumming of hooves and the rumbling in the skies got louder. Sankalp looked up; the moon had disappeared to the west. A few large drops of freezing rain splashed to the ground.

His horse suddenly became fidgety and nervous. Its ears flicking, it stomped the ground with its right hoof. Within moments, the chilling wind picked up speed and began to howl. The earth shuddered once as it displaced a large quantity of rock and gravel, and then a second time. Sankalp looked intently at the snow line above before whispering a few unintelligible words. A moment later, he shouted out to his captains.

'Retreat towards the valley! Retreat now!'

The men immediately tugged at their reins and turned their horses half right. The night was dark and the torches burnt low. After several minutes spent manoeuvring in the dark, the men managed to break into a gallop. They rode down the precipitous trail, braving the stinging winds that hissed through the narrow passageway in a prelude to a great storm. They were followed closely by a battalion of the invaders. Sankalp crossed the ridge and moved towards the plateau. It was surrounded by steep formations and jagged rocks.

'Scatter and ride towards Death Valley!' Lieutenant Rigzin shouted and waved a bright orange flame. His men immediately began to break rank. The invaders thought they were fleeing in different directions. The captain of the invaders ordered his men to break file and chase the fleeing men. No sooner did the invaders break file than Sankalp lit the tip of an arrow and shot it into the sky.

The arrow pierced through the wind, rising high and streaking behind it a trail of shimmering red light that was visible till far. Bhumiputra spotted it in an instant. This was the signal he had been waiting for. With blood-curdling cries, he and his men rode out from behind the jagged rocks. Hearing the mountains resonating with their fearsome cries, a jolt of excitement raced through Captain Tshangpa and his soldiers. Despite the bold front they were putting up, they were on the edge both physically and mentally.

The first glimmer of light had appeared in the eastern sky. Sankalp raised his hand and called attention. The ranks immediately slowed in response.

'Left flank rally! Right flank turn!'

Captain Tshangpa waved a torch in a prearranged pattern, urging the right flank to break away and follow him. Sankalp meanwhile turned on the enemy with about three hundred fighters. Captain Tshangpa followed right with the rest of the soldiers to engage the enemy from the rear.

'Attack!' they commanded in unison.

The sudden change in tactic baffled the enemy. The invaders had presumed a bit too soon; they had broken formation to chase what they had believed was a fleeing army. Caught between two fronts, the enemy soldiers struggled to hold ground.

The invaders fought hard but could do little. By dawn, Bhumiputra and his men had landed a crushing blow on the enemy. The invaders lost many men, and with no reinforcements in sight, many retreated, while some surrendered.

Meanwhile, Divya Drishti and his battalion, led by Captain Rabtin, had attacked the base camp, cutting off vital supply lines to the enemy. This was one fierce battle, with the invaders putting up stiff resistance. Divya's force was numerically weaker, but his men fought hard. The battle lasted well beyond sunset, with neither side willing to retreat. Only escape or victory would decide the outcome. Before long, both captains faced each other in do or die combat.

The moment their swords met, Divya knew the enemy was as able as he. They tested their skills in every conceivable manner. Both battled for nearly two hours, matching their arsenals of blows and counterblows. Then suddenly, Divya altered his footwork and modified his attack. This unsettled his opponent and gave Divya an opening. The change in tactic ended favourably for Divya Drishti! The fall of their captain led to an immediate withdrawal of the enemy. Divya sounded the victory bugle, and a wave of celebration swept the ranks.

As it was too dark and dangerous to ride that evening, the battalion decided to set up camp and rest for the night. They were ready early the next morning and immediately started on their journey home. The morning winds were silent. It was unbearably quiet for the invaders. An avalanche had covered the ridge and the mountain passes the previous night, burying enemy camps and destroying the large cavalry atop the mountain. There was no hope of any more men joining them from the base camp. The information sent by the village elders and their knowledge of the land had proved fruitful.

As the sun rose higher over the vast Himalayan landscape, signs of victory were distinctly visible. The invaders were on the run. They had been cut down to a small number of men, who had decided it was best to escape with their lives. The lead battalion had surrendered and amongst them was their commander-in-chief, Tempa Dargaye, the man who had unleashed terror on the village of Shaka. He was the slayer of Sankalp's family and many in his village.

Tempa Dargaye knelt before Sankalp, drained of his power and ego. Sankalp narrowed his eyes and stared at the man, his mind racing back to the day of mayhem in his village. The cries of women and children echoed in his heart. He could never forget the sadness he had seen in those eyes.

'The time has come to atone for all your sins and bid farewell to this world,' Sankalp said, maintaining his calm.

'Spare my life and give me safe passage, monk!' Tempa Dargaye raised his head with a venomous smile and stared at Sankalp. 'I will make you a rich man—a very, very rich man!'

Sankalp was taken aback but only briefly.

Bhumiputra glanced at Sankalp—at the silent, expressionless stance that seemed to speak volumes.

'You...You think you can buy your life by making me rich?' replied Sankalp, his eyebrow raised in disbelief and anger.

'I have the finest collection of gold and gems and a harem with the most beautiful women! I will give them to you if you spare my life,' the commander declared.

Sankalp let out a huff and shut his eyes in an effort to forget what he had heard. And then, his usual composure was back.

'I will spare your life, but not for the gold and gems or the harem of beautiful women.' Sankalp shook his head. 'But in exchange for the life of the village headman, his family and all those you brutally murdered many years ago!'

'Even the gods cannot give them back to you,' he shook his head and growled in an undertone, 'But why do you care about an old man and his family when I can give you everything that can make you a king?'

'I am his son!' replied Sankalp. 'The kingdom I seek stands hidden from your eyes by a veil of lust, desire and hatred. My sword craves your blood! You are a murderer for me and for many in the villages. But by taking your life, I do not wish to deny my people a chance to serve justice.' He turned to Lieutenant Rigzin. 'Take him away and let the people decide his fate.'

Later that day, Bhumiputra shared vital information he had gotten from the prisoners. They had told him that two more cavalries posted to attack the kingdom of Lhasa stood devastated and lay buried under the avalanche. 'The news has been verified by our scouts,' reiterated Bhumiputra. Sankalp looked up, his eyes staring unblinkingly at the horizon. Slowly he dropped his eyelids and connected his mind to the surroundings. He could read their thoughts—the enemy was dejected and had lost their will to fight.

There was some good news from the palace too. The Mongol king had accepted the proposal of friendship from the kingdom of Lhasa. He wanted to seize this opportunity to teach the renegade general a lesson. He had sent a contingent of Mongol mercenaries to capture the general dead or alive! Darqan Doodra had realized he was trapped. Like his dreams, the rest of his army had deserted him. Afraid of his fate, Darqan Doodra was pushed to the edge. Dropping his sword, he had walked to a ledge on a high mountain. Below him stared a dark, unending emptiness.

Gathering what little courage he was left with, he had fallen into its realms!

Courier pigeons sent by the invaders to various outposts had confirmed the news.

With victory ascertained, Sankalp and Bhumiputra started their victorious ride back towards Lhasa.

The ride back was slow as the men carried injured soldiers. Some also carried the bodies of their close friends and brothers to give them a final farewell at home, while many lay buried on the battlefield. They were the immortals! The mountains would forever resonate with the stories of these courageous and gallant warriors.

They set up camp at the base of the valley where Divya Drishti was to meet Sankalp. There was singing and dancing as the men celebrated their victory at night. While his men celebrated, Sankalp sat quietly considering the task completed and what lay ahead.

The kingdom of Lhasa, though, was astir with just one thought: Victory! Of this, only a few had dared to dream, and one man had made that dream come true.

The sun rose early on the fourth day of the march back home. The winds were calmer and gentler, a sign that the bitter winter would soon be over. Sankalp waited that beautiful morning for Divya Drishti. He was to join them at the mountain pass across Death Valley. After waiting till the afternoon, Sankalp decided to proceed towards Lhasa. Many men in his army were tired and wounded. They wanted to get back to their families, which were waiting impatiently for their return. Sankalp was concerned about Divya, and the fastest way to get information about his whereabouts was to use his eyes in the sky. He whistled for his pet falcon, and when Zanzi came, he tied a note to his leg. 'Fly!' he commanded. 'Seek out Divya Drishti for me.'

The falcon immediately took wing and flew towards the high mountain ranges.

Sankalp turned to one of his captains. 'Follow him, Captain, and take some soldiers with you. He will lead you to my friend.'

The captain and his men promptly turned their horses southwest of the mountain pass, while Sankalp rode ahead with the rest of the cavalry.

Songs of victory rang out up and down the ranks as the men continued their march at a brisk pace. The days were getting longer; if they rode well, their harvest-laden fields would be in their sights by sunset of the next day.

A party of advance riders had ridden to the capital. They had informed the king and Princess Mayuri about their glorious victory. The city immediately broke out in joyous celebrations. The princess requested the king to let her welcome the heroes at the city gates.

The dwindling light of the setting sun was compensated by the glow of a thousand lamps that lit the path to the main gates. The victorious army, led by the warrior of Shaka, entered the city amidst much fanfare.

On a raised stand, Princess Mayuri stood eagerly in waiting.

'Victory to the warrior of Shaka! Our savior!' shouted the crowds gathered to welcome them.

Mayuri had never thought she would be so relieved to see Sankalp again. Amidst the shower of rose petals, she stepped down from the platform to greet him.

'This victory is for the king and, above all, the people of the kingdom,' Sankalp declared, smiling.

'Where is Divya? And I don't see Bhumiputra?' Mayuri looked at him eagerly. 'Why are they not with you?'

'My Princess, Bhumiputra has taken the captured men to my village along with their captain, Tempa Dargaye, the slayer of my family! He will be put to trial by the village council of Shaka.'

Mayuri nodded. 'And Divya?' she looked expectantly at him for an answer.

'I don't have any news of him yet. But his cavalry was seen moving south. I have dispatched some men to track them.'

It was a night of joyous celebration for the tired men. Sankalp spent some time visiting the homes of the soldiers who had not made it back. He and the princess consoled the grief-stricken families. Mayuri immediately announced suitable rewards that would allow their families to live comfortably in the years to come.

The king was also eagerly awaiting Sankalp's return, and when the monk finally arrived at the palace, he wrapped Sankalp in his arms and exclaimed, 'Welcome, my son, the priceless jewel of Lhasa! Rest for now, but we await your presence in the royal hall tomorrow.'

The king then left Sankalp in the care of the princess.

Meanwhile, all was not well for Divya Drishti. His battalion had many wounded soldiers and only a few horses to carry them. Their progress slowed further as they approached a forested valley. By afternoon, they neared the lip of a small ravine. As they crossed a grove of trees, Divya dismounted and walked to a warm water spring nearby. A few guards remained within calling distance.

Out of nowhere, an arrow shot from nearby pierced his armour! He immediately felt dizzy and short of breath. Gasping and choking, he fell to the ground. The arrow had been shot by a hired assassin. He and his cohorts had been lying in wait, camouflaged in the trees. Divya Drishti and his men were not used to the tactics of a defeated enemy. The inexperience of a few and complacency had led them to lower their guard. A mistake with dire consequences!

Divya lay wounded close to a mountain pass. One of his soldiers spotted the assassin and his companions trying to flee as they climbed down the trees they had been hiding in. They were killed by Divya's bodyguards.

Sankalp, tired from his journey, fell asleep with the court physician still tending to his wounds. It wasn't long before the desperate cries of his pet falcon broke the hold of sleep over him. He opened his eyes to find Zanzi with a message tied around his leg.

They had found Divya Drishti; he was badly wounded! With no time to waste, Sankalp asked the princess to arrange for his horse and requested the royal physician to accompany him. They rode out within moments, followed by Mayuri. She feared for Divya's life. Zanzi took to the skies, leading the way. They rode all night without stopping for food or shelter. And then, the falcon swooped down, close to the grove where Divya lay.

'Divya! Divya! Where are you?' shouted Mayuri in desperation.

'Calm down, Princess. I can see his men by those rocks, where Zanzi is perched. He must be with them.'

Sankalp quickly dismounted and ran to where a handful of men stood, their faces covered with gloom. They were surrounding a makeshift tent in which their captain lay. Rabtin stood with his hands hanging limply by his sides, feeling helpless and dazed. Sankalp could see Divya Drishti lying unmoving. He looked pale, but the men had managed to pull out the arrow that had pierced his armour. Sankalp quickly cradled Divya's head in his lap while the physician examined him. He ran his fingers from his wrist to the neck and down to his chest, gathering vital clues of life and how to save it.

'The blood is dark and his pulse feeble.' The elderly physician paused. 'He must regain consciousness, otherwise it will be difficult to save him,' he remarked with concern.

The princess, unable to control her feelings, broke into tears as she looked at him.

'Move him so his head is facing the sun,' Sankalp instructed. Sadness gripped him as he looked at the physician. 'Please do your best to save his life.'

He watched Mayuri tend to Divya's wounds. She refused to leave his side.

The day went by with little reprieve. Divya lay unmoving, his breathing erratic. The experienced physician used all his ability and knowledge of alexipharmic herbs to cleanse Divya's blood. He was able to stabilize his vital signs after nearly forty-eight hours.

The summer sun rose early, and so did Divya Drishti from his deathly slumber.

'Ahhh…' he groaned. 'Where…Where am I?' he muttered, dazed. He blinked a few times, trying to recognize the figure seated next to him.

'Divya, it's me, Mayuri,' the princess said softly, wiping his forehead with a piece of cloth doused in cold water. She was trying to bring down his high fever.

'Princess Mayuri! What are you doing here?'

'We found you unconscious by the grove. How do you feel?' she said with concern.

'Ah…Ahh…!' He let out a moan. 'I have a terrible pain in my back. Where is Sankalp? I need to tell him…tell him that we were successful in our mission,' he coughed. 'But we lost quite a few men in battle…' he mumbled, still groggy.

'He is here. Don't speak; conserve your energy,' Mayuri urged.

Divya had survived and returned from the very gates of death! Sankalp, unknown to anyone, had spent the past two nights meditating upon the powers that be…

Early the next morning, Sankalp made his way to the tent where Divya Drishti was resting. They all sat surrounding him, while the able physician checked his pulse. There was a long silence before he spoke.

'He has survived the crucial hours and his pulse is better!' The physician sounded and looked relieved. 'Rest, while I prepare a potion to get your fever down.'

'Feeling better?' quizzed Sankalp.

'I think…I will live,' Divya jested, confronting his contused reflection in a mirror across the table. 'I owe my life to you… or perhaps the falcon?' he said smiling. 'Princess Mayuri just told me how you managed to find me.'

'She has been awake the entire night,' Sankalp said and let out a chuckle. 'And if she doesn't leave your side soon, we will be carrying home one sick princess.'

His banter elicited a laugh from Divya, while Mayuri lowered her eyes, not knowing what to say.

'Thank you for all that you have done to save my life…'

'Rest; don't talk! Mayuri interrupted and allowed herself a small smile. 'Let me prepare some porridge,' she quickly added and left the tent.

The accomplished physician possessed great skills and knowledge of life-giving herbs. Bright sunlight, the altitude and unmerciful temperatures sustained unique medicinal plants deep in the high mountains. He rode with Sankalp to collect them, while Mayuri remained with Divya, never leaving him alone for more than a few moments. Her unrelenting care helped his recovery. His wounds healed quickly over the next few days, and soon Divya was able to walk unassisted.

The physician decided it was best to ride back to the palace. Divya would be comfortable and more at ease there. On the way, Divya Drishti narrated how they had emerged victorious in their endeavour in spite of being heavily outnumbered by the enemy. He then told them how a single arrow shot by an unknown assassin had managed to pierce his armour.

'I tried to call for help but couldn't. Slowly, I lost control of my senses and fell. I don't remember much after that.' He pressed his palms to his forehead, trying to recollect the moment. 'When I briefly regained my senses, I was happy to see Zanzi and a few men by my side. I must have lost consciousness then and when I woke up again,' he said and smiled, staring at the audience of three. 'I was laid up in bed with a charming woman beside me. Surely I am in heaven, I thought.' Divya smiled broadly.

Mayuri burst into a laugh, and so did the others.

'That arrow had a poisoned tip that paralysed your muscles temporarily,' the physician explained. 'The poison affected your mind and muscles. If it had not been treated in time, it could have proved fatal. Your armour proved its worth. The tip just grazed your body. Had it pierced you completely…' he fell silent, letting them imagine what he couldn't say.

'Saved by the handmaiden of destiny,' Divya smiled. 'My father's armour, I meant,' he said, pointing to the metal plate, which bore a female form.

Sankalp stirred in his saddle and looked at him with brotherly affection. 'What matters is that you are safe, healing and so yourself,' Sankalp chuckled, offering amusement in a bid to overcome the seriousness of the last few days.

By sunset of the third day, they had reached the lands owned by Divya Drishti.

'I will ride on to my house and see my mother; she must be eagerly waiting for me.'

Sankalp nodded at once.

'Bind my wound,' Divya told the physician. 'I don't want my mother to see it.'

The physician padded the area with cotton and tied a bandage around his chest. Divya wore his armour over it, concealing the damage that was already healing.

'Sankalp, I will join you later at the palace,' Divya said and urged his horse towards the entrance of his estate.

'I will come with you,' Mayuri declared and spurred her horse after him.

The people working in the fields saw their master ride in with a beautiful woman. They hailed him from a distance.

Their faces lit up with joy, and a few women rushed to inform his mother. She was overjoyed to see him.

'Divya...Divya!' she cried out with a loud gasp and embraced him, her hands running over her son's body as she looked for signs of injuries. She let go of the breath she had been holding, convinced he was well and unhurt.

'Mother, we are on our way to the palace. I stopped by to tell you that we were victorious in our battle against the invaders!'

Tears of pride filled her eyes. 'Your father would have been so proud,' she said, gazing at her battle-attired son.

Divya then excitedly turned his attention to Mayuri. 'Do you recognize her?' he asked, pointing at Mayuri with a tinge of amusement.

The old lady looked at her with an expression of love as she tried to place the face.

'Mother, this is Princess Mayuri,' Divya reminded her.

A gleam leaped into her eyes as she recognized the princess. She immediately embraced the young woman. She and the queen mother had been close companions once.

'You have your mother's eyes and are prettier still. May her blessings be upon you,' she murmured.

Mayuri held her in a genuinely loving and grateful embrace, her eyes fluttering with a hint of tears.

Later that day, Divya Drishti and Mayuri rode back to Lhasa. Trinyen Tsenpo had been awaiting their return to the palace. Though he had been duly apprised about the difficult but successful campaign against the enemy, he was worried about Divya. The king heaved a sigh of relief on seeing him enter the palace with the princess.

'My dear Divya, is everything all right? I was very worried when I came to know what had happened,' he exclaimed.

'I am fine, sir. Just a small wound. A reminder of a well fought battle,' Divya chortled with his usual good humour.

'My son, I am deeply indebted to you for what you have done. You have made us all proud!' The king paused. 'I know words cannot offer much solace after what happened to your family,' his voice choked a bit with emotion as he took a few steps towards Divya. 'But you must understand that I too fell prey to the plot of treachery and deceit hatched by the very man I trusted!'

Divya had not intended to remain at the palace, but the king's enthusiastic welcome prompted him to think otherwise.

In the meantime, Bhumiputra had taken Tempa Dargaye, the captive commander of the invaders, to Shaka and brought him before the village council.

The council, led by Rangdol, came to a quick decision. They decided to execute him but spare the others. The captured men would be set free after five years. Till then they would labour in the fields and rebuild the houses they had destroyed in many villages.

The city of Lhasa celebrated for nine nights. On the tenth day, a grand ceremony was held in the royal court. Honours were bestowed upon the soldiers who had bravely fought for the kingdom, for Lhasa. Representatives from many lands attended the ceremony. The kingdoms of the south had learnt of the brave men who had saved Lhasa from the treacherous invaders. The Mongol king too had sent his representative, thanking Trinyen Tsenpo. They were all part of the grand ceremony.

One by one, they declared their allegiance, thereby once again establishing Lhasa as a powerful and righteous kingdom.

The court brimmed with dignitaries. Rows of seats covered in rich velvets stretched across the hall. Close to the throne sat the king's advisors and ministers. After them were the representatives from various kingdoms, seated in order of the power they wielded. Overhead, the gilded, domed ceiling rose high. Around the lower part of the dome were small windows adorned with coloured glass that reflected the sunshine in varied colours. The dome was beautifully painted with figures of celestials, who gazed down at the august assembly.

Sankalp walked with the king towards a dais amidst the chanting of sacred verses. Consecrated water was sprinkled upon them as they passed. Sankalp took his seat on the dais alongside the king. He was accompanied by Bhumiputra and Divya Drishti. Across sat Princess Mayuri with the ministers and visiting dignitaries.

First, the soldiers who had fought valiantly and those who were slain in battle received due recognition. The crowd hailed Captain Tshangpa, Rigzin and Rabtin as they came forth one by one and received their honours.

The king then decorated the heroes who had led the army to victory.

Bhumiputra the lame was nominated as a general. He had under his command the armies of the north. When Divya Drishṭi was formally introduced, Princess Mayuri was the first to rise as he strode past her to the king. He gracefully saluted the assembly and the ministers, but reluctantly accepted being appointed governor of Lhasa, though he did not let his emotions show.

Once again, the gathering hailed their brave heroes with loud cheers.

Amidst the applause, Trinyen Tsenpo stood up and raised his hand. A gong sounded twice, bringing the audience to near silence. It was time to honour the greatest hero of Lhasa—Sankalp, the warrior of Shaka!

'To all who have come from far and near, and our guests from the distant lands of the south. Let me introduce the saviour of Lhasa,' announced the king. He walked up to Sankalp, who stood up in respect. He held the monk's hand and raised it high. 'Brothers, with your approval, I would like to honour Sankalp, better known as the "warrior of Shaka", by conferring upon him the title of "Makchi", the commander of commanders.' The assembly roared in jubilation at his appointment.

Mayuri watched with excitement as her father made the announcement. Sankalp was decorated with the many honours that came with his title. Yet he stood calmly, his expression conveying modesty. He watched composedly as attendants brought in trays and uncovered them to reveal gold and silver coins as well as precious gems and pearls. This was followed by an announcement that ordained him the absolute owner of large tracts of lands, including farms and orchards, in all four directions.

With the pronouncements over, the gong sounded again. The gathering proceeded for dinner.

During the banquet, Princess Mayuri divided her time between trying the many dishes and conversing with her guests. The feast was indeed lavish, and by the time the last course was served, it was nearing midnight. The gong rang once, marking the end of the meal, and then a second time, preceding an announcement.

The musicians and artistes immediately stopped their performance. The king stood up, and so did the others. Trinyen Tsenpo surveyed the gathering for a moment and then looked at Mayuri affectionately.

'The reign of your king is over,' he announced.

The bustle of activity suddenly slowed down, and the gathering fell silent at the king's declaration.

Clearing his throat, he continued, 'My duty is done.' He folded his hands respectfully and turned to face the gathering. Emotions brimmed over as he spoke. 'We will soon have an Empress of Lhasa,' he declared and looked at his daughter with delight. A moment of emotionally charged silence hung over the two and his close aides.

'Your mother would have been so proud,' he concluded with a smile.

Princess Mayuri stood up, and all eyes fell on her as she gracefully walked up to the king. Mayuri hugged her father with tearful eyes.

'Not now father. Not now,' she whispered, keen to avoid any further attention on her.

With inexplicable grace, she signalled to the assembly to continue with the celebration.

20

The Final Conquest

The city was lit with joy and bore a festive look. Many people thronged the streets, celebrating. The revelries honouring the soldiers lasted another two nights, and by noon of the third day, the city was again buzzing with its usual business-like activity.

Sankalp was in the palace garden, thinking how happy and proud his family would have been had they witnessed this glorious moment. He thought of Titla and almost immediately many images flashed through his mind, filling his heart with a host of sensations. But everything seemed so distant, so far in the past…

As always, Sankalp returned to himself, satisfied. He had achieved what he had set out to do. The realization had a calming effect on his mind. Despite this, he often felt a sense of unease. A recurring question arose in his mind. Should he be here or elsewhere? The whispers grew stronger as the days passed …

He conveyed his thoughts to the princess when she joined him in the palace gardens a few days later. Mayuri guessed his decision to leave by the sight of his face, even before he spoke.

'My Princess, I have enjoyed your hospitality for a long while and my work here is done. The kingdom is secure. I know you are more than capable of handling its affairs with the help of your father and his council of ministers.'

'Sankalp, please don't leave now!' The sadness in her voice was obvious. 'You have just returned from battle. The people need to know you are here, with them.' She walked around the patch of white tulips between them and, with a tender expression, held Sankalp's hand.

'My father places more trust in you than anybody else. And I still need to learn so much,' she sighed. 'What is it you seek? I promise I will find it and bring it for you,' Mayuri said rather innocently.

Sankalp listened, his gaze upon the setting sun. He looked deep into her eyes and then reached out to place his hand on her shoulder in a gesture that held far too much tenderness to be cited as indulgent.

'I care about you and the kingdom. After a long time, there is a chance of stability in the region. A time for new political alliances that will redefine Lhasa. My Princess, I see hope in you, and so do your people.'

They stood in quiet stillness till a gong alerted them that the evening's festivities were soon to begin.

'Let us join your father for the evening,' Sankalp urged her, gesturing towards the banquet hall. Mayuri nodded and followed in his steps, ever so dignified.

After a well-staged performance by various artists, dinner was served. Trinyen Tsenpo requested Sankalp to stay after the meal was done. He wanted to speak to him about something important. They met later in the king's private chamber.

'My dear Sankalp, I have no words to thank you for all you have done for this kingdom. Princess Mayuri has informed me of your intention to leave. It makes me sad,' he said wistfully. 'I am getting old, my son, and Lhasa needs someone like you to secure its future. Do me and the kingdom one last favour; accept the hand of my daughter, the princess. She is blessed with beauty, intelligence and grace and will prove to be a worthy wife. I can find no better match in all the lands for my daughter,' Trinyen spoke from his heart.

'Your Majesty, you have honoured me enough with many privileges.' Sankalp smiled, and drawing in a deep breath, he continued. 'In this elaborate drama of destiny, I have only played my part. Princess Mayuri is a woman with exceptional qualities. I am sure you will soon find a match worthy of her.'

Trinyen Tsanpo nodded, almost reluctantly. 'Sankalp, the depth of your words and understanding of life far exceeds my simple thoughts. All I can do is express gratitude for what you have done. The future of this wonderful city is in your hands, and so is the welfare of its people. I am sure that with you as king, the city will stand safe from marauding invaders and prosper greatly,' he said, pressing Sankalp in the hope that he would agree to stay.

'I cannot stop you from leaving, but may I request you to rethink your decision? And while you do so, please continue to be our honoured guest at the palace.' The king's voice was heavy with emotion.

Sankalp inclined his head in acceptance. He agreed to remain at the palace for some more time.

Yes, he could well be king. Have a beautiful princess as his wife. A conqueror he would be known as, commanding a powerful army together with all the treasures and the rich lands of the kingdom. A tempting thought! And it did cross his mind.

Sankalp spent the rest of his days at the palace enjoying the pleasures it offered. For once, he lived like many men of the world. At times he felt vulnerable, afraid and exposed to the hollowness of the world.

He realized how easy it was to sink into worldly pleasures and how equally difficult to give them up and return to a certain nothingness. The pull of materialistic attachment was indeed intense. The mind enjoyed indulgence. The more freedom it got, the more it strayed, chasing everything that offered superficial fulfilment and generated a false sense of pride. It was difficult to remain bathed in this pool of ceremonial existence and remain untouched. It was indeed challenging to survive the onslaught of power and wealth.

He recalled stories of kings who had enjoyed power and wealth beyond imagination but whose inner self lay corrupted with ego. Once the ego superseded conscious reality, the intrinsic balance between the mind and the higher intellect faltered. It clouded the power of judgment, causing a distinct lack of understanding between the self and the surroundings. Once that happened, one began to exist in a surreal world, hallucinating about a world completely different from the existing reality.

Like the living, nations too had a fate, their destiny intricately intertwined with that of their rulers. Often, when a ruler fell from grace, so did the kingdom. A good ruler, hence, ensured the survival not only of his kingdom but also of his people. Yet again, Sankalp was caught in a dilemma that life had presented before him. He would indeed make a good sovereign with the powers bestowed upon him. But did he see himself as one? For a short moment, a flash of emotion invaded his calm. But his mind was strong and remained connected with his true self. Sankalp composed his thoughts and realized he would be more at peace and his thinking clearer if he were not in the palace.

It was one of those bright spring mornings. Sankalp accompanied Trinyen Tsenpo to the palace gardens. It had become a daily ritual before they presided over matters in the royal court. They continued to walk and debate over the subject at hand till both came to an agreeable conclusion.

After a few minutes of silence, Sankalp addressed the king in all humility.

'My king, I wish to take your leave and spend some time in my village.'

Trinyen looked up, a little surprised.

'As your guest, I have enjoyed luxuries beyond compare. But I need to be on familiar ground before I make a decision.'

In a low voice that held regret, Trinyen asked, 'My dear Sankalp, please speak your mind. Is there anything you need? Something that is not available here? I am sure it can be brought from your village.' The king felt sad at the thought of Sankalp leaving Lhasa.

Sankalp smiled, searching for the right words to express his thoughts. An uncomfortable silence fell between them for a moment.

'My King, I need to go back to my village where nature predominates and the world doesn't.'

A pleasant quiet followed his words. The king smiled and preferred to listen rather than speak.

'I miss the air of my village. The feel of the mud that stands splattered on the walls of my house, and the twinkling of stars in a clear night sky.' His eyes glowed with an unworldly light. 'Once again, I wish my dreams to awaken to that unseen reality…' He broke away from his thoughts and continued softly, 'I will be back by the next full moon. By then, I will know.'

Trinyen Tsenpo nodded but said nothing until they reached the edge of the palace garden.

'Very well then, I shall eagerly await your return,' Trinyen Tsenpo finally said, making no effort to curb his sadness.

That same evening, the monk bid farewell to the king and the princess, assuring them of his return.

Sankalp rode out a little before dawn; he left his horse at the stables owned by Divya Drishti. A trusted attendant discreetly took charge of the horse. Sankalp then continued his journey back to his village on foot, preferring to walk as he once did on his way to the kingdom of Lhasa. By sunset of the fourth day, he had reached the narrow ridge overlooking Death Valley. He was followed closely in the sky by Zanzi. The saker falcon never left his master's side.

The warrior of Shaka crossed Death Valley, the place a reminder of the glorious battle that had liberated the mountain people from certain domination. The air grew colder through the night as Sankalp lay down to sleep under a clear night sky. By afternoon of the next day, the valley once again shimmered with cool spring air. Sankalp entered his village a little before sunset. The long journey had been refreshing.

He walked along the narrow lanes. A misty darkness formed by a mix of smoke and the brisk evening air hung over the village. He felt the difference from before; the atmosphere was calm and peaceful. A sense of well-being pervaded. The men sat relaxed around their fires after a good day's work, while the women worked in their kitchens, preparing the evening meal.

Sankalp slowly made his way towards his home, taking care not to attract any undue attention.

Children played around, while the elders sat smoking pipes and discussing the day's happenings. The fear and despair that had once stalked the village were no longer visible.

A village elder noticed the strangely clad man, resembling neither a warrior nor a monk, but with a persona that was far too intense to be ignored. The man immediately realized who he was.

'Welcome back, son of Lin!' he exclaimed. He was heard by many who sat nearby. They rushed to welcome the monk. Sankalp returned their greetings with a nod, his palms joined together in the customary way. The commotion made the women leave their chores to get a glimpse of their hero, the great warrior of Shaka! They looked upon him with reverence. For them, he was more of a mystical figure, the stuff of which folklore was made, rather than a reality they could see and touch.

The commotion alerted Bhumiputra. He sat up on his bed, where he lay resting after the day's work. All of a sudden, he heard the familiar call of the saker falcon. It flew by his window, alerting him of the master's arrival. Bhumiputra wasted no time and rushed out to meet the man who had led them in an epic battle. A struggle, a victory that would be remembered for a long time in the mountain lands. He was the one who had taken upon himself the responsibility of failure and crowned his men with the fruits of victory.

'Welcome home,' exclaimed Bhumiputra, holding Sankalp in a brotherly embrace.

'My dear Bhumiputra, I am happy to see you and the residents of the village, they look well!'

'Well enough!' responded Bhumiputra with a broad smile.

By this time, a large crowd had gathered in front of the house.

'Welcome, warrior of Shaka! Welcome to the great warrior of Shaka!' was the cry reverberating through the tiny Himalayan village.

This was an unexpected visit, and a delighted Rangdol and his son Rabtin were more than happy to receive Sankalp.

'How are things in our neighbouring villages? Now that justice has been served.'

A smile curled Rangdol's lips in answer to the question. 'Finally,' he said fervently. 'All is well here. And what about Lhasa?'

Sankalp smiled back. 'Every land lives its own destiny.'

That night, the village celebrated the return of their hero. The women put together a magnificent feast. The singing and dancing did not stop—not till the tired folks finally went back to their homes well past midnight.

'Please share my humble abode for the night,' a village elder offered Sankalp.

'I am indebted to you for your kind hospitality. But today I seek refuge in my home. The one that everyone in the village so passionately helped me build,' Sankalp smiled.

'My son, why be alone, with no one to look after your needs? Instead, go to your home in the morning,' suggested the elder.

'I won't be alone,' the monk answered simply.

He bid goodbye to the village elder and proceeded towards his house. He was accompanied by Bhumiputra.

'Master, do you really wish to be alone tonight? I would be honoured to share my simple home with you,' said Bhumiputra.

'Bhumiputra, tonight I need to be by myself and reach into my past,' Sankalp replied, his expression solemn. 'It

Then each one told their father what he wanted to be.

The house once again resounded with their laughter. He could feel the thread of his emotions connecting with theirs. At that moment, his subconscious pierced the fourth dimension.

His brothers stood before him!

'Dear Sankalp, you have indeed become the greatest warrior of all,' they said. 'And we have been with you all this time, sheltering you and helping you realize your dream. As you have been with us in the many lives before, making us realize ours.'

'My son,' said his father, 'we all stand witness to your journey through life. It has made us proud. Go forth and conquer your destiny, mind traveller!'

Sankalp gazed intently into the haze that surrounded them until another form became more visible. He could not contain his feelings on seeing his mother.

'Mother...Oh, Mother!' For a moment, his emotions flowed unchecked.

'My son, how wonderful you have grown up to be!' she exclaimed.

'Oh how I have missed you!'

'I have been with you, always,' she smiled with unworldly affection.

'I know...I have felt your loving touch when I needed you most. I have missed you all so much; please be with me now. There is nothing more I need—nothing other than to be here with you!'

'My son, we will soon part from this lovely moment. But it will only be temporary in nature. You will always feel our subtle presence around you,' she consoled him. Then she moved closer and, in a parting gesture, kissed him on the forehead. For a moment, Sankalp seemed to lose his self-control. His eyes welled with emotion. Then, as quickly, the images faded.

will help me decide my future.' So saying, he bid fare\ Bhumiputra and entered the gate to his home.

A full moon stood high in the firmament. Its brigh bathed the pathway that led to his house. Every grain of shown in the starlight reflected upon a memory. Sankalp v into the courtyard and placed his meagre belongings a the mud-plastered wall. It too seemed to resonate with (from the past. He settled down on his tigard-skin mat. A instantly, all tangible objects in sight receded into obli

Sankalp retreated into the depths of time…

The house stood lit with the rays of the mornin overlooking a heavenly landscape. The children sat in while their mother served them food. The sight of father entering the house filled their eyes with joy, anc ran to him screaming in excitement. He was their favc Whatever time he got after attending to his duties, he spend with them.

They would go to the open fields, where he taught to fly kites. They were shaped like dragons with long that hissed as they rose into the sky. The large kites much too big for little Sankalp to handle. He would a let them go, and his brothers would yell at him for so. At night their father would tell them stories of brav mighty men who lived in faraway lands. They listened t tales with rapt attention.

'Who would you like to be when you grow up?' he w often ask his children. All of them were fascinated b mystical heroes of folklore.

'I would like to be the greatest warrior of all,' replied Sankalp, his small wooden sword in hand.

All his brothers burst out laughing. 'You will be the gre shepherd boy,' they teased.

Through the mist of time, Kalimpong appeared!

'Sankalp, it's been a long time.'

'Yes, Master, but I have always felt your presence,' replied Sankalp, bowing low in reverence.

'My child, I understand your dilemma. But it is you who has to make the choice,' he counselled, reading Sankalp's mind.

Sankalp nodded with a smile, having understood Kalimpong's unspoken consent to his thoughts.

The mist receded, opening a magical window that gave Sankalp a peep into the fourth dimension. It gave him a unique understanding of how the necklace of life was woven across many lives, with the karmic pearls of action that illuminated the path to one's destiny.

Sankalp returned to himself, the words of the learned monk still echoing within him.

'My dear Sankalp, life is mostly about you and how you face up to your circumstances. The end of all human adventure is the same. How you live it is what truly matters!'

The warrior of Shaka understood well those words of wisdom.

He left his home in the middle of the night and proceeded to climb the hillock that overlooked his village. There, at a secluded spot, he sat in a sacred trance.

The invisible forces in the ether released the powers contained in his third eye. The vision unlocked the matrix spread across the universal sky. For two nights, Sankalp continued in that state of entranced communion.

With his uncertainty over, a ghost of a smile curled around his lips.

'I relinquish my powers to mother nature,' his mind called. The vibration travelled through the ether and subsided.

'Why do you do that, Sankalp?' A voice spoke from the heavenly skies.

After a brief silence, the voice once again echoed through the crisp mountain air. 'You have a life to live, and the powers can still be yours...'

'I live without fear and with faith and trust in that supreme, sublime consciousness.' A smile broke out across his face and lit his sombre eyes. 'And I would not have realized these doctrines without making the journey.'

'Dear Sankalp! By surrendering these powers, which are exceedingly difficult to attain and even more difficult to give up, you have further elevated your consciousness. By this noble act, it is bathed in divine light,' the voice resonated through the ether.

Nature crowned its new-found prince with a burst of golden rays. They penetrated the night sky, bringing forth light and warmth to the cold desert land.

A while later, Sankalp made his way back to the village. Upon his arrival, he immediately summoned Bhumiputra along with the elders. No sooner did the messenger bring word of his arrival than a large number of people arrived at his home. His absence had not gone unnoticed in the tiny hamlet. Soon, the entire village had assembled outside his home. A festive mood prevailed.

Sankalp came out of his house to greet the people gathered there. He was led to the village square by an elated crowd. Women came forward bearing flower petals in baskets. They flung them in the air, showering him and covering the path he walked on in yellow and purple blossoms. Many more joined in and walked him to the high platform that was once occupied by his father.

'Glory to the son of Lin! Please stay among us and never leave,' pleaded an old woman with a display of lament and affection alike. She had known him as a child. 'We hope you will take your rightful place as the village headman and remain with us.'

Sankalp smiled, 'I will always be with you.' Turning his attention to where Bhumiputra stood, he spoke to be heard by all in attendance. 'Bhumiputra is a brave and courageous man. He has risked his own life to save yours; respect him. He is my choice for the village headman.'

The crowd applauded his suggestion almost immediately.

'Does that mean you will leave us again?' the elderly woman protested.

She was joined by Rangdol's wife. 'Sankalp, you cannot leave now. Please choose a beautiful girl from the village and start a family,' she said with unabashed innocence.

The crowd roared with delight at her suggestion.

Sankalp remained quiet but lent a smile to her demand. An uncomfortable silence followed, eased by Rangdol, who quickly responded to the women.

'Didn't you hear what he just said? He will be here whenever we need him. There is so much to be done in Lhasa,' Rangdol said and smiled at the two women, trying not to look too effusive. He then turned towards Sankalp, his eyes filled with gratitude and understanding. Sankalp met his gaze with humility and nodded.

The crowd, pleased by the words of Rangdol, clapped happily. Sankalp smiled at them. He spent most of the warm afternoon with the people of his village.

Many more came from nearby villages to meet him.

They all had but one concern—would the warrior of Shaka remain in the village and start a family, or would he leave them for the kingdom of Lhasa? The news of the king's offer had travelled fast in the mountain land. Some were happy for him, while others wanted Sankalp to marry someone from the village.

'Will you marry the princess and bring her here to stay amongst us, or will you leave us and live in the palace? I would love to meet a real princess,' a little girl said to him innocently.

'I will certainly bring the princess here to see you,' Sankalp responded, placing his hand on her head in blessing.

'Sankalp, please don't leave. The people need you here! They derive strength from your presence. With you amidst us, we can look forward to peace and prosperity,' said Bhumiputra, sounding subdued, even depressed. He truly wished for the warrior of Shaka to take his rightful place as the village headman. But over time, he had seen and realized more about the man than most in the village. He knew Sankalp's words had a deeper meaning that the innocent people of the village would not easily understand.

An enigmatic smile spread across Sankalp's face as he spoke. 'Bhumiputra, my friend, I have treated you like a brother. I will be here whenever the need arises. But I must leave now.'

Bhumiputra nodded in acceptance.

Over the next few hours, Sankalp spoke to all the key elders before meeting with Bhumiputra again.

'My brave friend, look after the people of the village as your own family. Rely on the advice and experience of the elders to deliver justice. Live with honour and pride. And above all, follow what you preach.'

'Your words mean more to me than anything in this world. I will do as you command,' replied Bhumiputra and bowed low in respect.

'Master, is there anything else? Anything we can do in return?' he asked in a low voice tinged with emotion.

'Maintain the home of my family as if it were yours. Let it stand as a monument in remembrance of the village headman, Lin Thiampong,' said Sankalp.

The parting was prompt as he collected his belongings and quickly left.

He made his way through the narrow village lanes and proceeded once again towards Lhasa.

Two days later, a little after dawn, Sankalp once again stood on the battlefield that had been witness to a decisive war. A well fought battle between the invaders and the brave men of the land. Acquiescing, he bent down and picked up a soldier's broken armour.

'I salute you—the ones who faced death with courage! For we were enemies only on mortal ground; while some fought to save what was rightfully theirs, others to take it away. But you are not to blame. You were only pawns in the hands of those who lusted for more. May your spirits forever be free from the burden of this action, and may you be born again as brave men, standing for righteousness,' Sankalp prayed.

That night, Sankalp chose to stay at the cave. The light in the earthen pot burnt brighter. Everything seemed untouched, as if time stood still within its confines. He could feel the subtle presence of the learned monk beckoning him to take his seat on the elevated platform. His heart felt lighter. Sankalp sat in meditation all night until the morning light reflecting off the rock face snapped him out of his meditative state.

After a refreshing dip in the icy waters of a nearby stream, Sankalp, accompanied by his feathered companion Zanzi, made his way towards Lhasa. Many there eagerly awaited his return.

The sun was about to set as Sankalp neared the sprawling lands where Divya Drishti lived. He intended to spend the night at his friend's house before proceeding to the palace.

It was a pleasant surprise for Divya, being informed by one of his guards that a monk dressed in strange attire wanted to see him. He knew immediately who it was and rushed out to greet him.

'We meet again, dear friend,' Divya exclaimed, pulling him into a brotherly embrace. 'I have been eagerly awaiting your return.' A smile floated across his face, and his dark brown eyes flickered in anticipation.

'My dear, I felt a certain uneasiness in your mind and decided to stop here before proceeding further,' Sankalp replied, relishing the moment.

'Aha! The reader of starlight can decipher minds too?' Divya exclaimed, grinning widely with a slight bow.

Sankalp smiled and once again held him affectionately in a warm embrace. The two walked towards the house, engaging in light conversation.

'I hope you will accompany me to Lhasa tomorrow?' Sankalp looked at him expectantly.

Divya drew in a deep breath at the remark, even as memories from the past flashed through his mind. 'If you want me to,' he replied and walked Sankalp to his room.

Sankalp could read the look of confusion on his face but remained quiet.

'My dear Sankalp, rest awhile; you must be tired after the long journey. Meanwhile, I will ask Mother to prepare your favourite meal—rice pudding it will be.'

Sankalp smiled and lay down on the bed as Divya left. His thoughts immediately went out to Titla, and his mind filled with pleasant memories. The warrior of Shaka was calm. He was here for a purpose, an unfinished task. And then, he would be free from the karmic cycle that had brought him back.

Only a few minutes had elapsed when a slight movement broke his thoughts. He quickly rose to his feet upon seeing Divya's mother.

'My son,' she whispered, as her eyes welled with motherly emotions.

Sankalp was unable to speak, overcome as he was by those two words. He immediately hugged her.

'Dinner is laid,' she said with a smile, holding back the thoughts she had come to express.

'Ahh, the much-loved other son arrives,' Divya joyfully remarked with his usual levity.

The table was laid with a variety of food. Divya Drishti had ensured that his friend was well looked after.

'The rice pudding is well cooked, Mother. I know of only one other person who can cook it as you do.'

'I am glad you liked it. I will keep some aside for your journey tomorrow,' she said.

She paused and then hesitantly expressed what she could not earlier. 'My dear Sankalp, you are aware of how people in the palace have treated us. But for the sake of your friendship and the honour of this kingdom, my son fought bravely by your side.' She fell silent for a moment, holding back her tears as she continued. 'I feel he has done his duty to the king and the kingdom. I do not see why he should set foot in the palace again.'

It was clear she still felt anger and resentment against the regime for the way they had been treated in the past.

Sankalp met her eyes with understanding but did not let her misgivings undermine his own certainty.

'Trust me, Mother, you have nothing to worry about. All the wrongs will be undone in time. Your family shall have its rightful place in the kingdom. But for that, you must let Divya accompany me to the palace,' he urged her.

Her affection for Sankalp prevented her from questioning him further. 'My dear, I trust you. He will ride with you to the palace tomorrow,' she replied, with an effort to smile.

Sankalp bowed low and took his leave, understanding her state of mind.

Sankalp was up early the next day. He stepped out into the garden and was greeted by a pleasant sight. Divya was deeply engrossed in practising what he had taught him. When not practising, Divya would read the many scrolls Sankalp had written and given him.

'You still have to teach me how to use the mighty sword of balance,' Divya declared.

Sankalp considered his protégé for a moment before answering with a slight smile, 'I will, in time. You are one of my best pupils, and the sword of balance will be yours when you are ready for it. But for now, we must leave soon. Many in the palace await our return.'

'As soon as I am done,' replied Divya, wiping the sweat off his brow.

A short while later, the two men were on their way, traversing the picturesque winding roads leading to Lhasa.

As the two horsemen rode towards the palace, Divya Drishti remarked, 'My dear Sankalp, you know how my heart feels every time I enter the city, although much honour has been bestowed upon me because of you.'

Sankalp studied Divya for a long moment, trying to decipher his emotions.

'Divya, your courage on the battlefield earned you the honour,' he finally said. 'I understand the pain you feel because of what happened to your father and family. But you must realize this was all part of the devious plan hatched by the villain, Asudai! He wanted to get rid of all those loyal to the kingdom.'

Divya nodded but said nothing.

Sankalp drew in a breath of the crisp morning air before speaking again. 'Do not dwell too much on the past. It is time for a new beginning. Perhaps a new romance with Lhasa?' Sankalp remarked, with a smile and a twinkle in his eyes.

'Romance...' Divya smiled dismissively and shook his head.

They entered the city of Lhasa by late afternoon and were pleasantly surprised to see Trinyen Tsenpo and Mayuri eagerly waiting for them.

The guards had sent word to the palace about their arrival. The ruler of Lhasa, along with the princess, decided to receive the two decorated men at the city gates. The king embraced them both.

'My dear Sankalp, I have been expecting you.' Trinyen's expression held relief. 'You have kept your promise to this old man,' he said affectionately. 'I have been thinking much about you too, Divya. It is wonderful to have you here with us.'

'How have you been, Divya? It has been some time since I last saw you,' Mayuri said, her delight clear.

'I have been well, Princess. Busy with my duties at home, of course, after having done what I could for the kingdom.'

'You could have made time to come to meet us,' Mayuri chided. 'I had expressed my keenness to see your mother and spend some more time with her...' She paused and then her voice turned to a whisper. 'I do miss her, ever since...'

'I will take you to meet her one of these days,' Divya promised.

'There is so much that I need to tell her. I hope I will have the opportunity to do so.' Her expression turned pensive. 'Till then we will have you here, with us,' Mayuri said with a questioning glance.

'I agreed to accompany Sankalp to the palace and intend to leave shortly...'

'No, my dear,' the king protested. 'You are now the governor of Lhasa, and before long, you will occupy your rightful place here.'

Divya remained silent, allowing the king to express his thoughts.

'I urge you to stay with us and partake in the grand festival being held in the city square tomorrow.'

'Stay, my dear Divya! I need you here,' Sankalp urged his friend.

Trinyen Tsenpo then requested Sankalp to accompany him to his private chambers in the palace.

As they left, Mayuri engaged Divya in light conversation as she walked him to his room. She made sure he was comfortable and well attended. Mayuri's presence ameliorated Divya's discomfort over her father's proposal, making him more amenable to the invitation.

'I will wait for you in the palace gardens later in the evening,' Mayuri said before leaving his room.

Divya nodded with a smile.

Meanwhile, the ruler of Lhasa had much to ask the warrior of Shaka. He had spent many a night waiting for his return. And Sankalp had much to share with him.

After a brief rest, Divya Drishti strolled across to the palace gardens.

Under the cool light of a buck moon, Mayuri stood silently staring at the city. Her beauty was accentuated by the magic of the starlit night. Hearing Divya's footsteps, Mayuri quickly turned around. She smiled and instantly felt at ease in his presence. Divya returned the smile as Mayuri walked up to him and held his hand. For a moment, he stood overwhelmed by her alluring touch.

The view was breathtaking. Bright lights lit up the city in preparation for the grand festival.

They had much to say but words fell silent that night...

Meanwhile, Sankalp shared his thoughts with the king, and he agreed with what the warrior of Shaka had to say. His suggestions and advice would not only ensure the happiness of all but also bring lasting peace to the lands.

'My dear Sankalp, you have surprised me with your views.' He paused and drew in a deep breath. 'I place my trust in your wisdom. But I hope you will not leave us again?'

'My king, there is someone who awaits me,' Sankalp smiled. 'I must go. But I will always be with you and the people of this land.'

He then requested the king to make arrangements to bring Divya's mother to the palace. He wanted her to be a part of the celebrations. Finally, the two men parted company for the night.

The city of Lhasa continued its celebrations till dawn. The day of the grand festival was one of many surprises and one that would be remembered for many years to come!

They had indeed lived through memorable times. The bards, the keepers of history in these lands, had composed ballads about the epic war and sang about the heroes in the city square.

Sometimes, the destiny of an entire kingdom becomes enshrined in the deeds of just one man. Destiny had wisely chosen Sankalp to do its bidding, ensuring peace, prosperity and harmony for many years.

That night, amidst the grand celebration, the king announced the marriage of his daughter to the valiant and brave Divya Drishti! Her childhood companion had a very special place in her heart. Mayuri's happiness was palpable.

Divya Drishti too felt the same about the princess. But feelings of love had been shrouded by the anger and mistrust that had come between them after the death of his father.

However, that was in the past; a new beginning awaited them and the kingdom.

In time, their marriage was solemnized, and the wedding was attended by many kings and princes from far and near. On the highest seat sat Sankalp. He kept his promise to attend the royal wedding.

As time went by, the kingdom of Lhasa prospered. And so did the people, who had indeed made many sacrifices. But none could forget the warrior of Shaka, without whom their life would have been one of slavery. As the years passed, Princess Mayuri became a queen, and she ruled the kingdom of Lhasa with King Divya Drishti by her side. They had taken over the reins of the kingdom from Trinyen Tsenpo, who was now an old man, spending most of his time with his two grandchildren.

Divya Drishti was an able and just administrator. Bhumiputra was the commander of the forces that kept the kingdom safe from enemies, ensuring peace.

Often, they would wonder where the warrior of Shaka was. The cave was untraceable. But the apple tree remained, ever so beautiful…

On some days, the winds would carry the music of his flute to his village and to the palace. Enemies never dared to cross the Yarlung Pass. Many said they still saw the shadow of the great warrior, riding a bear and waving the sword of balance up on the mountain ridge.

No one had seen or met him for many years, but the legend of Sankalp, the warrior of Shaka, lived in the hearts of the people. They knew he was there, somewhere amongst the endless Himalayan ranges. Ever the wanderer, he was the protector of the lands and the people who inhabited it.